# PRAISE FOR GWENDOLYN WOMACK

"A master at blending the mystical, the philosophical, and the artful in a gripping and romantic story that spans eras and millennia, Womack enthralls us with her latest novel—and it's not to be missed. Written with beautiful prose and woven with characters you can't help but root for, *The Last Labyrinth* is a winner!"

—Heather Webb, *USA Today* bestselling author of *Queens of London*

"A monumental journey through the power of love, sound, and the indelible spirit of history's lost female composers, Womack's novel expertly weaves threads of magic, music, and time into a profound, geomantic tapestry of story and heart. *The Last Labyrinth* is a triumph from start to finish. Once I started reading, I could not step away."

—Ava Morgyn, *USA Today* bestselling author of *The Bane Witch*

"A thrilling time-travel journey that brings the past to life. It will keep you reading well into the night."

—Diana Giovinazzo, author of *Antoinette's Sister*

"A time-travel triumph—Gwendolyn Womack spins an unforgettable tale that fuses music, myth, and romance into an epic adventure. *The Last Labyrinth* is a breathtaking odyssey across centuries where love and destiny intertwine."

—Constance Sayers, author of *A Witch in Time*

# THE LAST LABYRINTH

# ALSO BY GWENDOLYN WOMACK

*The Memory Painter*

*The Fortune Teller*

*The Time Collector*

*The Premonitions Club*

# THE LAST LABYRINTH

GWENDOLYN WOMACK

This is a work of fiction. Names, characters, organizations, places, events, and incidents are either products of the author's imagination or are used fictitiously. Otherwise, any resemblance to actual persons, living or dead, is purely coincidental.



Published by 47North, Seattle

www.apub.com



EU product safety contact:
Amazon Media EU S. à r.l.
38, avenue John F. Kennedy, L-1855 Luxembourg
amazonpublishing-gpsr@amazon.com

ISBN-13: 9781662534935 (paperback)
ISBN-13: 9781662534942 (digital)

Cover design by David Drummond
Cover image: © FairytaleDesign, © mikroman6, © davidhajnal / Getty; © David Hughes / Shutterstock

Printed in the United States of America

*For my father,*
*Leo Womack*

# PROLOGUE

The diary arrived in the morning, delivered to the head curator at the Morgan Library & Museum by special courier from England. The curator liked to work alone on Saturdays when much of the staff was gone for the weekend. He signed for the package and retreated to his office, wondering who—or what—the Liron Institute was and why they were sending a package to him.

The letter accompanying it gave him pause for several reasons. The gold symbol at the top was an ancient Egyptian emblem. The letter bore no name or signature and read like something out of a spy novel. It literally said, "The fate of the world rests in protecting this book." The instructions were to safeguard the diary and ultimately deliver it and the accompanying translation to a woman named Magellan Brighton. She was to come retrieve the book personally, and time was of the essence.

The curator didn't know anyone by that name. He also couldn't imagine why an institute in England had sent such a request to him across the pond as if he were a delivery service.

He opened the package to find a small pocket-size diary, centuries old, made of parchment and encased in leather with a beautiful Celtic triskelion, a symbol of three interlocking spiraled rings, engraved on the cover. The artistry was exquisite. He slipped on his gloves to handle it more gingerly.

The translation was just as enticing. A collection of loose pages, meticulously handwritten and sheathed in a folio. The paper was not made of wood pulp but rag paper, which would have been used before the 1800s. The curator put the translation carefully aside to study later, not requiring it, and returned to the book. He was one of the world's foremost experts in medieval manuscripts written in Old English and preferred to read the original text himself.

When he opened the diary to the first page, a powerful yet graceful script leapt off the parchment.

> **You know my brother's name,**
> **but you do not know mine,**
> **though we were born twins, a boy and a girl.**
> **A grand secret lies at the heart of life**
> **that must be remembered**
> **if we are to save this world once more.**
> **Every atom on this planet sings the same song.**

The curator paused for a moment to study the line *Every atom on this planet sings the same song*. He knew Old English with all its nuances and musicality better than modern English. How could someone who had lived centuries ago know what an atom was? And just what did the word *sings* entail?

The direct translation was "every life-spark makes the same music," and "life-spark" was a *kenning*—the Old English way of combining two words to make another word. He thought he knew every kenning ever written, but he'd never seen this one before.

As he read on he began to grasp just who the author of this diary was, and his heart sped with excitement.

Could it really be *her*?

No record of this memoir existed. A record of her barely existed.

She and her brother had lived in the sixth century, and her twin had gone on to be fictionalized a hundred times over. His most famous portrayal had been written by Sir Thomas Malory in the 1400s.

How had an institute in England he had never heard of gotten their hands on this diary? Where had it been this entire time?

The problem was there was no name signed to the letter or phone number for the institute to call, only one for Magellan Brighton. He dialed her number, and it went straight to voicemail. On the recording, she had a young voice. He hesitated, unsure what to say. Given the cloak and dagger of the letter and the monumental importance of what he held in his hands, he decided not to leave any details.

"Hello, I've just received a . . . book, a very special diary, that seems to be yours. Please call me at your earliest convenience." He did not mention he was with the Morgan Museum. Instead, he left his private cell phone number and hung up, feeling dissatisfied. Had he said too much? Had he not said enough?

A knock at his door startled him, and he went to open it. A fellow colleague was hovering in the hallway with an excited look on his face.

"What is it?" the curator asked him, not sure if the day could get any stranger.

"You have to come outside!"

The curator followed, locking his office door and leaving the diary on his worktable. He'd be right back. He walked out onto Madison Avenue, and his mouth dropped open when he looked up at the sky along with everyone else.

"My God," he whispered.

A brilliant aurora borealis that belonged more in Finland stretched above Manhattan.

The curator was a logical man, a historian in love with words, but his mind was already quickly forming a kenning—linking the aurora borealis in the sky to the diary on his desk, because they both felt magical—because the world's most renowned wizard had a twin sister who had written a memoir, and she knew what an atom was and talked about saving the world.

The curator left the gaping crowd outside to return to his office to find out just what Merlin's sister had to say.

# Chapter 1

## Magellan

The aurora borealis appeared the same day as her birthday. Only later would Magellan Brighton realize the timing was significant. On Saturday, October 24, in what should have been any other Saturday, colorful ribbons of light hued and swirled across the sky in a rich palette of indigo, green, and violet above Manhattan like its own galaxy.

Her back to the window, the curtain drawn, Magellan ran delicate fingers up and down her electric piano with her headphones on, searching for the song from her dreams last night. Cocooned in her robe, her morning coffee growing cold, she closed her eyes and let her hands have free roam.

How did it go?

The melody began to crystallize as she carved it out with the keys, over and over, to find the beginnings of the song's shape. On the cusp of snatching more from the ethers, her cell phone shook and blared a ringtone belonging to one person: her best friend and roommate, Wren.

Wren's call broke her concentration and pushed the song back into the recesses of her mind. She took her headphones off with a sigh and answered.

"Happy birthday to youuuuuuu," Wren serenaded her as only an opera singer could and ended with a crescendo, hitting the A above high C.

Magellan laughed, taking a sip of her coffee, a delicious French roast Wren brewed every morning. "Thank you. That was magnificent."

"Happy birthday," Wren said and rushed on in excitement. "Have you looked at the sky yet? It's freaking incredible!"

"You do remember who you're talking to."

Of the top phobias people had in the world—fear of heights, water, flying, storms, spiders, public speaking, and the dentist—Magellan was pretty sure she had them all.

"Mags. No. Just no. You have to look. There's an actual aurora borealis in the sky right now."

"What?" Magellan jumped up and was at the living room window in two steps. Bracing herself, she pulled back the curtain and worked to keep her equilibrium. Their apartment was only on the third floor, but still.

What she saw made her momentarily forget her fear of heights. The sky was so beautiful she felt the urge to step out on the patio, something she hadn't done the whole time she'd lived there.

"I have to get back to rehearsal," Wren said. "Turn on the news. It's happening everywhere." Then she hung up.

Magellan hesitated and decided to keep the curtain open. The sky was amazing, like a stunning painting she couldn't look away from. She turned on the TV. Wren was right. The aurora borealis was breaking news and happening all over the world.

On one station the weatherman said with a cheery smile, "Well, folks, today we have a surprise party in the sky. Experts believe this is a passing global magnetic storm, and the National Weather Service is projecting it will be over in a week. So until then, sit back and enjoy the show."

Another station had a much less cheery take. A grim-looking reporter said, "Everyone needs to know this atmospheric phenomenon happens in the Arctic region," he stressed. "That's why they're called northern lights. Or the South Pole—which are southern lights. It should not be happening here during the day." He gave a dramatic stare straight into the camera. "Stay tuned. This could spell trouble on the horizon."

Magellan frowned, and her cell phone binged. She had missed a call while she was talking with Wren. An old man had left a voicemail saying he had a book of hers. A diary. She cringed as she listened to the creepy message. *He had her diary?*

She deleted it. Like she would ever return such a call. People these days were getting more creative with their scams. Checking the time, she abandoned her coffee and the piano. She needed to get ready to go see her parents. They were planning a birthday lunch. Although the thought of making her way across town from Queens to the Upper West Side stressed her out, which was ironic since she shared the name Magellan with the famous Portuguese explorer who'd attempted to circle the globe in the 1500s. Unlike the real historic explorer, she never went anywhere. Her elderly parents weren't big on travel, and even if they were, the thought of getting on a plane was too much for her.

Magellan often wondered if she had inherited all her anxieties from her birth parents. She'd been adopted at infancy, and for the first four years of her life she didn't speak. She was tested for autism and other potential causes for the delay, during which time it was discovered she had an extraordinary ear for music. So extraordinary, she could play any instrument and re-create any song.

It wasn't until she was four and her speech therapist told her "Did you know your voice is an instrument too?" that Magellan began to hum. From humming, her speech therapist encouraged her to sing, and from singing to talk, which she finally did, but only when necessary, because music, not words, was her language.

If Harold and Margaret Brighton had shared their daughter's gift with the world when she was little, Magellan would have been proclaimed a child prodigy the likes of Mozart or Beethoven, but they had not. Instead, she had been homeschooled, sheltered, and kept off social media due to her fragile nature. Her parents were extremely protective until they realized their protectiveness was only hindering her. Magellan's incredible talent was meant to be shared, not hidden away.

When Magellan turned seventeen, her longtime music teacher, Garesh, was the one who had talked her into auditioning for Juilliard. "Your gift is for the world. You cannot stay here forever. Your ship will depart one day, whether you are ready or not."

Magellan wasn't sure what metaphorical ship he was talking about, but Garesh often said such things. He had been her teacher for as long as she could remember. He was the tallest and most gentle man she'd ever met, with midnight hair, dark skin, and piercing brown eyes that held a special light. He spoke softly, with the hint of an accent, as if every word were perfectly measured because he preferred silence. Once when she'd asked where he was from, he only smiled. "I am from everywhere."

A brilliant musician, Garesh had taught her musical theories from around the world. He would come to her house, where they would sequester themselves in her parents' study. They would pick apart musical forms, the structures of symphonies, and look to what the composer's intention was within each movement. He would bring instruments she had never known existed and encourage her to play them. Instruments like the crwth, the nyckelharpa, the contrabass balalaika, the cimbalom, and the theremin. When she was older, he showed her medical journals about the latest scientific studies with music that demonstrated the power of harmonics to heal the body at cellular levels. He firmly believed the future of the world depended on sound.

Garesh was the one who accompanied her to her audition at Juilliard and sat and watched her earn the awe of the faculty and a full scholarship.

"Will you still teach me?" she asked him, unable to imagine a future without her beloved teacher. For years it had just been the two of them.

He shook his head gently. "You no longer need me." To which she shook her head back emphatically. She couldn't disagree more.

At their last lesson together, he brought his violin to play a duet. This was her special request, for Garesh rarely played. They played Sarasate's *Navarra* together, a virtuoso violin duet that contained lightning-quick passages demanding perfect synchronization. Their eyes stayed locked on each other as they trilled in harmony, their shared joy in playing infectious. As the song neared its close, Garesh segued into Bach's double violin concerto, a poignant piece. The violins played in tandem, their melodies cascading over each other in farewell. As Magellan played, she pushed back the swell of tears. Garesh had said he was leaving. He had work on the West Coast and overseas, while she would be going to college at Juilliard only blocks away. She didn't know when she would see him again.

The song came to a close, and the last note seemed to hover in the air longer than it should have; then they both dropped their bows in salute. He gave her a courtly bow, in that moment looking as if he belonged to an ancient land. Before he left, he presented her with a parting gift, a ring made of a bronze-like gold with decorative symbols engraved around the band.

"It has been in my family for generations, to remember me by when you are playing around the world."

Magellan didn't know about the around the world part, but the ring was a perfect fit. The metal gleamed on her finger in an array of coppery striations that caught the light. "Thank you." Impulsively she gave him a hug for the first time, afraid to say goodbye. "I'll always wear it."

---

In the years to follow, she wore the ring not only for luck but to remember all that Garesh had taught her. She threw herself into her studies at Juilliard wholeheartedly, receiving her undergraduate and graduate degree in music theory by the age of twenty-three. Her mentors helped her to work through the stage fright and anxiety that hit her before a performance. Technically called glossophobia, the fear of being watched and judged by others, it turned out many musicians suffered from it. But she found once she started playing, the fear went away, and over time her stage fright became less debilitating.

Right before graduating two years ago, she met Wren during a school production. Magellan had been the harpist in Juilliard's student orchestra, and Wren was the school's star opera singer. Nicknamed "the Voice" by her friends, Wren could actually break glass if she wanted to. During a rehearsal, the two discovered they were both about to graduate and needed a roommate. The result was the beginning of a wonderful friendship. Now they shared a one-bedroom matchbox apartment in Queens.

In all these years Garesh had not called or been in touch with her or her parents—except on her birthday. Every year he sent a gift and a card postmarked from somewhere in the world. Places like Madrid, Paris, Lima, and Wellington. But this year he hadn't sent anything. Magellan tried not to worry and hoped he was all right.

Maybe her parents had heard from him. She'd ask them today. Gathering her things to leave, her cell phone rang with a number she didn't recognize. She answered it, hoping it was Garesh. "Hello?"

"Hello, I'm trying to reach Magellan Brighton."

"Speaking." It sounded like a telemarketer. Immediately she regretted picking up.

"Yes, I'm calling from the Morgan Library & Museum. I left a message for you earlier about a special book I have in my possession. The diary?"

"The diary?" Magellan parroted back, now confused.

"I received it today from the Liron Institute in England with urgent instructions to deliver it to you."

This morning's message had been from the Morgan Library & Museum? She frowned, confused. "I'm sorry but are you trying to reach one of my parents? Margaret or Harold Brighton? They're historians and members of the museum."

"No, no. The instructions were clear, and this diary is most precious." He sounded so earnest when he requested she come to the museum and said the reception desk would be expecting her. She found herself agreeing, and they arranged a time tomorrow.

Magellan hung up, utterly mystified. Why would someone in England be sending a diary to the Morgan Museum for her?

She had never heard of the Liron Institute before in her life.

# Chapter 2

𝄢

## Rhys

***England, 1827***

Rhys Sherwood, the Earl of Liron's eldest son and heir, loved labyrinths, but he loved his family's labyrinth the most. Few in England were as legendary as Hereford Manor's. At the labyrinth's center was an ancient stone circle with three towering standing stones and nine smaller ones that, legend said, had been built by Merlin himself.

Rhys's ancestor, the first Earl of Liron, had built a circular labyrinth like a fortress to surround the stone circle, and then he had made the maze near impossible to penetrate. Perhaps it was the hardest labyrinth ever built, if Rhys had to place a wager.

Wickedly designed, it was full of puzzling false starts, twists and turns, narrowed passageways, sharp curves, and dead ends. In the summer, during the month of June, the infamous Hereford Labyrinth opened to the public, and travelers came from miles around on foot or in their carriages to challenge themselves to find the center. Few ever did. Hereford Manor's groundsmen were given carefully drawn maps and sent in every afternoon to fish anyone out.

Rhys had spent his whole life learning those pathways. He knew every hedge wall and square meter by heart. In his childhood, the labyrinth had been a mythical place. The one place he could be alone with his imagination. He had slayed dragons, been knighted, saved princesses, and gone on long voyages all within its walls. Years later, his childhood stomping ground had turned into a place of solace. The labyrinth's center had a rose garden surrounding the stone circle with a fountain and benches where he often spent hours alone reading.

Today he was sneaking off to do just that with a book in hand. *Decoding the Rosetta Stone* had been on his reading list for some time. Three years ago, Thomas Young, an English physicist, and Jean-François Champollion, a French scholar, discovered the stone was the doorway to translating Egypt's ancient hieroglyphs. Although Rhys had reservations about the Europeans' arrival to Egypt, he couldn't help but feel a twinge of jealousy at the groundbreaking semantic discovery. He had devoted his life to linguistic pursuits and learning as many languages as possible, firmly embracing the Czech proverb *Learn a new language and get a new soul.* Over the years he had become fluent in six languages and semifluent in countless others. He especially loved words that could not be translated into another language. Solitary words full of beauty and power that defied any other word to match its meaning. Words like *saudade*, the Portuguese name for the feeling of longing for someone you love who might never return. Or *mangata*, the Swedish term for the reflection of a silvery road the moon makes on the ocean when casting its light. Or *yuanfen*, a Mandarin word for the fate between two people.

His father, Godwin Sherwood, had encouraged such pursuits. Rhys rounded the labyrinth's last corner to find the man in question hard at work—doing what, God only knew. His father was busy stringing up musical instruments on ropes across the entire stone circle like a bizarre decoration.

Rhys let out a sigh. His private reading time with the Rosetta Stone would have to wait. "What in heaven's name are you doing?"

His father ignored his question. "You cannot marry someone named Flora. Your mother told me of your plan." He spoke over the chimes and bells as he tugged on the line. "I forbid it. She is a plant."

Rhys bristled. "Flora also means *flower*, from the Latin word *flos*, as you well know."

"Given to us by the Romans who conquered these islands. Will you allow Flora to conquer you?"

"Oh, good grief. Yes!" The words tumbled out of him in a rush of frustration. "At some point, yes. I have to marry and continue the line. She has a dowry, which the estate desperately needs. The Winslows have invited me to their house party, and I have accepted. If all goes well, she and I will be engaged by the end of the month."

His father harumphed at that. "To a weed with a dowry."

"To a *flower*. She is a flower." Not a very beautiful flower if Rhys's memory was correct, but he could not let that deter him. "She is a peer's daughter with a large dowry whose family wants the prestige of my title in exchange for their fortune." He ignored his father's snort. "It will be a fair trade to help alleviate the estate's problems."

"What problems?" His father truly sounded bewildered.

"You do know the roof is leaking all along the second story of the east wing?"

"Near the library?" he gasped in horror.

"No," Rhys assured him, though maybe he should have lied, because his father turned away in relief and resumed his work.

"As long as it's not near the books or conservatory." He pulled a complex brass protractor from a bag of supplies. "We have a roof, and that's all that matters. No need to marry just yet to fix a few shingles."

Rhys sighed again. It was impossible to talk to his father when he was caught up in one of his experiments. "What on earth are you making?"

"A time machine."

A bellow of laughter escaped Rhys. "Of course. How could I not have guessed?"

"You may laugh now, but did you know the King's Chamber in the Great Pyramid is a sound chamber?"

"What does the pyramid in Egypt have to do with all this?" He signaled to the stones.

"Everything, my boy! Everything." His father waved his protractor in the air with excitement, and Rhys resisted the urge to duck. "The world and all its dimensions is connected by sound. Some of these stones can be played like instruments. Who knows what worlds are waiting beyond the barrier."

Rhys pinched his nose, praying for patience. He so loved his father, but the man had grown up reading the world's canon of fantastical fiction about traveling into space and the existence of other realms. He had stuffed his head full of notions written by eccentric authors with ink-stained fingers. The library even had a special section devoted to such works, arranged by century, starting with the second-century Syrian author Lucian of Samosata's *A True Story*, which claimed life was an illusion, all the way to *The Voyages of Lord Seton to the Seven Planets*, published in 1765 by a female French author who gained popularity when Rhys's father was a teenager.

Currently his father was looking like an earnest adolescent as he said, "Never forget these standing stones were put here by Merlin. Our family, the Lirons, were tasked to protect them. And these symbols here—" He pointed to the symbols engraved across the largest standing stone.

"Are Atlantean. Yes, you've told me many times." Rhys checked his pocket watch. As much as he had loved hearing those tales growing up, right now he had more pressing matters, and the urge to read about

Egyptian hieroglyphics had left him. "Well, I suppose I should be going. I need to pack."

"Wait!" His father stopped what he was doing and suddenly seemed sincerely afraid. "You really are going to this house party? You can't. I need you to read a book." He pointed to Rhys's book. "And not that one. Though it's good. I've read it—"

"Father, please—"

"A very important book." He dropped his rope of instruments with a clang. "Come along to the library and I'll show you, dear boy. Stop dillydallying."

Rhys could only shake his head. His father was being impossible on purpose. Still, Rhys followed him out of the labyrinth, through the gardens to the library in the east wing where his father kept his desk in the back alcove. Rhys was the only other person to know the desk contained a hidden puzzle drawer. He had never seen his father open it until now.

"Watch carefully and remember." His father showed him the mechanism to make the hidden drawer pop open, and he pulled out a tray holding a small leather-bound book. An exquisite triskelion, an ancient Celtic symbol, was engraved on the cover.

"What is it?" Rhys asked him, his curiosity now piqued. His father gently laid the book on the desktop and showed him the text. Rhys whistled softly at the beautiful Old English script. "What century?"

His father smiled like a Cheshire cat. "Sixth."

Inside the little book was a folded letter not written in Old English, though the parchment appeared old.

"Read this." His father handed it to him. "Then you'll understand."

**October 31, 1468**

**Dear Thomas,**

In your quest for historical materials to aid in your research for Merlin, I have unearthed this memoir purportedly written by his sister. Although records for the renowned Bard from the sixth century are rare, I was able to confirm Merlin did in fact have a sister, a twin named Gwynedd, and her diary appears to be authentic.

You relayed in your letters however Merlin is to be a supporting figure in your tale, a sorcerer to the king, and your story will center around Arthur and his noble knights, along with many battles and romantic overtures. Therefore, I am uncertain whether this memoir will be of any use. The text is written in Old English and given its age, the pages are frayed with a few torn leaflets, which is not unusual for a manuscript this old.

I am afraid that is as far as I have delved. I intentionally withheld reading the diary so I may have deniability if I am questioned by the authorities. Given Gwynedd is the twin sibling of history's most renowned wizard and Druid, there must indeed be mention of magic within the pages.

Hence, I feel I should caution you before deciding to read its contents. Just this year magic has been declared to be "crimen exceptum," with people suspected of practicing it getting hanged, drowned, and burned. Women are faring the worst in a brute show of submission.

Due to the fear of the day, it may be unwise to write a wizard into your story. Geoffrey of Monmouth may have done so, but he was a bishop and the times of the 1100s are vastly different than they are today.

I truly do not wish to censure you my friend before you have begun, but please heed my advice.

However, as I do remain your devoted friend, for your research I will be sending along a copy of Robert de Boron's Merlin, along with translations for Geoffrey of Monmouth's Prophetiae Merlini, Historiae Regum Britanniae, and Vita Merlini, as well as Nennius' History of the Britons and the French materials we discussed.

I do hope your room in Newgate Prison provides minimal comfort and does not have a draft. I was most pleased to hear you have a window this time and have been given access to the common areas including the library. Perhaps prison with its lack of distractions will be the best place to write a novel. I look forward to reading the adventures of King Arthur and his noble knights of the Round Table with utmost excitement when you are finished.

My regards,

Stuart

Rhys reread the letter, utterly flummoxed. "Is this letter really to . . . ?"

His father nodded, practically dancing with excitement. "Sir Thomas Malory."

"The Sir Thomas Malory? And he was given a diary written by Merlin's sister?"

"Merlin's *twin* sister."

For a moment Rhys grappled with the fact Merlin had a twin sister. "How did I not know Merlin had a sister?"

His father waved his hand in the air as if the question was ridiculous. "You know women are written as the supporting characters in history. Yes! Our most famous wizard had a twin sister. Isn't it marvelous? And we have her diary."

Legends abounded for the great Merlin. Stories had been written. Tales told. The most famous being Thomas Malory's *Le Morte d'Arthur*, written in the fifteenth century. Malory had woven together real history and mythical legends into his epic adventure, including legends of Merlin. Yet the sister had never been mentioned.

Rhys picked up the book. "Where did you get this?"

"I've been safekeeping it for someone," he dismissed.

"Can we sell it? Is that why you're showing me?"

"No!" his father said sharply, taking it away from him. "We can never, *ever*, sell this book."

"Why? Just think what a sixth-century memoir from Merlin's sister would be worth."

"This diary is priceless, and it is not ours to sell. It is tied to the labyrinth. To the stones. To our family." His father laid his hand on the triskelion. "One day, a lady will arrive and you must give her this book. For it is hers."

Now his father was talking in riddles. "What do you mean a lady will arrive? Whatever are you talking about?"

"I can say no more, for I fear I've already said too much." His father twisted his signet ring on his finger, which he was apt to do when he was worried. "Keep the book safe, and give it to her when she comes. But first, you must translate it out of Old English."

"Why? I'm sure you've already translated it."

"Of course I have. That's beside the point. *You* must read the original text. With your own eyes. Your own heart." He tapped him on the chest. "You as my heir are a meticulous scholar. I have the upmost confidence in your ability to comprehend every nuance for yourself."

"Thank you, Father," Rhys said dryly.

"And do not marry Flora the potted plant until you have read this book in its entirety. Promise me." His father gripped his arms with surprising firmness. "I do not jest in this matter."

Rhys had never seen him so intent. "All right, I promise. I will read it before I do my duty and offer for her hand."

It was not the answer his father wanted. He seemed to be searching for the right words. "Dear God. Is this the moment?" he asked himself and his eyes grew bright. He took a moment to compose his thoughts. "Let me tell you of your duty. Your duty is to live your life and to love with a full heart. To not die regretting that you didn't. Your duty is to be everything you were born to be." He searched his eyes, as if willing him to take in every word he was saying. "Do you understand?"

Rhys nodded, moved by his father's conviction.

"Good." His father physically relaxed upon his agreement and repeated, "Good," as he patted his arms once more. "You will know what to do when the time comes. Have faith."

Rhys didn't know what he meant and was afraid to ask. His father was in one of his moods. Instead, he watched him stow the diary back in the hidden drawer and made mental plans to read it soon, although translating anything from Old English would take time. He would start when he returned from the house party.

---

The following day he did not go to the house party. His mother's screams from the garden were what woke him.

Rhys heard her from the window calling for him hysterically. Without a thought to put on his robe, he dashed downstairs and ran outside where he found her bent over sobbing in the garden near his father's laboratory.

He dropped to the ground beside her. "Mother?"

She threw her arms around him, holding him tightly and weeping "He's gone. He's gone." She could not stop saying the words.

Rhys held her as his own heart shattered. The whole household was roused, and someone rode to the village to fetch the town doctor, but it was too late. His father had passed away in his laboratory in the middle of the night from one of his chemical experiments gone wrong. Most likely a deadly combination of compounds in his quest to discover new elements.

On that day, the morning of October 24, 1827, Rhys's life changed forever.

# Chapter 3

## Magellan

Garesh once explained the vagus nerve was the longest-running nerve in the body. It started at the seat, ran through every organ, and ended at the top of the head—and the vagus could turn the anxiety switch in the body off. "With your vocal cords, by humming," he pointed out. "Your voice is a tuning fork, and you can reset the vagus and calm your body whenever you need to." He began to hum a rich and melodious sound. "Why do children hum? Monks chant? Or church choirs sing? They are tuning themselves to a higher frequency. So when you feel anxious, get out of your head and back into your heart by humming."

Magellan found humming did soothe her. Which is why she hummed all the way to the Morgan Library & Museum. She didn't technically have enochlophobia, the fear of crowds, or the close cousin agoraphobia, fear of open spaces, but walking the streets of Manhattan did make her nervous. Was there a specific anxiety for that? Manhattanophobia? Particularly now that the aurora borealis had arrived. Everyone was on edge. She could feel it in the air.

She made it to Madison Avenue where the Morgan Library & Museum spanned half a city block, and she was met at the front by the curator in charge of the medieval collection who had called her. He was somewhere in his sixties and had thick glasses and an earnest air. He ushered her through an employees-only corridor into his office and brought out the diary from a locked cabinet.

Magellan studied the exquisite leather-bound diary, utterly mystified why he thought it was hers.

"You have no previous knowledge of this diary?" he asked her for the second time.

"No, truly. I'm as surprised as you are." She leaned down to study the engraving on the cover. The braided circular design had three interlocking spirals.

He nodded to a stack of antique paper that looked closer to fabric. "It came with a translation for you."

"For me?" The meticulous handwritten translation made her feel even more bewildered. "Whose diary is it?"

"Merlin's twin sister." The man sounded serious.

She turned to him with a surprised laugh. "Merlin? As in Merlin the wizard from King Arthur?"

"Yes, though that is a fictionalized version of him."

"So this is a story too?"

"No, it is a diary." He seemed to be becoming impatient with her questions. "The legends for Merlin are based on historical accounts. Though there is some debate who Merlin was, many believe he was a Druid and seer who lived in the 500s, who also had a twin sister." He nodded to the diary. "To have anything survive from that time period is astounding for many reasons. But to have this memoir is simply incredible."

She was trying to keep up. "And the Liron Institute sent it to *me* why?"

"I was hoping you would know the answer."

She had no clue and looked at the institute's letter, wondering how someone in England had gotten her name and phone number. "What is this symbol?" She pointed to the letterhead.

"An ancient Egyptian symbol for Horus."

"What's a horus?" The symbol looked vaguely familiar, but she couldn't remember where she'd seen it before.

"Not what, *who*. Horus was the goddess Isis's son. The last superbeing recorded in myth."

They both stared at the letter. A strange choice in stationery. Not to mention the letter itself. *The fate of the world rests in protecting this book.*

Magellan wasn't sure what to make of it, and she was due at a bridal luncheon in an hour and she still had to get her harp. This book was definitely not meant for her. And even if it had been, it wasn't as if she could slip a rare sixth-century memoir into her purse and hit the subway. "Could you hold on to this until we can talk to the Liron Institute and straighten out the mix-up? There's been some mistake."

The man looked relieved by her request. "Certainly. Given its precious historical value, the museum would be happy to act as steward."

"Thank you. I'll be in touch." She checked her watch. She actually had two performances today, a bridal luncheon and an evening wedding. Her schedule was usually full thanks to her boss, Crystal. Because of Crystal, Magellan had become the most in-demand wedding harpist in Manhattan. Crystal had all but accosted her after seeing her play at Carnegie Hall and begged Magellan to come work for her after she graduated. New York City averaged anywhere from five to seven thousand weddings a month, and Crystal would have planned them all if she could.

The wedding planner was a forty-nine-year-old Latina cupid from the Bronx who had been married and divorced twice. She had a glamorous windblown look to rival JLo and literally power walked across the city in stilettos. She was also a hopeless romantic who believed life was better shared, and she was brilliant at her job. She managed Magellan's schedule, handled every last detail, and even had a driver shuttle her and her harp all over the city.

The partnership had worked out well, and if it kept Magellan in her own little bubble, then that was fine with her. She played the harp at countless events. Then at home she would stay up late at night with her headphones on, plugged into an electric keyboard to sift through melodies, always searching for a song . . . a symphony, a grand, epic movement of music she could feel inside her that felt unattainable.

Until now.

She had found the opening notes on her birthday. What a wonderful present it had been. She kept composing more and more of it over the course of the week, as if fueled by the aurora borealis's arrival. The vivid lights continued to dominate the sky and grow stronger each day, giving life an otherworldly feel.

Her dreams were becoming just as vivid. Every morning she would wake up inspired and head to the piano to work. She'd slip on her headphones and enjoy the intimacy of the sound in her ears. The music would be her symphony one day.

The first part of the first movement was becoming fully formed. A soaring opening that brought goose bumps to her arms every time she played it. Then she hit a wall, unable to compose further. Each time she tried, the notes faded into nothingness, and she had no compass to find them. It was entirely frustrating. So she would give up for the day, drink her coffee that had grown cold, and look out the window at the aurora borealis.

Monday, Tuesday, and Wednesday she kept the curtain open. By Thursday, she opened the patio door and stepped out, needing to get a clear view without the glass. If she stared hard enough, she swore she could see dark shadows moving behind the palette of colors.

The entire world was basically waiting with bated breath to see when the sky would return to normal. Every church organization, every temple and religious sect around the world was praying more than usual. Some groups claimed it was the end of times. Others thought it was the dawning of a new age. People had taken to the streets with signs and megaphones to share their opinion. And financial institutions were simply trying to keep everyone from taking out their life savings and stuffing it in their mattresses.

All week, news outlets continued to make the aurora borealis their top story, cycling panels of experts who argued and debated ad nauseum. The president in a public address from the Oval Office suggested the country "enjoy the Earth's dazzling planetarium show while it lasted." One guest expert appearing on all the networks explained in big, fancy words that the last auric event of this magnitude was the Carrington Event of 1859, when "a mass coronal ejection by the sun created an enormous burst of solar plasma."

Magellan had no idea what a coronal ejection was. Wren didn't know either. Friday evening when Wren came home from her rehearsal at the Met Opera, where she had scored a coveted role for the season, they popped popcorn and opened a chardonnay. Then Magellan surprised her by suggesting they sit out on the patio.

"For real?" Wren gaped at her.

Magellan laughed, stepping outside like she was dipping her toe into the water. Maybe the aurora borealis was helping her in some weird way face her fears. "Just keep the door open," she said and settled into a chair to watch the dancing lights. The sky was even more magnificent at night, steeped in iridescent fluorescence.

"Did you see the news today?" Wren asked.

"About the objects?" How could she have missed it? Today's newest aurora borealis headline had been about people finding old relics and prehistoric objects in the middle of open fields around the world. Objects were popping up out of nowhere with no explanation. A physicist from CERN had gone on record saying he thought the out-of-place artifacts had to do with the magnetic storm. "The planet's electrical currents control the iron in the Earth, *and that* controls the magnetic fields of space and time. So this whole magnetic storm could be messing with our atomic clock."

The reporter had asked him in disbelief, "You're saying these objects are time traveling?"

The Swiss physicist nodded. "Or jumping."

Time-jumping objects had everyone even more on edge. Magellan had been checking on her parents every day. They assured her they were fine, but she could hear the worry in their voices. They wanted her to move back home and bring Wren too. Magellan said she would think about it and promised to come see them again on Sunday.

Crystal had been adamant the wedding on Saturday was going to happen. She assured the bride the day would be gorgeous and aurora borealises were good luck for newlyweds. "That's why my second husband and I went to Alaska for our honeymoon."

Magellan listened to Crystal go on about all the luck an aurora borealis brought without mentioning her marriage had ended in divorce. Crystal had told Magellan more than once about her crush on her podiatrist, who might just become husband number three.

When it came to finding love, Magellan didn't have Crystal's optimism. She'd never been in love, although deep down she hoped one day she'd find her partner. Her person. But so far she'd only dated a tuba player for a short while but called it quits because he kissed her like she was the horn. Who knew if she would ever find anyone who could handle all her quirks and anxieties?

Tonight, after Wren said good night, Magellan lingered outside, gazing up at the sky, feeling utterly alone and yet part of something greater than herself. A feeling of momentum was building inside her, for what she wasn't sure. The night lights above her were twisting and swirling, laced with those faint shadows she couldn't look away from. It was as if a darkness beyond the aurora borealis was trying to get in. She told herself it was her anxiety playing tricks on her. Maybe sitting on the patio hadn't been such a good idea after all.

# Chapter 4

## Magellan

The next morning when the man from the Morgan Museum called she let it go to voicemail. He left a message asking if she had contacted the Liron Institute yet and what she wanted to do about the diary. She had yet to look up the institute and call to talk to someone. She could not imagine why they had sent the diary to her. Her only thought was if it could be connected to her birth parents.

Just this year, she had listed her name in the state registry to find them. She hadn't told her parents she'd done it, not wanting to hurt their feelings. But she yearned to know. Maybe her birth parents had sent the diary to her, like a family heirloom. Or maybe the diary was from Garesh. Maybe he was connected to the Liron Institute. But then why hadn't he included a card?

Absently twisting the ring on her finger, she wondered where he was now and what he thought about the aurora borealis. How she would have loved to play for him what she had been composing.

The song would be an epic symphony one day. She could feel it in her bones. She just needed to be patient. It had taken Brahms twenty-one years to compose his first symphony. She didn't have to compete with Mozart, Rossini, or Schubert's record timing. She had yet to even write down the opening and commit the notes to paper.

That morning she didn't feel like sitting at the piano sifting melodies, and she had to get ready for a wedding. Today the festivities were Halloween-themed, and guests were coming in costume. Technically she wouldn't be in costume, although her dress could pass as one. It was the dress Crystal always had her wear: a long, lavender Renaissance-esque designer gown made of heavy silk.

"That's the one!" Crystal had exclaimed when Magellan stepped out of the dressing room wearing it for the first time. "You look drop-dead gorgeous. Trust me, in that dress, I'll be planning your wedding in three months."

Magellan knew Crystal was just being Crystal. There was nothing drop-dead gorgeous about her. She considered herself passably pretty. Brown hair. Pert nose. Her eyes were her best feature. Her eye color often changed from greenish brown to deep green depending on her mood. She was on the shorter side with a few curves, but she did not have a wow factor—except when she played music. When she played music, people often told her she was beautiful. And she wanted to tell them it was the music that was beautiful, not her. But she agreed the dress did make her look very much "the harpist" in the romantic sense and was perfect for a wedding.

Her only jewelry was Garesh's ring, which she always changed to her left-hand ring finger whenever she worked. Doing so deterred flirty groomsmen and drunk wedding guests from hitting on her, because she did tend to get hit on a lot. When everyone had had too much to drink, the love songs coming from her fingertips and filling the air were potent.

Today Crystal had given her a wreath of flowers for her hair made of tiny silk rosettes to match the bridesmaids. Magellan put it on and laughed at her reflection. The look was definitely over the top.

Checking the time, she threw everything she might need into her bag and carefully stowed her harp into its towering aluminum travel case on wheels and rolled the monstrosity into the elevator. Downstairs the SUV was already waiting with Crystal in the back, and the driver loaded the harp. Then they were on their way to Lower Manhattan.

Crystal blew her an air kiss while rapid-firing instructions to the caterer on the phone. "I want the chocolate fountain free-flowing like *Willy Wonka*. And double strawberries." Crystal covered the phone and asked Magellan, "Did you eat?"

Crystal had a sixth sense, because Magellan had forgotten. She usually always had breakfast before a performance due to her hypoglycemia, but today she'd been distracted. Berating herself, she dug out a pack of trail mix from her bag and an apple juice. She had trouble opening the bag because her hands were starting to shake.

Fortunately, Crystal wasn't paying attention, having wrapped up the call with the caterer and now was talking to someone else, listening to whatever they were saying until she cut them off.

"Darren, wait! You're talking way too fast. The Earth's magnetic *what* is collapsing?"

Magellan paused eating the trail mix. She and the driver met each other's eyes in the rearview mirror as they waited to hear more.

"You're seriously saying the North and South Pole are about to flip? Can that really happen?" Crystal listened and cut him off again. "I don't care what happened hundreds of thousands of years ago. I'm talking about right now."

Magellan could hear the man's raised voice. "Yes! I'm telling you it's happening! You need to get somewhere safe. I'll call you later if I can." He hung up and Crystal stared at her phone in shock.

The car pulled up to the corner of Broadway and Fulton at St. Paul's Chapel. Everyone sat in silence until Crystal finally spoke. "My first husband, Darren, works at one of the observatories on Long Island. He said the North Pole has been moving for years, and it sped up today—like a lot—and is going to cause the poles to flip. It could be in weeks. It could be days." She went on in a quiet voice. Magellan had never heard her sound so grave. "As soon as this hits the news there's going to be a panic. He thinks we need to leave the city."

"Leave the city?" Magellan asked in disbelief.

"If the poles flip, he said it's the end of the world as we know it."

Magellan looked out the window, her thoughts in a whirl. What kind of end? The kind where no one survived?

Crystal rushed on, clearly floundering, "Look, I know it's crazy and I don't know—he could be wrong. I hope he's wrong."

"What if he's not?" Magellan studied the sky. Suddenly the aurora borealis didn't look so beautiful.

The driver asked, "What do you want to do? We can't sit here forever."

Crystal hesitated, her eyes on the church. "Could we just go inside there and give the wedding party a few hours of joy? Pretend like I didn't get this crazy call yet from my ex-husband? Please?" Crystal was practically begging her and about to cry.

Unable to say no, Magellan nodded. She would play the wedding and then head straight to her parents. She'd call Wren and have her meet her there. They would figure out what to do together.

"Thank you, you're the best." Crystal took a steady breath and forcibly put on a bright smile. She hopped out of the car and hurried inside the church, leaving Magellan overwhelmed and sick to her stomach.

The driver unloaded her harp for her with an *I'm out of here* look, and Magellan forced herself to go inside and get set up, placing her harp near the altar where Crystal wanted her. She sat down on her stool, tuned the harp's strings, and then played the designated thirty-minute pre-wedding set on autopilot as the guests began to arrive.

Right now, she was simply powering through "Over the Rainbow," "A Thousand Years," "All of Me," "Endless Love," and other wedding playlist classics from Debussy, Mozart, and Chopin. She ignored everyone and simply played to calm her nerves, trying not to think about how Crystal's ex had just told them the world might be ending.

Suddenly her whole short life felt wasted. Why hadn't she traveled yet? Why hadn't she composed anything magnificent? Why hadn't she fallen in love? Put herself out there more and taken risks? Why was she wearing Garesh's ring like a fake wedding ring on her finger when she wasn't even married? Yes, she was introverted, full of anxiety, and usually lost in her own daydreams with music, but this was her life and she had yet to fully live it. She'd always assumed she'd have more time. Now suddenly she was running out of it.

As her fingers instinctively flew over the strings, she took a good look at the guests filling up the church. They were outlandish in their costumes. A motley crew of superheroes, *Star Wars* characters, priests, pirates, vampires, butterflies, and fairies. Someone clanged up the aisle in real knight's armor. A trio of enchanting mermaids sat in one aisle with an inflatable Tyrannosaurus rex towering over them in the next.

The knight raised the visor on his helmet when he walked by her and winked. He would probably hit on her at the reception. Today she would let him.

If they lived that long.

If the planet's magnetic field didn't break before the bride and groom said "I do." Because if what Darren had said was true, the poles could flip at any moment. Yet here she was getting a stern nod from a stressed-out Crystal to start playing Pachelbel's Canon in D. The flower-wreathed bridesmaids began walking down the aisle with beaming smiles. When all six had made their way to the front, Magellan performed a graceful transition to the traditional *Bridal Chorus*, compliments of Wagner.

The bride and groom were dressed like a king and queen from some bygone era. Darth Vader, the bride's father, gave his daughter away. There were happy tears as the ceremony got underway.

Until halfway through, when everyone's cell phones started vibrating and lighting up. Soon phones were in people's hands, and the crowd was looking at something more riveting than the couple saying their vows.

Magellan knew it had to be the news. Darren's news. The poles' flip was really happening and had become public knowledge.

Then came the panic.

Someone started crying, and the whole wedding went to hell as everyone began acting like actors do in disaster movies when they discover they're all about to die. People rushed in every direction for an exit, jumping over pews to get out. Someone tripped over the decorative ribbons and a flower arrangement went down. As if on cue, an ominous crack of thunder rumbled outside, followed by the sound of pounding rain. The storm came out of nowhere. Less than an hour ago the sky had been clear. Today's weather forecast had been for "sunny skies and an aurora borealis." Now it sounded as if a hurricane was thrashing at the church doors.

Magellan sat poised at her instrument, in shock and unable to move while she watched the pandemonium as the church emptied. Even the priest went running out with his robe flying.

"Magellan, sit tight!" Crystal yelled at her across the stampede. "I'm going to try to get our driver to come back for us." Magellan nodded, still frozen.

Astraphobia was the fear of thunderstorms, which unfortunately she had in spades. Instead of serotonin, her body produced adrenaline during a storm, and the only way to get through one was to distract herself.

With a well of pure panic rising in her chest, she looked up to the balcony. If the sky was really falling and they were all going to die, then she was going to die playing music. Something epic and grand, and what better instrument to play it on than a pipe organ.

She hurried upstairs to the balcony and sat down at the bench. The organ towered above her, silent and majestic with its 5,300 pipes. She planned to use every single one.

Taking a breath, she laid her hands on the keys. Like a car revving to life, the instrument responded to her touch as she launched into Bach's Toccata and Fugue in D Minor, filling the church with all its power.

*Toccata* meant "to touch" and *fugue* allowed the pianist to embellish notes within the progression in an open invitation from Bach to join him in the song. So Magellan did. If this was going to be the last song she ever played, then she would be the storm raging. Her feet danced over the foot pedals as she played the progressions harder and faster than Bach could have imagined. She closed her eyes, feeling the music surround her, filling her up and making her whole body—even the metal of her ring—feel warm.

She didn't see the ring begin to glow in an ethereal light, the metal lit from within, or see the symbols turn blue like the center of a flame.

She didn't know St. Paul's Chapel was the oldest church in Manhattan and had been built on an ancient Ley Line.

She didn't know yet what a Ley Line was.

If she had, she would have understood the power her song was wielding, the door it was opening. She would have known Ley Lines were the magnetic currents circling the Earth, and the geomagnetic storm underway with the poles was wreaking havoc on those lines and opening dimensional doorways that had been closed long ago.

Magellan didn't know the key to opening such a door was *sound.*

As the song reached its pinnacle, Bach's mathematical perfection of notes turned that forgotten key, and Magellan fell into a spiraling light. The momentum felt like plummeting a great distance, as if she were a comet falling to Earth—and Magellan, named after the first explorer who masterminded how to circumvent the world once over, traveled across the world as well, to another time and place.

# Chapter 5

𝄢

## Rhys

Once upon a time Rhys had believed in fate. He had believed his scholarly pursuits were for a noble cause. But when his father died and forced him to take on the earldom, he all but abandoned those pursuits. He'd been too consumed with the problems he'd inherited: Tenant farmers who needed support. The estate's fast-creeping debt. Economic challenges brought on by the aftermath of the Napoleonic Wars. The dwindling livelihood of families whose farms had been on their land for hundreds of years was now his responsibility. Not to mention a crumbling historic manor with a leaky roof, still in desperate need of repairs. He had not been prepared for any of it. He didn't know the first thing about how to run an estate, and his father hadn't either. Rhys's love of language could not provide for his family, and if he didn't do something drastic quickly, then his tenants would lose their land.

Unfortunately, he had missed his chance to marry Lady Flora Winslow due to his father's untimely death and his family's mourning period. Flora had gone on to marry a duke three times her age.

Now the family's time in mourning was past and they were back in society, and Rhys needed to face his responsibilities, which was how he had arrived at the terrible idea of hosting a house party for two weeks to get to know a small, select group of eligible ladies he had invited to Hereford Manor.

To his surprise, his overly romantic and sentimental mother had tried to talk him out of it, not wanting Rhys to enter into marriage "like a sacrificial lamb chop." Her own marriage to his father had been a love match, and she wanted the same for her three children. Rhys replied that his younger brother and sister could have their love matches, but he was the heir. And as the heir, not only did he have to save the estate, their home, and the farms, he needed to save the labyrinth and the stone circle. It had been in the family's care for centuries. So he had hand selected the ladies and stubbornly sent out the invitations, including one to Flora Winslow's sister, Lady Fauna.

If his father were alive, he would have pointed out that *fauna* technically meant *animal life* in Latin. To which Rhys would have replied it also was the name for the goddess of the woodlands. Flora . . . Fauna, it did not matter to Rhys. What mattered was the ladies' father, Sir Winslow, could spot a good investment and had made a fortune on the steam locomotive's emergence only this year with Stephenson's Rocket. If Rhys married Lady Fauna, their financial woes would be solved. It was either that or sell part of the land or the library off book by book. Rhys knew his father would have approved of neither.

Now all the girls and their families had arrived today to stay a fortnight in the guise of a house party and enjoy the outdoors, hunt, fish, play lawn games, frolic, and picnic. But everyone knew the real reason was Rhys would choose a bride.

*Sisu* was the Finnish word for persevering with dignity through a crazy, hopeless situation, and *sisu* was exactly how he felt. Which is why, now that the guests were here and settling in, he found himself heading to the labyrinth, the one place he knew he could be alone because no one could find the center but him.

However, when he reached the center and saw the young woman lying on the ground in the middle of the stone circle, his first thought was, *Good God, one of them has found me!* But when she didn't stir or sit up to greet him, he realized the poor girl was unconscious.

He ran and knelt beside her, panic now setting in.

Who knew how long she had been there? His imagination began to run wild with the possibilities, each one perfectly horrible. She must have gotten lost in the labyrinth, stumbled into the center, and collapsed.

Was she dead?

She was lying on her stomach with her head turned away from him, her long hair a tangled mess and crowned with flowers. He touched her outstretched hand, finding her pulse steady. He puffed out a breath of relief and sat back on his heels.

Who was she? Whose daughter? From which family on the list? He thought he had met all the young ladies in attendance when they'd arrived in their carriages earlier today, but he had never met this one. He would have remembered her. She looked straight out of a fairy tale with a crown of tiny roses on her head, and her dress was practically medieval in design.

How on earth had she ended up here? He looked around. If they were found alone together like this, the scandal would be unthinkable. Her family may even force him to propose to save her reputation. He at least wanted to be able to choose the bride he was being forced to marry.

What a dreadful start to a dreadful house party!

"My lady?" he asked. "My lady?" He raised his voice and tried again, needing the riddle of her solved at once. "My lady, will you wake?"

The lady would not. As he continued to look at the sleeping woman, his imagination began to take over. His father, the day before he died, had said a woman would arrive and that Merlin's sister's diary was hers. Had he literally meant Merlin's sister would come to collect her diary? And somehow the labyrinth's stone circle would bring her here?

As the whimsical idea whirled in his head, everything tangible and logical in the world crushed it.

The very thought was madcap. Absurd. Ridiculous!

Still, his eyes went to the standing stones towering over them like ancient sentries. After his father's death, it had taken Rhys months to return to the labyrinth and collect all the musical instruments his father had strung up for his time machine that a child could have made. While dismantling it, Rhys had cried tears like a child for the father who had been his best friend and was now gone.

Rhys dismissed the whole wild notion for the woman. She was not a time traveler. She was either a guest or an interloper.

Becoming impatient, he took a blade of grass and tickled the back of her neck to wake her. Again and again he tried, until her hand came up to swat at him like a fly. Then her eyes flew open and she sat up, making him sit back, startled. For he found himself staring into the most extraordinary green eyes he'd ever seen. Eyes as green as the leaves on the labyrinth's walls. And for a singular moment he thought indeed the labyrinth had conjured her.

Even more astounding, she looked like the woman in the painting. The painting he had found in his father's studio after his death. Rhys would bet his life on it, although the painting in question had been dated 1799, years before both he or this woman had been born. The very idea she was the woman in his father's painting made Rhys feel like he was losing his mind. Of course she wasn't the woman from the painting. The possibility was ludicrous. Just as ludicrous as the fleeting thought she had time traveled from the sixth century.

The woman was gazing at him with the oddest expression on her face.

He finally found his voice. "Are you injured?"

"I don't know." She winced, touching her head. "I must have fainted." She had an accent that sounded like an American diplomat's he had met in London.

"You are a guest of the party?"

"No, I'm the harpist." She leaned forward and put her hand on his arm. "Were you at the wedding?"

Rhys struggled to find a polite answer to such a nonsensical question. What wedding? And why was she touching him? Such a breach of propriety. Surely she knew who he was. Drawing upon a cloak of politeness, he said rather stiffly as he pulled his arm away, "I'm afraid we have not been introduced yet. Did anyone accompany you? Were you escorted?"

"Escorted?" she parroted back and looked at the garden with surprise.

"Or did you become lost and find your way to the center by accident?"

"The center of what?" Her eyes were riveted by the standing stones. "Where am I?"

Rhys scowled, his suspicions growing. "Did someone send you in here to meet with me alone?" Truly it wouldn't be the first time some lady's mother had tried to put her daughter in his sights. But this was beyond the pale if the poor woman had been made to suffer by lying in wait for him in the labyrinth all day.

She ignored his question. "How did I get here?" Truly she seemed bewildered. "Where's the church?" Then her hand covered her mouth in horror. Her other hand landed on his arm again, and she squeezed it.

Rhys could only stare at her hand gripping his sleeve. She had the most exquisite hands he'd ever seen. He tried to focus on what she was saying.

"Did the poles flip? Were you at the wedding too? I don't remember you." Her eyes welled with tears. "Did we die? Is this heaven?"

*Oh dear. Oh lud.* Was she serious? Suddenly this encounter was becoming all too Shakespearean. She thought herself dead. He gently pulled his arm from her grip. The young woman was clearly delirious, and suddenly he felt like a complete ass for scolding her.

He tried again. "Rest assured, we are not dead. You've simply fainted and are obviously overcome. You must have wandered the labyrinth for some time." He stood and gallantly offered her his hand. "Here, let me assist you. I will lead you back to the house."

"What house?" She stood with a wobble, ignoring his hand. "Are we near the church?"

"You are at my estate, madam, in the center of Hereford Labyrinth." Clearly she was addled. Or else this was a ruse and she was a fine actress. Dressed like a maiden from a past century to await his discovery. Everyone within miles knew the lore for this place. Then just as quickly he dismissed the cynical thought. No, something was not right with her head. It was obvious she had a mental affliction, because now she had her eyes closed and was humming. What a shame for such a lovely woman. She was enchanting, really. Did Flora and Fauna have a third daft sister they were hiding away from everyone? Fiona or Festa or Merryweather perhaps? She must have escaped her room.

He spoke slowly, as if she were a child. "I'm afraid I have not had the pleasure of making your acquaintance yet, but you must be a guest. You are in the labyrinth at Hereford Manor. I am the Earl of Liron, at your service."

Her eyes popped open and she stopped humming. "*Liron?* From the institute?"

"What institute?" Now they were talking in riddles.

"The Liron Institute! You sent me the diary by Merlin's sister."

He froze in disbelief. "How do you know about the diary?"

"Because you said it's mine."

"Who did?"

Instead of answering, her eyes rolled up and she promptly fainted.

He lunged forward to catch her with a surprised "oomph" and swooped her up in his arms, almost losing his balance too. Now thoroughly alarmed, he looked down at her. This would not do. This would not do at all! Hefting her more securely, he hurried back through the labyrinth, muttering the whole way. This most certainly would not do. It looked like they had just had a private tryst. Fortunately, the labyrinth was some distance from the house behind the ground's expansive gardens.

When Rhys exited the labyrinth's entrance, he saw his mother in the distance. The countess was busy gathering flowers, no doubt to make girlish bouquets for today's luncheon. She saw him and let out a startled cry, throwing the flowers up in the air theatrically and hurrying toward them. If he hadn't been so concerned about their precarious situation, he would have laughed. His mother was a short blond cherub of a woman, adorably plump in her dotage and not used to running.

"Vhat has happened?" she asked in the thick Austrian accent she had never lost in all the years she lived in England. She reached him out of breath, her cheeks pink. "Who is zis?"

"I have no idea." Rhys forced himself not to look at the lady in question, who looked more and more like the woman in the painting the longer he stared at her. "I found her lying unconscious in the labyrinth. She awoke briefly and was highly confused. I assume she is one of the guests?"

"No, she is not!" His mother puffed out a breath. "I have never zeen her before."

"Are you sure? She's not a sister being hidden away?"

"Dressed like zat?" His mother was staring at the young woman in wonder. "She looks like a magical *fuh-ree*."

"Fairy," Rhys corrected automatically. His mother tended to butcher the English language, as well as possess a romantic sensibility that knew no bounds. His nostrils flared with impatience. He was the one holding the fairy. The mad fairy. "When she awoke, she had no idea where she was and then fainted."

He didn't mention the diary. Was it just as his father said?

His mother's eyes had grown wide as if she was suddenly remembering something, then she gasped and whispered in German, *"I do not believe it! It must be her."*

"Who?" he asked sharply, fluent in German too. "So you do know her?"

His mother shook her head, looking like she may faint herself.

"All right." Rhys glanced toward the house. "What do we do?"

"Vell, vee cannot just stand here vis her in your arms like you are starring in zome opera!"

"Should I leave her on the ground, then?" Rhys couldn't help but retort.

His mother shot him a reproachful look and hurried along the garden path away from the manor, ordering him, "Come zis way."

He dutifully followed but slowed when he noticed where she was leading him. "Not there." He stopped in disbelief. "Anywhere but there."

"Vee have no choice!" She arrived at the small cottage nestled behind the garden's back hedge and held the door open. "Hurry! Before someone zees us. Zhink of the scandal."

Rhys reluctantly stepped inside his father's old laboratory. A place he hadn't been since his death. A pungent sulfur odor assaulted his nose.

"Vee must revive her immediately," his mother was saying, heading to the open doorway in the back.

"Surely the rotting smell in here should do the trick."

He should have ordered this place cleared out after their official year of mourning had ended, but his mother had forbidden him. The laboratory looked like a madman's lair, littered with candle-powered contraptions, charts, and shelves lined with jars that were filled with dead animals and their organs. His father had kept a spare bedroom in the back for when he worked late.

Behind the bedroom was the art studio, where Rhys had found the painting. Now he was back with a real live woman who looked just like her. Or perhaps it was wishful thinking. He'd have to look at the painting again to be sure. It was hidden away in his closet.

His mother asked him, "Did you talk to her?"

"Briefly. She had an accent. American." He forced himself not to think about their strange conversation. How could the diary be hers? "She kept talking about a wedding. She thought I was a guest and with an institute."

"How strange," his mother said as she led the way to the back room. "Lay her on zee bed. I vill find zee smelling peppers." She hurried from the room.

"Smelling salts," Rhys corrected her, but his mother had already gone. He placed the woman gently on the bed and allowed himself to study her openly.

Not a houseguest, not a servant. Who, then?

She must have been visiting a neighboring estate and gotten lost. Or taken a dare by her friends to enter the infamous Hereford Labyrinth. But alone? Surely not alone. Then there was the question of the diary. She claimed it was hers, just as his father had said.

Rhys did not know why his father had been keeping it for this young woman. Perhaps he had been friends with her family. Rhys didn't know what to make of any of it. But his mother was right. She did look like a fairy. A medieval fairy.

His eyes traveled over her graceful curves revealed by her unusual gown. He had never seen silk shimmer in the candlelight like that. The material looked rare. Her head was turned to the side, exposing a long, lovely column of neck. His eyes traveled farther along . . . he cleared his throat and turned away to study her feet, a much safer view. Then he noticed her strange slippers and peered closer at them.

"Here vee are!" His mother came rushing back, waving a cloth like a white flag and holding the smelling salts. Rhys turned away, not wanting to be caught gazing at the lady's shoes, or her ankles either, which were lovely too.

His mother placed the smelling salts under the woman's nose, causing her to lurch awake with a startled gasp. Rhys immediately turned to stare into the woman's eyes, and for the life of him he could not look away because she did look like the painting.

He was hit with a feeling he could not describe, and his mind searched for the right word and settled on the Persian word *goya*, the moment when a fantasy feels so real it becomes reality.

# Chapter 6

## Magellan

Magellan was wrenched back into consciousness by some god-awful smell. She opened her eyes to find herself staring into the piercing blue ones of the man she'd met before. They had been outside together in a garden he called "a labyrinth," which made no sense. And his name was Liron, but he'd never heard of the institute. Which made no sense either. Now she was lying on a bed, in a creepy dark room, and he was gazing down at her with an intense scowl on his face.

He was wearing a Halloween costume. A full-blown *I paid good money for this costume* with leather boots, britches or breeches—whatever they were called—and a tailored waistcoat.

A petite older woman somewhere in her fifties hovered beside him and gazed down at her with a concerned wide-eyed look. She was also in an elaborate costume. Her platinum-blond hair was done up in an intricate twist with perfect corkscrew ringlets that belonged on a doll.

Magellan's mind was totally blank. How had she gotten from the garden to here? How had she gotten from the church to the garden? She couldn't remember anything. She was seconds away from teetering into a freefall panic when the woman leaned over her with a raised voice and said, “Hello? Can you hear us, dear?” She had a thick accent, but unlike the man’s, hers sounded German, not British. They were probably both fake.

Earlier the man had proclaimed he was an earl with all the gravitas of a Broadway actor in full character. Truly he had the arrogance part down pat. He was charismatic, tall and broad shouldered, most likely one of those actors who modeled on the side. He must have come late to the wedding and sat in the back. Otherwise she would have remembered him.

Magellan asked the woman, “Are you from the wedding?”

“You see?” The man turned to the woman, raising his hands in exasperation. “She’s befuddled!”

“Rhys, hush. Do be kind.” The woman laid a soothing hand on top of hers. “My dear, you have had a *frightening*.”

“A fright,” the man corrected her.

Magellan took several long, deep breaths, trying to keep the panic attack at bay. Garesh always said, “You can’t take a deep breath if you’re being chased by a tiger.” Breathing deeply told the body everything was going to be all right.

While the pair watched her with concern, Magellan let out another long breath and inhaled again, and again, as if she were trying to blow up an invisible balloon. She started over, speaking slowly, in case the woman couldn’t understand. “Are we near the church?”

“Zee church?” The woman gave an owl-eyed blink.

The man’s lips pursed in irritation, but he said nothing.

“No, vee are in zee countryside,” the woman answered with a smile, as if that explained everything. “Can you zit up?” She helped Magellan slowly rise.

Magellan winced at the pounding in her head. She had a splitting headache. Had she passed out at the reception?

Had there been a reception after everyone saw the news?

*The news.*

Then it all came flooding back. The chaos. The desertion. Crystal running off to find the driver. The last thing she remembered was playing Bach on the pipe organ.

The pipe organ! She gasped, remembering the bright light . . . the sense of falling . . . then everything afterward was blank. She must have fainted and hit her head on the church floor. Had she cracked her head open and died? The man had said she hadn't died, and he'd seemed certain. Maybe she fainted from not eating enough. She hadn't had a full-blown blood sugar attack in years. Maybe she was in a coma in the hospital and this was all a dream.

"I can't remember anything," she said in a daze.

"Oh dear oh dear." The woman looked to the man. "Rhys, she has had an accident. Did you zee her horse?"

"She was in the labyrinth, Mother. There was no horse."

"Then maybe zee horse is grazing nearby?"

The man sighed painfully. "I can assure you there was no horse."

Why were they talking about a horse?

"No need to be testy, darling." The woman turned back to her. "Vhat is your name?"

"Magellan Brighton. I was playing at the wedding."

"Are you zee vicar's daughter?" The woman was frowning now too, looking just as confused. "Is zee vicar married?"

The man tried again. "Do you know how you came to be in the labyrinth?"

"Please." Magellan was unable to stop the pressure building in her chest. "I can't remember how any of it happened."

"Well try." The man sounded frustrated. "You were found trespassing on our estate."

"Rhys!" the woman reprimanded him. "Do not be cross."

Magellan glanced past them to the open doorway to see a laboratory looking straight out of Mary Shelley's *Frankenstein.* The room was filled with beakers, weird gadgets, and strange contraptions, like the set of a play or a movie. Except the horrid stench wafting in was worse than a city dumpster rotting in the sun. Her eyes landed on a shelf lined with jars, where she saw a brain in one of them. An actual brain. Then came the terrifying thought, *Had she been drugged and kidnapped?*

A heady mix of adrenaline and fear hit her all at once, and she slowly slid off the bed on the other side away from them.

"What are you doing?" the man asked sharply.

"She is standing," the woman said.

"I can see that, Mother."

The woman tsked, "You frighten zee poor girl." She smiled at her. "Don't be scarred, my sweet."

Don't be scarred? Magellan's eyes widened in alarm. Who talked like that? People who put brains in jars and cosplayed "the earl" in warehouses before they killed their victims.

"*Scared*, Mother. Scared." The man pinched the bridge of his nose.

"Do not correct me vhen you are zee one *scaring* her."

Magellan needed to get away from these people. "I'm so sorry. I didn't mean to trespass on your estate." She backed away toward the door. "I'll just be going."

She turned and ran.

At first the man and woman were too surprised to move. Magellan bolted for the door, dashing past dusty rows of smelly experiments, dead worms, and more jars filled with gooey things in formaldehyde.

She heard the woman yell, "Rhys, stop her! Zee guests! Zee guests!"

Magellan threw open the main door, expecting to find a back alley in Lower Manhattan. Not . . . *an estate.*

A garden extended for acres. A real garden unlike anything she'd ever seen, full of manicured pathways, rosebushes, trickling fountains, marble benches, and Greek statues. Athena and her owl were right beside her.

Crisp air filled her nose, the purist air she'd ever breathed, along with the sweet scent of flowers. In the distance stood a castle. A real castle. And behind it was a forest.

She stopped running so abruptly, the man chasing her barreled into her from behind. His arms banded around her waist and pulled her back to keep them both from falling forward. The air left her lungs in a whoosh, and she was dizzy all over again. Because everything in front of her eyes was *wrong*. So wrong. The gardens, the castle, the beauty. Her brain couldn't compute the sensory overload. As the man went to let her go, her body listed forward. She felt like a puppet whose strings had snapped. The ground rose up to meet her as her vision faded, and the man caught her in his arms.

"I seem to be making a habit of this," he grumbled. The other woman reached them, out of breath. He said to her, "We're not going back in there. It obviously frightened her to death." He began to walk toward the castle.

Magellan kept her eyes closed. She felt like she was floating, and the two strangers' voices sounded far away. She was no longer able to deal with reality, whatever reality this was. Because these two people weren't crazy. She was.

The woman sounded fretful. "I do believe you are vright. Zee poor girl is obviously suffering from amnesia."

*Amnesia?* Magellan's brain settled into a fog. Either she was experiencing a very vivid dream, or she had died—those were the only two possibilities. Right now, she was most likely lying unconscious on the balcony floor of St. Paul's with a traumatic head injury while her brain hallucinated her own *Bridgerton* Netflix special starring an earl with windswept black hair, ocean-blue eyes, and a mouth made for kissing in every episode. Now her brain must have concocted her own story as she lay in a hospital bed dying. She could feel herself drifting off, being pulled under a blanket of sleep.

The woman said, "Take zee back stairwell. Place her in zee room next to mine."

"We need to keep her out of sight," the man said. "Let me know when she wakes."

The last thing Magellan remembered before slipping off to sleep was the man gently taking the wreath of flowers from her hair. Then he touched her hand, and she fleetingly thought it felt like fingers playing the first keys to the beginning of a song.

# Chapter 7

## Rhys

After Rhys left their unexpected houseguest asleep in a bedroom far away from the other guests, he marched straight to his suite of rooms where the painting was hidden in the back of his changing room closet. He took it out from its hiding place and removed the cloth draping it. His eyes raked over the canvas, studying the woman's graceful profile, the quarter moon of her face. She was turned away from the viewer, giving only the glimpse of a smile. A smile meant for a lover. Rhys had never been able to ask his father who she was—or if she existed at all. The only clue was the painting's title and date inscribed on the back:

*The Lady of the Labyrinth, 1799.*

The more Rhys looked at it, the more he was convinced their strange visitor only slightly resembled her. They had the same hair color and delicate profile, but that was all. It wasn't as if she could have been alive in 1799. Not to mention, his lady from the labyrinth was an American and mad as a hatter.

How had she arrived at the labyrinth? And how had she come to possess such a diary? His father had known so many people, both alchemists and antiquarians in England and abroad. Had her family lent it to him? Rhys had yet to keep his promise to read it. Which is why he decided it would be best to skip tonight's dinner party altogether and go to the library. He could visit with the guests tomorrow.

With barely a guilty conscience at being such a horrible host, he sent his regrets through the butler, saying he had an urgent matter to attend to. He did not share the matter was a book.

He headed to the east wing, well away from the bustle of the staff and guests. The library had been his and his father's favorite room, a vast space with vaulted ceilings holding one of the largest collections of historical texts and rare manuscripts in Europe. His father had collected them like candy, including an assortment of alchemy manuscripts spanning the last five centuries. The library even boasted having the coveted thirteenth-century text *The Sum of Perfection* in its collection, written by a Franciscan monk from southern Italy who had found great success tinkering in his laboratory. The man's opus was considered the bible of modern science where he'd detailed how to refine metals—and somehow known matter was made of invisible particles. His revolutionary ideas helped pave the scientific revolution occurring in Rhys's lifetime.

Other treasures gracing Hereford's library were worth a fortune as well, which is why Rhys had been considering selling off the collection. He had even extended a house party invitation to a colleague from the Historical Society. Lord Erickson, a lofty baron, had arrived armed with his quizzing glass to appraise the alchemy texts over the course of the week. Rhys had yet to speak with the man, and instead of showing Lord Erickson the library this evening as he had planned, he came alone.

The room welcomed him with its familiar scents of old leather, parchment, and beeswax polish. A hint of apple spice cake wafted from the tea tray a footman had just delivered.

Settling in at his desk in the alcove, Rhys got out a clean notebook, inks, and his dictionaries to conduct his translation. Then he opened the hidden puzzle drawer. The diary gleamed in the lamplight, and he was hit by a strange melancholy. He had not opened this drawer since his father died. Nor had he kept his word to translate the diary. But he would rectify that at once.

He laid the book in question front and center on his desk, again captivated by the cover's beauty. The intricate carved triskelion of three interlocking spirals looked like a labyrinth itself.

If the diary was indeed authentic and penned by Merlin's sister, the ramifications would be extraordinary. Merlin was not only a most celebrated Bard from antiquity with a life steeped in myth and legend, he also had been one of the last Druids—and Druids never wrote down their history. They were notoriously secret in safeguarding their esoteric knowledge. Merlin had lived at the end of the Dark Ages, at the very edge of the country's recorded history. But even with all the lore attributed to him, little was known about the man. If his twin sister truly had written about their lives, an actual memoir, Rhys couldn't imagine what it might say.

The Old English text spread out before him like a treasure map, and for the first time in a long time, he felt the old thrum of excitement stir his blood. He settled into the first page, ignoring the goose bumps trailing up his arms. He told himself he would translate only a page or two tonight—until he began to read, and the cavernous depths of the past opened its mouth up wide and beckoned him inside.

# Chapter 8

## Gwynedd

*The night we were born two comets appeared in the sky.* Cathan would later say, one for each of us.

Ailith, head Druidess and the most talented midwife in Strathclyde, had known ours would not be an easy birth. Months before, she had foreseen our delivery in the twilight of her dreams. She told no one of her vision in the hope she was wrong. For in her dream, the birthing room became my mother's grave. Ailith worried, even with all her knowledge of ancient medicine, she would be unable to stop what would come to pass.

The Druidess searched the whole countryside for the legendary Holy Flower, which bloomed for one hour in the light of a full moon next to a stone circle's most northern stone. Picked within that window of time, the bud contained immense healing properties to extend one's life threefold. Picked at any other time, the flower was deadly poison.

Centuries ago, Holy Flower grew near every stone circle along the Ley Lines, those powerful streams of Earth's energy. But knowledge of the flower, like the Ley Lines themselves, had become lost to time.

Now only the legend of Holy Flower survived as a memory from the magic of old.

Ailith wondered if Cathan secretly had Holy Flower in his purse, harvested in the days before the Roman occupation. He was the oldest Druid in the land, and no one knew his age or could remember when he had not been an Elder. He was a towering man who looked like a winter tree with his long white robes and silver hair—and he had not aged further in all the years Ailith had known him. His skin still glowed, his teeth were strong, and his eyes held the brightness of youth.

Ailith, either from pride or embarrassment, never asked Cathan if he had Holy Flower or knew where to find its bloom. She had been unable and felt if the Earth would not relinquish the herb to her, then she was not meant to have it. Instead, she used every medicine in her arsenal she could for my mother. She made tinctures of black haw and burdock root, and brewed dandelion with lady's mantle. The risks of childbirth were always great, but my mother was strong and full in her maidenhood. On the eighth moon, Ailith gave her a daily infusion of motherwort and lemon balm to strengthen her. The time for our arrival had come.

When the twin comets appeared, streaking across the sky in a trail of heaven's fire, the celestial event caused Cathan to leave his observatory on the Druids' island and make the journey to Cadzow, where my father was chieftain. Our lands were the wealthiest in the Strathclyde kingdom, and my father, the great warrior Morken, was the king of Strathclyde's right hand.

Cathan arrived at our doorstep looking like he had stepped from the mists of an ancient dream. Brilliant gold plates adorned his neck and wrists, and he was dressed in his finest white ceremonial robes. His right hand gripped an enormous wooden staff that extended from the floor to his shoulder—a staff most assumed was for walking, when really its purpose was to measure the stones and the stars.

Morken greeted Cathan with surprise and hoped the High Druid's presence would bring good fortune for our birth. My mother had only recently revealed to my father she believed there would be not one of us but two.

My mother's labor was surprisingly short. The pains came quickly but were well managed by the herbs, and much to my brother's chagrin I was born first. Ailith cut the cord, and my mother sat back on the birthing chair to calm her breathing again.

"We'll call her Gwynedd," she said, having already chosen our names many moons ago. She often had dreams of us in the chasm of sleep while we grew in her belly. She knew with certainty we would be a boy and a girl. She foresaw my fire-red hair, red as Boudicca's, and she bet her favorite gold pendant my brother's hair when he arrived would be black as pitch like our father's.

Ailith's assistant took me to the birthing waters to be cleaned while Ailith rinsed her hands and prepared for the second birth. She gave my mother a sip of warm bone broth. "Well done, Vanora. Now once more."

My mother nodded when pain lanced through her like a sword, causing her to cry out. My father abandoned his seat by the hearth where he was sitting with Cathan and pulled back the curtain.

"There is trouble?" He knelt beside them and took Vanora's hand.

Ailith looked to him. "The baby has not yet dropped. He is turned." She tried to right the wrong but could not. Too much time was passing. "I believe the cord is wrapped around him." Her dream nine months before had not been a dream but a prophecy.

My mother had aided in enough births to know my brother's life was in peril. Her tone brooked no question at what must be done. "Then make haste. Do it quickly."

Ailith nodded and readied the dagger, but still her hand waivered.

My father paled when he saw the blade. "Wait," he said, suddenly breathless. "Will she survive?"

Ailith's stricken look was answer enough.

Cathan, who had stayed silent in his chair by the fire, watched the flames bend and bloom in the hearth and spoke softly to the room. "Ailith. One twin cannot survive without the other. They both must live."

Still tethered to her pain, my mother managed to give my father a smile. In that moment she was the vibrant girl he had married in the sacred grove on Partickhill, the young beauty the Bards sang songs about. "I will see you in the next life," she promised, knotting her fingers tightly in his. "Remember my wishes."

My father nodded, unable to speak. He was the fiercest fighter in all the North, but on this night his back was bowed, the weight of the Fates too much to bear. He watched helplessly as Ailith guided the blade.

"Forgive me," Ailith pleaded to them both, for in the end she had failed.

With the blade's cut, my mother's blood became a newfound river on the floor. Ailith dropped the knife with a clatter and pulled my brother out. She worked quickly to unravel the cord wrapped tightly around him and help him find air. My brother let out a wailing cry, his chest blowing a bright horn announcing that he lived. My mother reached out to touch his face and said his name. Then she closed her eyes.

My father was the one who held my mother's hand as she died. His eyes remained fixed on her with the unflinching gaze of a warrior on the battlefield, watching another leave this world. When her life ebbed and her spirit departed, a new vacancy filled the room where she had once been. No one spoke in the aftermath.

He carried her body from the birthing chair and laid her gently on the bed, where he sat beside her and smoothed her hair. His eyes met Ailith's, and his gaze settled on the midwife's hands covered with blood. He turned to Cathan, barely able to contain his anguish. "Did you know she was to die? Is that why you came tonight?"

Cathan shook his head. His eyes held no answers, only the reflection of the firelight. "I knew they were to be born."

Morken turned to Ailith. The Druidess midwife was a seer, and she must have foreseen the death. "The truth!"

Ailith nodded, the salt of tears on her tongue. The price for our survival had been too great. "I dreamed of it once. But I'd hoped I could change the outcome."

Morken turned away, no longer able to contain his grief. He and our mother had been married barely a year. In that time, he had given her all his tenderness, and she took it with her to the afterlife. The door to my father's heart all but closed on that day to everyone, including us. He turned to Cathan, his voice harsher than he ever would have dared to talk to the High Druid before. "Tell me. Why did you come tonight?"

"The twin comets in the sky," Cathan said softly. "Twins bring the waters of magic into the world, and I believe your children will bring an ocean."

Morken scoffed with a bitter laugh. "An ocean of magic? Yet not enough to save their mother."

Years later when my brother and I learned how to sift memories, we sifted this moment. My father's words wounded us the most because they were true. My mother had surrendered her life for us, and my father never forgave us.

Ailith's assistant held my brother swaddled. Her white Druid's robes were stained with blood. Red and white were the colors of the Netherworld, the place where the living cannot go.

A hard, cold flatness entered my father's eyes as he stared at his crying son with hair as black as his own.

"Would you care to hold him?" she offered.

He ignored her and strode to the door. His grief unbridled, he barked out orders to ready his horse as if there were a great battle to be waged outside.

After he had gone, Cathan allowed the full weight of his remorse to show. "Ailith, forgive me," he whispered, because he knew Ailith, deep in her heart, believed he had the knowledge to save my mother. "Some magic cannot be wielded. Some paths cannot be changed. In the wild of the world, there are happenings set in stone."

Even if Ailith understood, she did not agree. There were many myths of divine children left motherless in order to set their feet firmly on their path. But Vanora had died in her care, not some legend of old.

The Bard to Cadzow, a man named Oli, appeared at the door in solemn silence with the birthing book in hand. Crushed befuddlement rested in his eyes. Only the eve before, he had been leading the court in merry song for preparation of our birth. How quickly life had turned.

"Record their names in the book," Cathan ordered. "Both their names."

Usually a girl, unless she was born a queen, was not recorded in the birth registry. Oli did not question Cathan's order, for the Druids followed the Old Way, with the belief there was no difference between sex.

He wrote our names in the finest script:

*Gwynedd and Merlin, born in the year 540.*

Before Cathan left, he hung a birch tree branch above our cradle. The birch is the first tree at the edge of the forest and marks the beginning of a journey. The tree possesses both male and female catkins. So too did the birch mark the beginning of ours.

The fact you are reading these pages now means your journey has begun, and the time has come to unearth my memories, for the world is depending on us. You are wondering how my diary came to be in your hands. The simplest answer is by design. Merlin had the idea, and Taliesin swore he would help protect the book, and we have tied these words to each other through time with a powerful triskelion. For a single lifetime is only a small part of a much bigger story, and to understand the part you play, first you must know mine. We may not share the same memories, but we are the captain of an ancient ship, and as powerful as the mightiest magicians of old.

# Chapter 9

## Magellan

Magellan opened her eyes to be greeted by blinding sunlight streaming through a wall of windows framed by gold-brocaded curtains. She sat up and squinted at the brightness, only to find herself lying on top of an enormous four-poster bed with a regal canopy draped on top.

She blinked and blinked. This could not be happening again. For a third time she was waking up in a strange place. She squeezed her eyes shut and struggled for breath as an anxiety attack hit hard. She tried to call upon her coping exercises to calm the hell down. There was one, "the 5-4-3-2-1 countdown," to help someone in a panic connect back to their senses. See five things. Hear four things. Touch three things. Smell two things. Taste one thing.

She opened her eyes, noting right away the entire room looked straight out of a museum. Which did not help! Fighting back another surge of panic, she tried hard to look for five specific things. A dainty writing desk sat in the corner. An elegant sofa and side table was on the far wall with a mirrored antique dresser on the other side. The fifth thing was the wood floor's intricate design was partially covered by a soft-piled carpet.

Next came four sounds, except she couldn't hear anything. The background noise of the city was noticeably absent. Instead she focused on the sound of her breathing, hummed a bit, and snapped her fingers a few times. Moving on to touch three textures, she slid off the bed, feeling her bare feet on the floor. Her shoes were tucked in the corner nearby, and the flower wreath from her hair sat on the dresser. Her toes sank into the carpet as she moved about the room. She touched the bed's wooden banister and ran her fingers along the luxurious down blanket, soothed by the feel of the billowy fabric beneath her fingertips.

She sniffed about for two smells. The scent of lemon oil wafted in the air, along with a floral fragrance from the fresh roses on the dresser. The flowers were magnificent, an enormous bouquet of roses in pinks, yellow, and white. Their beauty alone calmed her significantly.

The last in the countdown was one taste, but her mouth was too dry and her stomach rumbled. She would need to eat soon or risk a blood sugar crash.

She padded over to the window and found she was able to look out at the breathtaking view without any dizziness. She was on the third floor, the same height as her apartment, but the stunning sight muted her fear. Green stretched for miles, and beneath her window was an enchanting garden lined with fountains and sculptures.

It felt like a dream. *Was it a dream?*

If this was a dream, everything felt stunningly real. Maybe she really was at an estate, just like the man said. The gardens were spectacular from the room's vantage point, and an actual labyrinth loomed in the distance, a majestic maze in the shape of a circle easily the size of a football field. She could see the stone circle and garden in its center where she'd woken up. That man, "the Earl of Liron," had been telling her the truth. About all of it.

His name was Liron, yet he'd never heard of the institute.

Magellan looked around the room and caught her reflection in the mirror. She was a mess. Her dress was rumpled with grass stains, her hair a tangle. She laid her hands on her body. Her skin and clothes felt real, physically real. Too real to be a dream.

She went to the bedroom door and tried to open it, only to find it locked.

Someone had locked her in.

A surge of adrenaline exploded through her body, infusing every cell with the primal urge to run, and suddenly she could not catch her breath. Every coping method flew out the window. She was trapped in an alternate reality and locked in a room. She pulled on the handle, frantically trying to force it open.

Should she scream for help? Did she want her captors to know she was awake? She dropped her hands from the handle, unsure what to do.

This wasn't a dream. It was a nightmare. She stood paralyzed, her thoughts racing too fast to come up with any kind of plan.

At the sound of the doorknob turning, she frantically looked around for a place to hide, but there was no time. She backed away in terror.

The same woman from yesterday bustled into the room with a bright smile that seemed forced. She was wearing another elaborate full-length gown. Yesterday, she'd said she was the earl's mother. Maybe she really was. Two women dressed in simple black gowns with white collars followed behind her. One woman was holding a tea tray.

"Splendid! You are avake." The woman's accent was thick. "Did you sleep vell, my dear? Vee have brought you tea."

Magellan stood there frozen, unable to find her voice.

"Do not vorry if your memories have not returned because of zee *amnesia*. I have heard *amnesia* can be long lasting." She kept emphasizing the word. "Zee only cure for *amnesia* is to vrest and recover until your memories return. You must look on me as your nursemaid. I am Lady Liron, and my son who you met yesterday is zee earl."

Magellan cleared her throat, desperately needing to clarify. "From the Liron Institute?"

The housemaids giggled and Lady Liron frowned. "No, my dear, you are at our estate, Hereford Manor, and vill be my guest vhile you convalesce."

"Convalesce?"

"From your *amnesia*," Lady Liron stressed again, looking as if she wanted to say more. The two maids hovering behind her seemed unsure what to do. Magellan wasn't sure either.

Was she making this all up in her head and actually lying in a Manhattan hospital?

One of the maids stepped forward and asked, "Milk and sugar, miss?"

"Yes, please," Magellan whispered, feeling lightheaded as she watched her prepare the tea. "Extra sugar, please." Then she gathered her courage to ask Lady Liron, "Do you think I might be able to go back to the labyrinth today? Where I was found? It might help me to . . . remember."

To her relief, the woman nodded. "My son can escort you vis a chaperone." Then the woman's eyes lit up. "Along with zome of our other guests! Our house party has just gotten underway, and you must be included in all zee festivities." She clapped her hands in delight.

Magellan raised her eyebrows. Though it was a relief to know they weren't going to keep her locked up in this room, she didn't want to join any festivities. She wanted to go home.

Lady Liron's gaze was riveted on her dress. "I vill have to give zome story to introduce you. My daughter Vivianne vill lend you clothing."

Magellan needed to know. "So I'm in England?"

Lady Liron glanced nervously to the maids but said, "Yes, of course. Not far from Wiltshire."

Magellan had no idea where Wiltshire was but nodded as if she did. Then she inwardly cringed when she asked the next question. "And what year is it?" She had to ask because she felt like she had wandered onto the set of *Pride & Prejudice.* One of the maids giggled nervously, and Lady Liron shot the girl a look.

Magellan reminded them, "My amnesia."

Lady Liron gave a strained smile and turned back to her with a swish of her skirts. "Of course." She patted Magellan's hand. "It is zee year 1829, vhich I'm sure you vill remember soon."

Magellan licked her lips, trying hard to stifle the urge to run hysterically from the room.

1829? She grabbed her tea and downed it like a tequila shot.

"Now vrest," Lady Liron was saying, "and I vill have a breakfast tray brought up." Then the woman hurried out as if she couldn't leave fast enough. Her maids trailed behind her.

The sound of the lock turning filled the room, leaving Magellan alone again.

Dread and a new kind of panic assailed her. How was she in 1829?

She looked around, trying to rein in her fear, and she rubbed her fingertips together over and over, another coping mechanism to ground herself. But it wasn't working. Anxiety was triggered either by being afraid of the future or regretting the past, and you only got out of it by being in the present. But what did you do when the present was the wrong freaking year? Her vagus nerve was in meltdown. There was no humming herself out of this.

Could it really be 1829? Had the polar shift catapulted her through time like those artifacts on the news?

Which triggered another terrifying thought—was she stuck here forever? She fought back the rising panic and forced herself to think. Somehow, she needed to get back to the center of the labyrinth. She needed to go there and figure out what the hell happened.

The sound of the lock turning made her pivot. A maid entered with a breakfast tray, set it down, curtsied, and left, locking the door behind her.

The tray was a feast of bacon, eggs, sausage, sautéed mushrooms, and thick slices of bread, along with a fruit bowl and dainty pastries. If

Magellan was in her right mind, she would have enjoyed it. Instead, she wolfed everything down to stave off the blood sugar crash she could feel coming on, barely tasting a thing. Only fleetingly did it register when she poured herself a second cup of tea that it was the best tea she'd ever had in her life. A strong English Breakfast that turned a rich caramel color with the milk.

She took her cup and went over to the window to study the labyrinth. The view was mesmerizing, the labyrinth a stunning masterpiece of architecture that looked like a beautiful mandala made out of green hedges.

Squinting hard, she attempted to pick out the route from the beginning to end. Surely if she studied it carefully enough, she could remember the path to the center. Labyrinths were nothing more than a pattern—like a challenging song—and she could remember any song.

Her gaze traveled along the hedge lines, and she memorized each turn by assigning it a musical note. She started over countless times until a mental map of a song formed in her mind. She stood there for well over an hour, humming the tune that would get her from the labyrinth's start to the center. Now certain she could find her way through it, she just needed to sneak off by herself.

Looking back at her demolished food tray, she took a napkin and hid several mini scones and an apple to make sure she had provisions for later. Then the door unlocked, and Lady Liron returned with four maids this time trailing behind her like a little army. Three maids held long satiny dresses in their arms. The fourth had a stack of white linens. The maids laid the selection of gowns on the bed. Then they all departed except for the fourth maid.

Lady Liron said, "Zis is Polly. She vill help you dress and do your hair."

Polly gave a quick curtsy. She was a small girl with wispy blond hair and a big gap between her front teeth that looked endearing when she smiled—which was all the time. Polly stared at Magellan with open curiosity.

"Polly vill assist you vhile you convalesce."

Polly curtsied again. "I'm so sorry to hear you've gone daft, miss."

Magellan found herself nodding in complete agreement. She stared at the mountain of gowns. "Surely, I only need one dress." This was a day-long hallucination at most. "I'll be needing to get back to—"

"Of course, my dear." Lady Liron cut her off and took both of her hands in hers, holding them tight. Magellan startled at the woman's firm grip and the folded piece of paper being pressed into her hand. Lady Liron squeezed her palms closed, holding her gaze as if trying to communicate. "Do not fret," she said. "Polly vill return and help you get ready. Vee vill make zee introductions zhis afternoon." Lady Liron squeezed her hands once more and swept from the room with Polly following behind her.

Magellan stared at the note Lady Liron had slipped into her hand, a small piece of parchment folded over several times into a tiny square.

She sat down in one of the chairs and opened it to find a bold handwritten message addressed to her.

> **Magellan, my dearest friend,**
>
> **You have arrived in the labyrinth at Hereford Manor. I am certain at present you are most confused. I have asked my wife to deliver this message upon your arrival, for I do know when you arrive from the future, unfortunately I will no longer be alive. She does not know the full extent behind your appearance, for I fear if I say too much I will unintentionally alter the course of the future for us all with disastrous results. I am taking a gamble in penning this note, but I feel I must, and it is as much as I dare.**
>
> **I have given my son, Rhys, the diary. He will translate the pages for you. If he resists, force him. You must read Gwynedd's words for yourself and read**

**them quickly. I am not understating facts when I say the fate of the world is in your hands.**

**Safe journey into the labyrinth.**

**Your servant and devoted friend,**
**Godwin**

**Post scripta: I do not wish to alarm you but please know when you play the song, forces beyond this world are waiting at the threshold to possess it. I have seen that hell with my own eyes.**

Magellan reread the letter over and over again, trying to unravel its riddle, and her heart beat faster each time. Her whole body was viscerally reacting to Godwin's message.

The letter made no sense. *Dearest friend?* And he mentioned the fate of the world just like the letter from the Liron Institute. An institute no one had ever heard of. And she assumed *Post scripta* meant *PS*—but she had no idea what song he was talking about.

Crazy as his message was, at least one person seemed to know the truth of her arrival here. The problem was the man was dead.

Godwin, the late earl, insisted she read the diary and his son, Rhys, would translate it for her. She had no idea how on earth she was going to get the earl with the scowling face to do that.

The door behind her opened, and Magellan quickly hid the note in the desk drawer in front of her where she had stowed her apple and scones.

"Are you ready, miss?" Polly rolled in a cart on wheels brimming with vials, jars, and an ancient-looking curling iron nestled in heated embers. She began to take charge with bristling efficiency.

Magellan couldn't believe she was being forced to change and tried to insist she didn't need to, but Polly wouldn't hear of it. The young woman helped her out of her old dress and then eyed Magellan's bra and underwear askance, asking if ladies wore those kind of undergarments in the United States of America. Then she held out the 1829 version of underwear: ankle-length pantaloons made of cotton and a matching shift-like gown. The pants had a slit down the middle so she could easily use the chamber pot, which Polly pointed out was "in the water closet." Over the shift went a corset-like bodice—the equivalent of an 1829 bra—and then a petticoat. Finally came the dress, a long billowy gown fit for a ballroom.

Polly beamed at the transformation. "You look so beautiful, miss! Now sit and let me do your hair." She pulled out the hot iron tongs from the embers.

Magellan watched in the mirror, trying to remain calm, but she was still reeling from the letter. How did Godwin know her? And how had a diary belonging to Merlin's sister followed her to 1829?

"Now for the gloves," Polly announced, slipping them on her hands as she chattered on about the house party, but Magellan didn't hear a word. The last thing she clearly remembered was playing the pipe organ, then waking up here. She had no clue how long she had been gone or if Crystal was still at the church. Did Crystal think she was missing? Was she missing? Maybe she was in a parallel world. Or maybe the world did not exist anymore. The deluge of questions whirling in Magellan's mind made the panic inside her surge higher until she couldn't breathe. She was trapped at an estate straight out of a Regency romance with a dead earl warning her about hell if she played music. Maybe she had lost her mind. The diagnosis did not look good. She began to hyperventilate.

Polly looked alarmed. "Are you all right, miss? Did I tie your corset too tight?"

Magellan grabbed Polly's arm, becoming desperate. "Do you have a piano?"

"I'm sorry, miss, you're asking if we have a piano?"

Magellan nodded emphatically.

"Of course, we have two."

"Could you take me to one? Right away?" She was too distraught to have it make sense, but she needed to play to calm herself.

"Should I call for a doctor?"

"No! I just need a piano. It will help." After she played something epic and complex and impossible until her fingers went numb and her thoughts stopped spinning. Twelve piano pieces were considered the hardest in the world, and Magellan could play them all. Beethoven's Sonata No. 29, Liszt's *La campanella*, Chopin's Étude Op. 25 No. 11, Ravel's *Gaspard de la Nuit*, Sorabji's *Opus Clavicembalisticum* . . . Today she would simply go down the list until she could breathe again. She would play until she couldn't remember she was stuck in 1829, and then when she was calmer, she would find a way to the labyrinth and try to get home.

She took hold of Polly's hand. "Please, Polly, I must play or I am going to lose my mind more than I already have!"

"You poor thing, if you think it will soothe you. Of course." Polly helped her into a dainty pair of shoes resembling ballet slippers. "I'll let the countess know you'll be in the east wing. She won't mind your tinkering if you're somewhere the guests can't hear."

Polly led her down a hallway and then a back staircase to the first floor. They passed through countless hallways and closed doors as Polly told her, "The formal conservatory is never in use anymore since the previous earl died. You shouldn't disturb anyone there."

When they reached the ground floor, they went down several more hallways and finally arrived at a pair of imposing double doors. Polly opened the doors wide to reveal one of the most breathtaking rooms Magellan had ever seen. Opulent mirrored panels gilded in gold extended up to a vaulted ceiling. The wood floor gleamed with an intricate inlaid geometric design, and three sets of beveled French glass doors opened out to the gardens.

Magellan looked around in wonder. "It's like a concert hall."

An elegant grand piano was the centerpiece. Chairs and settees were draped with white sheets, the room not in use.

Polly opened the garden doors to let in fresh air and the sunlight. "Play as long as you like. I'll check on you later and take you to the countess for the introductions to the other guests."

Magellan was already planning to escape to the labyrinth before then, but still she asked, "Are you sure I should meet anyone? What if someone guesses I'm not really a guest?"

Polly shook her head with a grin. "But you are a guest now, and you look splendid, miss. No one will ever know you have a medical affliction."

Magellan grimaced and turned toward the piano. As she approached the instrument, she gasped in disbelief.

The piano was a Streicher! A bona fide Streicher from Vienna. She had only seen one in a museum. This one was immaculate and brand spanking new. She reached out and touched the keys in wonder.

This piano would have been made by Nannette Streicher. Her father, Johann Andreas Stein, had been a famous organ and piano maker back in his day. When he died, his children, Nannette and her brother Matthäus, along with Nannette's husband Andreas Streicher, took over the business. Nannette had a hand in all things, including the instruments' designs. She was a musician, a close friend to Beethoven, and a great patroness of the arts who forged her way in a time when women had very little freedom, and Magellan was about to play one of her pianos.

As she laid her hands on the gleaming new keys, Magellan finally began to believe she might really, truly be in 1829.

Reverently, she sat down and slipped off the gloves, flexing her fingers.

First, she tested every key to acquaint herself with the instrument's range and tonal power. She'd never played an actual nineteenth-century piano before. The modern piano wasn't set to make its debut for another forty years.

Polly hovered by the door with a pitying look, most likely assuming her hen pecking was the extent of her musical ability. "Well then, I'll just leave you to your . . . playing. Ring the bell over there when you've finished, and I'll come fetch you." Magellan nodded, barely listening.

After Polly left, Magellan ran scales up and down the piano as she came to terms with the situation. Somehow, she was in 1829, and right now she was sitting in the most breathtaking conservatory in front of a brand-new Streicher. She tried not to dwell on the fact somehow a dead earl had known she would be coming—and a diary belonging to Merlin's sister was being given to her *again*, and she had to read it quickly because the fate of the world was at stake and according to Godwin in her hands.

Either this was actually the past or a parallel world or a very real-feeling delusional dream in which she was the star, or maybe they were all one and the same.

She launched into Chopin's Étude Op. 10 No. 4, one of his most difficult and acrobatic pieces, in order to quell her thoughts. Her fingers flew over the keys in the equivalent of an Olympic race, and she gasped with delight at the sound, knowing this was the exact instrument Chopin would have played with an identical resonance.

Magellan closed her eyes and gave herself over to the music, not planning to return anytime soon.

# Chapter 10

𝄢

## Rhys

Someone was playing in the conservatory. Rhys wondered who it could be. The room had been shuttered ever since they'd gone into mourning, and he had never opened it back up. He hadn't seen the point.

He was on his way to the library in the east wing when he heard the music, a haunting melody that curled in the air. The pianist was clearly masterful. But why they were playing in the conservatory and not the salon filled him with irritation. He was already out of sorts, having stayed up way too late last night translating the diary's opening pages. Now the last thing he wished to do was converse with houseguests—and a wayward guest was presently in the conservatory playing like a maestro. His curiosity was too piqued not to find out who possessed such astonishing talent. He had invited four families and barely spoken with them. The Winslows had brought Flora's sister, Lady Fauna. The other families, the Westbrooks and the Eastons, had brought their daughters, and he couldn't even remember the name of the fourth family, the Bailfrys or Balfords? Unfortunately, the daughter was just as forgettable.

Lord Erickson was the lone male guest, who had come to inspect the library. Presently, Rhys was too distracted to talk to the man. He only wanted to question the woman from the labyrinth and read the diary.

The irony was not lost on him. The first day of his house party where he'd finally decided to do his duty and marry and a woman shows up in his labyrinth looking like she'd stepped from the mists of a fairy tale and all his good intentions had gone up in smoke. The timing seemed intentional, which only made his suspicions rise.

Where had she come from? Now thanks to his mother, who had invited their mystery guest to stay, it looked like he would have plenty of time to find out.

Earlier that morning at breakfast, his mother had entered the dining room looking more frazzled than usual. Then she astounded him by announcing to the guests, "I'm pleased to share vee vill have an additional guest joining our party! Miss Brighton, zee daughter of my late husband's dear friend."

Rhys blinked, listening to the outrageous lie.

"She has just arrived overseas from America and is most tired from her travels. Unfortunately, her trunks have gone missing, hence zee delay in her joining us, but vee are overjoyed to include her in zee festivities."

Rhys's eyebrows shot up. *They were?* Had his mother gone mad? He held up the gold quizzing glass hanging around his neck to his eye and gave her a pointed look. Only she would know he was irritated. It was his father's quizzing glass. Rhys had borrowed it last night, using the little magnifying glass to study the diary.

His mother ignored his signal and continued. "She vill join us later today."

Rhys scowled and dropped the quizzing glass while his mother avoided looking at him. He waited until the guests finished breakfast and then led her into his study, where he dropped his voice to a fierce whisper in German. *"What in blazes are you doing? We can't let her stay!"*

"Rhys, don't be unkind. Vhere vould zee poor girl go?"

"Home! Back to her family who is surely looking for her. I will send out inquiries right away to the neighboring estates."

His mother looked alarmed. "No! Don't zend her away. You mustn't."

"Why ever not?" He raised the quizzing glass to make a point, and she swatted it away.

"Vhat if she needs our protection? Vhat if she is running away? Amnesia is triggered by trauma. Terrible, terrible trauma! Who knows vhat kind?" She fisted her hands in determination and stomped her foot like a child. "She *must* stay here. Vivianne vill lend her clothes, and you vill be kind."

"Mother . . ." He sighed. "That is your problem. You are too kind. And naive. Does she truly have amnesia? She knew her name. Magellan Brighton. And she thought she was a harpist at a wedding. That doesn't sound like amnesia."

His mother pressed, her eyes wide with worry. "Zhen she is afraid. Surely vee must give her time to recover before vee alert anyone to her vhereabouts."

Rhys sighed again and of course gave in to his mother's wishes. But he would need to have a private audience with Miss Brighton and question her.

"Now enough of zis talk." His mother headed toward the door. "Our guests are vaiting."

Rhys swallowed his frustration and followed, ready to perform his duties as host. He took a brisk morning ride with the guests and thought of Miss Brighton only once. Then he led everyone on a tour of the gardens and out to the pond for a picnic, where he tried not to think of Miss Brighton at all.

Lady Fauna seemed to be on his arm the most, needing assistance to step over rocks and such. She also kept dropping her handkerchief repeatedly to his ire. He didn't know if he wanted to encourage her handkerchief dropping. Lady Fauna's laugh was quite high-pitched and her face had a pinched look, as if she wasn't taking in enough air. Not to mention they had run out of conversation after discussing the weather.

Rhys found the perfect moment to excuse himself from the picnic early. Back at the house he enquired about Miss Brighton and was told she was convalescing in her room. With nothing to do but wait for her appearance, he returned to the library to translate more of the diary until dinner. Everyone else would be doing archery or needlepoint or some other fluff. If Miss Brighton did not present herself at dinner, then he would go find her himself.

---

He had made his way to the east wing to sequester himself in the library when he heard the haunting music coming from down the hallway. He bypassed the library and headed to the conservatory and quietly opened one of the doors.

Not knowing who to expect, it definitely wasn't to see her seated at the piano.

Miss Brighton's back was to the door, her arms spread wide over the keys. Her hair was upswept, and she was dressed in an elegant gown. She was playing with a mastery he'd never witnessed before, and she had no sheet music. He could only watch spellbound, his feet rooted to the floor.

The song traversed every possible emotion—hope, love, loss, rage—until the music distilled into a poignant melody. She bent low over the keys to play it tenderly. All the while Rhys stood riveted by the door, not daring to move, not daring to breathe. Her playing felt like an arm was reaching inside his chest and squeezing his heart.

Then the song ended.

Miss Brighton sat in silence for a suspended moment, the silence just as much a part of the music. Her hands stayed poised above the keys. Rhys waited, holding his breath to see if she would play again. When she didn't, he hesitated, about to step forward and announce himself. He'd only been wanting to talk with her all day. Before he could, she stunned him by laying her head down on the piano to weep.

Rhys hovered, unsure what to do. Witnessing any woman's tears was one of the singular worst experiences in life. He'd seen his mother cry only once, when his father died, and it had almost broken him. To intrude on such a private moment felt wrong.

He gently pulled the door closed and waited in the hallway as he listened to her muffled cries. The sound was simply dreadful. He tried not to fidget. He checked his pocket watch. He fiddled with his quizzing glass and studied the carpet. Then he studied his boots, noting how they gleamed. He would have to compliment his valet.

Finally, she grew quiet.

All he could think was his mother was right. The poor woman was suffering from some kind of trauma and needed their protection. He would give her time to compose herself, then he would announce his presence, and they could speak frankly, but he would be gentle with his questioning.

Several minutes passed as he waited with bated breath outside the door, desperately wanting to go in. He heard only silence, but at least she'd stopped crying.

After a few more minutes, he expected her to resume playing, but she did not. Unable to wait any longer, he peeked through the door to find the room empty.

The doors leading to the gardens were open. She was gone.

# Chapter 11

## Rhys

Rhys stepped outside onto the terrace and caught a flash of dress disappearing into the labyrinth. What the devil? She was going back in! The woman couldn't be so foolish to enter the labyrinth again. She could get lost for hours. He took off after her, the wide expanse of the garden between them.

When he reached the entrance, he called out, "Miss Brighton? Wherever you are, stop now and I'll assist you." She did not answer. "Miss Brighton, I'm here to help. Have no fear. We met yesterday."

He waited at the first juncture where a person usually got lost and retraced their steps. When she didn't appear, he continued on and decided to stop calling for her after a wild thought occurred to him. Was she meeting someone in a secret rendezvous? Perhaps with whoever had dared her to enter the labyrinth in the first place.

Rhys waited at every juncture, expecting to see her round the corner to backtrack, but she never did. It wasn't possible she could have made it to the center on a second try. Especially if the first time had been an accident.

But that was where he found her. In the center, alone, gazing up at one of the standing stones. Her hand was resting on it with her back to him.

The image struck him because he had seen something similar before.

*In the painting.* The same russet hair and graceful back. The same exquisite hand. The same woman?

The possibility was simply impossible. Yet she did resemble the woman from his father's painting, and Rhys was letting his imagination run wild. Because *this* woman was the real mystery. Which is why he did not step forward and announce himself.

She was studying the ancient symbols inscribed on the largest standing stone with a perplexed air. Reaching out, she traced a finger along the markings in wonderment. She began placing her hands all over the stone while he watched, bewildered, as she gave each stone the same careful inspection. Then she stopped and leaned against one as if she'd grown dizzy. She drew in a shaking breath and fished something out of her gown's hidden pocket—a biscuit.

She ate it quickly and took out a second, eating that one too just as fast. Then she drew in several steadying breaths and pulled a third biscuit from her pocket to nibble on as she returned to investigating the stones.

Rhys felt like a schoolboy spying on her. Why did she have biscuits squirreled away in her skirts? Had no one fed her today? The thought made him livid. He would have his butler reprimand the entire kitchen staff. The third biscuit, he was relieved to see, she ate more gingerly. Her attention now on the ground, she began walking and stomping all along the grass while she ate. He could watch the bizarre spectacle no longer and stepped forward.

"Miss Brighton, *what* are you doing?"

With a gasp she turned to him. "You," she said, her mouth full of biscuit.

*No, you,* he all but said. The labyrinth was his private sanctuary, and she was invading it with her presence just as she'd invaded his thoughts all day. "We meet again." He gave her a stiff bow, retreating behind a facade of politeness.

Her eyes traveled over him, then her face colored in embarrassment. "You were the one who found me yesterday."

"Yes, I'm pleased to see you are recovered, though it seems you are in dire need of sustenance." He frowned at the biscuit in her hand. "Were you not fed?"

"I was." She shoved the half-eaten biscuit back into her pocket. "But I get dizzy if I go too long without eating. I lost track of time."

He scowled at that. Perhaps that was why she'd fainted twice yesterday. She hadn't eaten.

Why had she been crying in the conservatory? All evidence of her emotional distress was gone. Thank goodness. "What are you doing here?" He sounded more abrupt than he intended. To distract from his discomfort, he stared at the carved symbols on the stone she had been tracing. They were as mysterious as the stone circle itself.

"I was hoping to remember how I got here."

"*Ah.* The amnesia." His mother might believe it, but she had always been gullible. The lady's crying in the conservatory was perhaps because she remembered all too well who she was. His eyes went to the ring on her finger, which she quickly hid in her pocket as if she didn't want him to see it. Was she running away from her family—or possibly a man? Maybe she wanted everyone to think she didn't remember so she wouldn't have to leave.

He decided to speak frankly. "If you are afraid and are dealing with . . . challenges that made you run away from an unfortunate situation, you can tell me. I'll protect you." He found his offer to be true. Whatever she was facing, he would help her. This mysterious woman who could play the piano better than anyone he'd ever heard before. He wanted to help her.

She shook her head. "I don't remember how I got here. That is the truth." Her eyes met his, her gaze open and guileless.

He considered the facts before him. “How did you know how to arrive at the center? Not once but twice. This labyrinth is a fortress.” His fortress.

She looked away. “The first time when I woke up, I really don’t remember. The second, I studied the path from my bedroom window.”

“Impossible.” He squinted at the house, imagining which window was hers.

“Not impossible. The path to the center is a pattern, like a song.”

He cocked a brow in challenge. “And you play music?”

“A little.” She brushed away the question.

“Come now,” he scoffed. “That is quite a severe case of false modesty. You play unlike anyone I’ve ever heard.”

“You heard me?” she asked, disconcerted.

“A little,” he retorted. “Is being here helping you to *remember*?”

She shook her head and then stunned him by saying, “Your father said you had Merlin’s sister’s diary and would translate it for me. You must, because I need to read it.”

“You need to read the diary?” Finally, he could question her about the book.

“It’s from the sixth century and written in Old English,” she told him as if he didn’t know.

“Yes, I have it in my possession. How did you know my father?”

She hesitated. “I didn’t, but he did write to me. He said you would translate it for me when I arrived.”

Rhys was at a loss for words. He could just imagine his father promising such a thing. But he couldn’t explain the irritation thrumming within him. Nothing about her or this situation made sense. How had his father known her or her family? “Yes, it is true my father asked me to return the diary to you when you arrived, although I have only started translating it. I have it in the library.” He would have to work quickly on the translation to keep his promise before she left with the book or her family came knocking at his door to claim their wayward daughter.

"Could you please show it to me?"

"Of course. I was just on my way there," he offered.

She hesitated, looking reluctant to leave but nodded, twisting the ring on her finger as she followed him out.

They walked the labyrinth in silence. Rhys was unsure what to say. He needed to solve the mystery of her for his own peace of mind.

"Miss Brighton—"

"Please, call me Magellan."

He shot her a look of surprise at giving him license to use her given name. That was usually reserved for people on intimate terms.

*Magellan.* Momentarily distracted, he wondered who on earth had named her after a Portuguese explorer and a man of all people. And once he started thinking on her name, he could no longer imagine her solely as Miss Brighton.

"Then please call me Rhys." He surprised himself by offering such an informality. Only his family called him by his first name.

Before he could continue his questioning, they were intercepted by one of the maids who met them on the lawn. He believed her name was Polly. She was holding Miss Brighton's gloves.

"There you are, miss! My lord." She gave him a curtsy and said to Magellan, "I came to the conservatory to collect you. It's almost time for the introductions, and you need to change into your evening gown."

"Evening gown?" Magellan exclaimed, sounding appalled. She looked down at her dress. "What's wrong with this one?" Rhys couldn't help but glance down at her gown too and think absolutely nothing. Then Magellan shocked him by placing her hand on his arm. "Rhys, could we still go to the library to see the diary? Please?"

He was too riveted by her hand on his arm and his name on her lips to care about Polly's surprise at Magellan's stunning intimacy. He made a smooth tuck of Magellan's hand into the crook of his arm as if he'd offered it first. "Of course." He cleared his throat and said to Polly, who had yet to stop gaping, "Miss Brighton and I were just going to the library to view a book. Please accompany us as her chaperone, and she can change for dinner shortly after."

There, that was sorted.

They strolled through the rest of the garden, and Rhys tried to ignore the warmth of Magellan's hand tucked on his arm. As they neared the library, her face lit with recognition when she saw it shared the same hallway as the conservatory.

As they entered the grand room, she gasped with pleasure, and Rhys felt a puff of pride. Hereford Library was breathtaking indeed. An immense cathedral of books assembled under one roof. They extended up to the vaulted ceilings. Ornate book ladders on movable tracks rested at each corner of the room like cardinal points on a compass.

He led Magellan to his desk tucked away in the back alcove. Polly took a seat on a sofa in the center of the room, affording them privacy.

As he retrieved the diary, a myriad of expressions crossed her face . . . confusion, astonishment, and something that looked like fear. "Yes, that's it," she said, glancing down at it but not touching it. "Was Merlin's sister a wizard too?"

He hesitated. What an odd question. "I don't know. By all accounts her brother possessed magic in the myths and could see the future. In reality, he was a Druid, and Druids were mystics. They never wrote anything down, so they're shrouded in mystery. Most likely she was a Druid too."

"But she did write something down." Magellan fingered the pages of his translation. "May I read your translation, please?"

"Of course," he quickly agreed. "I would like to translate it in its entirety. We can return after the evening's entertainments." Even as he offered, he had no idea what he was about anymore. He had a house full of guests, and here he was scheduling a private tête-à-tête with the one lady who hadn't been invited. "Polly will accompany you, of course, as a chaperone."

Magellan touched his arm again. "Thank you. I really appreciate it."

Good Lord, she had to stop touching him. He forced himself to step back and drop his gaze and gave her a formal bow. "Of course. The pleasure's mine. I will see you at dinner." He marched from the room as if he had somewhere important to go, leaving Polly to escort Miss Brighton. Her reaction to the diary was not what he expected. Not only did she recognize the book, she said she needed to read it, as if it were of great importance.

How had the book ended up with his father?

Goose bumps reappeared on his arms. As if to tell him the answer was not so simple. The explanation *of her* was not so simple. Then he pushed that thought away. He was being nonsensical. Of course there was a logical explanation for her and the book.

And yet . . .

Unable to stop himself, Rhys strode upstairs, straight to his closet where he found the painting. Ripping the black cloth away, he stared at the portrait, suddenly winded.

Good God. *Was it her?*

Could this be Magellan Brighton? Just the thought filled him with a sense of vertigo.

Could she have been alive in 1799? A woman who did not age?

Then he laughed out loud at himself. By Jupiter, he was losing his marbles and turning into one big oatcake to even consider it. He sank down onto the bed and put his head in his hands, trying to clear his thoughts. He rubbed his face and let out a pained laugh.

The painting stared back at him like a challenge. A puzzle. A parting gift from his dead father.

Rhys had never shown the painting to anyone, especially his mother, for fear the painted woman had been his father's mistress. Godwin had done the painting in 1799 before he'd met Birgit, his future countess, and Rhys's parents' union had been a love match. They had fallen in love over the course of a waltz at a ball in Vienna almost thirty years ago. Rhys had heard the story countless times. Godwin had gone there on a trip and come back with Birgit, a grand piano, and a carriage full of instruments he had bought from a shop in Salzburg. His father had so many endearments for his mother. He had called her his *Beautiful B*, his *Beloved B*, his *Lady B*, and sometimes just *B*.

Rhys had grown up witnessing their love, and yet he had found a painting of another woman hidden away.

How many nights had Rhys stared at the canvas?

*Duende* was the Spanish word for the mysterious power behind a work of art to deeply move one's heart. For over a year the painting had obsessed him, until last month he'd finally put it out of his sight. If he was to take a wife, he couldn't be mooning over a woman in a portrait who didn't exist.

He shook his head and whispered, "Father, why the bloody hell did you paint this?"

He draped the black cloth over it and tucked the painting back into its hiding place. The Lady of Labyrinth may look like Magellan Brighton, but it wasn't her. End of story. He would not be looking at the painting again.

Feeling resolute, Rhys dressed for dinner and hurried downstairs. When he entered the room, most of the guests had already gathered, sparkling in their evening attire and ready to begin the night's festivities. His mother was busy leading Magellan, who was in a new gown, around the room and making introductions. He tried not to stare as he listened to his mother spin her tale like a master about how Miss Brighton was the daughter of a treasured friend from America. Then she brought Magellan over to meet his brother, Cecil, who was next to him. Rhys found himself standing up straighter.

"This is Rhys's younger brother, Cecil."

Cecil winked. "The better, kinder, funnier one."

Magellan laughed, and Rhys could only stare at her.

Cecil needled him by telling her, "See how he glowers at us so seriously?"

It was true he was glowering, and he tried to stop, instead making his face a mask of indifference. A look he practiced in the mirror for such social occasions when he was on display. It was also true he and Cecil were nothing alike, either in appearance or personality. Cecil had lighter hair, lighter eyes, and a lighter heart. Cecil was the epitome of *sprezzatura*, the Italian word for making any action seem effortless and graceful.

Presently, Cecil was attempting to make Magellan laugh again, but she was back to looking about the room with a petrified gaze, as if she'd never seen a salon full of people in her life.

Then the fantastical notion wormed its way into his head again. Could she actually be from another century? Had she magically appeared in the labyrinth from the sixth century?

He brutally pushed those whimsical thoughts aside. A mystery surrounded Magellan Brighton to be sure. She was a woman with secrets, he could see them in her eyes, and they were secrets he intended to find out quickly for his own peace of mind.

# Chapter 12

## Magellan

The diary Rhys had shown her in the library was the same one Magellan had seen at the Morgan Museum—and her visit to the labyrinth today had given her another shocking discovery. She snuck a glance down at her ring again. The symbols on it were *exactly* the same as the ones on the standing stone in the labyrinth. Ever since she'd seen the markings this afternoon her thoughts had been in a whirl.

If the stone's symbols and the ones on her ring were identical, it could only mean they were tied to her traveling hundreds of years into the past, although that still didn't explain how the diary had found her again.

Right now, Magellan wanted nothing more than to hide in the library and read it. Instead, she had been stuffed into a pink evening dress by Polly like an 1829 Barbie doll and escorted to a dinner party with thirty strangers. She felt like an actress trapped in *Downton Abbey* without a script. In the salon there'd been a whirlwind of names, bows, curtsies, and hand kissing. She'd barely uttered three words, her social anxiety peaking at an all-time high. It was all she could do not to start humming.

Now she was in a dining room looking straight out of Buckingham Palace, with men in uniform standing at attention along the wall to serve the food and pour the wine. She looked around and for the countless time wondered what the hell she was doing here. The diary and her ring seemed to be her only clues. She'd always thought the symbols on the ring Garesh had given her were simply a design. Was it an ancient language? Or a spell? She couldn't believe she was even contemplating the idea.

Her thoughts were interrupted by the first course, a cream of asparagus soup. After that came a parade of unidentifiable dishes. Custard, strange balls, an unidentifiable meat—rabbit or lamb—then fish, vegetables, and pickled vegetables. Course after course was paired with different sets of silverware and wine. She kept sneaking peeks at the young woman with the pink feathers sitting across from her and copied her every gesture like a bad mime. Every time the woman took a bite, she took a bite. Then she would look over at Rhys sitting at the head of the table brooding at her, as if he knew she was a fraud.

Magellan was sitting between Rhys's sister Vivianne and their brother Cecil. Vivianne was vivacious, somewhere around seventeen or eighteen, and the friendliest of the bunch. Magellan quickly switched utensils to match hers. Vivianne caught her and gave a conspiratorial grin.

Magellan admitted to her, "I'm not used to formal dinners." That was putting it mildly. She was used to Pollo Loco bowls and sushi from the grocery store. "And I must thank you for lending me your dresses."

"I dare say you wear them better than me. You look quite fetching. My eldest brother seems to think so." She grinned. "He hasn't been able to take his eyes off of you all night."

Magellan couldn't tell her he was probably worried she would steal the silverware.

Rhys was still staring. He raised his voice and said, "Lord Erickson, you're the history expert at the table. Did Merlin the Magician truly have a twin sister?"

Magellan startled at the question, and he cocked a half smile at her, noting her reaction.

The older man sitting to his left had a distinguished air about him. He took his time putting his fork down and patting his mouth with his napkin before saying, "Yes, it is often overlooked but Merlin had a sister, and he also had a wife. Though not much is known about either woman. The sister rose to political prominence in her day as queen of Strathclyde. She was married to King Rhydderich 'the Generous.' An interesting fellow who, legend has it, possessed a magical sword, one of the Thirteen Treasures of Britain. Perhaps a gift from Merlin, his brother-in-law, who collected them."

One of the ladies asked what the Thirteen Treasures were. Everyone at the table listened raptly as the man explained they were objects from antiquity imbued with magical power. "A chariot which can take someone anywhere in the world, a chessboard made of gold and silver that plays itself, a cloak of invisibility, and so on and so forth. Merlin supposedly went on a quest to find them all." Lord Erickson asked Rhys, "What is your interest with the sister?"

"I've been reading a diary supposedly written by her. If it's authentic." His gaze returned to Magellan.

She couldn't help but frown back at him. What was he doing?

"How marvelous," Lord Erickson drawled with a haughty air. "I would love to see such a treasure."

"If Miss Brighton agrees. The book is hers."

Magellan froze as all eyes at the table suddenly turned to her, and she couldn't help but notice Rhys's smirk. He was intentionally baiting her. Lord Erickson looked down the long table. He raised his monocle to his eye and gave her a squint.

"Isn't that correct, Miss Brighton?" Rhys added, then had the audacity to wink at her.

Magellan felt her pulse race to a gallop. Everyone was now waiting for her to speak. The number one phobia in the world—which she had—was fear of public speaking, and she was being forced to do it at a dinner table in 1829. She could hear the nervous quiver in her voice as she grappled to come up with an excuse. "It's from my father's collection. He thought the earl would find it fascinating." She risked a glance back to Rhys. He had barely swallowed the amnesia story before. Now he might assume the father story was true. Whatever he believed, he *knew* she was lying. Could she tell him the truth that she had been catapulted to another time by playing Bach on a church organ? He'd think she was crazy. Perhaps she was. The jury was still out. And as much as she hated lying to everyone, telling the truth wasn't an option.

She shot a glance to Lady Liron, who gave her a reassuring smile. The woman was the epitome of kindness and seemed to know Magellan was struggling. Magellan wondered how much the countess knew about her situation. Rhys's mother had been the one to deliver Godwin's mysterious letter and also insist Magellan be a houseguest. The countess even had given her a cover with the amnesia story. Now all Magellan could do was pretend it was true.

It didn't help when Cecil began peppering her with all kinds of questions during the rest of dinner. He wanted to know how her travel across the Atlantic was and had she ever met an Indian. What did she think of Andrew Jackson becoming president? How could such a man have been elected, and did he still pay to have his runaway slaves whipped?

Magellan choked on her wine and brought her napkin to her mouth.

"Brother!" Vivianne scolded him. "Don't ask Miss Brighton such horrid questions. It's not as if she could have voted for him. She's a woman."

"My apologies, Miss Brighton. My sister is quite right. I should not have tarnished your delicate ears with such ugly matters."

Magellan puffed out a breath and downed the rest of her wine.

Dinner soon mercifully ended. After dessert, the group turned festive, exclaiming it was time to retire to one of the salons for port and sherry and pianoforte playing and who knew what else.

Magellan stood up and followed everyone to another stately room filled with rows of chairs facing a pianoforte. Before she could catch herself, she gasped with pleasure when she saw the harp.

The countess heard and turned to her with a smile. "Do you play zee harp, my dear?"

Magellan bit her lip.

Rhys came to stand beside her. "When we first met, she told me she was the harpist." He smiled glibly back at her. "At least you remember that much. You must play for us tonight."

"Oh no, I couldn't." She didn't want to be the focus of any more attention.

"I insist," Rhys challenged. "Surely you can grace us with one song."

"You play the harp?" Vivianne joined their group. "Miss Brighton, you must! You simply must!" She clapped her hands in delight, bouncing up and down.

Magellan turned to Rhys's sister. "Perhaps one song, only after yours, and only if there is time."

The countess patted her hand. "My dear girl, we have all zee time in zee world."

Magellan smiled faintly, tamping down the panic those words brought, and took a seat next to Vivianne. Tonight was the equivalent of a Miss 1800s Beauty Pageant—the talent show segment—and Magellan couldn't help but feel Rhys was the star judge. It seemed all the women were performing for him, particularly the one in pink, who looked like a Victorian burlesque queen with all her feathers and could not sing for the life of her. To Magellan it was too surreal. She was sitting in an 1829 parlor being subjected to a deluge of off-key notes. The performance finally came to an end with a smattering of polite applause. Vivianne went next, playing a sweet song called "I'd Be a Butterfly" that Magellan assumed must be popular for the time.

Then the countess was announcing, "Miss Brighton will now play zee harp for us!"

No one had played the harp yet, and a murmur of excitement circled the room. Magellan stood up, trying to calm her nerves and remind herself she'd played before plenty of crowds, countless weddings, and concerts. She would treat this the same. Plus, she'd wanted to play the harp since she stepped into the room.

The harp was easily one of her favorite instruments with its crystalline sound. There were ten different kinds, and she could play them all: lever harps, pedal harps, Paraguayan, Celtic folk harps, cross-strung harps, and bell harps. She had never questioned how she could play any instrument. She just could.

She sat down at the stool and slipped off her gloves, draping them artfully on the table nearby like the others had done while she thought about what to play. Everyone was staring at her expectantly, and the perfect song settled in her mind about a girl stuck in a strange land and needing to get home. Just like her.

She wondered if she dared to play it. She'd already played Chopin in the conservatory, and the space-time continuum hadn't collapsed. Chopin was only nineteen right now and yet to finish his studies at the Warsaw Conservatory or move to Paris, where he would compose some of his most famous works. No one would know, and she'd drunk way too much wine at dinner to worry about it. Though *The Wizard of Oz* wouldn't make its debut for another hundred years, she lavished the crowd with a beautiful rendition of "Over the Rainbow." She played with her eyes closed as her fingers flew across the strings, and she wondered if, like Dorothy, she could wish herself out of here.

Too soon the song was over, and she was opening her eyes back to 1829, to a sea of mesmerized faces. A hush held the audience until they erupted into applause. People asked for an encore, which she demurely declined. She could feel the weight of Rhys's gaze on her, and she avoided looking at him.

Now that all the performances were over, card tables were being set up for the next round of entertainment. Rhys came to stand beside her, his hand on her elbow as he gently guided her toward the door. They were escaping to the library as planned. He murmured close to her ear. "You play exquisitely."

"Thank you." She sounded breathless, which annoyed her. The last thing she needed was to develop a crush on anyone in 1829.

"Did you make up the story about your father giving you the diary?"

Of course he would circle back to that. She stuck as close to the truth as possible. "I didn't know what else to say. You caught me by surprise."

"I suppose I did. My apologies." His eyes trailed over her face. "I'm just trying to understand who you are and why my father was safekeeping the diary for your arrival."

"I'm sorry I can't remember . . ."

It seemed the safest answer. Rhys pursed his lips, dissatisfied, and opened the door to the library. "Shall we?"

Polly was already waiting for them. She bobbed a quick curtsy and retired with a book to the far corner while Rhys guided Magellan to his alcove. He set everything out on the table in a precise array and offered her the chair beside him. She took the translation from him, eager to get started. Rhys's penmanship was neat, compact, and the pages were dense with text. This must have taken him some time.

Before she began reading, he surprised her with the question, "Did you know the stone circle in the labyrinth was supposedly built by Merlin?"

"It was?" She gaped in astonishment, and her heart began to beat in a staccato rhythm. Did that mean Merlin had written the symbols on the stones? And her ring as well?

"You truly didn't know?" Rhys gave her a prolonged stare and she shook her head. Then he flashed her a rueful smile. "At least that is the legend the first Earl of Liron started. Imagine growing up with such a legacy in your backyard." He put on a pair of little round glasses with a bashful smile she found strangely endearing. The alcove suddenly felt incredibly intimate.

Readying his pen to get to work, he glanced at her over the rim of his glasses with a crystal-blue gaze and nodded to the pages in her hand. "Take your time, Miss Brighton."

# Chapter 13

## Gwynedd

*The first telling we were not ordinary was when the flowers in our nursery refused to die.* Our nursemaid, Brica, had placed the vase of winter jasmine beside our bed four months prior, thinking the yellow flowers would brighten the nursery after my mother's passing. Every day Brica waited for the flower petals to wilt and bow against the weight of the world, but they never changed, remaining outstretched and coursing with life. She reached out to touch a petal in marvel.

"These two must be charming the flowers just like the dogs." Mari, our wet nurse, nodded to the floor, which was a weave of brown and black fur. Every one of my father's Gordon setters had taken to sleeping in the nursery since our birth. All seven dogs were curled up beneath the cribs.

"And the birds," Brica noted. Dozens of collared doves, starlings, and wood pigeons had been nesting all along the windowsill outside, placing their homes against the glass. More arrived every day.

"Maybe the wee ones can talk to the animals," Mari said.

Brica laughed. "Speaking with animals only exists in the legends."

"So it is my imagination, then?" Mari swept her hand to the window and the floor.

Brica let out a breath, unable to refute her. She knew we were calling the animals but tried to make light of it. "Then we must take good care of these two or they will sic the crows upon us."

From the window she spied a large group of riders in the distance. The nursery was on the third floor and faced the backside of the lodge near the riverbank. She watched the band walking at a steady pace. "Morken is home."

The day after my mother's death my father had gone to his smaller residence in the royal town of Partick, the Kingdom of Strathclyde's administrative center, where he often stayed for several weeks throughout the year to hold council with the king. This time he had been away for months.

Partick was eighteen miles to the north of Cadzow and took half a day to reach on horseback. Last night a rider had arrived with the message our father would be returning home. The lodge had become a beehive of activity as everyone in the village prepared to celebrate his return. Janneth had been cooking in the kitchens with her helpers since dawn. The aroma of fresh bread and garlic baking on the hot stones permeated the lodge. The dogs were already standing and stretching, as if knowing their master's homecoming was near.

A figure in white robes led the procession. "A Druid is with them," Brica said in surprise. "An important one from the looks of it." There was no mistaking the glint of Cathan's gold headdress and neck plate.

Mari joined her at the window. "I hope Janneth knows the High Druid's coming or she'll throw a mighty fit she didn't make the feast grand enough."

"I wonder why he's come." Brica sounded nervous. "Do you think it's for the children?"

Mari and Brica gave each other a look of alarm. Their fears were confirmed when Cathan came up to the nursery, alone, soon after his arrival. Without a word, he came to our cribs and gently felt our hands, our feet, our faces, and laid his palm on the crown of our heads. Mari and Brica were both too afraid to speak.

Cathan had many talents. One was to peer into the hearts of a man or woman and know their spirit. "You have been good to them," he said. "Both of you."

Brica gave a wispy "thank you," her eyes riveted to the gold crescent moon around his neck. Cathan looked with a smile to the dogs sitting at attention and the birds on the windowsill. Then he left. Brica and Mari stared at each other in question.

Brica finally said, "What do you think that was about?"

Mari shrugged helplessly. "You must go down to the hall and find out. Is he to take them to his island?" she fretted, twisting the ties of her apron around her finger. "I still have months of milking. I can't leave Cadzow to go live on an island full of Druids!"

"Calm down, Mari. I'm sure it won't come to that." Brica shook her head, unable to fathom the possibility.

Then she saw the ring lying beside me.

"What's this?" She picked up the ring and held it to the sunlight. Strange fiery copper riddled the gold. Runelike symbols wrapped around the whole band in an engraving. The design was unlike anything she'd seen before. "The High Druid must have dropped it." She could think of no other reason for its appearance.

"Take it to him," Mari urged. "It will give you an excuse to find out what is going on." She motioned frantically with her hands for Brica to go, as if she were an animal to be herded. "Go on! Shoo! Shoo!"

Brica pocketed the ring and hurried downstairs to the Great Hall, her heart now beating furiously both from holding the High Druid's ring and being tasked to deliver it to him. Whatever his purpose in the nursery had only confirmed what Brica already knew: Ancient magic coursed through our blood, and the High Druid knew it.

When Brica reached the Great Hall, cheers and laughter were erupting. Oli was playing a bawdy song to the crowd. The whole village had come to welcome their chieftain home, and the hall was bursting at its seams. Ale and wine flowed freely down the tables. A feast was spread on all three tables with platters of roasted game, savories, and sweets. Even Morken's Gordon setters had come down to find scraps on the floor.

Morken sat at the head table with Cathan beside him, facing the band of musicians. Brica made her way to their table, slowing as she drew near. She steeled her spine and approached. "Excuse me, I believe you accidentally dropped this in Merlin and Gwynedd's crib." She placed the golden ring on the table.

Cathan could only stare at the ring in astonishment. "No. I did not."

"But . . ." Brica faltered. "The ring was not there before you came."

Cathan picked it up with a noticeable quiver in his hands. In the firelight the copper-gold glowed with an incandescent hue.

Even my father, thickheaded as an ox, could sense there was something special about the ring. "What is that metal?"

Cathan was staring at the ring's markings with wonder. "*Orichalcum.* The lost gold of Atlantis."

Morken's startled gaze lifted to his. Stories were still told of the sunken island city. All Bards could recount the epic tale. But no one had ever seen Orichalcum before.

Cathan placed the ring in my father's hands with great care and folded his fingers over it. "A most precious gift has been bestowed upon your children. Keep the ring safe," he advised him quietly. "Wait for Merlin or Gwynedd to find it. When they do, bring the children to me."

Morken barked out a laugh in disbelief. "Your magic took my wife. It cannot have my children." He pocketed the ring without another word.

---

The next morning, my father buried the ring deep in the woods where no one could find it. What he did not know is that objects have their own way of being found.

Five years later, the time came. I was running through the forest, past the creek, when something in the ground began calling to me like a song. The sound raised the hairs on the back of my neck. I told my brother, and we scurried like two animals to dig with our hands in the dirt.

I found the ring buried like a golden seed, and I squealed in delight. We decided we would give the ring to my father as a gift. We raced back to the lodge and found him on the field. Merlin ran up to him. "Father! Look! We found a ring for you."

That is the first clear memory I have of my father—a warrior who commanded armies, being felled by a piece of jewelry.

"Merlin, where did you find this?" he asked in a hushed tone as he knelt beside us.

"Gwynedd found it in the woods." Merlin pointed to me. "She . . ." He almost said I'd heard it singing but then stopped himself. We'd made a pact to keep our secrets.

My father gave me a searching look. "If I bury this, do you think you can find it again?"

We promised we would try, excited our father was playing a game with us for the first time. He called for his horse, instructing us we could set out to find the ring tomorrow.

The next morning the whispering song led me right to the spot. Even Merlin heard it this time. The melody stirred the leaves around us.

When we returned before midday with the ring, my father was dumbfounded. Two more days he buried the ring. Two more days we retrieved it for him. He then tried destroying the ring with his hammer and melting it in the fires, but the ring was indestructible, and he had to declare defeat.

On his following trip to Partick, he brought us with him. We had no idea why. All he said was Merlin and I were going to visit the Druids and it was a great honor.

The island where they lived was small and their last remaining sanctuary. A young Druid ferried us across from Partick in a boat. Never had I seen a more beautiful place. Thistles, harebells, and primroses bloomed in the gardens, and thousand-year-old oak trees towered above us like guardians. Ringed around the grove were cottages, and an observatory for the stars rose high above the treeline like a spire.

Cathan descended the stairs from the observatory and greeted us. He wore long robes like a woman, as did many of the men. He led us to his personal library, a vast room full of relics and art, musical instruments, and astronomical tools the likes of which I had never seen before.

Merlin scurried to produce the ring from his pocket and presented it to Cathan with great ceremony. "Father said we were to give this to you."

"Why, thank you, Merlin." Cathan placed it on the table. "It appears lost treasure has found its way to you and you to it. Shall we determine why?"

"Is it enchanted?" I asked.

"I would hope so, Gwynedd. I would hope so." Cathan nodded. "Who is the one who found this ring?"

"I did," I said. Happy warmth bloomed inside me that he had asked. "What do the symbols mean?"

"They are Atlantean. I believe it means, 'Know the way.'"

Merlin and I stared at the ring in wonder.

*Know the way.*

Cathan went on. "One day its purpose will reveal itself to you. Until then, I will keep it safe."

The ring remained with Cathan for many years until the time came for me to understand its purpose. I share the story of the ring because it is the same ring on your finger. A ring with extraordinary power forged to navigate a labyrinth. A labyrinth in time created millennia ago for one singular purpose:

To protect a song.

A song that can break worlds or make them whole again. An ancient song of such unspeakable power it was split into parts and hidden in time. Now we must reassemble those parts to keep the Earth spinning.

The death of this planet has been orchestrated and foiled many times. The scope of the ongoing battle between worlds and their dimensions cannot be contained within these pages. For brevity's sake, I can only stress if we do not find the song before the Winter Solstice, our world will be lost forever.

So read on and read quickly, and I will tell you what you must do.

# Chapter 14

## Magellan

Magellan could not read anymore. Her brain felt fuzzy, like it was ready to give up and stop thinking altogether. Right now, she was yearning for the oblivion of her feather bed and down comforter upstairs. She'd read the diary's beginning about Gwynedd and Merlin's birth and finding the ring. But she had to stop when it began to feel as if Gwynedd was talking to her, because books weren't supposed to talk to people.

Gwynedd had written she was the captain of an ancient ship, which was something Garesh had told her more than once. Magellan stared at the ring's symbols. They were the same symbols Merlin had carved on the standing stone in the center of the labyrinth. Cathan had said the writing was Atlantean—as in the lost civilization of Atlantis—and meant *know the way*.

Know what way? How to get out of 1829? She didn't understand—didn't even want to understand. Gwynedd had written about a labyrinth in time and alluded they had only until Winter's Solstice to save the world as if Magellan was somehow a part of that plan.

Right now, in a moment of weakness, she wanted to tell Rhys everything, to have him share in her shock at what she was reading. To show him her ring matched the standing stone. But who knew what he might do? He'd think she was crazy. No, she could not confide in Rhys. Tears welled in her eyes, and she fought them back.

"Are you all right?" Rhys asked.

Magellan blinked, trying to mask her emotions. "I'm afraid I have a headache."

She and Rhys had been sitting together in the library in quiet solitude with Polly snoring nearby. Magellan had been reading while Rhys worked on translating. She still had several pages to get through, but she couldn't manage any more tonight. She stood up, feeling overwhelmed. This was all too much. 1829. Gwynedd's memoir. The earl beside her. And this ridiculous pink dress.

Rhys jumped to his feet. "Shall I have someone bring you a cold compress?"

A cold compress was not an ibuprofen. "No, thank you. I just need to sleep." Forever maybe.

"Well. Good night, then, Miss Brighton." He took her hand and gave a polite bow. "Until tomorrow."

Unless she woke up in the morning back in her time. Back in her apartment with the world on the brink of destruction. At this point anything was possible. Rhys was studying her with that intent look of his. She gave him a wan smile and wished him good night, unable to escape the room fast enough. Polly escorted her, thankfully, or she would have been lost in the hallways for hours.

"Polly, what is today's date?"

"November 2nd, miss." Polly slid her a look. "And the same year as the last time you asked." Polly was speaking to her as if she was the most clueless person on the planet. Perhaps she was.

"And when is Winter Solstice?"

Polly lit up at the question. "December 21st. Do you celebrate in America with a fire festival too? At Stonehenge the sun sets right between the two largest stones. It's quite a sight. Everyone comes from miles to watch it. Have you ever been?" Polly seemed to remember herself. "Forgive me, the countess said I wasn't to ask you any questions and tax your feeble mind."

Magellan gave a faint laugh, silently thanking Rhys's mother.

Gwynedd had written she had until Winter Solstice to find a song that could save the world, which sounded completely unbelievable.

What song was Gwynedd even talking about?

Magellan realized Polly was asking her something and tried to focus. "I'm sorry, what?"

"Would you like a bath tomorrow morning?" The simplicity of the question threw her. A warm bath versus the end of the world. She would take the bath.

With Polly's help, she changed out of her dress into a soft nightgown and freed her hair from its hundred pins. Mentally exhausted, Magellan crawled into bed and slept without dreaming.

---

The next morning she woke up and blinked at the same sunlight streaming through the same windows in 1829. The light was blinding. She looked out at the labyrinth, an emerald fortress in the distance bathed in serene silence, and wondered if Gwynedd was actually writing to her in a magical diary that was following her through time. Was there really a song that could save the world, and how insane was she to even be considering it?

Magellan looked down at her hand to the ring Garesh had gifted to her. Was he somehow a part of the story?

Today she would sequester herself in the library to read more of the diary, and she'd try to find the right time to ask Rhys about the symbols on the standing stone.

Fortified by her plan, she waited for Polly to arrive. A crew of maids came with her, carrying a large metal tub and buckets of steaming water.

Magellan felt guilty they were literally lugging a bathtub for her, but she was also desperate for a shower. After the bath and a breakfast tray, she felt like a new person and ready to face 1829. Then Polly returned with the horrible news the house party was going riding to the lake for a picnic and she was to join them.

"Horseback riding?" Magellan squeaked. Being forced to ride a horse was not in her plan for today. She tried to get out of it, but Polly said the earl insisted she come.

Polly helped her change into Vivianne's spare riding habit, boots, and a hat with a feather sticking out. "There." Polly tilted the hat fashionably. "You look quite the horsewoman."

Magellan stared at herself in the mirror, trapped in a nightmare. The gown weighed at least twenty pounds and was made of wool. How was she supposed to ride a horse in this? She'd never ridden one before.

Polly escorted her to the stables. Most of the guests were already mounted and heading toward the pasture. The scene looked straight out of a historic painting with everyone on horseback and all the ladies with feathers on their hats. Rhys was waiting for her, holding the reins of a magnificent stallion.

"You've got to be kidding me," Magellan muttered under her breath. His horse was white.

"It is a perfect day for a ride, Miss Brighton," he said to her, his eyes taking on an appreciative gleam at her attire.

"Yes, truly." She forced a smile. If she admitted she'd never ridden a horse, it would open up a whole new line of questioning from him. Rhys would either not believe her or want to know how she had arrived at the labyrinth if she couldn't ride, and they'd be back to square one. She decided it was best not to say anything. How hard could it be?

He led her to her horse, a mottled brown mare with a difficult look in its eyes. "This is Mudcake. She's very gentle." Mudcake snorted as if to negate the fact.

Magellan hesitated, not sure how to climb aboard. To make matters worse, her saddle didn't look normal. She glanced over to Vivianne, whose body was twisted to the side with one leg dangling down and the other hitched over the saddle. Magellan realized in horror the women were riding sidesaddle.

"Here. Let me assist you," Rhys offered. Before she could prepare, he grabbed her waist and lifted her into the air and onto the saddle sideways. Magellan let out a yelp, and her horse took a few agitated steps.

"My apologies." Rhys held on to the reins and steadied the horse. "I thought you were ready."

"I'm fine!" she assured him and patted the horse's neck like a dog. "Good boy—good Mudcake." She clumsily arranged her legs like Vivianne while Rhys mounted his horse with expert precision.

Rhys's horse took off in a regal walk, and Magellan tried to prompt Mudcake with her one usable leg in the stirrup, wondering when women got to ride like men. Maybe in a hundred years when they were finally allowed to vote and they all voted against sidesaddle.

Mudcake started walking. Magellan sat rigid in the saddle, trying hard not to fall off. Soon the gardens and the labyrinth were behind them in the distance. The wind felt refreshing on her face, and the surrealness hit her hard. She was on a horse, in England, in 1829 with a feather on her hat, riding sidesaddle while the world might be ending. Maybe God was really a woman and this was her idea of a twisted joke.

The other riders were well ahead while she and Rhys brought up the rear alone. Now was the perfect time to ask him. "Rhys? In the labyrinth, I noticed symbols carved onto one of the stones. What do they mean?"

Rhys glanced over to her, looking relaxed in the saddle. "I don't know. My father swore the symbols were an ancient language known to the Druids and that Merlin himself had carved them there. He said I had to find out for myself what the symbols meant. I spent many an hour in the library looking for clues. Perhaps he didn't know either, and it was a game for him to watch me try."

Magellan glanced down at her hand, her ring encased in a glove. Or perhaps Godwin did know and just didn't want to tell his son for fear of altering the future—just as he had said in his note to her.

Rhys interrupted her thoughts. "There is something I wish to speak to you about privately. It is clear you feel you must keep your circumstance secret. But you may tell me, in confidence, and I swear I'll protect you from whatever it is. You have my word."

Magellan glanced over to him in surprise. He wanted her to confess.

"Miss Brighton?" he prompted.

"You wouldn't believe my circumstance." She barely did, and she was living it.

"Magellan," he bit out, a stormy look now on his face. "I must know. For my own sanity. *Who* are you? Are you purposefully trying to pretend you're from the sixth century?"

"What"—she let out a stunned laugh and almost fell off her horse—"are you talking about?"

He waved his arm impatiently. "You show up in costume with a crown of flowers in your hair looking absolutely medieval. Then you say you can't remember how you got here?" He had that mocking tone back in his voice. "So you conveniently settle yourself into the manor as an invited guest to convalesce—"

"I didn't settle in. And your mother was the one who insisted I convalesce!"

He kept on as if she hadn't spoken. "All the while you walk around with this bewildered air as if everything is new to you. Then you proceed to enchant us all with music like . . . like some angel." He stopped for a moment, as if he'd admitted too much. "Tell me, Miss Brighton, who are you?"

Magellan grappled with what to say. His accusation would have been funny if she could find any of this funny. He was accusing her of pretending to be from the sixth century. She wanted to shout, *Wrong century, dude.*

"You have nothing to say?"

She finally spoke. "I swear on my life I am not pretending. I don't know how I came to be in your labyrinth. That is the honest truth. But

I will tell you everything I remember *after* you finish translating all of the diary. I really do need to read it."

He scoffed. "So you admit there is more you could tell me?"

"Yes. But I need to read the diary first." She added, "While I convalesce," throwing the word back at him.

He made a growl of frustration. "Do you know how many pages are left?"

With a determined tilt to her chin, she said nothing. She couldn't tell him the truth. Not yet.

He brought his horse close to hers. "At least tell me this: Was it arranged for you to appear in the labyrinth, the same day I've invited ladies I am to consider . . ."

"Consider?" she prompted, not understanding.

"Courting," he finished, looking embarrassed. "The purpose behind this whole ridiculous house party. Which I didn't even want to have to do, but I must because it's my duty, and now you've arrived to distract me, and I'm in the library translating Old English as if I have nothing better to do with my time!"

As Rhys vented his own confession, she couldn't decide whether to laugh or be offended. Suddenly the festive group up ahead made sense, as well as the hostile looks she kept getting from some of the women. Only Vivianne, Rhys's sister, was being nice to her. "So that's what this gathering is about? A matchmaking party? And you think I crashed it to 'be courted' by you?" Of all the pompous, convoluted, 1829 ideas. "Dream on, buddy."

"Buddy? Is that an American term?"

"Yes, it's kind of like *sir* but not as polite."

"Thank you, madam, for the clarification. I will send out inquiries to search for your family posthaste. They may come and collect you at their earliest convenience."

"Good!" Magellan's mouth set in a grim line. "Please do, my lord. Then I can be on my way, and you can get back to your courting. I'm sure all the ladies are beside themselves because you're showering attention on me. Especially when I didn't ask for it."

Right now she could happily hate him. He was arrogant, presumptuous, and too damn attractive with his hair all windblown like that. She did *not* have a princess complex or need a man on a white horse. She was a modern-day woman who wore yoga pants and flip-flops and tank tops. She lived and breathed music, had graduated top of Juilliard, and was starting to compose a truly epic symphony. But no, now the world might be ending and she was stuck in Jane Austen–land riding sidesaddle with a man who seemed to think she had some covert plan to get him to court her. Well, Rhys could go jump in a lake and then dry himself off and translate more of the diary. Because he was the only one who could read it, and that was all she needed from him.

Mudcake must have sensed her upset because she started trotting to get away from their fighting. Magellan wobbled, trying to stay on. "Whoa, Mudcake." Then they were off.

Rhys called out for her, "Pull on the reins!"

"I'm trying!"

Mudcake raced downhill in a full gallop. The last thing she heard was Rhys yelling her name before Mudcake reared up on its hind legs and threw her.

Magellan went flying and hit the ground hard, rolling downhill until she stopped, face-planted in the grass. Her entire body hurt. She couldn't move. For a moment she was floating and could almost believe this was all a dream. In a minute she'd open her eyes and wake up in her bed. Wren would be making coffee while doing her vocal exercises, and Magellan would shuffle out of the bedroom to sit at the piano and chase the symphony she'd started composing on her birthday.

How did it go?

"Magellan! Magellan!" Rhys's voice wrested her from the dream.

"Not yet, please," she begged with her eyes still closed. She wasn't ready to come back.

Rhys pulled the silly feathered hat off her face and was touching her cheek. "Your neck is bleeding," he gasped. She kept her eyes closed, wanting only to go to sleep, wake up, and have life make sense again.

He was gentle as he tried to move her. "We need to get you home."

*Home.*

She opened her eyes and stared into his eyes. They were as blue as an infinite sky, and for a singular moment she wondered if he was the one who had called her here to this time and place.

"I don't know how to get home. It's not possible," she admitted on a whisper, feeling the traitorous slip of tears escape. She closed her eyes to his piercing gaze, not wanting to see the questions in his eyes because she'd already said too much.

# Chapter 15

𝄢

## Rhys

Magellan's fall brought everyone running. Rhys reached her first. They'd been quarreling. He had caused the accident. His anger. His accusations. So bloody stupid of him and badly done. It was clear from the start she wasn't skilled in the saddle, though she had said nothing. And he'd purposefully not challenged her since Magellan refused to offer up anything about herself. She was an absolute mystery. And like a buffoon he had confessed the machinations behind the house party and then accused her of trying to get him to court her. When they were together, he found himself saying exactly what was on his mind, and now it might have killed her!

When he saw the blood, his heart stopped and he almost passed out. Then she opened her eyes and he expelled the breath he'd been holding, trying his best to remain upright.

"Oh dear God, can you move?" he asked anxiously. He'd heard of riders becoming paralyzed after a fall. He didn't understand why women fell from their horses so much more frequently than men.

When she nodded she could, his relief was so profound it caused him to blink back the surprising urge to cry. Everyone was watching them. This was an unmitigated disaster.

He helped her to sit up. She was dazed and still in shock. Vivianne had turned back to help, wanting to cancel the picnic and return with them, but Rhys encouraged them to go on. To make matters worse, in the midst of the chaos, Lady Fauna slipped off her horse too, injuring her ankle, and was squawking on the ground like a chicken. Rhys called to one of the footmen accompanying them to go help her. He might be ruining his chances with the Winslow family, but right now, he simply did not care.

He lifted Magellan carefully and carried her to his horse. "Grab on to the saddle," he instructed, hefting her up and then mounting behind her. Without a word he settled her across his lap and wrapped his arms around her. Wincing, she leaned back against his chest and closed her eyes. They headed to the house at a slow pace with Mudcake trailing docilely behind. He tried to ignore the intimate feeling of her in his arms and settled his thoughts. She was wounded, and he was assisting her in a time of need. Nothing more.

He tried to focus on the matter at hand. "Have you never ridden before?"

Her silence was her answer. He pursed his lips and reined in his urge to lecture her. Instead, he said, "Forgive me for quarrelling. I will not press you further on your circumstance, and I will translate the diary for you. But then you will tell me everything?" he asked, his words quiet but firm. He was offering a truce and more time to keep her secrets.

"Yes. Thank you," she whispered.

They finished the ride back without speaking, and Rhys wondered what heavy burden she must be carrying. What secrets were so unspeakable that she had to pretend she could not remember herself?

When they reached the stables, there was a flurry to help when the groomsmen realized she had been in a riding accident. Rhys insisted on carrying her to her room.

"Vhat has happened?" His mother and her brigade of maids met them in the entryway and followed behind him in a fretful parade.

Magellan's cheek was scraped, and she had a cut on her neck. When Rhys reached her room and laid her on the bed, she winced again in pain, grabbing at her right side.

"Fetch the surgeon," he ordered.

"The surgeon?" Magellan sat up horrified and grimaced again at the sudden movement. "Rhys, I'm not dying. It was just a little fall."

"A little fall? You were hurled through the air by your horse! You're bleeding." He waved a hand over her tattered riding habit. "He must inspect you," he said, praying an actual blush was not blooming on his cheeks.

"I don't want to be inspected. I'm fine." Magellan lay back on the bed and covered her eyes with her arm. Her whole body began to shake.

Was she . . . was she laughing?

Rhys could only blink, utterly confused and captivated at the same time. "What is so funny, Miss Brighton? You're bleeding and hurt."

"She is embarrassed, Rhys," his mother said. "You must leave." She was already ordering a water basin brought with willow bark and healing herbs and a hot bath be readied.

"We'll tend to your lady," Polly teased him.

His lady?

*Well.*

Now it was Magellan's turn for her cheeks to color. She lowered her arm and looked at him. They stared at each other a suspended moment.

*Iktsuarpok* was the Inuit word for the sensation of obsessively waiting at the window in anticipation for someone to arrive. Rhys felt like he had been waiting for something or someone for years, and now she was here. Their agreement she would tell him the truth once they were finished with the diary hung in the air between them. He turned and left the room without another word.

He strode straight down to the library, even though the last thing he had time for was to translate Old English. He really should be rejoining the house party at the lake. He really should repair the damage he'd done by turning his back on Lady Fauna. But translate Old English was precisely what he was going to do. Not only for Magellan and their agreement, but for the promise he had made to his father. The sooner he made good on it, the sooner Magellan would tell him the truth and the sooner he could be done with this wild infatuation for her that was burgeoning inside him.

However, as he began to read, all those thoughts fell away and he sat forward in disbelief. For Gwynedd had indeed broken the Druids' renowned shroud of secrecy and written about England's most ancient history. She had written about Stonehenge.

# Chapter 16

## Gwynedd

Cathan was the oldest Druid in the land and remembered our island's deepest and most ancient history. He taught us everything he knew, including how to chart every constellation in the sky. For eight years I studied Venus's cycle as it made its way around the Earth. The path's geometry formed an exquisite five-petaled symmetrical shape, like a perfect flower in bloom. Cathan enjoyed filling our minds with such wonders of the universe, knowing it was feeding the magic inside us.

During this time, I began to have dreams of Stonehenge, though my young mind did not know its name yet. I could feel Stonehenge tied to me like an umbilical cord. In my dreams I often saw a towering woman in iridescent robes standing within the ring of sarsen stones with a quartz hammer in her hand. With great care she would tap on the stones until they began to ring, and the humming sound would travel out across the land like music.

I kept seeing this vision and hearing the song in my dreams—dreams that felt more like memories. Every time I woke, I knew with certainty I would have to travel to Stonehenge one day to understand why.

Merlin knew of my dreams. We were twins, our minds joined together like a Dara Knot, and yet looking back on my life, my brother and I had very different paths because he was a boy, and I was a girl.

Though we practiced the Old Way, as I grew older, I began to observe the differences between our sex in the outside world. The imbalance of power between men and women had not always existed, but in the time I was born, as a woman the choices for my future were limited.

My brother announced he would become a Bard, a Druid storyteller and wielder of words. To become a Bard is not an easy path. Bards have to possess the highest mastery of language and memory. They are the storytellers, the history keepers, and the entertainers of a court. They used to train with a wizened old Druid name Alistair to learn how to recount the epic tales of the past. Bards are our living libraries, our poets and singers. A Bard in his element is a powerful force, and it is believed some Bards—the most masterful Bards—can weave spells with their words like the magicians of old.

My brother became such a Bard. When we turned sixteen, I watched him don a Bard's robes for the first time, and I was filled with jealousy. Becoming a Bard was not an option for me solely because I was a girl. Not since before the Roman occupation of our lands had there been a female Bard. With my brother's course set, I wasn't sure what my future held. I was almost a woman, coming fully into my maidenhood, and soon my father would marry me off to form a political alliance. I had already heard whispers he was angling for a match with the king's son, and I knew my time of freedom was limited. If Merlin was to be a Bard, I needed to discover what I was meant to be.

---

The next time we arrived for our lessons, Cathan led us to the far side of the island where Alistair lived in a cottage overlooking the water. Cathan knocked and moments later the door swung open.

Standing on the threshold was the most striking young man I'd ever seen. He looked to be a few years older than me. His hair was golden brown and almost as long as my own. He had pulled it back at his crown with a single braid, showing both his ears were pierced and decorated with silver cuffs. He was wearing more jewelry than a woman, with an enormous belt buckle, bracelets, and a neck cuff. I had the feeling each piece told a story. His eyes were a startling azure, and he was staring at me just as intently.

Then he turned to Merlin. "You are here to see Alistair, no doubt, my torturous master." His face broke into a grin. "I am Taliesin."

I had heard of Taliesin, the youngest Bard in all the land, as well as the brashest and the brightest. He had not yet finished his apprenticeship and he could outspeak, outsing, and out-letter anyone. The young maidens said Taliesin could reach for the stars and force one down just with his voice. He knew words in Brythonic, Gaelic, Welsh, Celtic, Latin, and a myriad of other languages. He knew the roots of the word, their dimensions and power. He knew how to make vowels breathe, consonants crack, and every sound sing with perfect meter. He was beautiful in his Bard's robes, which were blue, not white, for blue was the color of truth. And right now, he was looking at me as if I were the subject of his next poem. "You must be the fair Gwynedd."

I could not help but laugh. No one had ever called me fair. I had been called fierce, stubborn, and headstrong, but never fair.

Merlin had a silly grin on his face too. We were all three starstruck with each other. Seeing Taliesin felt like we'd just found a long-lost friend we had not seen for lifetimes. Even Cathan could sense the immediate bond between us.

I was halfway in love with him already. I left my brother with him, while Cathan and I returned to his cottage.

Suddenly I felt alone and adrift. My life before me seemed to be a wide, cavernous abyss. What was my path?

Cathan in his wondrous way intuited my thoughts and said, "I think it's time we see if the ring fits, don't you?"

I nodded, not surprised by his ability to know my mind. He disappeared into his workroom and soon returned. Only now a lilting song permeated the air. He opened his hand and laid the ring on the table. I had not gazed upon it in years.

I picked the ring up reverently and slipped it on my finger. A perfect fit.

"Does the ring still sing for you?"

It did. A soul-stirring melody that filled me up on the inside.

"Can you play the song you hear inside your mind?" Cathan challenged me. He brought out a beautiful lyre and set it before me.

I frowned. I'd never tried to play an instrument before, yet somehow my hands knew what strings to pluck, as if I could conjure the melody from my own heart. I did not even need to see with my eyes what my hands were doing.

Cathan listened to the music, too stunned to speak.

For I had found my gift, my magic—*music*—and I could play like a master.

---

All my life, Cathan had shared with us the legends of powerful songs. How sound once upon a time could move mountains, build pyramids, and even open portals in time.

My musical ability was gifted for a purpose, and the answers lay at Stonehenge. Answers to the riddles of my dreams and why I had a ring from Atlantis. However, to reach Stonehenge in the far south would take a month on foot. It may well have been on the other side of the world. I had never traveled farther than Partick.

My father unknowingly helped me accomplish my quest. When he and his armies had to go north for an extended period to fight off Angle invaders, Merlin proclaimed the time for our journey had come. Of course, my brother had foreseen it. His ability to see the future was growing stronger as he aged. Although even without Merlin's gift of foresight, I knew my whole life had been leading up to this moment.

Taliesin, my brother, and I set off alone. The journey took us thirty days.

The men did not wear their Bards' blue robes, for many had not seen a Druid south of Hadrian's Wall for centuries, not since Rome had come to conquer. After we passed the wall we began to see the ruins and abandoned towns from Rome's exodus a hundred years ago when their empire fell. Overgrown weeds filled the aqueducts. Public baths were empty shells. We passed deserted houses with fallen roofs and a Roman amphitheater left to an audience of ghosts.

We camped in dense woodlands, keeping to ourselves and encountering few travelers. No one ever visited Stonehenge. Rome, during its four-hundred-year occupation, had outlawed gathering at any stone circle across the land, and the fear the Romans had planted was rooted deep. Many thought such places were haunted.

Only the Druids knew how to read the stones and the stars. The stones could chart years, predict eclipses, equinoxes, and solstices. The stones were guides to the cosmos and some even said ancient doorways to Ley Lines, Earth's energy pathways, and only Druids from the ancient past knew how to make the stones sing.

As we journeyed south, the closer we neared to our destination, the song inside me grew like a beacon. When we arrived at Stonehenge, we set up our camp right in the center of the sarsens' ring under the dome of the sky. The stars stretched above us like a peaceful canopy, and I knew I had arrived at the one place on Earth I was meant to be.

Then we waited. On the third day I saw a figure in the distance. A man walking toward us, coming across the field. As he drew near, I could see he was enormous. Quite easily the tallest human I'd ever seen. He was a dark-skinned, black-haired warrior, adorned with metal, and he moved with the fierceness of a wolf. When he closed the distance, a feeling of recognition stirred within me. I knew this man—or had known him in another life—though the memory escaped me now. He stared at us with weary eyes, looking as if he'd weathered a war and lived to tell the tale.

"You've come," he said to us. His unwavering gaze never left mine.

"We have, but we've not yet gone." Merlin grinned, deciding to play the jester to offset the man's fierceness.

The warrior said to me, "There is a price for the answers you seek."

Taliesin cocked a brow in question. "What is this price?"

Whatever it was I would pay it. I'd come too far to turn back now. I'd been waiting my whole life for this.

"A lock of hair." The warrior held out his dagger to me.

I hesitated. From my lessons with Cathan, I knew the power a single strand of hair held. The hidden code to the body and the imprint of the soul. Though after the Golden Age ended, humanity had lost the ability to access it. Perhaps this mysterious man still knew how.

Merlin, Taliesin, and I looked to each other, suddenly wary.

"What is your name?" I asked the man. If I was going to give him a part of myself, at least I deserved to know that much.

"Garesh."

# Chapter 17

## Magellan

Magellan set down the pages Rhys had sent up to her room, certain she had lost her mind. The ring on her finger winked back at her, as if confirming Gwynedd's words were true. Except that was impossible. *Her* Garesh could not be the Garesh in this story. That would make him over a thousand years old. They shared the same name. That was all. And perhaps they looked the same. But that was all too.

Wasn't it?

Magellan stared at the ring's symbols. The same symbols Merlin had carved on the standing stone in the center of the labyrinth.

*Know the way.*

Garesh had said the ring was old and had been in his family for generations. He could not have been alive in the 500s—just as she should not be here in 1829.

Tears welled in her eyes, and she let them fall. She didn't understand what was happening to her or what was real anymore.

She was alone in her room and had been all day. After her accident on the horse, the village doctor had come, an elderly man who had given her medicinal tea and prescribed a week of bedrest. A week! After the man left, she had argued to the countess and Polly that was ridiculous. All she needed was an ice pack and two Advil, though she didn't tell them that.

She had found the pages with Rhys's translation tucked under her dinner tray that evening. He had sent them along as promised. She read them over several times and then fell asleep mentally exhausted, unable to consider what it would mean if her Garesh and Gwynedd's Garesh were one and the same.

---

The next morning when Polly came, Magellan pleaded to let her get dressed. She had to read more of the diary, but first she desperately needed to play the piano. "Please? I can sneak into the conservatory. No one needs to know." She grabbed Polly's hands, not above begging. "You don't understand. I have to play!"

"All right, miss. Don't upset yourself so. Let me see what I can do." Polly left, and minutes later Rhys was barging into her room looking indignant with Polly skirting behind him.

"Polly says you're trying to get out of bed?" he demanded and then stopped, taking in her appearance. She was in her nightgown with her hair down. The white gown was high-necked and as modest as a grandmother's robe, but it still seemed to make him blush beet red.

"Yes. I need to play the piano and then go to the library."

"You almost died from a fall off a horse, and you want to play a piano?" His voice rose in disbelief.

"I did not almost die. I was barely hurt."

"You *were* hurt and you could have died. Do you know how terrifying it was to watch?" Running a hand through his hair, he expelled a breath and turned away to go to the window. Momentarily distracted by the labyrinth, he murmured, "You really can see it clearly from here."

"I know. That's what I said. And I am going downstairs with or without your permission."

He turned to her again with an unfathomable look. "Then I will escort you. In your delicate condition you might slip and tumble down the stairs."

"Tumble down the . . . ?" She put her fingers to her temples, trying not to scream.

Rhys strode to the door. "Polly, inform me when Miss Brighton is dressed," he said imperiously and left.

Polly giggled. "I do believe the earl is sweet on you."

Which was the last thing she needed. She shouldn't even be in this century. "Then it's a shame I don't remember who I am."

"Your memories will come back to you, miss. Not to worry." Polly helped her into one of Vivianne's day dresses. Another frilly gown in pale yellow. With a sigh, Magellan sat in front of the vanity while Polly did her hair in a simple twist.

Rhys reappeared at the door and offered her his arm. He assisted her down the stairs, walking in front of her and practically backward, clearly believing she might fall. She'd lived her whole life afraid of so many things, trapped in a different kind of corset, held back by anxiety and her insecurities. Now Rhys's incessant coddling was showing her how much she didn't want to be afraid anymore. She wanted to be strong. She was being treated like a helpless female in 1829, and she wasn't helpless at all.

"Rhys, I'm fine. Truly. When I'm done playing, I'll come to the library."

Although part of her didn't want to read anymore or see Garesh's name again. The possible ramifications were too much to consider. Suddenly she was looking back on her life with an entirely different lens. Garesh had taught her so much about the power of music and how it connected the world. Had his lessons been orchestrated for this reason? Because she had to find a song hidden in time?

When they reached the conservatory, she sat down at the piano bench like it was a lifeboat. Rhys hovered next to her and asked, "May I stay and watch you play?"

She stared up at him. If he stayed, she wouldn't be able to lose herself fully in the music. "I'd rather be alone."

A shutter came over his face. He was taking her rejection personally. She tried to soften it. "It's just that—"

"No, of course I would only intrude." He stopped her, sounding stiff and formal, and marched off, shutting the door before she could say anything more.

She stared at the empty room. The conservatory felt colder, or maybe he'd taken the warmth with him. Somehow in the short amount of time she'd been here, the connection between them was becoming undeniable. He was translating a diary that seemed to have been written for her—a diary with instructions of how to save the world. She wasn't ready to read yet how she was supposed to accomplish such a feat. She was just one person, not a hero or a superhero. She wasn't even courageous. She was just a woman, full of anxiety about life and how to live it.

Trying hard to shut off her thoughts, she laid her hands on the keys.

# Chapter 18

## Rhys

Rhys stood outside the door listening to the stirring music. The song's melancholy wrapped its arms around him and would not let him go. Magellan was playing a well-known sonata by the famous composer in Vienna, Beethoven, who had died a few years ago. She was playing without sheet music. Of course she was. She must have studied her whole life to become this masterful. Everything about her fascinated and flummoxed him. Since her arrival he had abandoned all his duties and left the house party's entertainments to his mother and Vivianne.

Feeling guilty, he headed outside to find the guests. They were in the middle of an enthusiastic game of croquet. Rhys pretended to watch, sipping on a glass of lemonade and cordially making the rounds to visit. He was informed that Lady Fauna and her family had left early after the lady's unfortunate fall off her horse. Rhys should have been affronted by the slight since they had gone without a personal farewell, but he was in fact relieved. The entire house party had become a plague.

He checked the time and called for tea to be brought to the library along with food. Ever since Magellan had told him of the affliction she faced by going too long without eating, he made sure trays were brought to her regularly.

He set out for the conservatory with a determined stride. She'd had more than enough time to play. *Alone.* When he neared the conservatory, the music wafted down the hallway. She was playing a vibrant piece by a composer he did not recognize. One of the conservatory doors was half open. He stepped inside to discover his mother and Lord Erickson sitting in the chairs. Seeing them hit Rhys with a jolt of irritation.

She had allowed them a private audience but not him? He tamped down his resentment, knowing he was being irrational. It wasn't as if she could have kicked the countess out if she had asked to sit. He pasted a serene smile on his face and joined them in the front row.

Magellan's eyes darted to him without missing a key. She had color in her cheeks that had been missing before, and he realized playing for an hour had indeed rejuvenated her.

He sat back to watch, letting the music ease his ire. Everything about her as she played was beauty in motion. When the song finished, his mother sprang up from her chair. "Zis room has never had such talent. You must give a concert! I insist! Have you zeen my husband's collection of instruments?" She went to the mirrored panels and pressed on one. It clicked open to reveal an enormous hidden closet full of instruments. "He brought zhese back from Vienna."

Magellan jumped up in excitement and went to join her. The cabinets contained a whole treasure trove. His father had collected every kind of instrument, another one of his eccentricities. He even had a set of ancient bagpipes that supposedly came from Egypt.

Magellan picked up a small wind instrument from the shelf, brought it to her lips, and played the loveliest folk song sounding straight from the Highlands. His mother clapped along in delight. Rhys could only watch in awe as Magellan's fingers flew over the little pipe's six holes to conjure the most amazing tune, and in that moment he fell a little bit more in love with her.

She brought the song to a close with a laugh and a blush on her cheeks. "Sorry, I'm afraid I got carried away. This is a beautiful little penny whistle."

"You are quite the maestro, Miss Brighton," Lord Erickson complimented, his eyes keen. "How did you learn to play such a variety of instruments?"

Magellan looked uncomfortable by the question, her smile dimming. "It just comes naturally, I suppose." She placed the whistle back on the shelf.

That was when Rhys saw her hands were shaking and then she swayed, no doubt from fatigue. He jumped up in alarm, announcing, "I'm afraid Miss Brighton is taxed and must return to her room. She is in no state to be up and about."

"But the pages—" Magellan tried to protest.

"I will have them brought up right away with your tea tray."

To his relief, she relented. "Thank you. Yes, maybe that would be best."

Rhys escorted her to the stairs, where she was met by Polly. He asked for a tea tray with food to be sent to her immediately.

With Magellan now escorted to her room, he headed to the library to finish translating the diary. For the sooner he did, the sooner she would confess and he could put all the fanciful notions about her to rest.

He worked hard for hours, noting Gwynedd's story was beginning to take an even more fantastical turn with her, Merlin, and Taliesin's travels to Stonehenge. In the diary Gwynedd called the three of them a powerful triad.

*Two comets and a North Star.*

In recorded history, Rhys knew Merlin and Taliesin would go on to become the most famous Bards in antiquity, and Gwynedd would be married and become the queen of Strathclyde. Rhys did not understand how real history fit into the puzzle of this memoir. It was as if Gwynedd was sharing the secret shadows of their lives as she recounted her magical discovery of music, her time at Stonehenge, and her growing love for the great Bard Taliesin.

Up until now Rhys had dutifully translated every word. Even when Gwynedd explained in some detail how music connected all living things in the world. How a musical scale contained twelve notes. How the heavens were divided into twelve houses. How our bodies had twelve pairs of rib bones to protect the heart. Gwynedd had written it wasn't accidental time was measured by the number twelve, or that the day ended when the sun was below the horizon by twelve degrees. For within the connection between math and music lay the answers to the mysteries of the universe, because one single musical note could be divided into an infinite number of them.

Her treatise on the mystical nature of music was heady, and as Rhys worked, he couldn't help but notice the similarities between Gwynedd and Magellan. Magellan could play music quite magically too. She had arrived wearing a medieval dress and a ring on her finger similar to Gwynedd's, although he hadn't gotten a close look at it.

Then another thought occurred to him. A much darker one.

Did Magellan already know Gwynedd's story and was trying to act out her own fantasy? The ring on her hand, her being talented in music as well, and now in the diary, Gwynedd was falling in love with a Bard who had a mastery with words.

Had Magellan come here for her own love story? Young women often had overactive imaginations from being trapped in their cloistered lives, which is why these kind of romantic tales enticed them. Even he had become captivated with Gwynedd's story. Even he had had a moment of whimsy and contemplated Magellan being Gwynedd—or the woman from his father's painting. Fortunately, he knew the difference between fantasy and real life. He only hoped Magellan did too.

Now that Gwynedd had arrived at Stonehenge and shared what happened with Garesh, Rhys took off his spectacles and rubbed his eyes.

*Oh lud.*

The story had completely veered into pure make-believe.

"Is that more of the translation?"

Rhys glanced up to find Lord Erickson approaching, and he struggled to keep his displeasure from showing on his face.

The baron truly was becoming another thorn in his side. The tedious man had been asking repeatedly to view the library's collection and the diary. Rhys had finally relented and shown the man last night. He had watched with unease as Lord Erickson traced his fingers over the diary's leather cover and remarked, "What a glorious triskelion."

In that moment Rhys had wanted nothing more than to swat Erickson's hand away. Erickson had read the letter to Sir Thomas Malory with his quizzing glass, then turned his attentions to Rhys's translation with a sniff of approval. "You can read Old English. I'm impressed." He glanced up, a wolfish grin on his face. "If this diary is in fact authentic . . ." He trailed off and went back to reading.

Rhys knew what he was implying. The Druids were notoriously secretive, and Gwynedd had written about her Druid tutelage with Merlin, breaking the Druid code.

*If* it was real. The more Rhys translated it, the more he doubted it. Now, after this last bout of translation, he was sure it was pure fiction.

"We will have to conduct a careful study," Erickson said, and Rhys tried to hide his ire at the "we" as the baron went on. "This could likely be a fabrication by an imaginative nun in the 1100s, when it became quite popular to write about mythical figures of antiquity. Though I cannot make an informed decision as of yet."

Rhys did not like seeing the baron handling his translation or the diary. He was feeling quite possessive of the little book—and every other book in the library. He would have to make his apologies to the baron and send the man home empty-handed.

At this point he didn't know how he was going to save the estate. His house party was a failure, and he was back to where he started. *Luftmensch* was the Yiddish word for someone who was an impractical dreamer with no business sense. It seemed he had inherited that trait from his father. What a horrible Liron he was turning out to be.

Now Lord Erickson was back to read more of the translation, and Rhys could find no excuse not to let him. Erickson greedily took the pages and sat down. When the baron finished, he handed them back with a sincere, "Fascinating," and then proceeded to quiz him about Magellan's father, who he assumed was the owner of the diary. "I look forward to meeting Miss Brighton's father when he arrives. Perhaps he will wish to sell the book."

"Unfortunately, I've never met Miss Brighton's father. Only my father seems to have known the man. He was safekeeping the diary for the family." Rhys still had not solved the mystery surrounding Magellan, her family, or why his father had the book. But he would demand the answers from her tomorrow.

Feeling resolute, he wiped his ink-stained fingers. He would send these last pages up with her dinner tray, but come the morning, he would refuse to tell Magellan one more word of this lunatic story until she told him hers.

# Chapter 19

## Gwynedd

Garesh was a Sumerian name and an ancient one. I could see the weight of years in his eyes. All Druids knew the Sumerian tale of a man and woman, the only two people in the world given the gift of immortality who could not die. I believe this man was the Sumerian.

I had a hundred questions for him. Instead, I took his knife and recklessly cut off a lock of my hair and handed it over. I watched him wrap it carefully in a small swath of silk and pocket it in his purse. "You as well." He nodded to the men.

Silently I pleaded with Taliesin and Merlin to follow suit.

They reluctantly gave Garesh their hair, and he said, "Come," turning and walking away.

We followed him across the fields away from Stonehenge until we reached another clearing with an enormous mound of raised earth, a barrow almost four hundred feet long. I knew right away the woman from my dreams had been laid to rest there in an ancient burial ground. This warrior must be the guardian of her grave.

"Only she may enter." He barred the way to Taliesin and Merlin, and I signaled them to wait. I lit a candle and walked into the small cave-like opening to find out what this woman's bones had to say.

She had been laid to rest in the open air. Her skeleton decayed by millennia. Even so, I could tell she had been buried like a queen. Her body was extraordinarily long, and her skull was strangely shaped with an extended brow, much like a drawing I had seen once in Cathan's library of an ancient Egyptian pharaoh. The air inside her tomb was distilled with remnants of power.

I could sense memories waiting to be sifted and closed my eyes to chase them. I could not tell if they were her memories or mine from another lifetime I had lived and forgotten. Ultimately, it did not matter. The past's horizon opened in my mind's eye like a doorway, and I saw everything all at once:

I saw the Great Cataclysm from long ago in the ancient world. The meteors and earthquakes came at dawn, and by sunset the same day Atlantis, Lemuria, Shangri-La, Aztlan, and other empires across the world had fallen. People either took to boats on the waters or traveled deep into underground caverns, using whatever means they had to survive. I saw whole cities sink beneath the sea, their tallest spires disappearing beneath the ocean. I saw Atlantis, the most magnificent circular island city and pinnacle of technological feat, break apart as its ships sailed away from its ports with thousands on board hoping to survive. Captains maneuvered their boats through raging waters and towering tsunamis. These men and women were powerful *Torsionists*, the last from the Golden Age who were able to manipulate matter. The ships pushed through the ocean wall. In a testament to their mastery, not a drop of water touched the bows.

No one was meant to survive this planet-wide destruction. I will not burden you with talk of other worlds and the Great War with those forces who still seek to destroy this planet—or the guardians who made the decision to abandon us and sanction our annihilation.

All except for one guardian. One guardian who loved humanity so much she saved us with a song. A song of infinite power that holds the key to creation and all the elements—a song that controls the atomic spin of life itself. For *music* is the Force. Music is the very fabric of the universe. Music can alter fields of energy, lift objects in the air like leaves in the wind, and transform atoms at their core. The harmonics of the universe are encoded into our DNA. A song created this Earth and saved it once, and there are factions who never want this song wielded again.

After our guardian rescued the world, she created a protective shield around the planet and hid the song in a labyrinth of time. It was the only way she could ensure its survival. She split the song into six parts and entrusted a part to five women. The sixth, she gave to her son, Horus.

The ring holds the map to finding the women when the Earth will need the song once more.

As I sat beside the guardian's grave at one of the most powerful Ley Lines on Earth, I finally understood and my vision became clear. For not only did I hold a part of the song inside me, I had been entrusted by her to find the other women and the parts they safeguarded. This was the vow I had made to her lifetimes ago, because I had been a captain of a ship on that ocean too.

In that life, I swore an oath to assemble the song when the time came—when the poles began to break apart.

I do not know what year this will happen. I do not know what lifetime I will be living. Merlin has the gift to see the future. I do not. My future lives are unknown to me, but the soul's calling transcends lifetimes, and the soul is more than the sum of a single life.

Sitting in the cave, I saw how when the time comes, the Ley Lines will open her labyrinth, and my real journey will begin to find the women. I will know them by their mastery of music. These women are scattered in time, and I must find each one and the part of the song they hold.

I say I, but I really mean you. For I am writing to my future self. To a future life I've yet to live. Merlin has warned me repeatedly there is a chance we will fail our mission. That we will not remember what to do or the ancient vow we made lifetimes ago. Which is why I have left my memories on parchment.

To travel the labyrinth will be a perilous journey. Once inside, you must find the woman in the time the labyrinth has sent you to. However, when you do find her there is great risk. Each time you play the song's part, the song will splinter the labyrinth's walls, opening dimensional doorways that should remain closed. Beings of lower vibration will be drawn to the song's power and want to possess it. I believe stories of demons from hell defined in various religions attempt to describe such forces. Your only safe course is to get to hallow ground where the Earth's natural resonance is too high for them to follow. The only way to escape their reach is to leave the time you're in. They will not have the ability to follow.

After you have retrieved one part of the song, never linger in that time. To do so will be at your own peril. Lower vibrational beings will hunt you, and if they capture you, the labyrinth will close to you forever. Which is why I must impress upon you, once you have the song's part, leave or risk not getting back at all.

Only music can open the labyrinth's doorway to the Ley Lines, and the ring on your finger is the key to opening the right door. When the Ley Lines open, the ring will send you to your next destination. Only after you have the other women's four parts of the song can you return to your time where Horus will be waiting with the sixth and final part.

You must return before Winter Solstice or we will fail. I know these words seem fantastical to you now, but soon enough you will discover they are true.

Her song is the only chance we have to save this world once more.

# Chapter 20

## Magellan

Magellan had begun playing the song the morning of her birthday with the backdrop of the aurora borealis outside her window. Now sitting by the light of an 1829 oil lamp, she could hear the music clearly in her mind, illuminating the truth behind Gwynedd's words. She could no longer doubt.

She had stayed up late into the night reading Gwynedd's account of her trip to Stonehenge, and finally she understood why she was here in 1829. It wasn't to play houseguest to an earl's family but to find a piece of music buried in this time and the woman who had it. The opening of the symphony Magellan had begun crafting on the piano at her apartment was only the beginning. That string of notes still echoing inside her led back to the labyrinth's center like a lit pathway. It was the reason she had not been able to compose any more of the song yet. A woman in 1829 had the second part.

Magellan kept hold of her certainty like a lifeline and brutally pushed aside her logical mind, which was questioning whether she was insane for believing Gwynedd's diary was not only real but written for her—and she personally knew an immortal named Garesh. But the reality was, she was here in England in 1829 with Gwynedd's diary, Garesh's ring, and the music inside her. She had the compass and needed to believe; she *was* the captain of an ancient ship. She could feel it in her bones. Here and now, this moment, this awakening, was what she had been searching for her whole life.

Only when she was playing music did she feel truly alive and fearless. Now she would have to draw upon that power. The song had been split into six parts and hidden in time. She held one part and Garesh's ring had brought her here on the eve of global destruction to retrieve the other four. She could almost feel Garesh beside her, whispering words of encouragement.

A woman in 1829, a master of music, had a part she needed.

Magellan searched her mind for who it could be. She had studied the greats—both men and women. Although only men were ascribed as the canon, the "columns" that held up the symphonic traditions. Beethoven, Tchaikovsky, Mozart, Strauss, Bach, Brahms, Mendelssohn . . . Only men's music had been allowed to soar and spread wings around the world. But Garesh had made her also pay close attention to the women who were only now being unearthed and celebrated. Then Juilliard had rounded out her education with some of the best scholars in the world intent on shining a light on our musical past.

Certainty filled her with who it was. Felix Mendelssohn, the famous composer from Germany, had a sister, Fanny—and Fanny was just as much of a prodigy as he was. Felix even assigned his name to several of Fanny's songs so they could be published. Only later in life did Fanny shock society and start publishing her music herself.

*Fanny Mendelssohn.* It had to be her. In 1829 Felix had come to England for the first time and conducted his music in a concert. The siblings were very close. Fanny could be in London with her brother.

Magellan had no idea how far away London was, but somehow she needed to get there—and she needed Rhys to finish translating the rest of the diary. She needed all of Gwynedd's instruction.

---

Galvanized with newfound purpose, in the morning when Polly came to help her, Magellan rushed to get ready and hurried downstairs to breakfast. She was surrounded by well-wishers who were relieved her accident had been minor. She politely declined the group's offer to ride to the lake, saying she was still recovering. She planned to go to the library.

At breakfast she sat next to Vivianne and caught Rhys's searching gaze. He declined the morning ride too and offered to escort her. It seemed Lord Erickson was already in the library and could act as chaperone.

When they arrived, Lord Erickson was sitting in the far corner at one of the long tables. He had Rhys's translation spread out and was handling the diary with gloves like a serious archivist.

Magellan stopped and pulled Rhys back from walking any farther into the room. She whispered in shock, "You're letting him read the diary?"

He whispered back, "I couldn't stop him. He's an expert in ancient texts and wouldn't stop pestering me."

"Fine," she said, even though it wasn't. "Just please finish translating it today."

He searched her eyes and slowly shook his head. "No. I won't translate anymore until you tell me your circumstance."

"That wasn't our agreement."

"I've changed my mind. I've had quite enough of Gwynedd's tall tale. Whoever the author was has veered into pure lunacy. Atlantis indeed. A lost guardian at Stonehenge. A war with other worlds." He finished with a fierce whisper. "It's utter poppycock!"

With a sinking heart, Magellan listened to him vent. He'd been the one having to translate every word, and he was obviously done.

Rhys strode to the tea tray and surprised her by pouring her a cup. He added cookies to a napkin. "For your pockets," he said, giving her the cookies, and then he set the tea down in front of her. He busied himself making a cup.

She looked from the tea to the cookies to him, at a loss. She would have to tell him the truth and show him Godwin's letter. There was no other alternative. The time for pretending was over. She needed him to believe.

She glanced over to Lord Erickson, who was still across the room and absorbed in reading.

Rhys said in a low voice, "I'm not translating another word until you tell me everything." He cocked an imperious brow, leaned back, and took a sip of his tea.

She never had a chance to reply because the countess arrived breathless in the doorway. "Miss Brighton, your father has arrived!"

"My father?" Magellan was sure she misheard her.

Rhys's mother nodded and said fretfully to Rhys, "Terrance Brighton is in zee salon right now." She lowered her voice so Lord Erickson could not overhear and went on to say, "Apparently, he has been looking all over zee countryside for her. I invited him to stay as our guest, but he insists zhey leave today. He vas most adamant." The countess turned to her with tearful eyes. "Polly is upstairs vaiting to help you change into a traveling gown."

Rhys dropped his tea cup with a clatter. "A traveling gown! She's leaving?" he whispered in disbelief.

Magellan's whole body started to quiver. She felt like she was going to faint. What was happening? Who was Terrance Brighton?

Rhys's mother led her from the room. She lowered her voice further to whisper in confidence, "Forgive me, I did not know he vould be coming."

Magellan nodded, resisting the urge to run. She grabbed on to the only plan that made sense: She needed to get back to the center of the labyrinth right away.

# Chapter 21

𝄢

## Rhys

Rhys was still unable to move as he watched Magellan leave with his mother. Someone had come to collect her. A surge of panic hit him, and he launched out of his chair. He hurried to the salon to find Magellan's father.

Terrance Brighton was a well-dressed heavyset man from America who seemed both anxious and mortified to find his beloved daughter being housed by the Earl of Liron. He and his daughter were in England visiting his cousin, a vicar at one of the neighboring estates to the north. Magellan's horse had returned without her days ago, and they'd been scouring the countryside, frantic and fearing the worst. His eyes glistened as he spoke, and Rhys felt guilty he had not sent out the inquiries.

His mother joined them after depositing Magellan with Polly. Flustered, she waved her lace handkerchief around in the air as she talked. "Vee sought she might have suffered an accident. She doesn't zeem to remember who she is."

"My deepest apologies, my lady. I'm not sure that's the truth," the man said, wringing his hat in his hands.

Rhys stepped forward. "What do you mean?"

"She's probably worried I'll be upset with her. Your father, God rest his soul, was safekeeping a diary for us until I was ready to sell it. He offered to hold on to it until my return. We had met in London while I was visiting the Historical Society. When Maggie discovered my plan this trip, she ran away. I never imagined she would turn up at your doorstep or I would have come sooner."

*Maggie?* Rhys listened perplexed as Magellan's father fully explained the situation.

"One of her favorite stories, it is. Her mother used to read it to her."

Rhys's eyebrows shot up. "Her mother reads Old English?"

The man chuckled. "No, no, of course not. I have a translation."

Everything Terrence Brighton was saying was causing Rhys's fury to rise. The hours he had spent squinting over candlelight with his father's spectacles. How she must have laughed at him when she already knew the story quite well!

"I see" was all Rhys could get out.

"Your father was quite aware my daughter is a special girl, full of imagination. She loves her fairy tales and her music. I'm sorry if she's been a burden." He looked so remorseful.

"Why did she say she had amnesia? Did she say it out of fear?" An alarming thought hit Rhys. "That you would take your anger out on her?"

The man put his hat over his heart and swore, "I would never lay a finger on my girl. She is my precious angel."

Rhys relaxed at hearing the promise. Yes, Magellan was precious. And a liar. His thoughts were in a tailspin. While his mother offered Magellan's father tea, Rhys hurried back to the library and retrieved the diary from Erickson, who sputtered in surprise when he heard Magellan's father had arrived.

Erickson of course had to follow him back to the salon, where he introduced himself to Mr. Brighton. Rhys did not know how to handle the situation. He handed the diary over to the man. "Here is your property returned, sir. Your daughter should be down any minute."

"Thank you, my lord." The man slipped the diary into his coat pocket. Then he sipped his tea while they waited.

"We have been admiring your glorious book," Lord Erickson said and politely enquired if he had any interest in selling it, to which Mr. Brighton replied he had already secured a buyer in London. Erickson looked crestfallen. An awkward silence ensued.

"May I call on her when she is settled?" Rhys asked, still needing to talk to Magellan. This could not be their end. Now that he knew the truth he had so many questions.

"Of course, my lord. Give us a few days to help her come to her senses again."

Rhys expelled a breath, running his hand over his face to cover a pained laugh. Come to her senses? That was putting it mildly. Her medical affliction was so much worse than he had thought. His heart was breaking in this parlor in front of Magellan's father and his mother. She looked as stunned as he was.

"Where did Magellan learn to play the piano and harp so well?" he asked her father.

"She was born with the gift, and I hired the finest teachers." Mr. Brighton gave him a tight smile and went back to his tea, clearly uncomfortable.

His mother asked, "And vhen do you return to zee United States?"

"In less than a fortnight. I own a small business and must be getting back."

Rhys frowned. That didn't give him much time to decide the best course of action. "And Magellan's mother? Did she travel with you?"

"Her mother died years ago," the man said bluntly. "Which is probably why my daughter's a bit wild, running off alone all the time. She hasn't had a mother's hand to guide her."

Rhys glanced toward the door, impatient to see her, to watch her face when she saw her father.

Only Polly returned alone, looking nervous. "Miss Brighton . . . she's gone."

Rhys jumped up. "Gone? What do you mean? You were with her."

Polly's lip quivered. "She seemed quite upset and asked for a few minutes alone after I helped her change. When I came back to get her, she was gone."

Springing into action, Rhys issued orders to the servants to search the house and to check the stables to see if any of the horses were missing. Magellan's father looked just as alarmed, and Rhys rushed to assure him, "Do not worry, sir. We will find her."

Rhys strode away to join the search, heading immediately to the conservatory in the east wing. When he walked into the empty room, his eyes went to the glass doors, and he knew exactly where Magellan was. He hurried outside, keeping to the side path, and ducked into the labyrinth. The second he was inside the maze he began to run.

His heart was beating furiously with a mixture of anger and worry coursing through him. When he turned the last corner leading to the center, at first he didn't see her and fear slammed into him he had been wrong. She hadn't come to the labyrinth.

Then he spied her on the other side of the standing stones. She was sitting on the ground with her knees drawn up. She had changed into a simple brown travel gown with a high neck and long sleeves. Vivianne had given her an old pair of travel boots as well.

Magellan looked up at him. Tears streaked down her face.

Her despair took away all his anger. Whatever lies she had told, it was because she was ill.

"Magellan," he said gently.

"He's not my father." She did not seem surprised to see him, as if she knew he would figure out where she'd gone. "I swear, Rhys. He's not, and that's the truth. I was adopted in New York by a couple named Harold and Margaret."

Harold and Margaret. Her father said she had an active imagination. "He said you ran away because he was planning to sell the diary. Your horse turned up days ago, and he's been worried sick."

She swiped the tears from her cheeks. "I didn't run away. And you know I don't know how to ride."

No, he didn't know. Her lies hardened him. "He said he has his own translation, and you've read it many times," he gritted out.

She jumped up in outrage. "He's lying! Rhys, I've never read it before."

"He knows about your musical ability. He knows you!" He was yelling now too. "Magellan, stop. You don't have to lie anymore!"

"I'm not lying. Maybe I lied before about not remembering, but it was for a good reason."

"Why? Is your father cruel? Are you afraid of him?"

"No! My father is kind. He is the sweetest man, and I didn't tell you because I didn't think you would believe the truth."

"Why don't you let me be the judge what I'll believe?"

"Fine! The truth is I'm not from this time. I'm from the future."

Rhys's heart fell as he watched her pace back and forth. His eyes went to the standing stones, remembering the ridiculous "time machine" his father had tried to construct. Had he and Magellan been in conversation by letters? Had Godwin encouraged her whimsical notions?

She began to babble, waving her arms as she explained. "I was playing the harp at a wedding. There was a panic because the North and the South Poles are about to flip just like Gwynedd wrote about. I ended up playing Bach on the church organ, and I think the music brought me here on a Ley Line. You said Merlin himself built this stone circle." She turned to face him, wild-eyed. "Gwynedd wrote her diary for me, and somehow . . . somehow your father ended up with the book. He wrote me a letter, knowing I would end up here."

"How? He's dead!" Rhys felt like he was losing his mind.

"He wrote it before he died." She took a step toward him. "He said you're supposed to help me."

"Help you what?" He held his breath and prayed she did not say save the world.

"Find the song? Save the world?"

Good Lord, she said it. He rubbed his brow.

She held up her hand in front of his face. "This is the ring, Rhys. I have Gwynedd's ring. Look!"

He refused to look. Instead he took her hand in his. "So you think Gwynedd's diary is real?" he asked gently, as if she might break.

"It is real." She began to sob, the words tumbling out of her. "My whole life has been about music. I can play any instrument, and I never knew how or why. For the first time I have answers. And I know Garesh! He is just like Gwynedd described. He was my teacher and gave me the ring. I don't know how he was there in Gwynedd's time, but he was."

"Magellan, the story is make-believe."

"It's not! Can you for one moment suspend your disbelief?" She took a pleading step toward him. "Please, Rhys. I need your help. The world might be ending on Winter Solstice, not just in my time but yours too. It's all connected. That's only six weeks away. Gwynedd said I need to find the women's four parts of the song in order to get back."

If she said "to save the world" one more time, he was going to lose all reason. Why couldn't he have fallen in love with a normal, sane woman?

"I have a part of the song. I've always had it. Now I need to find the other women. It's why I'm here. Fanny Mendelssohn has part of the song."

He blinked in surprise. "Who?"

"Felix Mendelssohn's sister. It must be her."

Rhys had no idea what she was talking about. He knew who Felix Mendelssohn was, of course. He was the famous composer from Germany.

She said, "In 1829 Felix came to England for the first time to conduct a concert."

Rhys frowned but nodded. "With the Philharmonic Society. I believe I received the invitation."

"You did?" She looked at him with hope. "He's in London? Then maybe Fanny is here with him!"

Rhys was having trouble keeping up. "Who is Fanny?"

"His sister!" Magellan was waving her hands in the air again and talking too fast. "She's a composer too. Her brother, Felix, was called the child prodigy, but she was one too. She lived in his shadow. If she has the song, it will prove I'm not crazy. Help me get to London and see her before she leaves for Germany again." She took his hands and squeezed them.

He stared at their joined hands, his feelings in turmoil. How could he extricate her from this fantasy? Was her mind this unstable? He'd heard of musical geniuses who buckled under the weight of their gift and succumbed to madness. Even his own father had been half mad all his life. Godwin had often spouted off strange ideas and proclamations. The late earl had been an alchemist and an artist to boot. Now it looked like he had encouraged Magellan in his letter writing.

But her real father was here now and had come to collect her.

Even so, Rhys would not abandon her. He would do everything in his power to help her get well. Because the painful truth was somehow she had stolen his heart without his permission, and he could not lose her today. *Agape* was the ancient Greek word to love someone through all obstacles, and he truly believed with time he could help her rein in her unbridled imagination.

He spoke to her gently. "I will not abandon you, but going with your father to your relative's house to rest will be the best course. I will come in two days' time, and we will speak more then."

"Rhys, did you hear anything I just said? I don't know that man. I'm not even from this time. I'm here to get the song because the world is dying!"

He took a step toward her, at his wit's end. "It. Is. A. Story."

Instead of cowering, she took a step forward and yelled back. "It! Is! Not! Read your father's letter." She held up her hand. "Or look at my ring. Look at it!"

"I don't want to look at your bloody ring!" He grabbed her hand in his, and she put her other hand on his heart imploringly, causing his pulse to skyrocket. They were neck in neck, breathing furiously down each other's throats. It was either shake her to make her see sense or kiss her.

The kiss won. Before he could change his mind, he grabbed her, his mouth devouring hers. The kiss was a raging, burning, helpless twist of need in the face of her delusions. She was mad as a hatter, yet he still wanted her with a soul-crushing desperation that terrified him.

By the deuce, he wanted her.

"Rhys," she whispered. "Don't let me go."

"I'll never let you go. Never," he swore with another kiss. His hands were on every curve of her, just as hers were on him. Their mouths were insatiable, drowning in each other.

When they finally pulled away for air, she let out a pained, choked laugh. "You don't even believe me."

"I don't." He kissed the corners of her mouth, her cheeks, her temples. "You were in a riding accident. You're confused and becoming lost in your favorite story. You just need rest. I will come to you in two days." He was convincing himself as much as her. He would give anything to have her stay, but she needed to go with her father. It was the best thing for her and would only help put her feet back on the ground. Perhaps if he had tried harder to help his own father find his footing in this world, he might still be alive today.

Rhys pulled away gently. She expelled a breath and leaned her head back to look up at him. The two tears escaping her eyes lanced his heart. He kissed them away, tasting the salt on his tongue. "Everything will be all right."

She closed her eyes as if in pain. "No, it won't."

He disentangled himself from her with a weary sigh and helped straighten her travel dress as if she were a child, because maybe she was a child, mentally, on some level. She was certainly as stubborn as a child, determined to cling to her delusions.

"Help me find Fanny Mendelssohn. It could prove—"

"Magellan, enough!" he cut her off, his voice sharp. He pulled himself together, becoming every inch the earl. "I will return you to your father, and I will come visit you in two days' time."

With steely determination he took her hand and all but pulled her back to the house where the others were waiting. He ignored her continued pleas and fresh tears.

It was time for the Lady of the Labyrinth to go home.

# Chapter 22

## Magellan

Magellan's first thought when she was told her father was here—crazy as it was—was maybe she did have a father in 1829. Or maybe he had also time traveled to find her. Maybe he was part of the mission. Maybe he knew Garesh. Her mind was concocting the wildest theories to explain the man waiting for her in the parlor.

Rhys, on the other hand, preferred to think she was mentally ill. She choked back a sob, letting him drag her to the house. She was still reeling from their kiss and wished it hadn't happened, because now she knew what it would be like between them. Never had she experienced such passion, and she didn't know if she would ever see him again. She had tried to make him listen, but he had decided this was the best course.

By the time they drew near the house, she'd stopped begging him to let her stay. Her whole body was quaking with fear. She pulled her hand away from his, trying to be strong.

"What about the diary?" she asked, unable to hide the tremble in her voice.

"I gave it back to him, since it's his."

She fought back another sob. The diary was the only thing anchoring her here, and Rhys had given it away. She would have to figure out how to get it back. She needed to know the rest of Gwynedd's instructions before they ran out of time.

This was a nightmare. She was being kicked out of Hereford Manor with Rhys thinking he was doing the best thing for her. Returning her to her family "to rest" at a vicar's house. He kept promising he would come for her in two days. When he did, she would pretend to be cured. She would pretend anything to get back here to him, to finish translating the diary, and somehow get to London to meet Fanny Mendelssohn.

When they arrived at the salon, the countess was there with Vivianne, Cecil, and Lord Erickson, as well as a few servants. Everyone had been looking for her.

A balding man in a suit clutched his hat in his hands. "There she is! My girl." He came toward her. "My darling girl."

The world began to spin, and Magellan fought back a panic attack. It was a miracle she didn't throw up. She had never met this man before in her life.

Were those tears glistening in his eyes? No wonder he had convinced them all.

Rhys assured her again, "I'll come visit you in two days." He looked to the man. "If that is acceptable with you, sir?"

"Of course, of course! I'll tell my cousin to expect you."

Vivianne said, "I'd like to come too, please." Rhys's sister was tearing up, seeing how distraught Magellan was. Even Cecil was upset. The countess was the most emotional. She had her face buried in a handkerchief, weeping.

One of the servants hurried into the room and handed Rhys a satchel. Rhys then handed the satchel to "her father" and said to him,

"I asked the kitchen to pack some provisions for you and your daughter for the carriage ride, for her physical condition."

The man looked confused for a brief moment but took the bag. "Of course. Of course, my lord, thank you so much."

Rhys was sending her away and yet he had packed her snacks for the road so she wouldn't feel sick. The gesture was so sweet it made her want to cry again. She didn't know how to try to convince him anymore.

He took her hand and kissed the air above it and met her eyes. "I will come," he reassured her, the echo of their kiss still in his eyes.

She nodded stoically, pulling her hand away.

"Off we go, then." The man claiming to be her father kept a firm hold on her arm and led her to the carriage, saying "There, there, my girl . . ." in a soothing manor as if she were a horse about to bolt. But where could she go? The man had the diary, and she needed it back. She needed to bide her time for two days. Then Rhys would come. She knew he would.

She turned back before she got into the carriage. It looked like Rhys was in physical pain. The countess clung to his arm. Magellan got into the carriage and settled into her seat facing forward. The man got in and sat across from her. Then he waved a jovial goodbye to everyone out the window.

Magellan was too busy focusing on her breathing to look back. If she looked, she would suffer a panic attack the likes of which she might never recover from. Right now, she was in a carriage with a stranger. Everything was wrong. So wrong. She knew it in her bones, and her breath started to quicken out of control as the carriage got underway.

The man posing as her father sat back with a satisfied sigh. He stared at her silently, his smile gone.

Magellan said while puffing out little breaths, "You and I both know," *puff*, "you are not," *puff puff*, "my father."

"'Tis true, 'tis true. That we do know, girlie," he agreed with a thick cockney accent and reached into his jacket pocket.

Swift as a snake striking, he put a cloth over her mouth, cutting off her scream. She clawed at him, but he held her in a vise. "Rhys!" She tried calling out for help, her voice muffled as the reeking fumes struck her like a hammer and the world around her went dark.

# Chapter 23

## Magellan

When Magellan woke up some time later, blind terror hit her first. Her hands were tied in front of her with rope, her mouth bound. Night had fallen. The man who claimed to be her father had tossed aside his fine coat and hat. He had a knife in his lap and was thumbing through Gwynedd's diary by the light of the carriage lantern.

Magellan couldn't stop the surge of adrenaline coursing through her. She started to twist and writhe, pulling at her wrists. The rope was rubbing her skin raw and cutting off the feeling in her hands. The rancid rag in her mouth made her want to vomit.

"You're awake." He gave her an assessing look. "What is this book? Why's it so special?" He waved it in front of her. Then he seemed to realize she couldn't talk. "If I take that off and you scream, I'll cut you."

Her eyes widened, and she nodded frantically in agreement. He took the rag off, not too gently, and she gagged, fighting the urge to throw up.

"It's a diary from the sixth century." She tried to sound helpful, her voice shaking as she looked around wildly for a way to escape.

"Why does his lordship want it?"

She had no idea who his lordship was. "Is that who had you kidnap me?"

"I ask the questions, girlie." He pointed the knife at her. The nine-inch blade gleamed in the lamplight as his eyes swept her. "Didn't know I was being paid to fetch someone so pretty. I may have to sample the goods before we arrive."

He leered at her, and Magellan tried hard to calm her breathing before she passed out. Her blood sugar was dropping dangerously low. Garesh was the one who'd taught her basic self-defense before she went off to college in case she was ever in a scary situation. This was beyond any scary situation she could have imagined. Her brain felt fuzzy, her vision going in and out of focus. If she died here, she would have failed Gwynedd. Would the world end?

Garesh was the one who'd always told her, "You are stronger than you can imagine—if you believe it." Right now she had to believe it. She had no choice. It was either do or die.

She drew a deep breath into her lungs. Her only weapons were her feet, which weren't tied. Without waiting to deliberate, she brought both feet up blindingly fast and kicked the man full in the face with Vivianne's heavy boots. The man reared back in shock, his nose bleeding. Enraged, he roared and backhanded her. She tasted blood and raised both feet again and kicked him in the chest with all her might over and over like a wild bucking horse as she screamed a primal scream born from the fury of wanting to live.

In the struggle, the man blindly swung out his knife repeatedly. Only the basest instinct to survive gave her the strength to lean back and strike his face with her boots again and again. The third time he lost consciousness. Blood was everywhere. She didn't know whose it was. Both her hands were still bound. She was shaking too hard to use the knife to cut the rope.

The carriage barreled on in the darkness. Frantic, she looked around, needing to escape before shock rendered her immobile. The carriage door was locked but the window was just large enough for her to fit through.

With both hands still tied, she grabbed the diary, trying not to get blood on it, and tossed it in her bag. Then she hitched up her skirts. She climbed halfway out the window and looked up. The driver was sitting high up on the carriage toward the front. If her kidnapper woke up, she was certain he would kill her. She had to jump.

When the driver slowed down for a curve, she flung her bag into the wooded darkness. Then she struggled to climb out of the window and hurled herself to the ground.

She forced herself not to cry out when she hit the dirt road and rolled to a stop. Frozen, she waited in terror for the carriage to slow down, but the driver kept going. She watched as the carriage light on the road grew dimmer and dimmer until it finally turned a corner and was swallowed up by the night.

For a long time, she could only lie there, in shock and gasping for air. She sat up, fighting dizziness, and realized her arm was bleeding badly. A cut ran down her calf too. She needed to find help before she passed out—and she needed to get off the road. Once they realized she'd escaped, they would turn back to search for her.

Getting to her knees, she groped around in the dark until she found the satchel. Forcing herself to stand, she wavered for a moment as the knife wounds began to throb. She had no idea where she was. Surrounded by the dark, the night's coldness crept into her skin, and she started to shiver violently from shock.

"I'm sorry" was all she could say over and over again, even though she had no idea who she was apologizing to. To Gwynedd for failing? To the guardian? All she knew was she never should have left Hereford Manor or allowed herself to get in that carriage. She should have tried harder to convince Rhys. She had caved in a moment of weakness when she should have stood by her conviction. Now she was alone, lost in a time not her own, and she desperately needed help.

"I'm sorry. I'm sorry. I'm sorry. I'm sorry." She kept saying the words like a mantra, putting one foot in front of the other and forcing herself to go on. She didn't know how long she had walked until she crested the hill. Then she heard it:

Music.

Music sounded in the distance. A jubilant, rowdy song led by a group of fiddlers. Claps, cheers, and laughter accompanied them, calling to her like a siren's song and forcing her to keep limping forward. For wherever there was music as joyful as this, there had to be sanctuary.

Within minutes she saw the glowing lights of the tavern and choked on a cry. Hobbling toward the open door on the side of the building, she heard the sounds of pots and pans clanging from inside the kitchen along with a woman's voice. The woman's commands rose over the den as she gave orders to the kitchen staff.

Magellan rounded the corner to stand on the doorstep and came face-to-face with the woman, who took one look at her and said, "Sweet Mary, mother of Jesus."

Magellan promptly crumpled to the ground.

The woman knelt beside her and called out for help. "Curtis! Get Ned! And ready a room. We'll be needing boiling water and fresh linens." She cradled Magellan's head in her arms. "Lass, who did this to you?"

Magellan whispered, barely able to get the words out, "Don't let them find me."

A fierce light came into the woman's eyes. "No one's going ta find ya here, love, or hurt you again, that I can promise."

A group gathered around, their faces full of concern. Magellan felt two burly arms gently pick her up and carry her upstairs. She floated in and out of consciousness, vaguely remembering another man. Whatever he was doing to her arm hurt like hell. They gave her whisky to drink, but it didn't stop her from screaming. The burly man with gentle hands held her down while the other poured what felt like liquid fire on her cuts.

Magellan thought her whole body might go up in flames and disappear altogether. The last thing she remembered was the pain when something sharp stabbed her arm. The fiddlers were still playing somewhere in the distance, but she couldn't hear them anymore. She had been hurled into the silence of oblivion.

# Chapter 24

𝄢

## Rhys

Rhys couldn't sleep. Every time he closed his eyes, he imagined Magellan begging him not to make her leave. Desperate, he even got out the painting from his closet. For the first time, it did not soothe him. In the portrait the Lady of the Labyrinth was resolutely turned away from him.

She did indeed look like Magellan. Which brought his thoughts full circle back to his original angst. He'd done the right thing, hadn't he? That man was her father. Even an earl couldn't keep a daughter from her father. This wasn't the Middle Ages.

Rhys just couldn't shake the feeling he'd made the wrong decision, and then another wellspring of panic would rise up again, until he was drowning in doubt. He would go to the vicar's in the morning and make sure all was well. He would stay at a nearby inn and call on her every day.

Feeling better with that plan, he fell into an exhausted sleep, tossing and turning as he ran away from the nightmares of Magellan begging him to let her stay.

When he woke the next morning, he felt ragged. He went down to breakfast to find the guests had departed early, sensitive to the drama that had unfolded and wanting to give the family privacy. The house was empty now. It was just his mother, Cecil, and Vivianne.

Rhys sat down wearily, taking a coffee, and apprised them of his plan to travel to the vicar's that day.

"I think it wise," his mother surprised him by agreeing.

He nodded. "I should have accompanied them yesterday." Not doing so was his mistake. Why hadn't he ridden out with her in their carriage or followed behind on his own horse? He had just sent her off in tears like a coldhearted arse because it was the "right" thing to do. She should be here, dammit. Why did he let her go?

"She did not vant to go, and I did not know vhat to do." His mother began to cry. "I did not expect zomething like zhis to happen. He never varned me."

Rhys shook his head. "Who?"

"Your father."

"What does Father have to do with this?" Rhys tried to muddle through what his mother was saying.

His mother dabbed at her eyes. "He told me she vould come to zee labyrinth. He made me promise to help her, and he gave me a letter to deliver to her vhen she arrived."

His father had asked his mother to deliver the letter?

Rhys sat forward. "What did the letter say?"

"I do not know. He made me promise not to read it. He said zee future vas at stake." She gave a little laugh. "You know how dramatic he vas. But he knew she vould come one day and he vould not be alive to meet her." She lifted tearful eyes to him, showing Rhys the pain in her heart. "He never varned me her father might come. Yesterday, I did not know vhat to do."

"When did you give her the letter?" he demanded.

"Zee morning after she arrived."

Blast it to hell. Had he made the wrong decision?

*Yes,* his heart whispered. He had sent her off with a stranger who he had believed over Magellan, because he had no other answers to explain how she had arrived in the labyrinth. He thought back to the moment he had handed Magellan's father the satchel of food for her and mentioned her physical affliction. She needed to eat at timed intervals to not grow dizzy. Terrance Brighton had stared at him blankly before covering his mistake.

*Because he hadn't known.*

A chill coursed through Rhys.

The man hadn't known Magellan needed food because *he didn't know her.*

Dread overtook him and Rhys huffed out a painful breath, his whole body quaking with fear. "He did not know of her propensity for getting dizzy if she does not eat." He'd been trying so hard to be reasonable and logical and nothing like his father that he had missed the most obvious clue. He stood up, choking on the words. "I have made a grave error."

"Rhys?" his mother whispered.

"Did you tell anyone of her circumstance? Anyone of her amnesia and how she was found?"

His mother shook her head. "Only Lord Erickson."

He turned to her in surprise. "You told him?"

Vivianne and Cecil were looking back and forth between them, not understanding.

She tried to explain. "He kept questioning me about her and zee diary. But he's your friend."

Erickson was no friend. He coveted the diary. "I will go to the vicar's immediately." Rhys strode from the room, barking out orders to ready his horse and pack a bag.

Cecil was beside him, understanding the gravity of the situation. "I'll ride with you."

The vicar in question lived on an estate three hours north in Oxford. They rode hard, making excellent time, and arrived at the man's cottage. Only to find the vicar was an elderly man who lived alone and had no family, certainly no relatives living in America.

Rhys questioned him fully, his heart squeezing tighter with every word until he feared he might stop breathing. The man posing as Magellan's father had indeed been a fake. Rhys was paralyzed with fear. He didn't know what to do.

For once his younger brother took charge. "We'll split up and take both roads. We'll stop at every inn and tavern."

Rhys covered his mouth with his hands, feeling ill. "Cecil, what have I done?" Hot tears burned his eyes. "My God, she doesn't know him. I sent her away with a stranger."

"Rhys, we will find her. You will find her." Cecil laid his hand on his arm firmly. His little brother who had idolized him all his life was witnessing him fall apart.

Rhys nodded, forcing his emotions into check. He spent the rest of the day riding hard and stopping at every inn and tavern, looking for Terrence Brighton's carriage and asking proprietors if anyone had seen a father and daughter traveling together. No one had. It was as if she'd disappeared.

Night was falling, but he couldn't go home. He would go mad if he had to sit and wait for news. He needed to get to London and hire an investigator. He would hire a whole team of Bow Street Runners to find her.

As he rode, a suspicion wormed its way into his mind. His mother had told Erickson the truth about Magellan. Erickson had also taken a keen interest in the diary. Could he have acted in secret to steal her away? Created a ruse to obtain the diary?

Erickson's estate was another two-hour ride to the north. Rhys paid for a room and a hot meal at an inn and slept for only a few hours to give his horse time to rest. Then he set out at dawn's light. He would question Erickson first and head to London.

The wind pushed against him, and he tried not to give in to the despair pressing on his chest like a lead weight. His horse seemed to sense the urgency and stretched harder to cover ground.

When they arrived at Erickson's, his horse was frothing at the mouth. Rhys dismounted and whispered soft words of praise before handing him over to the stable master.

He made his way to the house, only to be met at the door by Erickson instead of the butler. The man looked worse than him. His hair was wild, his eyes red, and his clothing was in disarray. He was on his way to being drunk.

"Did you find her?" Erickson asked, his voice a pained whisper.

Rhys could only stare at the man dumbfounded. There was no way Erickson could have heard Magellan was missing.

In a blind fury, Rhys grabbed him by the shirt and shoved him hard against the wall. "What did you do?" He shook him. "What did you do?"

"I only hired him to be her father. He was supposed to bring the diary to me. That was all!"

Suddenly the missing pieces fell into place. How a stranger had known about the book and just enough about Magellan to convince him. Rhys shook him again. "Where is she?"

"I don't know! She never arrived."

Rhys staggered back. He wanted to break something. He wanted to pummel Erickson's face badly. *Backpfeifengesicht* was the German word for that. He raised his fist to strike him but before he could Erickson fell to his knees, weeping.

"I just wanted the book. A diary from Merlin's sister. Liron, think of it. It's priceless. I never meant to hurt her."

Rhys realized there was something Erickson wasn't telling him. "What happened?" he demanded, suddenly winded.

"Only the carriage returned. The driver said . . ." Erickson was unable to go on.

Rhys eyes widened in horror. “He said what?”

“There was a struggle. When he stopped to water the horses, the man I hired was unconscious. Miss Brighton was missing. She must have been thrown from the carriage.”

Rhys shook his head, unable to process what he was hearing. “Where’s the man? The father—the pretend father.”

“I don’t know.” Erickson broke down. “He ran off.”

Rhys yanked him to his feet. “Show me the carriage at once!”

Erickson led him to the stables, to the back garage. Seeing the carriage Magellan had left Hereford Manor in brought her departure back in vivid clarity. He’d waited on the steps for her to look out the window and wave to him, but she hadn’t.

Because he had forsaken her.

When he saw inside the carriage, he ran to the corner of a stall and threw up, casting up his accounts although there was barely anything in his stomach. In the carriage, blood was everywhere. The cushions had been tossed, the seat covers torn by a knife. Had she made it out alive? How could she have withstood the man’s attack?

*She couldn’t. She didn’t.*

His knees began to buckle. “How could you do this?” Rhys choked on the words. “How could you?”

Erickson was frozen. “I never meant—”

“Bring me the driver! Right away!” Rhys staggered back against the wall.

Erickson admitted the carriage driver must have gone into hiding, and his family did not know when he would return. Rhys needed to hear the driver’s account, but he didn’t have time to wait. He had to get to London to hire the Bow Street Runners. He would get a whole team to find Magellan—and the driver and the impostor. He would offer the driver’s wife money to convince her husband to come forward and give his account of what happened. It might be the only way to find Magellan.

He left his instructions and secured his horse's safe return to Hereford Manor. Then he took Erickson's fastest steed and rode straight through to London.

Rhys was not a religious man, but he cast up his prayers to heaven for the first time in his life and prayed Magellan had survived.

# Chapter 25

## Magellan

Mary Callahan was an angel with a temper and didn't want Magellan getting out of bed. Magellan had woken up to find her left arm was wrapped in a bandage from her wrist to her elbow and her right calf too. She was wearing a chemise, and her body was thrumming in pain like the rhythm of a drumbeat. She tried to stay immobile and focus on her breathing.

From the countdown method she ascertained she was in a small bedroom on the second floor of a tavern. She could hear the people below and smell roasting meat. The room was sparse with only a bed, dresser, and chair. Soon after she woke, Mary, a buxom woman in her fifties, informed her both knife wounds had required stitches, and she'd been lucky Ned, the local doctor, was at the tavern or she might have bled to death.

"You've been in and out of fevers for two days," Mary told her as she tidied the room and delivered broth and tea. "Ned wasn't sure ya were going to make it."

Magellan tried to sit up and winced, lying back again. "Has anyone come looking for me?"

"No, and whoever did that to ya will have to get through me first," Mary said fiercely. "Tell me his name. I know a few fellas who'd be happy to go find him for ya."

Magellan shuddered, the violent attack in the carriage still too vivid. Her eyes welled with tears and she blinked them back. "I don't know. He said his name was Terrence Brighton, but it was an alias."

"Where's your family, lass?" Mary asked gently. "Across the sea in America?"

Magellan nodded. It was easier than explaining she had no family in 1829.

"Ya poor thing. Ya shouldn't be alone."

Until now she hadn't been alone. She'd had Rhys and his family. She tried to focus on breathing and the throbbing of her wounds to keep from succumbing to despair. "Where am I?"

Mary said they were near the town of Leicester, which didn't mean anything to her.

How far away was Rhys? Not that she could go to him. He hadn't believed a word she'd said. She tried to mute the pain in her heart and put him out of her thoughts and instead focus on the situation at hand.

Fanny Mendelssohn was the real reason she was in 1829 and her only hope of getting home. When she found Fanny, Magellan would be able to confirm whether Gwynedd's instructions were real. *If* Fanny had part of the ancient song Gwynedd described, then Magellan truly was on a mission inside a labyrinth of time to save the world—and she only had until Winter Solstice to find the women. Only Garesh's ring knew where they were. Garesh, her beloved teacher, who knew the world's music better than another living soul, was either a time traveler or immortal. She didn't know which. Had he known the journey she would have to make? Had her parents? It made her wonder how much of her life had been engineered.

Or, if she did find Fanny Mendelssohn and the woman had no idea about the song, then Magellan would check herself into an 1829 mental institution herself and call it a day. Because she wasn't so far removed from reality to admit a cracked head on the floor of St. Paul's Chapel was looking more and more like a possibility. But until she woke up in a Manhattan hospital coma ward, she had to carry on. "I need to get to London to see someone."

"Do ya now?" Mary asked tartly. "Well, you're not fit to travel yet."

Not to mention she had no clothes. All she had was the satchel. Magellan motioned to it. "Could you hand me my bag, please?" she asked, trying to keep her voice steady.

Mary handed her the satchel. For a moment Magellan was afraid to look inside. Her memory of the carriage was a blur. She thought she had grabbed the diary, but she wasn't sure.

Except there it was nestled against the cheese, bread, and apples Rhys had given her. She sagged in relief and closed her eyes.

Mary moved to the door. "Drink your broth and rest. Ned doesn't want ya moving about for a few more days."

Magellan pursed her lips but didn't comment. She didn't have a few days. Somehow she needed to regain her strength and find a way to London. But she only said, "Thank you for all your help. I don't know how I'll ever repay you."

"Nonsense," Mary tsked. "Kindness to strangers is the best kindness worth giving." She set out fresh water and a basin on the table. "Ned will come around tonight to change your bandages. Don't let them get wet if ya wash up. And I would avoid the looking glass for a while. Ya have some nasty cuts and bruises."

Magellan nodded. Her face did feel swollen. She was sure she looked terrible. She glanced down at her hands and flexed her fingers. At least the feeling was back, although angry welts circled her wrists, and the skin was scraped from the rope. She lay back in bed and closed her eyes with bone-weary relief that she wasn't dead.

The next few hours she dozed in and out of consciousness and roused herself to sip the broth. Then she dug into the food Rhys had sent and ate a slice of cheddar cheese and crusty bread. When evening came, the music started up again downstairs. The same fiddlers from before were playing. Magellan nibbled on an apple and enjoyed listening to the lively performance coming from the first floor.

Her ear could pick out two fiddlers bandying back and forth and a third musician who alternated between a guitar and a flute as the audience clapped and cheered them on. Magellan closed her eyes, feeling the music float up to her like a soothing balm.

Later, Ned "the doctor" came to visit her. He was a spindly man somewhere in his sixties and quite drunk.

"Ah! My patient is awake." His face was flushed and his speech slurred. He began to unwrap the bandage on her arm.

Magellan offered a tentative smile, which disappeared the second she saw the stitches under the bandage. Her arm looked like the Bride of Frankenstein. Rows of coarse thread ran up the whole inside of her left arm from her wrist to her elbow, and the skin around it was inflamed.

"You're lucky the cut wasn't deeper, or I would have had to take the whole limb."

Magellan recoiled at the thought of a half-drunk doctor trying to saw off her arm. As he cleaned the stitches, she hissed with pain and watched him sloppily spread honey across it. Her leg didn't look much better. When he was finished changing out the bandages, he gave her a medicinal tea and told her to keep the bandages clean and apply honey regularly.

It sounded like Ned considered himself done with his services. After he left Magellan lay in bed worrying.

How was she going to get to London? What if her arm got infected and had to be amputated? What if she died?

Horrible what-ifs began crowding her brain like passengers on a train as her mind raced forward to an unknown future. How could she find the song like this? Her body was broken. Her mind and her heart felt broken. How could *she* save the world? She was just one person. A girl. Weak and pathetic. Not good enough. Never good enough. What could she do but fail? She would fail. The world would be destroyed, just as she would, and her deepest fear that she would cease to exist forever would come true.

Her wounds burned like fire as her thoughts raged on alongside her fever. If Garesh were with her, he would tell her she only had to climb down the ladder of her mind back into her heart. Delirious, she could almost believe he was beside her whispering the words.

Her body racked with pain, she surrendered her fear, her self-judgment and doubt on the wings of a long breath and opened her heart. The moment she did, the music coming from downstairs so full of joy and life, burst its way in and offered her its hand.

# Chapter 26

## Magellan

When Magellan woke, her fever had broken. It took some effort but she got out of bed and tried to walk. She had to sit back down several times. Mary had given her a simple gown made of brown wool. The fabric itched her skin, but she was grateful for it. Mary had also lent her a hairbrush and ribbon to tie her hair back.

Magellan put her arm into a makeshift sling to keep it cradled and made her way downstairs to see if she could offer to work in exchange for a meal. Mary had been taking care of her for days without payment, and she needed to reimburse her somehow. The tavern was almost empty. It was between mealtimes, and only a few stragglers were about.

Mary put a hearty plate of roast beef, potatoes, and green beans in front of her. When Magellan broached the subject, Mary said, "I'll not be putting ya to work just yet, love. But what are ya good at?"

"I'm actually a musician."

"Are ya now? A wee girl like yourself?" A teasing glint came into Mary's eyes. "What instrument do ya play?"

"Anything," Magellan said simply. "What would you like me to play?"

"With that arm, I'd say nothing today." Mary wiped down the counter and called out to the three young people eating at a table near the stage. They were two young men and a woman, all with bright red hair and freckles. "We've got another musician here who says she can play anything!"

The three perked up. One of the young men grinned at Magellan. "Even the fiddle?"

Magellan smiled back, realizing. "Are you the musicians who played last night?"

"We are." The other young man stood up and gave her an exaggerated bow. "The Lucky Horseshoes, at your service."

Magellan laughed, delighted by their name. "You're very good. I enjoyed listening from upstairs." She didn't tell them their music literally had saved her life.

"We're even better when you're downstairs," one of the boys teased.

The young woman beside him elbowed him and told her, "Don't mind him. I'm Nessie. These are my brothers Tim and Oliver."

They all looked to be the same age, and Magellan's mouth parted in surprise. *Triplets.*

Tim explained, "Mary's our aunt. She lets us play here in exchange for her delectable food and fine ale." He said it loudly enough to reach Mary, who snorted from behind the bar.

Oliver asked Magellan, "You really can play the fiddle?"

Magellan nodded. A fiddle and a violin were no different except for the way they were played, and she could play any style of violin.

"But you're a woman."

For a moment, Magellan had forgotten the time she was in—a time when the violin was deemed unsuitable for a woman to play and some even said indecent. The violin was considered too sensual, too erotic. No thanks to Paganini's dramatic and sexually charged performances. The violin was likened to a woman's body being strummed. The parts of the instrument were even named like a body: the belly, the neck, the ribs. Many in this era believed only a man could "master" the instrument.

Magellan could count on one hand the number of female violin players who were recognized before the 1900s, and they all encountered great resistance. Regina Strinasacchi, Catarina Calgano, the sisters Milanollo, Wilma Norman-Neruda, and the trailblazer Maud Powell, who traveled the world with her violin at the turn of the twentieth century.

Oliver or Tim, she couldn't remember which, said, "But women aren't supposed to play it."

"Well, I do." Magellan didn't try to hide her irritation, although it wasn't his fault women were not given the simple freedom yet to play a violin. She was itching to play, even with her injured arm. Fingering the strings might hurt, but she still had mobility. "May I?" she asked Mary.

"Not today, ya won't." Mary cast her a stern look. "That arm's still healin'. But ya can stay downstairs tonight and have a listen. Just stay close to Curtis so no one gives ya trouble."

Curtis was Mary's son, big as a bear. He was the one who'd carried her that night and whose gentle hands had held her down while her wounds were stitched. She had no idea where Mary's husband was or if she had one. The Hen House was the name of her tavern, and she ran it like a tight ship. Everyone walking through the door seemed to know Mary. The Hen House had clean rooms, good food, and hospitality known far and wide.

That night Magellan sat by the bar, drinking ale and enjoying the Lucky Horseshoes' show. They were even better in person. Oliver and Tim kicked up a musical storm as they dueled each other with their fiddles, while Nessie played a small guitar and a flute. People were yelling and singing and dancing on tables.

Magellan felt the music loosen the knot of despair gripping her since she had left Hereford Manor. Today was the first day she began to feel a glimmer of hope. She'd lived through a nightmare and still had music surrounding her, lifting her up.

Then sometime during the night a way to London presented itself. It came about while the band was taking a break over a cup of ale. The triplets were arguing about what song they would play in an upcoming competition in London.

Magellan perked up. "You're going to London?"

Oliver nodded and leaned closer, his face flushed from an evening of playing. "We're entering a competition in Covent Garden. There's a large purse for the winner."

"When do you leave?"

"In two days' time."

Magellan's mind raced. Two days didn't give her much time to convince the band to let her come along. But she had to get to London right away, so she made a plan. Tomorrow would be the equivalent of an audition.

That night when she went to sleep, she allowed herself to think about Rhys, though it hurt. She replayed their kiss in the labyrinth over and over until the longing inside her felt close to physical pain. Then she tucked him away like a treasured memory and steeled her heart. Her time at Hereford Manor was over. Now she had to get to London and find Fanny Mendelssohn. She fingered Garesh's ring on her hand, trying to draw strength from it, and envisioned the song in her mind. She had the symphony's opening—the first part of the first movement. Now she needed to find the rest.

---

The next day she woke up feeling stronger. She wiped down with water from the basin as best she could, then braided her hair and tied it back with the ribbon. When she came downstairs, Mary was bustling about, preparing for the lunch crowd. Magellan offered to clean all the tables, convincing Mary she could do it with her good arm.

By the afternoon the Lucky Horseshoes were setting up, and it was time to audition. Magellan flexed her hand. The stitches still burned, but it wasn't enough to keep her from playing. The band kept spare instruments by the back wall in case they broke a string during a performance.

Magellan joined them and nodded to one of the extra fiddles. "May I?"

Oliver laughed and gave her a gallant bow. "It would be our pleasure, my lady. Do your worst."

Magellan removed the sling holding her injured arm and tucked the instrument under her chin, savoring the feel of the chin rest. She warmed up with a series of tricky strokes and scales. Her arm immediately started to throb, but she pushed past it. Now in the zone, she transitioned to a flashy progression to make sure she had the band's attention, crossing strings and playing long bows with a speed and mastery no other violist could emulate.

She looked up to realize everyone in the tavern had stopped what they were doing. Tim, Oliver, and Nessie stared at her with stunned expressions. She gave them an impish wink, one only a fellow musician would understand, and they all laughed and picked up their instruments to play together. As she suspected, Oliver and Tim didn't care one whit if she was a woman. They only cared if she was good.

The Lucky Horseshoes launched into one of their songs, and Magellan easily followed along. She knew all the music from the previous nights. As if to prove a point, she playfully sped the tempo up, forcing Oliver and Tim to do the same. Soon it became a war of the fiddles, while Nessie stayed constant on the guitar, cheering for Magellan. Oliver began to circle Magellan in a flirtatious challenge, playing faster and harder. Magellan laughed out loud and took the dare, splaying the melody over three octaves, her fingers flying. Round and round they went. Magellan didn't notice the people clapping. She didn't know how long she played until her arm hurt too much to ignore. At the end of the song she gracefully bowed out with a curtsy, and the crowd went wild.

She left the stage to rousing cheers. Reluctantly, the triplets moved on to their next number without her. Magellan took a seat at the band's table, now an honorary member. Her arm was killing her, and she'd give anything for a bottle of ibuprofen, but it'd been worth it. Mary came over beaming with a mug of ale. Magellan carefully wrapped her arm in the sling again and sat back to sip her ale and enjoy the rest of the show. She stayed up late into the evening, drinking ale and eating sausages with the band. The siblings could not believe a woman could play the fiddle so well. They were talking over each other in excitement as they said they were heading to London tomorrow and begged her to come with them. With her playing, they'd be the talk of the competition.

Fleetingly, Magellan thought of Rhys, knowing she was traveling farther and farther away from him. But she could not go back. She told the band it would be an honor to go with them, because London was exactly where she needed to be.

# Chapter 27

## Rhys

*Won* was a foreign word Rhys had notated long ago from a book on the Far East about a hermit kingdom called Korea. The word meant being unwilling to give up hope for a lost cause. He had been fascinated by the word because it was the same spelling as the past tense of *to win*.

Last week had been the bleakest of his life while he waited for updates from the Bow Street Runners. When the driver of the carriage finally came out of hiding, after accepting his promise of coin, Rhys rode to the man's village. The driver was tearful and contrite. He had not been aware of any deception until the end. He actually thought Magellan and Terrance Brighton were father and daughter. The driver had been hired by Lord Erickson simply to deliver the pair to his estate by evening, although Terrance instructed the driver to take a roundabout route. Whenever the driver stopped to take care of the horses, he asked Terrance if he or his daughter had need of anything. Terrance always said she was sleeping.

"The blinds were drawn, so I could not see inside."

Rhys's eyes burned as he listened to the driver describe how the last time he stopped, the carriage window was open. He peered inside to find Terrance unconscious with his face bloody and nose broken.

Rhys startled at that, for the first time feeling the faint stirrings of hope. Had Magellan fought him and gotten away?

"There was no one else in the carriage?"

"No, my lord." The man swallowed.

Rhys forced himself to remain calm. "Then what happened?"

"I shook him awake and asked him what had occurred. He said his daughter attacked him and ran off."

Rhys felt a rush of dizzying relief so strong he leaned forward and steadied himself—so she had escaped—but then the driver went on to say more.

"But I could tell he was lying. I saw the knife in his hand. All that blood. I demanded to know what happened. I'm a good citizen and would never turn a blind eye to something nefarious," he insisted, though he had in fact been hiding for days. "All that blood did not come from a man's nose. He still had the knife, or I would have chased him. So I brought the carriage back round to Lord Erickson and told him what happened."

To Rhys, every word was like a dagger. Erickson, the bastard, had known the first night everything had gone wrong with his scheme and still he had done nothing to find Magellan. Rhys glared at the man. "I need to know the exact route you took, where you watered the horses, where you discovered him unconscious. Every detail."

Magellan had disappeared somewhere on the road between the driver's two stopping points. Rhys would visit every home, inn, and tavern along the way.

The man gave him all the information he could. She was somewhere in Leicester. But was she alive? The question squeezed Rhys's heart in a vise. Then a thought occurred to him. "When you found the man, was there a satchel of provisions with him?"

"No, sir, there was no satchel."

"Are you sure? Did he have a book on his person? A small diary?"

The driver shook his head. "No, sir, nothing that I saw. Just the knife."

Rhys was unsure whether to hope further. Magellan had to have escaped and taken the diary with her. She wouldn't have left it behind. He ran his hands over his face, fighting the urge to cry, imagining what she had gone through. This was all his fault.

He paid the driver his coin and headed north to find the road the carriage had taken. Riding hard, he finally reached the carriage's first stopping point. The proprietor had not seen anyone by Magellan's description. Rhys made his way up the road, knocking on every door to ask if they'd seen a wounded young woman in a brown traveling dress and offered her aid.

When he finally made it to the Hen House, the hour was late. He was bone weary and ready to give up. He sat down at the bar to order supper and a large tankard of ale. When he asked the woman behind the counter if she'd seen a wounded young lady in a brown dress last week, he expected the same answer he'd received all day.

To his astonishment, the woman leveled a savage look at him and demanded, "Were you the bastard who tried to kill her?"

At first Rhys could only stare at her dumbstruck. "She's alive?" He leaned forward with urgency. "Madam, is she alive?"

The woman yelled to the kitchen. "Curtis!"

Suddenly a huge lumbering man appeared. With a growl, he grabbed Rhys's neck with an iron grip and began to squeeze while the woman watched with a hardened gaze. "My boy loves nothing more than ta pummel bad men."

Rhys struggled to get the words out, unable to breathe. "Wait! I'm trying to find her. To save her!" With both hands he tried to break the man's grip before he passed out.

"You're a bit late for that," the woman snapped. "And I made her a promise not ta let anyone find her." She nodded to Curtis to let him go.

Rhys fell back into his seat, gasping for air but not about to be deterred. "You don't understand. I've been searching for her ever since . . ." He didn't even know how to explain what happened. "I can pay for information."

The woman's eyebrows rose high. "I don't want your money."

"Please, I swear on my honor as a gentleman. I've been trying to find her to help her." Rhys went to rise from his chair, and Curtis growled low in this throat. Still Rhys bowed. "The Earl of Liron, at your service."

"An earl, is it?" She did not look impressed. "I don't like seeing a woman harmed, and I don't care for earls who allow it to happen. Best eat your food and be on your way."

Thoroughly chastened, Rhys reluctantly sat back down and tried to remain calm. "How badly was she injured?" He forced the words out.

"She was damn near killed is what she was. The surgeon had to stitch her up."

Rhys closed his eyes and covered his face with his hands. "Please, I beg you." He was trying not to break down. He cleared his throat. "You cared for her?"

The woman nodded, studying him closely. "Kept her upstairs until she could walk again."

"I will pay you handsomely if you take me to her."

"I said I don't want your money." She scowled again, looking offended, and the woman's son grumbled at her. She told him, "He may not have hurt her, but he had something to do with it, else how'd she end up wandering the road in the dead of the night alone and bleeding?"

Rhys winced. "May I see her? Please?"

"She's no longer here."

"What do you mean?" He shook his head in disbelief. "She left here wounded?"

"There was no keeping her. She was all bent to get to London."

London! Magellan had not thought to send word to him? *But then why would she?* he grimly thought. She must hate him for what he'd done. She'd begged and pleaded with him and almost lost her life because of his mistake. Now the thought of her wounded and heading to London filled him with a new kind of terror.

"You just sent her on her way, all alone, to London?" he demanded. The son made a grunt of warning, but Rhys was beyond caring. Let the big lug try to take him down.

The woman smarted at the accusation. "She went with my niece and nephews! They're all together."

Nephews? She was traveling with strange men? "How can I find them?"

A guarded look came over her eyes. "Ya can't."

"Then I believe we're at an impasse. I'm not leaving here until you tell me. I have a whole team of Bow Street Runners searching for her as we speak." He saw the woman's eyes widen. "If I must get the chief magistrate here to question you, I will. I personally know the man." The woman gasped at the threat, but Rhys wasn't above making one. He was desperate. "I'll even offer assistance to your niece and nephews when I locate them."

The woman's son nudged her. "Ma, they did leave with little coin."

That news only made Rhys's worry grow. What was Magellan thinking going off to London by herself with a group of strangers?

The woman finally relented. "They've gone to a music competition."

Now Rhys was the one who wanted to growl. A music competition? He pinched the bridge of his nose. Only Magellan.

"My niece and nephews call themselves the Lucky Horseshoes. They're quite talented," she said with pride. "There's a hefty purse for the winner."

"Where is this competition?"

"Covent Garden. Next week."

Covent Garden was one of London's most notorious neighborhoods, chock-full of brothels, theatres, and coffeehouses. The thought of Magellan heading there left his stomach rolling. Tomorrow morning, after a few hours' sleep, he would set out early to London and start scouring the neighborhood. If he got back on his horse tonight, he might fall off.

He reached into his purse and pulled out a generous number of coins, more than enough to pay for a week's lodging. "Thank you for taking care of her," he said. Both the woman and her son's eyes widened at the amount. "I insist I reimburse you for your kindness. And may I have a room for the night? Her room?" He needed to be where she had slept, if only to be closer to her.

The woman nodded and took him upstairs to the room where Magellan had stayed. Rhys looked around at the spartan space and touched the mattress.

He asked the question he had been dreading. "What were the extent of her wounds?"

"Two knife wounds. A savage one down her arm and another on her leg. The fevers almost took her, but the girl is a fighter. A strong lass. I hope ya find her in London and see that she's well."

"I will. I swear it."

"I wouldn't have let her go, but she said it was urgent she get there before the lady she's seeking left."

It took a moment for her words to sink in. "What lady? Did she say who?"

"Some lady musician she needed to meet. Said it was a matter of life or death."

Rhys closed his eyes in disbelief. Magellan was going to London to find Felix Mendelssohn's sister. He didn't know whether to laugh or cry. Magellan was still entrenched in the diary. But at this point he didn't care if she told him it was possible to fly to the moon and back. Ever since he found her in the labyrinth, their lives had become entwined. He could no longer fight the reality she held his heart in her hands, and nothing, *nothing*, not even a thousand-year-old diary, would change that fact.

# Chapter 28

## Magellan

London, the birthplace of the Industrial Revolution, was the most populated city in the world in 1829. To Magellan, it was awe-inspiring and disgusting and ten times more terrifying than New York City could ever be. The River Thames was thick with human sewage. A rank fog hung in the air, especially in the morning and at night. Horse dung piled along every street. She was constantly assaulted by rank smells and the bustle of too many people, along with a motley of stray dogs, raggedy children, scavengers, and pickpockets. Over a million people were crammed inside the city space, where extreme poverty lived right next door to decadent wealth. The dismal cityscape was exacerbated by the coal smoke rising from all the chimneys and settling soot on the ground like black ash.

Magellan maneuvered past street vendors, prostitutes, drunks, and beggars. She clutched her violin—technically Oliver's violin—to keep it from being bumped or broken, or worse, stolen. Right now it was her only source of income. The band had played on a street corner yesterday for coins and earned enough for meat pies and ale. It was their only meal for the day.

At the time, leaving Mary's and traveling to London had seemed like the wisest course, but now Magellan was questioning her decision. The Lucky Horseshoes, which she had been inducted into, could barely afford to eat and were sleeping in a park. She was dying of thirst for a glass of water and had not been able to drink her medicinal tea or change her bandages for the past two days. All her care had been neglected while trying to survive. The competition, and the purse they planned to win, was still five days away. She was literally homeless in 1829 with nothing but Rhys's satchel, Gwynedd's diary, and Oliver's borrowed instrument. All the food Rhys had sent with her was gone. She and the band had eaten the last of it for breakfast. She tried not to think about Rhys as she set out on her own.

Today she had to make her way to the Argyll Rooms on the West End and see if she could find Fanny Mendelssohn. Magellan had seen a flyer proclaiming this week was Felix's debut performance. It was the equivalent of a blockbuster movie's opening, and all of London was talking about the show. Magellan had told the band she needed to meet someone before the woman left London. She had not told them where, because she had to go alone. Fanny might not connect with her if anyone else was with her. Yesterday, she'd asked Oliver to draw her a crude map so she would not get lost and promised she'd be back at the park before sundown.

This morning for breakfast she and the band had split the last apple and cheese, and Magellan tried not to worry about what she would eat later. She planned to play for coin on the corner and hopefully have enough to buy food afterward.

The Argyll Rooms was the only place she could think to have a chance to run into Fanny Mendelssohn in a city this size. Her brother, Felix, would be there. The question was, would Fanny? Magellan had no idea if Fanny had come to London for her brother's debut.

She found the building and set out the collection hat Nessie had lent her on the corner. Her plan was to play and hopefully spot Fanny. As she did, some of the people walking past her recoiled. Not only was she a woman with a violin in 1829, she was a dirty, scruffy, injured woman with a violin.

Magellan did not play any of the popular music the crowd would know from composers who were already immortalized: Bach, Beethoven, Mozart, Handel, Haydn, and Paganini. She ignored the canon of men and instead played Fanny's songs—songs Magellan knew wouldn't be published or played until well after the woman's death. It was a gamble, playing Fanny's own songs the woman might not yet recognize, but Magellan had no other ideas to gain her attention.

To anyone passing by, Magellan looked like a beaten-up homeless woman. Her cheek was still bruised, her wrists red with welts. The few coins landing in her hat were only because her playing was so extraordinary.

By the end of the day, she gathered her earnings and had enough to buy a savory pie and fresh milk from a nearby vendor. The pie was filled with ground meat, potatoes, carrots, and celery. She ate it quickly, her hands shaking, and wished she could afford one more. She had not found Fanny and now had to hurry back to Covent Garden before nightfall.

Fortunately, the return was much quicker. She found her friends in the park at their designated spot. They had earned more money than her playing that day and had bought sausages and ale for everyone. The group ate while playing silly songs under the moonlight, which buoyed Magellan's spirits. She tried not to think on the fact it was almost mid-November and time was passing quickly.

Attempting to sleep, she lay down next to Nessie. The two were sharing blankets to keep warm against the chill. That night her dreams were filled with images from the pages of Gwynedd's diary—and Rhys and the labyrinth and Hereford Manor—until they all blended together into a kaleidoscope of yearning and loss.

---

The next day she woke feeling exhausted, as if she hadn't slept at all. Still, she struck out again and spent all day playing in front of the Argyll Rooms without any luck. On the third day Fanny still had not come, and Magellan did not have the energy to walk back to the park. The last reserves of her strength were fading. Her arm throbbed dreadfully, she had a fever again, and she was officially out of food. Earlier she had stopped at a vendor to buy a piece of fruit only to feel a hole in her pocket. A London pickpocket must have stolen her coins, the few she had.

But she had made a promise to herself that morning—she would play today until she couldn't play anymore. Dirty and bedraggled, she tucked the violin under her chin with all the dignity of a world-class performer and launched into another one of Fanny's songs.

Used to the stares of those passing by, the pity, the disdain, she steeled herself and channeled all her energy into the music. Someone even spit at her feet, but still she played on. She might be stuck in 1829, but if the world was really ending and she didn't do everything in her power to save it, then she didn't deserve to live.

Her heart was still beating, her body was still alive, and so she played on, even as she felt her vision begin to dim. She played on to shut out the dizziness and the pain, the thirst and hunger. She played on, unwilling to stop, vowing she would only stop playing when either the Earth ended or she did, whichever came first.

# Chapter 29

𝄢

## Rhys

Rhys couldn't help but feel he was running out of time. He could not eat or sleep or function properly. He could not wait for the musical competition, which was still days away, to find Magellan.

His only course of action was to discover Felix Mendelssohn's whereabouts and hope Magellan would turn up nearby. The composer was performing with the Philharmonic Society this coming week at the Argyll Rooms. If Magellan was looking for his sister, she might go there.

His carriage turned onto King Street when he heard the music. A lone violinist playing in the distance. The notes, heart-wrenching and pure, moved through the air and struck him like a blow.

No one could play like that.

*Except her.*

He jumped from the carriage without waiting for his driver to stop and yelled at the man to circle around. Rhys dashed down the street toward the violinist. As he rounded the corner, there she was.

He stopped with a gasp when he saw her across the street. She looked like a vagrant, a broken angel. Her face was bruised with a dried scab on her chin, and dark shadows ringed her eyes. A thick, soiled bandage padded her left arm, and an old brown dress many sizes too big hung on her slight frame. The satchel he had given her was slung over her shoulder.

The sight of her undid him. Even gaunt and weak she still played magnificently. Rhys hadn't even known she could play the violin.

Her eyes were closed, a look of pain etched across her face.

As Rhys ran to her, he heard a woman frantically call out, "Stop the carriage!" And the woman hopped out.

She and Rhys both rushed toward Magellan from opposite directions, like two traveling points on a map about to collide.

Rhys was barely aware of the woman in his periphery. Magellan's eyes were still closed, and her body listed as her playing slowed down like a music box about to stop. Her arms, unable to hold the violin up any longer, lowered in defeat. Rhys reached her right as she crumbled, and he lunged to catch her.

She was unconscious in his arms.

"I've got you." He held her tight. "I've got you."

The woman, winded from running, swooped in and caught the violin, right as Magellan let it go.

Rhys turned to the lady who had raced from her carriage to meet them and choked out the words, "Thank you," unsure what else to say.

"Is she all right?" the woman asked, breathless with concern.

"I don't know." Rhys frantically looked to the street for his carriage. He needed to get Magellan medical attention right away. He could see his driver caught up in traffic, slowly turning the carriage around at the corner to come meet them.

"How did she know?" the woman asked in a daze, shaking her head as if trying to clear it. "How did she know my music? I haven't even finished it yet."

Rhys blinked, taking in the woman. She had the accent of a foreigner. He almost didn't dare to ask, switching to German. *"Are you Fanny Mendelssohn?"*

The woman looked at him with startled eyes and answered in German too. "Yes, I am."

Rhys could barely think straight. Here was the woman Magellan had put herself at great risk to find. He quickly made a decision and rushed on, still speaking in German. "I am the Earl of Liron. My driver will give you my card. I'm afraid my fiancée was in an accident and is not well. She is a musical aficionado and would love to speak with you when she has recovered. Please call on us in three days' time at my town house in Mayfair." He didn't know how else to explain their situation to her. All he knew was Magellan had asked for his help once and he'd denied it. He would never make that mistake again.

He didn't give Miss Mendelssohn time to ask questions. He climbed into his carriage with Magellan in his arms and ordered his footman to go fetch his physician quickly and meet them at his residence. Miss Mendelssohn handed his driver the violin and took his card. Then the carriage was off.

Rhys cradled Magellan, dizzy with a heady mixture of profound relief and stark terror. She was injured, unconscious, and burning up with fever. The carriage ride was brief, but the minutes felt like an eternity as they jostled and crept alongside London traffic. When the carriage entered his house gate, footmen stood at the ready. Rumors had been running rampant with his staff ever since Rhys's arrival to town. All the servants believed the lady he'd recently betrothed had gone missing with her father after a carriage accident. It was the only story Rhys could think to put forward.

When the staff saw Magellan in his arms, they broke into action at once. Gibbons, his head butler, and Mrs. Weathers, his housekeeper, took charge. Rhys strode up the stairs with Magellan, listening to his housekeeper order boiling water and fresh linens be brought up. The doctor should be on his way. He reached Magellan's room with Mrs. Weathers fretting behind him.

"Put her on the bed, my lord. Then you may go."

"No, I will help." He wasn't about to leave.

"But my lord . . ."

"I will tend to her myself." Propriety be damned. He gently laid Magellan on the bed and removed the satchel from her, tossing it aside. "Help me with her boots." He pulled them off to find her stockings worn with holes, and her heels and toes riddled with blisters. "Throw those shoes away," he bit out. "Burn everything."

"Of course." When Mrs. Weathers pulled the ruined stockings down Magellan's legs, he saw the other bandage on her right calf.

Two knife wounds from the monster he'd given her to. Rhys felt the pressure back in his chest, suffocating him, and the room began to spin. He staggered to sit in the chair by the bed, leaning forward and putting his head in his hands.

"I'll be back with the linens and water," Mrs. Weathers said and scurried off.

Rhys was left alone, unable to stop the tears even if he could try. He took Magellan's hand, bringing it to his face, and closed his eyes, whispering, "Please forgive me." He could never make amends for this. "Forgive me."

The metal of her ring felt cold against his forehead. He opened his eyes to look at the band and there engraved across it were the symbols from the standing stone. He stared at the ring, dumbfounded. How could Magellan's ring match the stones? Rhys searched for a logical answer but could not find one.

He barely realized when Mrs. Weathers returned or when the doctor arrived. Rhys kept hold of Magellan's hand, unwilling to let go while he watched the doctor unwrap the bandage on her arm. His heart seized when he saw what lay beneath, a horrific wound with stitches inflamed and oozing.

The doctor went to clean them with some astringent, and Magellan screamed, her eyes opening wide, wild with pain. Rhys shot up in alarm and braced her shoulders, trying to calm her. "Shhh. It's all right. We need to clean your wounds."

Her eyes focused on him. "Rhys?" She raised a hand to his cheek in shock and blinked several times, still delirious. "What are you doing here?"

"You are at my London home. The doctor is here." He didn't know if she understood. Her eyes closed, and she was unconscious again.

After the doctor was finished cleaning her arm and leg, the man dabbed a thick ointment over both and instructed Mrs. Weathers on the treatment to administer. "I'll come check on her again tomorrow."

"Will she recover?" Rhys asked anxiously.

The doctor sighed. "If the fever subsides. The lady has been through a serious trauma."

Rhys nodded, unable to speak. Mrs. Weathers saw the doctor out. Rhys sat back down at Magellan's bedside and took her hand again. Closing his eyes, he willed his strength to her. *Take it.* Take all of it.

Mrs. Weathers returned with another maid carrying a tray with broth and water. She insisted he leave so they could change Magellan into a fresh nightgown. He reluctantly did and tried to be productive. He wrote a letter to his family, explaining Magellan had been found and they were in London. For propriety's sake he knew he should secure his rooms at the club and spend the night elsewhere, but he couldn't bring himself to leave. He sat by her bedside all night, waiting for her to wake. Finally, the next day after her fever broke, her eyes fluttered open.

They stared at each other for a long moment. Neither said a word.

He had water, tea, and broth at the ready, but for the life of him he couldn't move as he watched a myriad of expressions cross her face. What was she thinking now? Was she pleased to see him? Did she hate him?

"What happened to Oliver's violin?"

Her question broke the silence. He shook his head to clear it, for a moment not understanding. *Who was Oliver?* Then he realized it must be one of the Lucky Horseshoe persons. "Do not worry. I have it downstairs."

"And my satchel?" She looked around in a panic. "Did I lose it?"

Disconcerted by her practical questions, he went to the corner of the room where he had stowed it and brought it over. "Do not worry. It is here."

She quickly opened it and drooped in relief as she pulled out the diary.

Rhys stared at the book, not knowing what to say. That blasted book. How much misery it had caused, from Magellan's near death to Erickson's covetous treachery. Still, the last thing he wanted to do was express those sentiments and upset her. He'd just gotten her back. He gently steered the conversation to where he needed it to go and softly said, "I don't know how to ask for your forgiveness. How you ever could . . . I'm so sorry I didn't believe you." He choked the words out while she watched him with solemn eyes. "That your father was an impostor. How can you ever forgive me?"

She wasn't looking at him anymore but staring stoically straight ahead. She clasped the diary to her chest. "How did you discover the truth?"

"I couldn't wait to see you. I went to the vicar's the next day, only to find the man had no cousin. It took me some time to unravel the truth. Erickson hired someone to lure you away."

She looked back to him in shock. "Lord Erickson?"

"He hired a man to pose as your father and tell us enough truths to believe him. He wanted the diary." Rhys stared at her wrists, at the bruises from where she had been tied up. "Tell me what happened," he pleaded in a whisper.

For a long time she didn't speak. She stared into the distance as if remembering. "As soon as we were down the drive, he drugged me."

Rhys uttered a curse and stood up to pace.

"When I woke, it was night. I was still in the carriage," she recounted in a quiet voice devoid of emotion. "He tried to hurt me, but I fought back and escaped." She shook her head in disbelief. "I can't believe Lord Erickson would do such a thing."

"He wanted the diary. He had some foolish belief—" Rhys stopped, realizing what he was about to say.

"That the story's true?" She turned bright eyes to him.

He resumed pacing, unable to hold her gaze. Could he really take the leap of faith and truly believe she was a time traveler from the future? If he did, he would be as whimsical as his late father, with his head in the clouds and believing in the impossible. Doing so went against every grain of logic inside him. How could Magellan have come from the future? How could a song save the world? A song! As if music had such power.

He turned back to her. They locked eyes, and then he looked at her ring. She glanced down to it, realizing he'd seen it, and he said honestly, "Magellan . . . I don't know what to believe. But right now, it is not important. What is most important is for you to be safe and whole." He knelt by her bedside. "I will spend the rest of my life making this up to you even though I know you can never forgive me."

She looked weary and leaned her head back against the pillow. "That is not necessary. I already forgive you."

"Why? I sent you off with a monster! I don't deserve your forgiveness!" He could hear his voice rising, but he couldn't stop it.

She was scowling at him now. "Well, I do. You didn't know who he was."

"Stop being so kind."

"I'm not being kind. I understand why you did it. You thought I was crazy." She motioned. "You still think it. I can see it in your eyes.

If you came to my time and told me you were from the 1800s and believed in a mythical diary written by Merlin's sister, I would think you're crazy too."

Rhys forced himself not to comment. She sounded so accepting, and he did not want to upset her. They could discuss her convictions another day. Right now he needed to help her heal. "Let us put the debate of the diary aside."

"The debate? Is that what this is?" She gave a weary sigh. "Rhys, I don't think you fully grasp the magnitude of what's happening. I only have until Winter Solstice and I haven't even gotten yet the first part of the song I've been sent here to find. There are four parts out there somewhere and I'm running out of time."

Rhys didn't comment, uncomfortable with where this whole conversation was going. "Could we please, *please* put aside your quest to save the world momentarily?"

Magellan choked on a laugh and closed her eyes in exhaustion. "All right. How did you even find me?"

"I've been searching all over England for you. I finally found Mary at the Chicken House."

She opened her eyes again in surprise. "You went to the Hen House and talked to Mary?"

He leaned forward. "Who is Oliver?" he bit out, his jealousy ridiculous given the circumstances. But who was he? Was he a suitor? Was he sweet on her? "He gave you a violin?"

Her eyes widened. "Oh my gosh, they must be worried sick."

He sat back. At least she said *they* and not *he*. "Who? The Lucky Shoes?"

"Horseshoes. My friends. I was traveling with them. Is there some way to get word to them that I'm okay? I've been at the Argyll Rooms every day and walking back to the park to sleep with them."

"You've been sleeping in a park? Do you know how dangerous that is?" He stood up to pace once more. "Why didn't you send word to me from Mary's? You could have told her you were under my protection."

"Was I?" she asked frankly.

"Yes!" he exclaimed. "Do you know how worried I've been? I told you I would come in two days."

"Well, forgive me for getting kidnapped!"

"And instead of sending word from Mary's Hen House, you came here with a group of unlucky horseshoes to sleep in a park? Do you know what could have happened to you? What did happen?"

"I was looking for Fanny Mendelssohn."

"Yes, I know." He took a deep breath, trying to calm down. Upsetting her further would not be good for her condition. "You found her too," he said bluntly and noted the shock on her face. The bruise on her right cheek made him want to go hunt the bastard down who'd given it to her.

"What? Rhys! How?"

"Miss Mendelssohn heard the music you were playing and arrived when I did. I invited her to come speak with you the day after tomorrow."

"You did?" Her face lit up with hope.

"I will do anything for you," he swore quietly. He would invite every damn female composer in Europe to his house if it made her happy. "Surely you know that." Tears welled in her eyes and he begged, "Don't cry. It will make my own tears return. I've already shocked Mrs. Weathers enough." He actually did feel the threat of tears and cleared his throat. "I'll have her bring you a tray and assist you. The important thing is for you to rest now and recover."

As he headed to the door she called him back. "Rhys? If you'll truly do anything for me . . ." she repeated his words softly.

"Anything. You have only to ask." He stood at attention in the doorway.

She held the diary out. "Finish translating it for me?"

He forced himself to keep his face expressionless. That bloody damn book was becoming the bane of his existence. He nodded. "Of course. After you've recovered." He didn't step forward to take it from her outstretched hand. Instead, he left and closed the door. He would put off translating the rest of the diary for as long as he could.

# Chapter 30

## Magellan

Magellan had found Fanny Mendelssohn. The woman was coming here. Rhys had helped make it happen. The reluctant earl who desperately wanted to believe she was off her rocker was still doing everything in his power to help her on her mission.

She still needed his help to read the rest of the diary, and time was running out—and even more pressing, she needed to figure out what in the world she was going to say to Fanny Mendelssohn when the woman came here.

*Um, excuse me, Fanny, but you have a song trapped in your head that can save the world. Could I please have a listen?*

What if Fanny Mendelssohn had no idea what she was talking about? Magellan only hoped she was one of the four female composers Gwynedd alluded to. She had to be.

In 1829 Fanny would be twenty-four, a lovely woman with raven-haired ringlets, if the historical portraits were anything to go by. She would die young at the age of forty-one from a stroke. By the time of her death, Fanny would have composed over four hundred and fifty pieces. But all of her life she had stood in the shadow of her brother, Felix. Her father had limited her, ruling that Felix could become a composer, but she could not. Her music was only "an ornament."

Fanny would fall in love with the famous painter Wilhelm Hensel but only marry him on the condition she always be allowed to compose. He was besotted with her and agreed. She even composed her wedding song the night before their ceremony because her brother forgot to do it.

In her lifetime, women were not allowed to give public performances. So instead, she would host salons at her home and perform there, sometimes with over a hundred people in attendance. Near the end of her life, when she was forty, she pushed to start publishing her songs under her own name instead of her brother's. Sadly, only a year later, she died. To Magellan, she was a hero—a heroine—a shooting star whose light was extinguished too early. Soon she would meet her.

A quiet knock sounded at the door, and a young woman named Jane brought a dinner tray, a simple medley of fresh bread, sliced ham and cheese, and carrot soup. Magellan ate every bite. When she was finished, she crawled back into bed and propped herself on a mountain of pillows. She must have drifted off to sleep in exhaustion, for she only had the vague memory of Rhys visiting her in the middle of the night. Hazily, she felt him applying ointment to her stitches with the gentlest touch. The next time she woke it was late morning, and Jane helped her bathe and change into a soft house robe. Magellan could think of nothing but Fanny's arrival tomorrow, and what would happen if she did get the song from her. Gwynedd had warned her she would need to leave the time she was in because staying would be dangerous.

Magellan didn't know how to prepare for such a possibility. And she wasn't sure she could coax Rhys into translating the rest of the diary before Fanny came. He didn't even want to talk about the diary right now, much less give her more pages. Yet tomorrow was looming along with the definite chance she would be leaving 1829.

If she got the song from Fanny, could she leave Rhys? She didn't know if she had the ability to say goodbye to him again. In her heart, she knew they were supposed to be together. The Ley Line had delivered her to *him*. He was the translator of Gwynedd's diary, and he hadn't finished it yet. Surely that meant something. She couldn't just leave Rhys and vanish on a Ley Line. They were a team. Partners. Even if he didn't know it yet.

With that realization, she began to think ahead. Fanny would be here soon, and she was a bundle of nerves. If she received the song from Fanny, she wouldn't have much time to convince Rhys.

She started to hum to tamp down the anxiety that possibility brought and looked around the room. Packing a bag seemed the most logical thing to do. To start with, she needed food. The currant scones from her breakfast tray should stay fresh for a while. She wrapped them in a cloth napkin and tucked them away in her satchel along with the diary. Then she added tooth powder, soap, and a spare nightshift and stowed the satchel in the dresser drawer.

Next she needed to find a piano to play to help her mounting anxiety. She ignored the picturesque view from her bedroom window of a park across the street and the horse-drawn carriages passing by the wrought iron gates. Instead, she made her way down a sweeping staircase to the main floor, though she hadn't gotten back her strength yet. The house was enormous with a library and a ballroom, but she found the best room to be off the back hall, a cozy parlor where a charming upright piano was tucked against the wall.

Relieved by the find, Magellan sat down on the bench. Gripped by the urge to play something from her time, she played U2's "Where the Streets Have No Name" and afterward went through the band's *Best of*. She could feel the pent-up tension running away down her fingertips and being absorbed by the keys.

After U2, she turned to Sting, Coldplay, Imagine Dragons, and the Lumineers. Then she hit the ladies. Katy Perry, Beyoncé, Taylor Swift, Pink, and Lady Gaga. It was her version of shuttling through the stations. All modern. All from her time. She played song after song, lost in the fluidity, and thought of Rhys.

They had been tethered to each other from the moment she arrived at his labyrinth—they both felt it—and yet he didn't believe her. Now tomorrow she might have to leave and didn't know what to do.

As if she'd conjured him with her thoughts, she looked behind her to find him leaning against the doorway, listening to her play.

# Chapter 31

𝄢

## Rhys

Rhys could have stood in the doorway for hours listening to Magellan. He wanted nothing more than to go to her and kiss her like he'd done that fateful day in the labyrinth. But the room may well have been an ocean between them, and he didn't know how to cross it. She stopped playing when she realized he was there.

"Forgive me. I didn't mean to disturb you." He went to the window and looked out, standing stiffly with his hands behind his back.

"You didn't."

"You're playing is unequivocally lovely," he complimented, knowing he sounded formal. "I'm glad to see you're feeling better."

"I am. Mrs. Weathers and Jane have been taking good care of me."

"Good." His eyes held hers. "I found your friends today and assured them you were fine. I put them up in an inn near the competition. And Oliver has his violin back." He tried not to grimace. Oliver was a strapping red-headed buck with the swagger of a young man who thought he was the best at what he did: play music. Rhys did not want Magellan playing the man's instrument. He had found himself irrationally jealous of a boy who called himself a lucky horseshoe. "I have violins in the house you are welcome to play."

"Wonderful. I will play your instrument, then." She gave him an innocent smile.

Was she teasing him?

"Excellent," he strangled out, running his hand through his hair. So much needed to be said. Too much. He'd told the household staff they were to be married and he hadn't even proposed. He'd also promised his dead father he would not ask for anyone's hand in marriage until he read the diary in its entirety—and he'd yet to finish translating it. The truth was he didn't know what to say to her. He backed away to the door to make his escape. "I'll have a dinner tray brought up."

"Rhys, I don't need any more trays. I am in desperate need of a hug, though." She stayed sitting on the piano bench.

He hesitated, unsure what to do. "A hug? As in an embrace?" She simply nodded, her luminous eyes pulling him to her, and without thought, he took three brisk strides as she rose up on the piano bench to her knees.

Their arms wrapped around each other and he held her tightly, their chests pressed against each other like two magnets snapping back into place.

"Magellan." He breathed into her hair. She smelled like fresh flowers.

Suddenly she was kissing him, her hands weaving into his hair. His last rational thought was *cafune*, the Portuguese word for such a gesture. Then their kiss turned heated, laced with desperation. Their embrace was madness. The door was open. Anyone could walk in. Rhys's heart was thundering as her hands guided his face. Her fingers moved to his neck and down his back. Those glorious fingers. He was her instrument now. He lost all sense of propriety and sat down on the piano bench, pulling her onto his lap. Her legs wrapped him into the cocoon of her body and he leaned into her, his whole body on fire. The kiss raged on until his lips moved down to devour her neck.

"You have bewitched me. I don't care what your circumstances are, Magellan, I don't care," he said, his mouth returning to hers again. "I just want you to stay with me."

She broke off the kiss to search his eyes. They were both breathing heavy, as if they'd just run across a field together, their faces inches apart. "I need you to finish translating the diary, and I need to see Fanny Mendelssohn."

He nodded, feeling like he was about to fall into an abyss and never return. He would keep his promise. Felix Mendelssohn's sister would come, and then they could sift fiction from truth. He set her gently away from him and stood. "I will finish translating the diary. You have my word. Miss Mendelssohn will be calling in the early afternoon tomorrow. We can talk more . . . about your circumstance after her visit."

"Could you please translate it today?"

He hesitated and declined gently. "I prefer to wait until after Fanny Mendelssohn's visit." Before she could argue with him, he excused himself with a bow, needing solitude to compose his thoughts, and he escaped to his study.

He wrote to his family again and apprised them of the events. He did *not* mention the wedding proposal he had yet to make, nor that the staff thought they were engaged, nor that Magellan was sleeping in the countess's room as if they were already married, nor that he was most likely creating a scandal of unknown proportion by having a single young lady stay at the house unchaperoned. He tried to rein in his stress. Fortunately, his staff was discreet. No one would talk. He had increased their wages just this week to ensure the fact, not above bribing his staff in the delicate matter of safeguarding a woman's—and his future wife's—reputation.

He asked his family to delay coming here. The last thing he needed was everyone descending on them in London. Magellan needed time to heal, and he needed time to understand what was happening. Hopefully the meeting with Fanny Mendelssohn would shed light on the situation.

One could only hope! He knew why Magellan wanted to meet with Miss Mendelssohn, but the question that kept circling his mind was, *Why did Fanny Mendelssohn want to meet Magellan?*

Magellan had asked him twice to finish translating the diary, and in truth, he didn't want to read one more word of Gwynedd's story. Merlin's sister truly had become a pariah to him. Now he understood why Thomas Malory had never used a word of it. Could anyone imagine if Merlin's sister had been trouncing about in King Arthur's tale?

In legends, Merlin could walk through time, and here his sister was purporting one could cross time's thresholds with sound. Magellan believed she had been sent back into the past to find an ancient song hidden by a guardian from another world. Well, tomorrow she would meet Fanny Mendelssohn and have to face the truth.

# Chapter 32

## Magellan

Magellan couldn't fathom how music could stop a polar shift from happening. Inherently she knew sound's fundamental power was yet to be understood. She had heard of musicians taking part in cutting-edge studies and how sound could cure diseases, including cancer. She'd even been invited to take part in a medical study herself in Boston. When—or if—she made it back to her own time, she might need the help of actual scientists to play the song. *If* the song Gwynedd described was real. Because right now, she was running on faith and waiting for Fanny to arrive.

From the stormy look on Rhys's face when she brought up translating the diary again, she would have to wait. The problem was she had no idea what would happen after Fanny's visit. According to Gwynedd, she would need to find a Ley Line and leave, like finding the nearest emergency exit. This morning Magellan had woken up paralyzed by the thought and had to do every coping mechanism she knew just to get out of bed.

After she played the song with Fanny today, she would need to find a church organ to play Bach again. It seemed the safest bet since that had worked the first time. Gwynedd had said Ley Lines' crossroads were often marked by sacred sites, churches, and temples. When she had asked Rhys if they could visit a church after Fanny's visit, he expelled a pained sigh, but she had gotten him to agree.

She looked down at Garesh's ring and tried to fight the panic blooming inside her. The first course of action was to finish packing. She hid more food from her breakfast tray, extra bandages, her ointments, and added a few fresh hand towels. She slipped a hairbrush into the satchel too and looked around the room for anything else she could take. Eyeing the breakfast tray again, she wrapped the butter knife in a heavy cloth napkin and hid that as well. Then she stowed the satchel back in the cabinet.

Mrs. Weathers came to help her dress, and Magellan said firmly, "No curls today." Instead her hair was styled into a bun with a braid wrapped around it.

Mrs. Weathers told her, "I went through Vivianne's dresses from last season and found something you might like." She returned holding a frilly pink dress that made Magellan wince.

There was no way in hell she was going to wear that today. She needed something functional to travel in, not a dress that looked like a design from an 1800s lace convention. "Do you have something plainer to help not draw attention to my arm? Perhaps a darker color and long sleeved." She was busy binding her arm carefully with a clean bandage.

"Of course." Miss Weathers came back with a simple navy dress with long sleeves and a high neck. Magellan slipped it on, relieved.

After Mrs. Weathers left, nerves hit her hard, and she began to feel sick to her stomach. Soon the moment of truth would arrive. She headed downstairs, unsure where to find Rhys. He was most likely avoiding her again. She made it to the back parlor and sat down at the piano bench and took a deep breath. She stared at the keys for a long time, remembering the opening of the song but not ready to play it yet. She needed Fanny Mendelssohn.

A soft knock on the door interrupted her thoughts. Rhys stood in the doorway. They stared at each other, neither sure what to say. He gave her a nod and cleared his throat, looking every inch the earl today. His quizzing glass hung from his jacket vest, lending him a formal air. The only sign of his unease was the subtle fidgeting with his signet ring as he twisted it back and forth in a pensive manner.

"Miss Mendelssohn has arrived and is waiting for you in the salon."

*She'd come.* "Could I meet her here instead? I'd like to use this piano while we talk."

Rhys arched a careful brow. "Of course."

Before he turned away, she said, "Alone, please."

His face shuttered and he nodded before leaving. This was the second time she had sent him away when she was to play. She felt guilty for hurting his feelings, but she needed to be alone with Fanny.

A minute later the butler arrived. Rhys was notably absent. The butler announced, "Miss Brighton, may I present Miss Mendelssohn." Then he ushered Fanny in.

"Thank you," Magellan said, feeling breathless as she stood to greet the woman she had been sent back to 1829 to find. The butler shut the door, leaving the two women alone. Magellan was tongue-tied, unable to believe she was meeting *the* Fanny Mendelssohn.

Fanny gave her a hesitant smile. "I'm relieved to see you are much recovered." Her voice was rich and melodious with a German accent.

"Thank you. Yes, I heard you were there when I fainted." Magellan left the rest unsaid, unsure how to explain.

Fanny's eyes went from her to the piano and back again. "The music you were playing the other day on the street is the same I am composing. It was incredible to hear. I had to meet you."

Magellan could feel the powerful connection between them. "I had to meet you too."

"How is it we share the same music?"

"I believe . . ." Magellan measured her words slowly, "music connects us all in a special place, in a perfect world we cannot reach yet but can feel in our hearts."

Fanny's lips parted in wonder, and she nodded, saying softly, "Yes. I believe so too."

Magellan pushed on, knowing here was the defining moment. "A song has been in my own heart I'd like to share. Perhaps you know a part of it and can help me complete it?" She sat back down at the piano, feeling the air around her become charged. She had never played the song's opening for anyone else or without headphones. Magellan knew her part of the song like she knew her own body. It was the symphony inside her bones she'd been born with. The first part of the first movement.

She began to play, her hands flying over the keys faster than a pianist should be able to. The symphony's opening was grand and complex, a musical vortex expanding with momentum and energy. The full orchestra existed in her imagination, an epic movement of harmonies and counterpoints only she could hear. Trumpets and French horns, the loudest instruments, would come in like nightingales. The percussion would follow right behind with bass drums, snares, timpani, xylophones, and marimbas, in a towering wave of rhythm, heralding the beginnings of the song that would keep the Earth spinning.

Fanny watched transfixed as Magellan played on until she reached the end of what she knew.

"That's all I have so far," Magellan simply said. "Do you know what comes next?"

Fanny brought her hand to her heart and nodded. "Yes," she whispered, sitting down on the bench beside her, and she laid her hands on the keys.

# Chapter 33

## Rhys

The music Magellan and Fanny Mendelssohn were playing inside the parlor was incandescent, truly a soaring achievement. Rhys hovered in the doorway of the library, close enough to the parlor to hear but not near enough to hear whatever the women were saying to each other. They'd been sequestered together, even declining tea. They played the magnificent song again from start to finish.

Was this the song, though, that could save the world? On a piano? The reality was it was a song on a piano being played by two ladies in a parlor. To Rhys, now more than ever in the light of day, listening to the music coming from the room, Magellan's belief in the diary and "her mission" seemed incredibly delusional. By Jove, he was embarrassed to admit she almost had him wanting to believe it as well.

Earlier she'd even requested they go to a church after Fanny's visit. She had said, "I need to visit the most ancient church in London with a pipe organ."

Rhys had choked on a laugh. "A pipe organ?"

"Please?" She looked at him hopefully, her green eyes making him forget himself for a moment. As green as his labyrinth.

"Rhys?" She was waiting for his answer. "I need a pipe organ in the oldest church."

Who *needs* a pipe organ? "In the oldest church," he repeated her request. "May I ask why?"

"Because I need to play it," she said vaguely, blushing prettily.

Of course he would take her to a church. Perhaps not today but sometime soon. Where he would one day kiss her under God and say his wedding vows. He had already decided he would marry Magellan. It didn't matter if she was penniless. He would find another way to help the estate's finances. He would sell the whole library off for her. He didn't care either that she was from America and slightly addled with an overactive imagination. In the light of day, everything was becoming clear. Who knew how she'd really ended up in the labyrinth. He simply Did. Not. Care. Nothing mattered anymore except keeping her with him. If the future Countess of Liron required an ancient church with a pipe organ, then so be it. That's what he would get for her. His father had been most eccentric too, and his mother had managed him quite easily enough.

Several minutes later, Magellan opened the door and she and Fanny came out. They were both laughing, looking radiant and full of joy. Fanny was even wiping happy tears from her eyes. Rhys resisted the urge to raise his quizzing glass at them. Magellan was glowing, as if the nightmare she'd been through the past week had never happened.

The women saw him hovering with uncertainty in the hallway.

Fanny beamed at him. "Lord Liron, thank you so much for inviting me to meet Miss Brighton! It has been a most illuminating day."

*What did that mean?* He was fiddling nervously with his quizzing glass and forced himself to stop.

He gave her what he hoped was a pleasant smile. "Would you like to stay for tea or luncheon perhaps?"

"Thank you, but I should be going." She turned to Magellan. "I hope we meet again, Miss Brighton, even if it's only in our dreams," Miss Mendelssohn said, waxing poetic, and she gave Magellan a firm hug.

Rhys stood there awkwardly watching, astounded by the women's overt sentimentality with each other. The two had literally just met and were hugging like old friends—like sisters. He had no idea female musicians were so romantic at heart.

I hope we meet in dreams, indeed!

Magellan looked vibrant, even dressed in a somber dark-blue travel dress meant for a long carriage ride. Rhys frowned at the ensemble. Why was she wearing such plain garb? Did Vivianne have nothing else in her closets? He would need to take Magellan to the modiste today to order a proper wardrobe befitting a future countess. But first she needed to eat before she got dizzy. And just as pressing, at some point he would need to garner his courage and propose before the housekeeper or butler did it for him. He prayed the staff had not mentioned their engagement to her. Another worry to add to his plate of worries. His one and only marriage proposal and he'd already botched it.

Miss Mendelssohn left, leaving the two of them alone together.

"Thank you for letting Fanny come." Magellan grabbed hold of his arm like she had once been prone to do. He gave her a foolish lopsided smile, stifling his worries for the moment, simply happy she was happy.

"I take it the visit was a success?" he asked, though he could tell it was.

"It was amazing." Magellan's whole face was shining as if lit from within, making him feel momentarily breathless. "She had the second part of the first movement!"

"The first movement of what?" He led her to the salon and offered her a chair. Then he prepared her a plate of food.

"The symphony I've been sent to find." Instead of sitting, she quickly crossed the room to the window and watched Miss Mendelssohn's carriage depart. She was keyed up with excitement and a jittery nervousness. "You see, a symphony generally has four movements. Now I have the first movement, and I need the other three. I believe we should go to the church now. Gwynedd warned me." She stayed by the window, looking riveted by something down on the street.

Rhys prided himself by nodding as if what she was saying made perfect sense. Because he loved her. He would help her move past this fantasy. Even if it took years. He would surround her with instruments and other composer friends and whatever she desired to make her forget her delusions.

Then she gasped and took a step back to hide behind the curtain.

"What is it?" He looked out the window to find dark storm clouds gathering on the horizon.

"Strange men are outside the gate, looking up at us. It must be them."

"Who?" He followed her line of vision, surprised to find there were several questionable fellows at the gate. They looked like seedy criminals who had somehow wandered into Mayfair. He drew the curtain. "Do not worry. Those ragamuffins wouldn't dare climb the gate. I'll have my footmen run them off."

She stood frozen like a startled deer about to bolt. "Do you hear that?" she whispered. A fierce frown was on her face as she strained to listen to something. She backed away farther from the window in terror. "Rhys, we need to leave now."

"After you eat something." He nodded to her plate and poured her a tea. "I thought this afternoon we should go and have you fitted for new dresses." He watched her grab the food and shove it into her mouth. Her hands were noticeably shaking.

She said with her mouth full of biscuits, "I need to get to the church a-s-a-p."

"What do the letters *a s a p* mean?"

"Sorry." She looked flustered. "It means right away." She downed the tea in a single gulp and headed to the door.

He got up to follow her, suggesting, "Are you sure you wouldn't prefer a carriage ride in Hyde Park perhaps?" Although that would attract attention. He was trying to minimize the possibility of a scandal.

"No! Let me just get my bag." Magellan was already running upstairs, taking them two at a time as he watched astounded.

The butler interrupted him. "Pardon me, sir, but there seems to be a commotion outside the gates."

"Yes, the ruffians. Do have the footmen handle it."

"I believe they might be dangerous, perhaps escaped from an asylum. They're trying to climb the gate."

Magellan, overhearing, leaned over the upstairs balcony and called down to him. "Rhys, it's happening. The labyrinth is breaking. Can't you hear it? I need a church and a pipe organ right away!" She disappeared into her room.

To the butler's credit, he did not change his facial expression. Rhys tried to smooth over his acute embarrassment. "Do see to those men, Gibbons, and call for the carriage to be brought around back." They could leave from there and avoid the front gate.

Rhys went for his coat and gloves and grabbed his purse, newly filled with coin. They could go shopping after the church, and he would buy her the dresses she required. Then tonight they would talk. He would work hard to help her put her feet firmly back on the ground. She only needed an anchor. *Him.* By Jove, the anchor would be him. Then he would propose. She would say yes. After they were married, he would put a piano in their bedroom where they could kiss on the bench whenever they liked and not stop there. He blushed at the thought.

He waited at the bottom of the stairs. His smile quickly turned into a frown when he saw her come downstairs with the satchel he had given her before. It was bulging with items inside.

*Why* in blazes was she bringing the satchel?

"Why do you still have that bag?" he all but spit out. He should have burned the atrocity.

"I need to bring some things with me," she said vaguely. She was wearing one of Vivianne's heavy cloaks over her dress, and his heart fell. She really thought she was going to time travel.

"I'll carry that for you," he insisted, taking the satchel from her. He'd be damned if he'd let the bag—or her—out of his sight.

They climbed into his carriage, and he told the footman to take them to All Hallows by the Tower. It was the oldest church in London and had been there since the 600s. That should be old enough for her, and the church did have a grand pipe organ. He may have to bribe some priest to let her play it, which is why he brought his heaviest purse.

Magellan didn't say a word in the carriage ride. She sat ramrod straight, staring out the window and startling at every jolt and bump on the road as if they were going to be attacked any moment.

Getting across town took some time. The church was on Byward Street near the Tower of London. Rhys kept the windows up to minimize the rotting stench of the city. Magellan was looking out the window wide-eyed, gazing up at the darkening sky. "We have to hurry. There's not much time."

He crossed his arms, refusing to engage in the conversation.

"Rhys, I know you don't want to believe me, but now that I have Fanny's part of the song, I have to leave 1829. I can't stay here."

He scowled again. He was itching to wrench open the satchel and see what "things" she had brought with her to leave 1829. He looked glumly out the window, his arms still crossed as he brooded on this madcap situation. Darker clouds were rolling in. "Perhaps we should save the organ for another day and turn around?"

"No!" She grabbed on to his arm so tightly he startled. "We must keep going. Can't you hear those vibrations?"

"I believe that is thunder rumbling in the distance."

She shook her head as if he had no idea what he was talking about. "Maybe you can't hear it. Maybe only I can. But do you see how they're all looking at us?"

"How who's looking at us?"

"The people. It's like they know I shouldn't be here anymore." Her gaze was fixed outside the window in pure terror. Rhys did notice a few disreputable fellows watch the carriage pass by. Their prolonged stares were odd, perhaps unnerving if he were to let his imagination have free rein. He knocked on the ceiling to order the driver to go faster.

Magellan turned to him and took his hand in hers. "Do you want to come with me? I don't know what time I'll land in. It could be dangerous."

He could only stare at her. How on Earth did he handle her when she was like this? "Of course I will go with you. I never want to be parted from you again." *There! Let her stew on that.*

She searched his eyes. "Even if we wouldn't know how long we'd be gone or where we were going?"

He tried to stay calm. "Even then."

She expelled a heavy sigh and looked out the window. "I have no idea how to convince you it's real before it happens, and by then it will be too late."

Suddenly the carriage lurched and she screamed. Rhys braced her as the carriage almost tipped, but somehow the driver stayed in control and maneuvered the horses to the side of the road.

Rhys got out to investigate.

Magellan jumped out after him. "What's happened?"

"We've broken a wheel, but never fear, we have a spare. Wait in the carriage while we change it, and then we'll return to the house."

She was clutching the satchel and looking wildly about. "No! We must go to the church. It's getting louder. They're coming. We can't just wait here like sitting ducks!"

Sitting ducks? Whatever did that mean?

Thunder cracked across the sky and the horses startled. Rhys had never heard thunder so loud. He tried to reason with her. "Today is not the best day for an outing. Look at the sky." Storm clouds were forming quickly, obscuring the daylight. Thunder crashed again and she yelped.

"Today is the only day." She pointed up. "That is the labyrinth breaking. I'll go on foot if I have to."

The sky opened up and poured rain down on them. He tried to usher her into the carriage, but she resisted. His patience was at its wit's end. "Fine! We're going! Just get inside and stay dry."

Instead, she was looking at something behind him and took a step back in horror. She covered her ears as if to block out a painful sound. "She was right. They're here!"

Who was right? Rhys turned around to see what else could have upset her so. Four men were moving toward them. Two blocks still separated them, but they had a deadly intent in their eyes. "Those men?"

"No, the shadows," she whispered, still plugging her ears with her fingers. Gripped by full-on hysteria now, she started weeping and backed away, her tears mixing with the rain. "Either help me now or I swear to God I'm running!"

Her absolute terror was real—and contagious. London criminals were the deadliest in the world, and these men clearly had their sights set to rob them.

He could not fight all four and ensure Magellan's safety. Moving quickly, he brought out his dagger and within seconds freed one of the horses from the carriage. Using the undercarriage as leverage, he jumped up and mounted the horse. "Hurry! Give me your hand."

The men saw them trying to escape and broke into a run. Rhys shouted to his driver to take shelter and he wrenched Magellan onto the horse, taking off at a gallop.

"Hold on," he yelled over the wind and whipping rain.

He raced to All Hallows by the Tower as if he were competing in the Derby. By the time they arrived, their pursuers were nowhere in sight. He and Magellan were drenched, and the streets around them were beginning to pool with water.

He dismounted, helping her down, and they rushed into the church out of the rain. Throughout their whole escapade, she still had the satchel with her. He took it from her without a word and slung it over his shoulder.

Once they were inside, Magellan sagged against the door and closed her eyes. She stopped covering her ears and fought hard to slow her breath.

"Are you all right?" He wanted to comfort her, but he was shaken by the whole encounter, by those criminals along with Magellan's terror over seeing shadows and hearing noises. Hallucinations were a clear sign of madness. Dear God, she truly did need medical help.

"I just need a moment." Magellan kept her eyes closed, fighting to calm down.

Then she started humming. Rhys did not know what to do. "There, there." He tried to soothe her, patting her back. "All is well now. You've had a fright, that's all. Let me go enquire about the organ. Then you can play and feel all better." He led her to sit in the back pew.

The church was empty midafternoon. Services were over. No priests were about. Rhys found a man busy mopping the floors and gave him a shilling to allow them upstairs to the balcony.

He escorted Magellan to the organ, feeling proud he'd at least accomplished this one request. Perhaps if she played, she would return to her senses. He stared up at the towering pipes. It was the grandest instrument he'd ever seen. He could barely believe Magellan knew how to play it.

Was there any instrument she couldn't play?

The question boggled his mind, and for a moment he thought of Gwynedd. They did share the same gift.

The same ring? Whose symbols matched the standing stones. In the diary, Cathan had said it meant *know the way.*

Goose bumps trailed up his arms. Had his father truly believed in the story, like Magellan? Rhys stood beneath the pipe organ's magnificence, a bit of heaven brought down to Earth, forged in metal, and once again questioned everything he believed to be true.

*Fate* came from the Latin word *fatum*, a divine decree of what had yet to happen would happen. Magellan entering his life was fate. He knew that with an unshakable certainty. She believed she was on a mission to save the world, and he had been chosen to help her. Well, here they were in a church with an organ. All she had to do was play it.

Magellan stood beside him, staring at the organ with a strange mix of apprehension and determination. Then she sat down on the bench as thunder quaked outside. She jumped at the sound, as if she would be its next victim.

Rhys hovered waiting for her to play, waiting to see what she purported to be true. But instead of playing, she turned away from the keys to face him. "I know you're waiting for me to come to my senses."

"Magellan," he began softly, "please just play."

"When I play, I will leave." Tears slipped from her eyes. "*It's real*, Rhys. I have to keep going. Your time doesn't want me here anymore." A wind howled outside and banged on the church doors as if a force was trying to get inside. "When I play this, I will end up in another time. I will disappear."

"All right, then," he said, sitting down on the bench beside her. "We'll go together."

"Why can't you take this seriously?"

"I thought I was." He scowled back. "I brought you here, didn't I?"

"Yes, but you think I'm crazy!"

"Just play the bloody organ!"

"But when I do—"

He kissed her to make her stop. It was either that or shake her to make her see sense. She soon turned into putty in his arms and then broke away, closing her eyes. "Is it wrong I want you to come with me?"

He kissed her again, whispering, "No, I want to go everywhere with you, even in your dreams." Even as he said the words, he found them to be true.

Magellan stared at him hard a long moment. "I promise this is not a dream." She kissed him tenderly on the lips as if this were goodbye. "I can't take you with me. You don't believe me and afterwards it will be too late. You won't be able to get back home." She shook her head, truly believing what she was saying. She was weeping now. "I have to go. I'm so sorry. I was born to do this." She clutched him in a desperate embrace. "I promise I'll come back to you if I can. I'll find a way to come back."

"Of course you will," he said, trying to soothe her. He just needed her to stop crying.

"Go stand over there. Please," she begged him.

"Of course." He hurried to stand where she wanted him. "I'll be right here while you play." He was six feet away, not far.

"Thank you for everything." She looked so solemn, her eyes shining. "I'll never forget you."

Rhys could no longer play the part. His mouth dropped in disbelief. Was she actually saying goodbye to him on a piano bench as if she'd go poof?

Then she gave him the most heartbreaking smile. "You have my heart."

With those words her hands resolutely came down on the keys, and powerful music filled the cathedral in a torrential wave of sound. The organ pipes opened, bellowing chords like an ancient bugle call on a mountainside to herald in something magnificent.

Magellan's hands flew over the keys as she played Bach's masterpiece in a wild tempest of notes. The grandeur was staggering. Rhys could only look on stunned as her hands moved faster and faster—the music growing louder and louder and more and more until the air around Magellan seemed to glow and crackle. She continued to play on like a charioteer riding into the eye of the storm. Then lights began to swirl around her.

At first Rhys thought his eyes were playing tricks on him.

He blinked, then he blinked again.

To his astonishment her body began to fade within a shroud of rainbows. The ring on her hand was glowing with the brilliance of a star.

She was disappearing right before his eyes.

Rhys didn't second-guess his actions. He lunged to grab on to her right before she vanished. Falling to his knees, he wrapped his arms around her waist and suddenly he was enveloped within the brilliance too, falling and flying, as the world around him fractured and then splintered into infinite prisms of light.

# Chapter 34

## Magellan

Magellan opened her eyes to find herself lying on a bed of grass and staring up at an open sky. She sat up slowly. Rhys was beside her out cold with her satchel slung across his chest. Back at the church, she'd been so upset saying goodbye, she'd forgotten to take it from him.

She looked around her. They were somewhere in a field on top of a sloping hill. An ancient standing stone—a stone well over ten feet—towered behind them like an *X* marking the spot where they landed.

"Holy crap." Her heart skipped as adrenaline flooded her body. She'd done it. She'd actually done it and gone somewhere else. She turned back to Rhys, and a rush of emotion hit her. He had grabbed onto her at the last moment. Right now he looked like a sleeping angel with his face in repose, and the enormity of what she'd done struck her. He had a family and an estate and responsibilities. He had a life she'd just forced him from. His life. Panic seized her. She laid her hands on his arms and shook him.

"Rhys? Rhys! Wake up."

She kept shaking him until his eyes fluttered open and he looked up at the sky in confusion. Then he sat up, slowly looking around.

Knowing how disoriented he was, she waited for his memories to come flooding back. When they did, he jumped up in alarm and turned a 360.

"What happened? Where are we?"

"I don't know." She rose to her feet, trying to stay calm for him.

Where this was and when this was remained a mystery, but she'd been through this once before. And she was more relieved to be out of 1829 than still there. After she'd gotten the song from Fanny, things had gone south quickly. The men at the gate, the storm, the criminals on the street. Then came the strange moving shadows and terrifying sounds. She didn't know what she'd experienced, but a malevolent force had come for her with sounds so painful—a screeching tangle of discordant wails both piercingly high and despairingly low. Within the wails was an abyss of human torment, a cacophony of pain. If hell had an orchestra, she had just heard it, an orchestra at war with itself and intent on destruction.

The vortex of shadows and sounds had wanted the song and wanted her. The song's resonance had drawn it to her, just like Gwynedd had warned. Magellan had only come to her senses when they reached the church. Now she was somewhere else in time's labyrinth, and according to Gwynedd, whatever was hunting her in 1829 could not follow here—until she played the song again and opened another doorway.

She shuddered, trying not to think about when that time came. Right now, she had to help Rhys come to terms with their new reality, wherever they were, and she had a feeling the Earl of Liron wasn't going to handle it well.

"Good God! Where are we?" he yelled to the open countryside. He walked a circle around the standing stone and reached out to touch it. "We were at the church. You were playing the organ, and everything began to glow. How in blazes did we get *here*?"

She shrugged helplessly, unsure how to explain. "Bach and a Ley Line?" she ventured to guess.

"You're telling me it's all true?" His voice was pitched high in disbelief.

She made a wild gesture around them with both hands like *What do you think?*

Rhys did another 360, as if their environment would change if he kept turning in circles enough. "I'm not dreaming this?"

"I don't think we can have the same dream. I tried to tell you we would end up somewhere else."

"Yes, I know. But I didn't think . . . this is madness!" He began to pace. "You're telling me what Gwynedd wrote in the diary is actually real? That you traveled on a-a-Ley Line from the future to my labyrinth?"

It did sound crazy, but they were standing in the middle of nowhere next to a twelve-foot ancient stone confirming that fact.

Magellan didn't know how to answer. Rhys looked livid, and her heart fell. Of course he was upset. She knew he hadn't believed her, and she'd tried to bring him anyway, because she was selfish and wanted him with her. Then she'd chickened out at the last minute and tried to leave him behind. She never should have let him come upstairs to the balcony in the first place.

"Rhys, I'm so sorry. I know you're mad at me—"

"Mad! Mad?" He whirled on her looking angrier than she'd ever seen him. "You almost came here alone without me!"

It took her a moment to realize what he was mad about. "Wait. You're not mad that I brought you?"

"If I wasn't here, you would be here all alone, and I would have"—he had to swallow to get the words out—"been unable to find you."

She was becoming emotional too. He didn't understand and was getting it all wrong. "I did want you to come. But I thought it was wrong to trick you when you obviously didn't believe me."

"So you knew this whole time you were leaving." His lips set into an angry line. "You had no idea where you were going, but you packed a bag." He sat down on the ground and rifled through it, muttering to himself. "I wondered what was in this bloody thing." He held out a scone, and his voice softened momentarily. "Please eat something."

Magellan sat down and took the scone grudgingly. Rhys always seemed to know when she needed to eat, because she was feeling lightheaded.

He continued to go through the bag. "We've landed in the middle of nowhere, but at least we have tooth powder and a butter knife for a weapon."

Magellan blushed. "There's food and my ointments and cloth."

He held up two flasks. "How did you get these?"

"From the carriage when you weren't looking." She was pretty sure one held wine and one held water.

"Here, drink something. You must keep your strength to face wherever in the world we are." He offered them to her, his eyes glittering with emotion as he waited for her to eat and drink. It wasn't as if she had wanted to leave him behind. Without a word she reached for the flask that turned out to hold the wine. She took two large swallows, needing a stiff drink to deal with this.

He was rubbing the bridge of his nose. "When did you start to realize the diary was real?"

"When Gwynedd started talking about our gift with music and my ring." A big part of her was relieved Rhys finally knew, because it'd been hard being alone and barely holding on to her sanity. "And Garesh." She still hadn't solved the riddle of Garesh. Gwynedd believed he was the immortal from an ancient Sumerian legend, which felt even more fantastical to her than landing in another time.

Rhys was staring at her intently, trying to puzzle it all out. "My father knew you would come, and he had the diary."

"The diary found me in the future too." Which was still a mystery. "On the morning of my birthday, a man left a message on my cell phone that he had my diary sent by the Liron Institute."

Rhys stared at her, utterly perplexed. "What is a cell phone?"

She bit back a sigh. "A way to talk and send messages. I'll explain later. Gwynedd said Ley Lines are mysterious things and objects find their own way to people. Wherever the diary came from, your father's past or my future, we still need to translate the rest."

Rhys nodded, looking overwhelmed and trying to take it all in.

"The entire week before I left my time and arrived in yours, an aurora borealis appeared in the sky all over the world."

His brow furrowed. "Celestial lights?"

She nodded. "Crystal said a magnetic pole shift is happening, and it's going to be catastrophic."

"Who is Crystal?"

"My boss." Poor Crystal. Magellan fleetingly wondered what Crystal thought about her disappearance at the church. Did her parents and Wren think she was dead, or kidnapped? Were they searching for her?

"What is a boss?" Rhys was picking apart every word she was saying. She tried to be patient.

"It's what we call the person you work for. That day I . . . traveled . . . to you, I was playing the harp at a wedding."

"Whose wedding?" He was sitting on the ground with his arms crossed, a scowl on his face.

"No one I know personally. I play music at weddings for work. During the ceremony the news broke about the poles shifting. Everyone panicked. I went upstairs to play the pipe organ. The next thing I knew I was in the labyrinth. I thought it was a dream and you were from my imagination."

She gave a faint smile, remembering that day, and her eyes traveled wistfully over him. So much had happened since then. It felt like a lifetime ago. And her old life was beginning to feel like a faraway memory—or worse, a dream. She tried to focus on Rhys and held out her hand. "Then I discovered my ring matched the symbols on the standing stone. It was the only thing that kept me from completely doubting my sanity."

"Yes, I saw the ring when you were sleeping." Rhys took her hand to study it. His fingers traced the symbols. "And still, I couldn't believe."

She could see the profound regret in his eyes. She told him, "Fanny had the second half of the symphony's first movement." She couldn't explain to Rhys fully what had happened with Fanny Mendelssohn. The song was a symphony of epic proportion with so many moving parts and instruments. What she was playing on a single instrument was the core, and the rest existed in her imagination. Just the first movement alone, made of hers and Fanny's parts, boggled her mind. She was already considering all the instruments she would need and the people to play them. Not to mention the singing and the voices. Voices were instruments too. Powerful ones. Like Wren's.

"You think you're meant to find a composer somewhere here in this vast wilderness?"

"Yes." At least she hoped so. It was a leap of faith, but Magellan had to believe the ring and the Ley Lines had brought them here for the same reason.

Rhys considered everything a long moment. "I think it's wise for us first to figure out where we are and find shelter before it gets dark." He held out his hand to help her stand. He was acting stiff and formal, or maybe he was distracted as he took in their surroundings. He shielded his eyes from the sun, squinting. "I think that's a road in the distance. Are you able to walk?"

"Of course." She bent down to get the satchel, but he beat her to it.

As they began walking into the unknown, her own anxiety returned full force. She had no choice but to hum.

Rhys asked, "Are you truly singing? At a time like this?"

"I'm humming. It calms my nerves."

"Humming," he clarified, as if he hadn't heard her right.

She hummed a bit more. "The sound resonates throughout your body like a tuning fork and calms your—" She almost said vagus nerve but didn't have the energy to explain what it was.

"That is the reason you hum sometimes?" he asked, as if a great mystery had been solved.

"I have a lot of anxiety," she hesitated, admitting, "and fear."

"Truly? I think you're the most courageous woman I've ever met."

She turned to him in surprise. "You do?"

"And reckless with no thought for your safety." He waved his arm at their view. They walked on in silence toward the road, a thin ribbon in the distance. Rhys kept stopping to turn a full circle and look at the sky.

"What are you doing?" she had to ask.

"Keeping track of our direction so we can make our way back. The standing stone might be the only way out of here."

She hadn't thought about that.

He added, "We find out where we are, find this composer of yours, and then get back to the stone."

"I'll need an instrument." But first, she needed to figure out who she was meant to meet.

When they reached the road, they saw travelers up ahead, a group of men and women with a horse and a wagon. The women's colorful gowns with decorative metal belts looked like something from a Renaissance Fair. The men wore long tunics or shorter tunics with boots. From afar she could see metal glinting in the sunlight.

"Are those swords?" Magellan asked breathlessly. One man had a spear as well. "What century did people stop walking around with swords and spears?"

"Apparently not this one. Bloody hell." Rhys started to hum under his breath.

She was so surprised she had to ask to make sure. "Are you humming?"

"You said it helped with anxiety." Then he announced, "But I find it is not minimizing mine." He stopped walking and pulled them behind a tree. He worked quickly to take off his cravat, vest, and coat and stuffed it into the satchel.

Baffled, she watched him. "What are you doing?"

"Trying to blend in with those medieval chaps up ahead." He untucked his shirt from his pants, letting it hang down long to slightly resemble a tunic. Then he stared at her, his eyes sweeping her from head to toe. She had dressed smartly in a plain blue gown and travel cloak. "Your skirts are too full and will call attention. Take off whatever is underneath them." A blush bloomed on his cheeks as he waved an imperious hand at her skirts. Then he about-faced and shielded her from anyone who could see. "Quickly now."

She reached under her skirt to slip off the voluminous petticoat. The skirt immediately flattened to resemble the other women's up ahead on the road. "You can look now," she said. Rhys turned and flushed even more when he saw the petticoat on the ground. She wadded up the fabric and put it in the now bulging satchel.

"Better. Take your hair down too like the other ladies."

Magellan started pulling out the countless hair pins, but she was making a knotted mess.

"Here, let me." Rhys stood in front of her and worked all the pins out with a gentle hand. She stared at his chest, watching him breathe. He was being infinitely careful finding all the pins, until she felt the knot of her hair give and tumble down her back. "I think I got them all," he said, his voice husky. Then his hands were in her hair searching for any stray pins. He found two.

She looked up at him. The wary hurt in his eyes pained her. She tried to explain herself again. "You don't know how much I wanted you to come," she pleaded softly, wanting nothing more than to kiss him, but he took a step back, deftly slipping the pins in the satchel's side pocket.

"As you said." He still sounded distant and busied himself with his coin purse, fishing out a handful of coins and putting them in the pocket of his pants. She hadn't even considered she would have come alone without any money.

"Will your coins work here?" she wondered.

"Silver and gold will always be in demand no matter what year it is." He took her hand in his and briskly set off. "We need to follow them and hope they're going to a town. Let us stay close, but not too close. We don't want them noticing us."

They trailed behind the traveling group for over an hour. After a while Magellan was too tired and hungry to hum anymore but refused to complain. Especially not when Rhys was still upset. His hurt was legitimate. If he had left her behind intentionally, she would have been devastated. They didn't talk and instead focused on following the group. The men spoke loudly and were laughing.

She whispered, "Can you understand them?"

He shook his head. "Only a few words. It's definitely an offspring of German, most likely its earlier form."

They crested another hill and finally saw the town. A huge, sprawling medieval metropolis with bridges connecting the city on both sides of a river. Relief hit her hard upon seeing it. At least they weren't stranded in the middle of nowhere.

Up ahead the road merged into a bigger one with more travelers, more wagons, and more swords and spears all heading to town.

Before she and Rhys got onto the main road to join the others, he said quietly, "Don't stare anyone in the eyes, and try not to speak. I will speak only German. With luck they will think us foreign travelers with a heavy dialect. It will be better than English. Just answer *ja* for yes and *nein* for no."

Magellan nodded, beginning to panic. Rhys gave her hand a tight squeeze, and they merged onto the main road. She could feel the stress oozing from him. He was the only man without a sword. She tried to keep her eyes downcast but couldn't help peeking up at all the people. Aside from the colorful robes, heavy jewelry, and weapons, everyone looked filthy, as if they hadn't bathed in weeks. The pungent odors of sweat and oil wafted in the air alongside the stench from livestock. The smells only increased as they made it over the first bridge to the outer wall of the city.

Boys in a nearby field were playing with what looked to be an ancient soccer ball. An enormous market loomed ahead, crammed with rows of vendors selling a dizzying array of fruits, vegetables, livestock both alive and strung up butchered, spices, fabrics, pottery, and glassware. They passed by booths selling foods being cooked in the open, and she eyed the grilled sausages and giant pretzels, her mouth watering.

Rhys stopped at a popular booth manned by two industrious women at an oven. He tried his hand at buying a round of rye bread and fresh cheese spread by paying with copper pennies and speaking slowly in German with hand signals. Then they were off again. Rhys seemed to have some kind of destination in mind. It'd been hours since they woke up at the standing stone. Magellan was about to ask if they could stop and rest when they rounded a corner and entered a small square.

Rhys tried to block her view but wasn't fast enough. A man hung from a scaffold, his back a patchwork of torn flesh and blood. "Don't look." Rhys's arms came around her, and she fought not to throw up as he led them back the way they'd come. "Just keep moving," he whispered. "Don't stop."

Soon they were back at the market entrance where they passed by several wooden pillars with pieces of parchment nailed to them. Rhys stopped to read one. Magellan looked up, still woozy, and saw the public notice with the date written on top.

# Chapter 35

𝄢

## Rhys

*1165. They were in 1165.* Rhys gaped at the date scrawled across the top of the town missive. His brain felt like it was about to stop functioning. He was drowning in disbelief and had been from the moment he opened his eyes in that field. They were standing in a town square in the year 1165, somewhere in medieval Germany.

It was too incredible to be real, yet they were here. His historian's mind quickly cataloged the century: A brutal time of open battle, crusades, and bloodthirsty knights. A group of such men were standing right over there. He grasped Magellan's hand tighter and clutched the satchel. To think she would have arrived here with nothing—basically humming her way through the countryside alone—made him lose all reason. She really had tried to leave without him!

The moment when he saw her body fading, not grabbing onto her had never been a choice. Now they were in 1165, which meant the diary was utterly real. And Magellan getting the song's part from Fanny Mendelssohn had happened.

If everything was real, and what Gwynedd had written was real, then *who* was Magellan?

Gwynedd had alluded she was writing to herself in the future, to a future lifetime, to remember exactly what must be done when the time came. Then the diary had taken a further dive into the fantastical, and Rhys had stopped paying close attention to what he was translating, especially that last chapter. Now he'd have to read it all again, as well as translate the rest. He needed to know, more than ever, what the diary said.

With his free hand, he reached into the satchel to reassure himself the book was still there. Trying not to panic, he looked around to get his bearings. If he had to take a wild guess, this had to be Frankfurt. "The City of the Franks" was the only city in medieval times to have been this thriving. It had been a meeting place for Charlemagne three hundred years before, and the kings of Germany were elected here. Its famous market drew tradesmen from all over, making it an international meeting ground.

As he and Magellan passed through the market stalls, he heard a myriad of languages. He was still cursing himself he'd led her into that square where the man was being whipped. Never had he seen a more gruesome sight. Right now, they needed a safe place to sleep for the night, and Magellan needed to eat. They'd been traipsing across the countryside for hours.

People jostled brusquely past them. He kept his hands tight on the satchel and Magellan, only wanting to get them behind the safety of a locked door. Then he spotted a sign down the road, possibly for an inn, and hurried toward it.

They entered the tavern and he asked the barkeep in German, speaking slowly, "Do you have a room?"

The woman looked them over, and he placed three shillings on the counter. She frowned at the silver and he gave her two more. Then she nodded and led them up the stairs to a door at the end of the hallway. She prepared the room and brought them a pitcher of water for the basin and a lit lantern. Rhys nodded his thanks, hurried Magellan inside, and bolted the door, leaning against it in profound relief.

At last. They were secure. Finally, he could breathe again.

"Sit down," he told her gently. She was not recovered from her abduction, yet she hadn't complained once today. In fact, she'd been deadly silent, casting him solemn looks.

He huffed out a sigh and took stock of the room. It was tinier than his closet and had a small bed. The mattress was straw and topped with a sheet questionable in its cleanliness. A linen sack stuffed with leaves was the blanket. A wooden table and two chairs sat next to a window that opened, allowing a breeze into the room. The washing basin along with a pitcher of water sat on top of a tall cabinet. He peered behind a large wooden screen in the corner to find the chamber pot. At least it had a lid, and at least they wouldn't have to step outside to take care of their needs. All in all the room wasn't bad for the 1100s. The accommodations could have been worse.

He put the satchel on the bed and set out their provisions on the table. Magellan sat down at the table with a glazed look in her eyes.

"You need to eat," he encouraged, sitting in the other chair and stretching his legs with relief.

"So do you."

He took a long swig from the wine and let out a weary sigh.

"You don't have to keep sighing," she said softly. "I know you don't want to be here."

"I don't want *us* to be here," he corrected her. "Specifically, you to be here. In case you didn't notice, 1165 is dangerous."

She scowled at him. "Are you mad that you came or are you mad that I had to come? Because I don't know anymore."

It took him a moment. Why in blazes was she upset with him? He said each word slowly, so it was clear. "I'm mad you would have left me. What is it about that fact you don't understand?" Then he crossed his arms and leaned back in his chair to glare at her, fuming all over again.

She leaned forward, her eyes bright with emotion. "I didn't want to leave without you. But it was wrong of me to force you to choose—"

"And I'm telling you when it comes to you there is no choice. Do you understand? This debate is over. What's done is done."

They ate in stony silence. He cut her cheese and apple and kept handing her pieces along with bread until she claimed she was full. "We'll buy more food tomorrow at the market," he stated, then couldn't help adding, "With the coin I fortunately thought to bring."

Her lips tightened with irritation, but she didn't offer a rebuke. He got up and went to the window, unable to stop another sigh. It was nighttime now. At least they were safe for the time being. Magellan could believe all she wanted that he didn't belong here with her, but, by thunder, he did.

Humorless laughter rose up inside him. His father had always told him he would travel far in life. Though 1165 was perhaps beyond even Godwin's imagination.

If the diary was to be believed—which now he had no choice but to accept it as true—right now they had to find a composer in 1165 in order to get out of the Middle Ages. He tried to focus. "I believe we're in Frankfurt, Germany. You need to think who it is you could possibly be looking for."

"I already know. I knew right away when I saw the year."

"You do?" he asked in surprise. Well, that was something at least. "Why didn't you say so?"

"You were too busy being upset."

They stared at each other a long moment. He bit back a retort and instead sat down. He gave her a polite smile, unable to stop the sarcasm. "I'll do my best to refrain from future upset."

"Thank you, my lord, for being so accommodating." She glared back at him.

Rhys pinched the bridge of his nose, praying for patience. "Who are we here for?" He stressed the *we* because they were a *we*, dammit.

Now it was her turn to sigh. "Hildegard of Bingen."

The name meant nothing to him. "Who is that?"

"Only the greatest composer of this time. Male or female."

Another woman he'd never heard of. He frowned, deciding to tackle the cheese and bread, suddenly starving. "You're sure?"

"Very." Magellan got up to pace. "Hildegard of Bingen was more than a composer. She was a visionary, a prophet, a poet, a scholar." Rhys ate while he watched Magellan's arms become animated with excitement as she explained. "She wrote books on biology, botany, medicine, theology, and the arts. She exchanged letters with popes, emperors, and kings who sought her advice. She even founded two abbeys and ran both of them. The woman was incredible."

"She was a nun?" Rhys asked, further surprised.

"Yes. A brilliant, unorthodox nun."

"And what of her music?" The reason why they were here.

"That's the most fascinating part. She only started playing music when she turned forty. She never had before, but she took to it quickly, composing on a ten-string psaltery."

"What is a ps-altery?" He tripped on the word.

"It's like an ornately decorated harpsicord."

"And how do you know so much about her?"

Magellan turned to him. "From college. I took a history class on women composers." She laughed softly to herself. "I actually wrote a research paper on her."

He could not have been more flummoxed. She had gone to college?

"Hildegard of Bingen was a great medieval composer, and her literary work is as vast as her musical compositions. There've been countless books and movies about her—"

"What is a movie?" His question seemed to catch her off guard.

She hesitated. "A moving picture, like a painting that has come to life."

He was still confused. A painting could come to life? Magellan had gone to college, and in her time there were living paintings. How did the paintings come to life? He didn't want to ask. The notion sounded like a fantastical fiction novel and made him self-conscious and embarrassed to know her world in the future was so vastly different than his. A part of him was afraid to find out how different.

He returned his focus to the medieval nun they were supposed to find. "So where does this Hildegard live? In Frankfurt, hopefully?"

Magellan shook her head. "Her two abbeys were in Rupertsburg and Eibingen in the countryside."

He had no idea where those places were. "Which one do you suspect she might be at?"

Magellan was back to pacing. She took off her cloak and laid it on the bed. Momentarily distracted, he tried not to stare at the lovely figure she cut with her hair down—or look at the bed where she would be sleeping tonight. He would sleep in the chair. She was saying, "If I had to guess I would say Rupertsburg."

"Then tomorrow we'll find out where the town is. Hopefully it's not far. We may have to buy horses." He saw her frown and they locked eyes again, both remembering her riding accident, and he amended. "Perhaps we'll buy a donkey and a cart for you to ride in." That caused her to laugh, and he caught himself gazing at her again. He cleared his throat and stood up stiffly. "I'll step out to give you some privacy to prepare for bed."

She hesitated but then nodded, her eyes darting all over the room, between the bed, the water basin, and the screen. "Thank you. But maybe I should go outside first and let you get ready?"

"There's no way you're ever standing outside this door."

"Rhys, I'm sure you'd like a private moment—"

"I don't need a moment. I need you not getting accosted in 1165." He crossed his arms, feeling his irritation rise again. Did she have no thought for her safety?

"Please, we're at an inn—"

"In medieval times! With drunk knights downstairs with swords that have recently been used!" he sputtered. "I'll be right outside. Bolt the door and let me know when you're finished."

He stomped outside into the hallway and waited for the sound of the door being bolted again. The last thing he needed was someone pummeling him in the hallway and then forcing his way in and attacking her. He tried not to let his imagination run wild, but it was hard not to do when everyone was walking around with sharpened blades. Not only swords and spears, but he'd seen axes, whips, and an actual mace downstairs at the bar. Maybe he should buy armor tomorrow or at least a shield.

He stood in the hallway. Fortunately, no one paid him any mind. An older couple was staying across from their room, and a rowdy family of six was down the hall. He began to relax somewhat as he leaned against the wall to wait, then Magellan's knock came. She unbolted the door and opened it.

She was in her chemise, her dress hanging on the back of the chair. He averted his eyes as he entered and bolted the door again. She was busy laying out her petticoats over the mattress and offered, "I thought we could sleep on this. It'll be cleaner."

The thought of sleeping with Magellan on top of her skirts was another kind of torture. He went and sat down at the table, unable to watch. "I'll take the chair, and you'll have the bed."

She turned to him. "That's ridiculous. You can't sleep in a chair."

"There's barely room for one person on the bed, let alone two."

"We'll make room. You need your sleep too. Stop being so Victorian."

What on earth did that mean? It didn't sound like a compliment. He crossed his arms. "Forgive me, madam, for being too Victorian for you. Whatever that descriptor means."

"For Queen Victoria."

"We don't have a Queen Victoria. We have King George."

"Well, you will have a Queen Victoria soon and for quite some time."

"Then I'm not 'Victorian' yet."

She gave a half moan, half laugh. "Rhys, can we please stop arguing? I didn't mean anything by it."

"How backward you must think me." He shared his thought out loud. She came from the future, hundreds of years from his time. He'd read plenty of outlandish fiction growing up. *Gulliver's Travels* was one of his favorite books as a child, and his father had a signed first edition of Louis Sébastien-Mercier's *The Year 2440* where a man falls asleep and wakes up in Paris in 2440. Now he had fallen for a time traveler who might be Merlin's twin sister reborn.

Gwynedd had written about the compass of the soul. What was his compass? Because right now he had never felt more lost sitting in an inn in 1165.

He took time straightening the table and repacking the food for the night so the rats wouldn't come out. He'd spied one earlier downstairs.

Magellan lay down on the bed, curling up on her side. She had taken his coat and rolled it up to use as a pillow. He disappeared behind the screen to use the chamber pot, in disbelief he was being so intimate in front of anyone, let alone her. When he came back out, he found her eyes were closed and she had dozed off. He rinsed his hands in the water basin and wiped his face with the towel she had set out. Then he settled down in the chair to sleep. He stretched out his legs, leaning his head back against the wall. The chair was hard and unforgiving, but at the moment he was too tired to care. The oil lantern had dimmed to a soft glow, casting the room in warm shadows.

"What are you doing?" she demanded. He opened his eyes to find Magellan sitting up, glowering at him. "You're not sleeping there. This bed is big enough for both of us."

He refrained from commenting.

"I know you're still upset with me—"

"I'm not upset with you," he sighed. Of course he was still upset.

"Then come to bed," she challenged him. "You need rest just as much as I do. Who knows what we'll be facing tomorrow."

He remained silent.

"Rhys Sherwood, if you don't get in bed right now, then I'm going to sleep on the other chair. I swear I'll do it."

He found he was too exhausted to argue and went around to the other side. He took off his boots with blessed relief, luxuriating in the feel of his feet finally being free. Slowly, he lay back on the lumpy mattress and stared up at the ceiling. He tried to ignore the sensation of Magellan being only inches away from him and he closed his eyes, willing his body to relax. He was trying his hardest not to let any imaginings of her in his arms fill his head.

He must have fallen sound asleep, for the next thing he knew it was pitch black and the middle of the night.

Magellan let out a startled yelp and climbed on him, startling him awake.

She was lying fully on top of him, her body covering his like a blanket, a very soft feminine blanket.

She whispered, "Are you awake?"

His chest started to rumble with laughter, unable to help himself. She couldn't be serious. "Of course I'm awake. You're lying on top of me."

"I heard something under the bed," she hissed. "I think it's a rat." She was trying to make herself as small as possible, staying splayed across his chest and using him as a new mattress. His arms came around her to anchor her to him.

"There might be one," he teased, not in a hurry to ease her fears. Magellan lying on top of him was pure bliss. Every one of her curves molded perfectly to his body, as if God had made them to match.

"Are you serious?" She lifted her chin off his chest to stare at him, her eyes two luminous moons in the dark.

"You're the one who heard it." He couldn't resist teasing her again. "Or did you simply need a reason to climb on top of me and have your wicked way?" His eyes gleamed, his whole body waking up.

They stared at each other for a long moment, too many unspoken words between them. Then she kissed him, her lips soft and full of tenderness. The kiss was the balm he needed, and he deepened it, his passion igniting. He twisted, flipping her over so he could be on top and kissed her neck, his body now covering hers.

"Rhys . . ." Her hands trailed up his back as her legs wrapped around him. Their clothes were the only barrier between them. His body was on fire, his head full of windmills. He couldn't think.

"We can't," he whispered between ravishing her with his mouth and pressing closer.

"We can't?" she asked breathlessly, returning kiss for wonderful kiss.

"I refuse to make love in a rat-infested room."

"So you agree there is a rat?" she said between kisses.

He laughed at her sauciness and raised himself up on his elbows to look down at her. *This woman.* She smiled up at him and his breath caught. "Magellan . . ." He needed to say this. There would never be a better time. These four walls had become their temporary sanctuary, with the world waiting for them outside an unknown. Who knew what dangers tomorrow would bring?

What must it had been like when she had arrived in his time? How terrified she must have been. How courageous.

He whispered in the dark, "I'm sorry I didn't believe you. Please don't regret I'm here."

"I don't regret you're here."

"But I can see it in your eyes. I wanted to come with you. *I had to come* with you. There was no choice. Do you understand? I don't have any choice when it comes to you." He willed her to believe him.

She blinked up at him, her eyes growing suspiciously bright, her mouth quivering, and she hugged him tight. "I won't be able to say goodbye again."

"Then don't." He buried his face in her neck and breathed her in as he listened to the soft rise and fall of her chest. "We go on together," he said. "Where you go, I go."

She smoothed his hair away from his brow and repeated his words back. "Where you go, I go."

The kiss that followed was their promise. A most tender kiss. Then he turned on his side and tuck her close to him. They drifted off to sleep in each other's arms, their limbs entwined in the very picture of devotion. He tried not to worry about what tomorrow would bring.

*Waldeinsamkeit* was the German word for the sublime spiritual feeling one had being alone in the forest. He and Magellan were deep in the forest, in the labyrinth, alone in time, and the feeling was sublime. He took a long, steady breath full of resolution. The world was depending on the woman in his arms, and he would do everything in his power to help her.

# Chapter 36

## Magellan

The next morning was filled with quiet tenderness and few words as they dressed and prepared for the day. Magellan's eyes landed on the diary, lying on top of the satchel. She only had until Winter Solstice to find the women. Now it was almost mid-November, which didn't leave much time.

Rhys seemed to be thinking the same thing. "We should find Hildegard first and then I'll finish translating it."

She nodded, her pulse speeding at the thought of going back outside into a medieval world to find Hildegard of Bingen. She didn't want to worry about what would happen after she found her, but they had to have a plan in place. Now was the time to make one before they unlocked that door.

"Rhys, after we find Hildegard of Bingen, we have to be prepared."

"What do you mean?"

"After I met with Fanny, things changed." She didn't know how to describe what happened. "Those men who were coming after us when we were on our way to the church. They knew I had the song."

"But they were thieves from the streets. How could they know?"

"They did. And there were moving shadows on the ground." She didn't even want to talk about the hellish sounds that had assaulted her. Within the noise had been a malevolent force seeking to annihilate life.

"You were distressed by the storm," he reminded her.

"Distressed." She frowned. Was he seriously trying to downplay what happened? She fought her irritation. They had just made up and she didn't want to argue again. "What I'm saying is after I get the song's part, we have to get back to the standing stone right away."

"Don't worry. We will," he reassured her. Magellan nodded, trying to assuage her fears, but the thought of what might happen after she played the song again was terrifying. He didn't understand. He asked, "So you think she'll be at Rupertsburg?" as he finished packing up the satchel.

She put her shoes on, the pain from her blisters not as bad this morning. "I think it's our best bet. I just don't know how far away it is."

Rhys put a few more coins into a smaller purse and tucked it into his pants. The larger purse went back into the satchel. "We'll find her," he said, slinging the satchel over his shoulder. "Especially given how famous she was in her own time."

That did give Magellan some hope, because it was true. All of Europe knew Hildegard of Bingen. She was a living legend, a mystic and musical genius. Truly one of a kind. Hildegard of Bingen believed in the splendor of being human and the divinity of women. She was a feminist, freely explaining her beliefs on the mechanics of sex and how Divine Love worked, and declared a woman's womb to be the most sacred seed on Earth. She believed ultimate truth lived in music, the language of God. For it was sound that gave birth to the world. Of course Hildegard held part of the song. How could she not? A sense of determination filled Magellan. She and Rhys would find her.

Before they left the room, Rhys gave her a final embrace, belaying his own fear of the outside. "Promise me you'll be careful today." He gazed down at her, consumed with worry. "And stay close."

"I promise." She wrapped her arms around him and pressed her cheek against his chest. Last night she had listened to his heart beating like a calming metronome as she drifted back to sleep.

When they left the room, Rhys gave the tavern woman several shillings for one more night, just in case they needed the room again.

He cautiously led the way through the market. First, he bought a salted pretzel, smoked sausage, and an assortment of apples to replenish their satchel. Next, they bought wine and ale in sturdy pottery jars with lids Rhys said were called flagons.

"I'd give anything for a glass of water," she grumbled. This morning they'd finished the flask of water from 1829.

"Only if you want to get sick. It's undrinkable unless thoroughly boiled. Everyone sticks to ale and wine."

"Is that why everyone looks drunk?"

"Precisely. Come on." He led her forward through the throng. The market looked even more sprawling today, full of traders from all over Europe selling every kind of good imaginable. Rhys bought a cloth hat and a colorful tunic that fell to his knees. He slipped it on over his shirt and belted it. Magellan laughed, and he gave her a rueful look.

She teased him, "You're looking very with the times, my lord."

"I look like a squire from a Shakespearean comedy—or tragedy," he said grimly. At least he wasn't so conspicuous now.

They continued through the wonderland of stalls with artisans performing metalworking, glass blowing, and wood whittling. "Look!" She pointed at a stall of musical instruments and dragged Rhys over to it by the hand.

A display of medieval violins hung on a thick cord. They were larger than the modern violin and had five strings instead of four. Magellan had never played one before. She'd only seen them in history books.

The man in charge of the booth saw her excitement and asked her a question. She shook her head in apology, signaling she didn't understand.

"Do you want one?" Rhys asked her.

She shot him a *Do you even need to ask?* look.

He grimaced. "To replace Oliver's?"

She laughed. "Oliver's was a violin and this is a vielle, a more medieval version of the violin. But yes, I need something to play for Hildegard when I see her." A vielle would do nicely. These instruments were lovely.

Rhys did his best to communicate with the man, but the seller didn't understand him. He tried another language and the man answered back.

"He speaks Latin," Rhys told her, excited. Then the two men were off having a chat. Magellan was only half listening, busy inspecting the vielles. The man gestured, encouraging her to try one. She took it under her chin, deftly adjusting the strings into tune, and played a simple melody. The man applauded with delight.

"He says you play well. I told him you were still learning," Rhys said with a teasing glint in his eyes. "I asked if he knew Hildegard. You're right. She is famous. He says she's here in Frankfurt."

Magellan turned to him in surprise. It was too much to hope for. "She's not at one of the abbeys?"

"Frankfurt's first-ever international fair is going on. She and the other nuns have come for it. Their camp is by the woods."

After Rhys paid, Magellan tried to convey her thanks to the instrument maker and set off with Rhys hand in hand. "Thank you. I love it."

They maneuvered through the throng of people until they were at the end of the market, where a huge field stretched to the beginnings of the forest. Various traveling groups and families had erected camps all along the grass.

Magellan scanned the field until her eyes landed on a quiet camp, nestled near the trees. A plain white banner blew in the wind with a rose in the center. Gazing at the banner, for a moment she thought of the roses growing at the center of Rhys's labyrinth.

Before they went any farther she grabbed hold of his sleeve. "Wait. Just say I do get the song—"

"You will. That is the plan."

"That's not my point. Afterward we might need to make a run for it."

"What do you mean by 'make a run for it'?"

"To the standing stone."

His eyes flashed with surprise. "You literally mean for us to run back to the standing stone? You realize how far a distance we would need to traverse, and you have blisters on your poor feet."

"Forget about my feet. I know you didn't want to believe me at the inn when I said I was hunted after I got the song."

Rhys looked around, but no one was paying them any attention. "It's not that I didn't believe you, but I do think in that particular moment, your emotions were running away from you."

"Are you for real right now?"

"What does that mean? I do believe this is real, yes."

She could feel her frustration growing. "That's not what I meant. Gwynedd warned us what would happen, and I'm telling you it happened and will happen again!"

Rhys looked embarrassed by her raised voice, but she couldn't help it. He said, "Magellan, my love," his cheeks becoming red. "The standing stone is a half day's walk, and I have not seen anywhere to secure an animal. By the time we get there it will be night, and if the stone doesn't take us somewhere else, we will be stuck in the wilderness with wild animals and rabid criminals who happen by."

She listened to him, wide-eyed. He did have a good point.

"I think the best course is we get the song and go back to our room, which has a door with a lock. We will stay one more night and set out early in the morning."

She deliberated, still worried. "And what is plan B?"

"Sorry, what is a *planby*?" He said it as one word.

"No. *Plan. B.* As in A, B, C, D. We have to have another plan in case we have to make a run for it."

He hesitated. "Is *running* something people do a lot in the future? Because you keep referring—"

"OMG. Forget it." She threw up her hands in surrender. "Let's just go." Determined, she took his hand with a firm grip and led the way.

# Chapter 37

𝄢

## Rhys

Rhys made a mental note that people in the future use single letters to communicate, like a secret code. He wondered what *o-m-g* meant but knew now was not the time to ask or tell her how adorable she was when she was huffing in irritation.

"What are you going to say to her?" He increased his pace to keep up as Magellan marched determinedly through a motley crew of scary-looking knights and medieval chaps to reach the abbey's tents. He tried not to focus on the grizzly men walking about. He had yet to buy a sword but would do so right after meeting the musical nun.

"More like what will you say. Not everyone speaks Latin." Magellan nudged his side with her elbow, and he could feel his chest puffing up with pride. Ridiculous though it was. Never had he thought his Latin studies would be put to so much use. Even though finding the song was Magellan's mission, he wanted to be useful to her. He still needed to translate the rest of the diary, which he planned to do later today.

She was heading toward the tent, pulling him by the sleeve and speaking quickly. "Tell her I'm a musician from a faraway land, and I heard of her music. Tell her I would like to present the gift of a song."

Rhys focused on the matter at hand. He agreed that was the best course as far as introductions went and said as much to the woman hovering at the tent's opening. Was she a nun too? All the women at the camp looked nothing like nuns. They were dressed in fine silk robes with fur trim and silver belts. Their long hair was adorned with flowers for the fair. The woman at the tent's opening looked to Magellan and her vielle with a bright smile and ushered them inside. The interior was roomy but modest, with an assortment of straw beds and simple furniture the women most likely had transported by cart.

In the back of the tent an elderly woman sat at a small table, her hand moving with incredible speed as she wrote on parchment. She looked small and frail but had a quiet strength about her.

The woman who'd escorted them went to her and bent over, speaking softly. The elder woman stopped writing and turned to them. Rhys felt Magellan stand up taller, as if she were meeting a queen, and Rhys knew they'd found Hildegard of Bingen.

The woman making introductions spoke in Latin so Rhys could understand. Hildegard kept her eyes trained on them both and answered with a soft voice.

As Rhys translated for Magellan, his eyebrows rose. "She says she had a dream you would come. She has a song for you too."

Magellan had told him the legend, how the woman was supposedly gifted with the ability to see the future. Had Hildegard foreseen their arrival?

She beckoned Magellan forward, and Magellan joined her at the table. Wasting no time, Magellan tucked the vielle under her chin and took a deep breath. Her eyes darted to the tent's opening to outside, and a glimmer of fear crossed her face. Her apprehension made Rhys apprehensive. He'd tried to ease her worry earlier about what came after she possessed the song. Had he been wrong to do so? They would hurry to the standing stone first thing in the morning. It's not as if he wanted to stay in 1165 any longer than necessary, but they couldn't just traipse around in the dark. That would surely lead to their demise. Plus, they had no lantern or compass. Returning to the inn and locking themselves in the room was the best plan.

He was so busy reassuring himself that when Magellan started to play, it startled him out of his thoughts. She was playing the same music he had heard her play with Fanny Mendelssohn.

The melody brought gooseflesh to his arms, and he felt a deep sense of peace descend over his body. The song was moving and powerful . . . and yet still a part of his intellect wondered, *Could this song truly save the world?*

The music didn't strike him as particularly "all-empowering" to produce magical effects or keep the North and South Poles intact. Still, he watched Hildegard listen to Magellan with an intent gaze. Then the woman placed a harpsichord-like instrument on her lap and began to play too.

Magellan knelt beside her, intently listening and watching Hildegard, as if trying to memorize every note. The two women didn't seem to need words to communicate with each other. After the woman was finished, Magellan took the harpsicord from her, sat down in the opposite chair, and miraculously played Hildegard's part of the song perfectly from memory. When she finished, the nun nodded and laid her hands on Magellan's and said a blessing. Then Magellan stood, looking a bit dazed.

"Is that it?" Rhys asked her gently. "You . . . heard what you needed to?"

Magellan nodded, a faraway look in her eyes, as if she were still hearing the song. "Yes, we can go now."

To Rhys it all felt a bit anticlimactic. That was all? They were done?

They bowed to the nuns and were shown outside again. The sunlight was blinding in comparison to the shadow-laced intimacy inside the tent. Rhys looked out to the swarming market. He wasn't sure if it was his imagination, but people were staring at them—or more like glaring.

The world around them suddenly felt incredibly and undeniably wrong.

"Should we head to the inn?" Rhys took her hand protectively in his, again cursing himself for not buying a sword yet. People *were* staring at them with a clear malice as if they knew he and Magellan did not belong in their time.

A band of those bloodthirsty knights from before were now studying Magellan with a wild lust in their eyes. Bloodlust. One of the men said something to the others, and they started making their way toward her across the field.

"Rhys." Her voice shook with panic. She had seen them too. "Do you hear that? It's here. It found us." She tried plugging her ears and looked to be in pain.

All he could hear was the racing of his heart. "Now I understand what you meant about plan B." He did an about-face and dragged her quickly toward the large crowd gathering for a musical performance on the other side of the field. A group of merry musicians had banded together to play. One of them was the instrument maker who had sold them the vielle. The man saw Magellan join the audience and motioned for her to come play with them.

Rhys led her toward him. "Get inside their circle. Play and maneuver your way to the church over there. I'll go around." She would be safer surrounded by people. Right now, they were deep in the crowd, and he could no longer see the knights.

"We should stick together," she said and circled about in terror. It was clear she was hearing something he couldn't.

"I'll follow in the crowd," he urged her. "Meet me at the church. Hurry."

She nodded and stepped into the circle. In one fluid motion she brought the vielle to her chin and joined the song. Only she was playing harder and faster than anyone, as if she were dueling with a force no one else could see or hear. In that moment she was a wielder of music, a force to be reckoned with.

Rhys couldn't help but stop for a moment to watch her in wonder. People began clapping, not understanding what they were witnessing.

He was so riveted, the snap of the satchel strap on his shoulder took him by surprise. He whirled around in shock to find the small thief running away.

A boy had cut the satchel with a knife.

"Stop!" Rhys called out, chasing after him.

Everything they had was in that bag. All their possessions. His purse. Their food. Her medicines.

The diary.

He ran harder, keeping sight of the boy who was about to enter the market's maze, where Rhys would surely lose him. He heard Magellan calling to him from behind, but he didn't dare stop. Stretching his legs farther, he leapt and grabbed onto the boy's shirt.

What he was not expecting was the boy's swift turn and the dagger he plunged into his chest.

The abrupt attack froze Rhys in his tracks. In one stark moment he saw the boy's vicious grin, the evil in his eyes. Then the boy wrenched the knife out of him and ran off. Rhys fell to his knees.

He was too shocked to call out as he watched the boy disappear into the market with the satchel. The world began to sway in his sights. A moment later Magellan was beside him, her hands all over him. She was crying and calling his name.

His vision began to blur. "He took the diary. I couldn't get it back."

"I don't care about the diary!" she said, hysterical, and called out for help.

"No! Don't attract attention. The knights." He had to get her away from the knights.

Suddenly his eyes were riveted to the ground. Dark shadows were approaching like an unnatural fog as the sounds around him became muted. He could no longer hear the world.

"What is that?" he whispered, unable to believe his eyes. His voice sounded underwater to his ears. Behind the moving shadows, the band of knights came toward them with their eyes on Magellan as if she was the prize.

She gripped him in desperation and forced him to rise to his feet with a strength he didn't know she possessed. "Run!"

His body shivering with shock, he grabbed Magellan's vielle. She would need it. Together they stumbled to the church.

She yelled again, "Run!"

The crazed knights were almost upon them. He and Magellan ran past the oak tree at the church doors. The tree must have marked the hallowed ground like a sentry, because the knights would not cross it. They stood screaming behind its trunk like demons as shadows writhed around them. The sight was paralyzing. To Rhys they looked like a visage straight out of Dante's *Inferno* and the Circles of Hell. He forced himself to turn away and keep going.

Inside the church was empty. He was halfway to the altar when his body could go no further. Crumbling onto the stone floor, he lay down.

Magellan bent over him. She was framed by the vaulted ceiling of the basilica like a beautiful angel, weeping and begging him to stay with her. The lights around her began to dim as his vision failed.

His thoughts fading, the Arabic word *ya'aburnee* faintly floated across his mind, and he thought how now he understood its meaning: *You bury me.* He would die and she would live, as it should be, because he could not live without her.

"Go," he begged her. "Play and go. You must."

"I'm never leaving you. Where you go, I go. Remember?" She straddled her legs on either side of his waist to secure him to her. "You made me a promise, Rhys Sherwood. Do you hear me? You will not die!" She raised the vielle to her neck and played a long, powerful chord. The lone note sounded like a wail in the silence.

As she played on, Rhys looked up to see light surrounding her, the glow from the ring on her hand beyond beautiful. The whole space was transforming into a brilliant prism, like a star being born. Bathed in ethereal light, his mind and body infused with peace; he thought surely this was death. He closed his eyes and listened, flying away on the wings of Magellan's music to somewhere else.

# Chapter 38

## Magellan

Magellan kept playing, afraid to stop. She closed her eyes and played on as the world around her transformed into a spinning wheel of light, and she prayed for the Ley Lines to take them somewhere safe.

When the blinding light faded and the tilting sensation stopped, she opened her eyes to find she and Rhys were no longer on the floor of the church, and the violent noise from the shadows' attack was not ringing in her ears. She fought the urge to be sick from the aftermath. The sounds had been worse the second time and felt like a visceral strike on her nervous system. Her whole body was still shaking.

Now they were on the floor of a different church. She couldn't tell if Rhys was still breathing. She placed her fingers to his neck and after a moment of panic felt a faint pulse.

Behind the altar, a door opened and a small elderly man in priest's robes came out. He gave a cry of alarm when he saw Rhys bleeding on the floor and rushed to help. Words tumbled from him, which Magellan quickly identified as Italian.

"*Per favore*, please help him," she begged. She didn't know enough Italian to communicate. She knew only a few words from her time playing operas.

The priest called out and two young men in long brown robes came hurrying from the back room. He spoke to them with urgency, and one of the men ran off, hopefully to get help. The priest and the other man lifted Rhys with some difficulty and carried him through the door behind the altar, leaving Magellan to follow helplessly.

The door past the altar led to a large sitting room, and beyond that was a hallway full of smaller rooms with sleeping quarters. They carried Rhys to the end of the hall, to a room with two twin cots and a small table, and laid him on one of the beds. The knife wound was still bleeding badly.

The priest fired off questions at her. She shook her head, unable to stop weeping. "I don't understand."

He lifted Rhys's shirt and tried to slow the bleeding with cloths. Magellan knelt by Rhys's head to stay out of the way.

Countless minutes later another man came, dressed in long black robes and carrying a leather bag. Magellan desperately hoped he was a doctor. Right away he took over, directing the men in a severe, no-nonsense way. Bowls of water were brought in and more cloth. He cleaned the stab wound and then poured a liquid from a vial over Rhys's chest, causing Rhys to scream in agony. Magellan shot up in alarm.

"What is he doing?" she cried out, but no one paid her any attention. Rhys was at these men's mercy. She watched as the doctor pressed hard on his chest, wrenching another scream from him. The knife wound was inches above his heart. The man directed the other men to hold Rhys down as he prepared the needle and thread.

Magellan stayed kneeling near Rhys's head, tucked in the small space beside the cot. She stroked his hair and tried to assure him. "I'm here. I'm right here."

When the doctor jabbed the needle into his chest, Rhys screamed, lurching off the bed, but the men held him down. The doctor didn't take long. He worked quickly, not seeming to care his patient was writhing in agony. The knife wound wasn't wide, but it appeared to be deep. Fortunately, Rhys passed out halfway through the procedure. When the doctor was finished, he placed padding over the stitches and wrapped Rhys's chest and shoulder in a binding.

After he finished, the doctor turned his focus on her and launched into a harsh slew of Italian. It sounded like a lecture, as if she had stabbed him. Whether he was asking her questions or giving instructions how to take care of Rhys, she couldn't tell. She shook her head helplessly, not understanding a word. The priest said something, then the doctor scowled at them all and stormed out. The priest gave her an apologetic look and hurried after him.

Magellan knelt beside Rhys, taking his hand. He was barely breathing, his skin deathly pale. They should have left 1165 quicker. They should have bought a horse before she met Hildegard so they could have ridden straight to the standing stone as soon as she'd gotten the song. Gwynedd had said never to linger, to do so at her own peril. Now Rhys might die.

Tears ran unchecked down her face. She stayed kneeling on the ground. She could only pray, *Let him live, let him live, let him live,* unable to stop repeating the words.

Sometime later the priest returned with a plate of food and drink. He set it gently on the table, then helped her stand.

He laid his hand on his heart. "Giuseppe."

Magellan put her hand on hers. "Magellan."

He repeated it back, haltingly. She took his hand, unable to hold back the fresh wave of tears.

"*Grazie*, Father Giuseppe. *Grazie.*"

Father Giuseppe patted her hand and motioned for her to eat. He blessed the food, lit a candle, and then left her alone again.

Magellan stood in the center of the room, unsure what to do. She sat down to watch Rhys sleep, taking small comfort in the rise and fall of his chest. The world was ending in the future, and they had lost the diary. She didn't even want to contemplate the ramifications of that fact. Right now, she needed to get Rhys out of here, wherever here was, but to do that she needed the song. The Ley Lines had sent them to this time to find someone. But she couldn't leave Rhys alone, not like this. She would wait for him to recover. If he recovered.

Her heart lurched at the thought. Of course he would recover. He had to.

She knelt by his bedside again, holding his hand. She must have fallen asleep that way, because when she woke it was the middle of the night. The length of the candle burning down was the only indication of time passing. Rhys was back to moaning, his face flush with fever. At dawn Father Giuseppe came and checked on them. He brought fresh water and encouraged her to sit down and eat when he saw she hadn't touched the tray. She forced herself to eat bread to keep from having an attack, but she didn't taste a thing. Right now she was adrift, unable to function until Rhys opened his eyes again.

She choked on a sob. Someone had stolen the diary from her. Now life was trying to take Rhys from her as well. She gripped his hand, willing her strength to him, trying to anchor him to her.

"Stay with me, Rhys. If you leave me, I can't do it. I can't do this without you." How had she ever thought she could do this without him? Leave him in 1829. This man who had her heart.

For hours she tried coaxing him awake. She threatened him, then pleaded and begged. She told him stories of her life, of the future, and everything he would miss if he didn't wake up. She even proposed marriage if he would just get better.

"You're going to wake up, and I'm going to court you," she whispered, kissing his hand and pressing her cheek to it. "I'll play you love songs. All the best ones." She would play every song from her playlists.

"You can sit beside me on the piano bench anytime you want." She choked back a sob. She would never send him away again.

---

Two more days passed. Two more days of waiting and praying in the twilight of despair as his body raged with fever. Magellan was trapped in a strange purgatory, a limbo she couldn't escape. They were somewhere in time's labyrinth. She had only part of the song, the first movement and the second, which Hildegard had given her in its entirety, a lyrical part full of beauty. Two women were still left to find, and she had to assume one was here in Italy, but Magellan couldn't rouse herself to leave the church. She'd been sitting by Rhys's bedside, praying and listening to the masses Father Giuseppe conducted on the other side of the wall. But Rhys wouldn't wake, and his fever hadn't broken. Had the world already ended and this was hell?

On the third day when Father Giuseppe came to Rhys's bedside and began to perform what looked like last rites, Magellan stood up in alarm.

"No no no!" Hysteria rose within her. "He's not . . . He's not . . ." *going to die*, but she couldn't say the words. She backed away, shaking her head in denial. Rhys needed another doctor. He needed medicine. He needed a better goddamned century than this one. Had antibiotics even been discovered yet? He could not die here. He had a life in 1829. He had a family who would never know what happened to him.

These last days sitting in a dark room in the back of a church, Magellan had become convinced Rhys had to survive because their love was part of the song. He was a part of the song—and a part of her. He was *her* love song, and she couldn't play a song for the world without him.

In a blind panic, she ran down the hallway to the doors leading outside the church. She had no idea what was waiting for her on the other side. Her hands hovered on the knobs, and every fear, every ounce of anxiety she had endured her whole life, returned all at once in a flood until she was drowning. She closed her eyes, breathing too fast and heavy.

She could do this. She just had to open the doors and walk through them.

Trying to calm down, she let out a long, deep hum, slow and steady, feeling the vibration from her voice fill her body.

She knew better than anyone nothing was more powerful than sound, and music was a universal prayer. So she stood at the church doors and hummed, feeling the sound's resonance filling her with power. *Her power.*

She threw open the doors to meet the outside world for the first time and blinked furiously at the sunlight. She was standing in the middle of a gorgeous city in some previous century with narrow cobblestone streets and vibrant buildings stunning in their artistry. Everyone was dressed in fine robes, speaking Italian and looking straight out of a Renaissance painting. In front of the church stood a pillar covered with public notices. Magellan scanned them to find the date.

1570.

The air puffed out of her. They were right smack dab in the Renaissance. But where?

She did a full circle, taking in the city, and her mouth fell open when she recognized the famous view from a postcard Wren had sent her when she had visited last year. A postcard with the famous lit dome of the Saint Mary of the Flower. In Florence.

They were in Florence, Italy, in 1570.

Magellan thought quickly. Only one woman in Florence could have the song. A woman whose quote was in fact framed on Magellan's wall. The first woman ever to publish her music. The first woman to also publicly chastise men for not allowing women to do so.

BBC radio had done a special on Maddalena Casulana for International Women's Day and performed a concert of her madrigals. A madrigal was popular in the Renaissance and Baroque periods. It was a vocal piece, performed by a group without any musical accompaniment. A form of musical poetry, madrigals reached their zenith in the 1500s, and Maddalena Casulana was the equivalent of Adele, Celine Dion, Mariah Carey, Aretha Franklin, and Alicia Keys all rolled into one. She also played the lute, which was the Renaissance guitar.

In her first book of madrigals, Maddalena had dedicated her songs to her patron Isabella de' Medici and had written in the dedication:

*"I want to show the world the vain error of men*
*that they alone possess intellectual gifts and believe*
*those same gifts are not possible for women."*

Maddalena was a giant in her own time and had fearlessly forged a path for other women in the future. She had shined so brightly, history had been unable to look away.

Filled with newfound determination, Magellan returned to the church and hurried back to their room. She would not lose Rhys to this place. She would find Maddalena and get him out of here.

She quickly ate the food Giuseppe had left for her, suddenly voracious. She shoved olives, bread, and cheese in her mouth and downed the wine. Then she braided her hair back and wiped her face. She slipped her hand into Rhys's tunic pocket hanging on the wall and found the few coins he had taken from the satchel.

Kissing his brow, she whispered, "I'm going to get the song. I'll be back." She tried not to think of the danger she would face or she would never leave this room.

Father Giuseppe was in the main sitting room behind the altar. When she found him, she held up her vielle and tried to communicate. "Maddalena Casulana?" Then she mimed playing and pointed to herself. "Student."

Father Giuseppe's eyebrows rose. "Maddalena Casulana? *Alluna?*"

Magellan had no idea what "alluna" meant, but she nodded and repeated it again. Father Giuseppe seemed to understand.

He led her outside, down the main street ending at the river, and they walked across an enormous stone bridge to a palace. It had to be the palace where Isabella de' Medici lived.

Isabella was Maddalena's influential supporter, a powerful woman in her own right. Magellan had watched a documentary on them both. Isabella had been murdered by her husband and brother. Magellan only hoped that tragedy was still years away or else she was walking into a murderer's den to find the song.

# Chapter 39

## MAGELLAN

Two guards stood at attention outside the palace like Renaissance bouncers. Father Giuseppe spoke imploringly to them and made several signs of the cross for good measure. Finally they were allowed inside. A guard escorted them, weaving his way through hallways and courtyards. Magellan's stress only began to lessen slightly when she heard the singing. Female voices were performing an exquisite madrigal, and she slowed down in wonder. She was listening to a bona fide Renaissance a cappella group.

They arrived at a grand conservatory where Maddalena stood at the helm, directing five young women while they sang. Maddalena was a large woman, gorgeous and voluptuous, a true Italian Venus. The group of women were alone, obviously rehearsing.

The guard directed Magellan and Father Guiseppe to take a seat in the row of chairs by the door. Magellan was too caught up in the performance to notice Father Giuseppe did not sit down with her. He murmured something in her ear and then left before she could stop him. Magellan tried not to panic at being abandoned and instead focused on listening to the women's performance. She tried not to think of Rhys still lying unconscious at the church or worry about the fact she spoke zero Italian and had only a medieval violin and a few coins in her pocket.

The nearby cabinet built into the conservatory wall caught her eye. It was opened to reveal a trove of musical instruments. Several lutes were toward the front.

Maddalena was a famous lutenist, and Magellan decided to forget the vielle in her hands. She needed to play the lute to make an impression.

The lute basically looked like an odd-shaped guitar. Technically it was the guitar before the guitar. The body was smaller, the neck wider, and there were more strings. The hole in its belly was called *the rose*. Two strings were often paired together and called courses. Magellan had no idea how many courses those lutes had. They were too far away for her to tell. She'd have to wing it.

Finally, the rehearsal ended. Maddalena made a speech to her singers, her voice rich and lush. No doubt she was offering a critique and instructions for next time. Then the group was dismissed.

A cleaning crew of servants came in as the singers filed out. They eyed Magellan with open curiosity. She was filthy. Magellan couldn't remember the last century she had bathed. She stood up and smiled, trying to hide her nerves.

Maddalena was following her singers out and looked to be in a hurry.

"Wait!" Magellan called out, but Maddalena only gave her a sniff and headed for the door.

Magellan ran to the cabinet and grabbed a lute. One of the maids started yelling, probably thinking she was trying to steal it. She was seconds away from being thrown into the palace dungeon, which no doubt existed.

Wasting no time, Magellan started to play as she hurried across the room toward the door Maddalena had just left. She played as loud and fast and hard as she could, using the lute in ways not imagined until Jimi Hendrix. The cleaning crew froze in shock as Magellan began an impromptu lute rock concert. She played in a fury of desperation. She played like Carlos Santana or B. B. King or Prince. She was Eddie Van Halen in a dirty dress. She couldn't even glance up, too busy managing the strings and the frets.

When she finally finished, she looked up to find Maddalena standing in the doorway with a stunned expression on her face. Then the woman rushed forward.

She ordered everyone out of the room in a loud, commanding voice, until they were finally alone. Maddalena's eyes were twin flames of intensity. She asked Magellan something, and Magellan shook her head in apology. "I don't understand."

They may not speak the same language, but they did speak music. Without hesitation Magellan played the song, the first three parts that she had, the symphony's two movements, and let every note speak for itself.

Maddalena listened with a riveted gaze. Then she went to the cabinet and pulled out a lute of her own. She sat on the stool, nodding for Magellan to join her, and began to play her part. It was magnificent. A lively dancing minuet.

In symphonies the third movement is often called the trio, the *scherzo*, or musical joke filled with joy, beauty, and laughter. The guardian's song's scherzo had been hidden within the Renaissance and entrusted to this woman.

Magellan felt like a young girl watching one of her heroes. Here was the artist who had trail blazed her way through her own time, where female oppression was rampant, and chastised everyone for thinking she couldn't be powerful. Maddalena was one hundred percent woman, unapologetic with her femininity, her generous breasts, rounded hips, and sensuality. Watching her made Magellan aware how her own fear had stopped her from putting herself out into the world, of risking failure and being judged. Instead, she had safeguarded herself. Only now was she realizing to truly live and love required risk, courage, and faith. The trio. For life at its core was a scherzo meant to be enjoyed.

Maddalena held her eyes as they played their lutes together, their heads inches apart, and the five hundred years separating their lives dissolved away.

When they finished, a sense of knowing passed between them. Magellan placed her hand over her heart in gratitude. Maddalena was overcome with emotion too and nodded back.

Magellan relinquished the lute and took her vielle in hand again. She could feel hope filling her. Maddalena had just given her the third movement of the symphony in its totality along with its energy. In this moment, Magellan felt invincible. She would make it back. She would heal Rhys. She would never give up.

---

Maddalena personally escorted her to the palace entrance. Outside the sun was setting, casting Florence in a golden light. Nearby a rough-looking group of young men sat on the wall's ledge and catcalled to them. Whatever they said must have been lewd, causing Maddalena to yell back, scolding them. Then she embraced Magellan, clasped both her hands in goodbye, and left.

Florence's rock star seemed to take all the sunlight with her when she went inside. The sky dimmed as rolling clouds began to gather in a mass to cover the sun. The wind picked up, and the men resumed their calling. One of them hopped off the ledge with a threatening glint in his eyes.

The rest of the men followed moments later like a wolf pack ready to hunt. Magellan tried to ignore them as she set out to cross the bridge. They were some distance away. Still they followed, jeering. She picked up her pace, the pathway over the bridge back to the church suddenly looking like a gauntlet she would have to run.

Her time in Florence had ended. She had gotten what she'd come for. Now she and Rhys had to leave before the labyrinth closed in on them.

She heard and felt the moment when the vortex arrived.

The streets narrowed and every cobblestone darkened with shadows as the city's golden light was eclipsed by a malevolence that had found its way in. The dissonant sounds that came were paralyzing, a deluge of discordant vibrations. Unmusical, unmelodious, screeching with pain and seeking to annihilate.

Her heart hammering in her chest, Magellan broke into a run, weaving in and out of the crowd as she tore down the bridge.

Right as she cleared it, the sound struck her like a blow and she stumbled. One of the men grabbed her from behind. She screamed and on pure instinct bashed his hand with her vielle. The man let go in pain, and she jumped up to keep on running.

The sound continued to attack her with sharp vibrations like sonic bullets, as if it had the power to invade her cells and destroy her from the inside. In a blind panic she began to hum a primal sound. A forceful chanting mantra to shield her body from its attack. It took all her breath to do it and keep on running. Her lungs were on fire.

She was right outside the church doors when the men caught up to her. Someone grabbed her and yanked her back, holding her neck in a vise while the other men circled her. He began choking her to stop her vocal defense. She kept the hum going as she clawed at his hands, knowing if she stopped the vibration she was generating in her body, the force would kill her.

People on the street erupted in Italian, witnessing the attack. An old woman began hitting one of the men with her cane, trying to help.

The commotion must have been heard from inside because the church doors flew open and Father Guiseppe and his fellow priests came running out with the entire congregation behind them. They poured onto the street and overcame the men, wrenching Magellan free. Father Guiseppe's assistants rushed her inside and then returned outside to help.

Magellan collapsed on the floor but forced herself to get back up. She ran down the hallway to her and Rhys's room and locked the door. When she turned around she screamed. Outside moving shadows covered the window, their vibrational force rattling the glass over and over, trying to find a way in. The glass was splintering and seconds away from breaking.

Frantic, Magellan gripped the vielle and sat beside Rhys on the bed, wrapping his arm around her waist to secure him to her.

She began to play—not Bach this time but *the song*.

More voices came from outside the door. She could hear Father Giuseppe yelling over the din. Not daring to stop, she kept on playing as the air around her began to sift with power.

A glowing light bloomed in her vision, becoming brighter and brighter from the ring on her finger as every note of the song reverberated in her chest. She played on, wedged against Rhys to not let him go, feeling the music spiral around them.

Father Giuseppe unlocked her door and walked in to catch a glimpse of them bathed in the music's brilliance before they vanished and dispersed into a thousand stars.

The priest sank to his knees in wonder, and Magellan heard the word from his lips right before she was gone.

*"Miraculum."*

*Miracle.* For it was.

# Chapter 40

## Magellan

Magellan lay still with her eyes closed, hearing only the blessed sound of silence. Then a soft wind brushed across her skin, and she could hear birds singing in the distance as the sounds of nature enveloped her like a healing balm. Opening her eyes, she found herself lying in the center of a labyrinth, Rhys's labyrinth at Hereford Manor.

Rhys was lying unconscious beside her. She stared up at the standing stones, dizzy with relief they'd landed someplace safe. They'd made it. They'd made it back. Then shock hit her hard and she couldn't stop shaking.

She sat up and felt her neck. The burning pain from the man choking her was gone. The song, when she played it, must have healed her.

"I'm going to get help. I'll be right back," she said, though Rhys didn't stir. She got up and ran into the labyrinth's corridor, still holding the vielle, and tried to remember the tune she had given the path.

While she hummed it, she fought the disbelief she was back in 1829. Right-left-right. Several times she made a wrong turn and had to retrace her steps, choking back sobs. She had to calm down. They were home. She thought she would never see this place again. She would find the countess and summon help. Rhys's mother would bring the doctor.

Magellan finally made her way out of the labyrinth. She emerged from the entrance and spotted a man in the distance near the gardens. He saw her at the same time and began to walk toward her with concern.

The closer he came, the more confused she became. He looked like Rhys. The resemblance was striking. They could have been brothers—even more so than Cecil—but she'd never met this man before. Did Rhys have another brother?

The man was puzzled by her as well. "May I help you? You are in distress." He grew more alarmed when he got a good look at her. She must be a sight in a dress that had been worn across seven centuries. He was dressed in fine clothes, and she saw Rhys's signet ring on the man's finger.

The ring only the earl was supposed to wear.

For a moment her thoughts turned fuzzy. Magellan looked around and realized the gardens seemed different. All the Greek statues were missing.

She turned back to him, unable to stop the quiver in her voice. "What year is it?" The man gave her a startled laugh, and she pressed, "Please. Tell me."

"1799."

Magellan's knees almost buckled. How had they ended up in 1799 and not 1829? Which meant . . . This could only be Rhys's father. Except right now he looked to be a few years younger than Rhys. "Are you Godwin Sherwood?"

His eyes widened in surprise, shocked either by the fact she knew his first name or had the nerve to ask him.

He gave her a playful bow. "The Earl of Liron, at your service." He nodded to the instrument in her hands. "Are you a forest nymph who has come to lure me into the timeless realm of Fairyland with your strange violin?"

She realized she was still holding the vielle in her hand. "No, I'm a . . . traveler." She grappled with what to say. "From America. And . . . my friend is lying wounded in the center of the labyrinth."

"Is this some kind of jest?"

"No. Godwin—sir Earl—please. I need your help. Right away." Without waiting for his answer, she turned and dashed back into the labyrinth.

She heard him call out "Wait!" But she was running ahead, humming the tune to get back to the center. She'd already left Rhys too long.

Godwin ran to catch up to her. "Wait! How do you know the way?"

She kept humming, right-left-right. She was almost there with Rhys's father following closely behind. Her mind was in a whirl. Why were they in 1799? This made no sense. She shouldn't be here. They had arrived thirty years off the mark. She reached the center with Godwin two steps behind her.

He saw Rhys lying on the ground and hurried to kneel beside him. "He's been stabbed?" he asked in shock. "How did you both get here?"

Magellan wasn't sure how to answer. She placed her hand with her ring on the standing stone beside its engraving. "I believe this was built by Merlin centuries ago?"

For a moment Godwin stared at her in disbelief. Then he looked to Rhys, and she wondered if it was feasible for a father to meet his unborn son. Were they disrupting the past and the future by being here? Right now, she was too terrified for Rhys to care. But surely Godwin saw the striking resemblance between them. Then he saw Rhys's signet ring on his hand.

"My word," he whispered and looked back to her, his eyes piercing. "Tell me quickly. The truth."

"We're both from the future, from different times. I traveled first and he ended up coming with me. The Ley Lines sent us here."

"The Ley Lines?" Godwin asked weakly, staring at her with a dazed look.

"Listen, we don't have time for you to process what I'm telling you. He needs help right away. Please! He's dying." Magellan choked on the hysteria rising within her. She was on the verge of falling apart.

Godwin seemed to realize how desperate the situation was and snapped to. "Let me get help to move him. I'll be right back." He stood up and backed away, looking afraid to turn his back on them. "You won't . . . vanish . . . will you?"

"Not unless I play this." She held up the vielle. "Please hurry."

Godwin hesitated, countless questions in his eyes, but he nodded and ran off.

Magellan wobbled for a moment, feeling faint with exhaustion. She sank down to her knees and grabbed Rhys's hand. "Rhys. You have to hang on." She closed her eyes and pressed his palm to her cheek, trying to keep her panic at bay. He couldn't die. He couldn't.

Minutes must have passed because Godwin was suddenly there with three footmen behind him. They had brought a makeshift stretcher made of canvas and wooden poles and carefully lifted Rhys onto it.

Magellan pulled herself to her feet and stumbled, her last reserves of energy gone. Godwin offered his arm to help her even though she was filthy. She shook her head. "Thank you, I can manage."

Godwin led the footmen out and she walked beside him, somehow making it to the manor without having to be carried too.

Godwin said, "I'm afraid I am at the disadvantage of not knowing your name."

"Magellan Brighton."

"And your friend?"

"Rhys." She almost added *Sherwood* but didn't.

Godwin gave her a sharp look but didn't comment. When they reached the manor, the butler was waiting with the door open. The footmen carried the stretcher through a series of hallways to an infirmary behind the kitchens on the ground floor.

Godwin said, "You're lucky you arrived when I was here. I was planning to return to London for the holiday season."

Magellan didn't even know what day it was anymore. Was it December yet? How many days had they wasted in the Renaissance? Time had become a blur. All she knew was they were running out of it.

She gave Rhys's father a faint smile, knowing luck had nothing to do with it. The Ley Lines had delivered them to this precise moment in time on purpose. Now she needed to find out why. But first, Rhys needed help.

"Tell me about his wound," Godwin said.

Magellan described what happened and what the doctor in Florence had done. Rhys had been unconscious with a fever for days.

Godwin instructed the housekeeper, "Bring me vinegar, honey, crushed garlic, and salt. Send someone to my laboratory. On the shelf is a crystal distillation of willow bark. I'll need all of it." The woman hurried off. He told another servant, "We'll also need boiling water, hot tea, and bone broth."

It took Magellan a moment to realize no doctor had been called. Godwin was to be the doctor. He put on little spectacles she recognized and was busy lifting Rhys's bandages and examining the wound.

"Nasty business. I'll need to reopen the stitches and flush it out."

Magellan nodded and sat down in a nearby chair before her legs gave way. The earl issued orders for a guest room to be readied for her with a bath, fresh clothes, and a tea tray. It sounded like a dream.

She shook her head. "I can't leave him."

"I don't need two patients, Miss Brighton."

"I'm not leaving. What if he wakes? He'll think—" She almost said *he died and went to heaven* but stopped.

Godwin seemed to realize she could not be persuaded. He went to the water basin at a large table and washed his hands. Then he doused them with a pungent liquid that smelled like alcohol. She watched him line up an assortment of clean surgical tools—a vast improvement from 1570—and select a pair of small scissors and tweezers. He ordered the remaining footmen to come and assist holding Rhys in case he woke.

"Hopefully he'll stay asleep through this."

He didn't.

Rhys woke up screaming when Godwin began taking out the inflamed stitches. Two large footmen had to hold him down. Magellan stood behind Rhys's head, her hands on his brow, trying to calm him.

She watched Godwin painstakingly flush the wound until the blood flowed bright red again. Then he cleaned it further with a concoction of things. Magellan had no idea what everything was. Rhys screamed the whole time.

He choked on her name. "Magellan."

"I'm here. I'm right here." She kissed his brow. "We're cleaning your wound to make it better."

Godwin lifted a brow at the tender gesture but kept on working. "Keep him steady," he told the footmen and then looked to her. "We're almost done."

At those words Rhys opened his eyes in shock and turned to him. "Father?" he asked before he passed out.

Godwin stared at him in bemusement. Then his eyes went to Magellan. Neither said a word. Godwin focused on stitching the wound. Then he coated it with a honey-like sludge and gently wrapped it with clean bandages. He placed cool towels on Rhys's neck, shoulders, and head. His eyes fell on Rhys's signet ring again.

Magellan was too weary to know how to explain. Fortunately, she didn't have to yet. Godwin said, "That is all I can do for him now. Let him sleep. I'll have someone stay to keep changing out the towels and give him the medicines to drink. Now I'm afraid my second patient desperately needs assistance as well."

She tried to protest. "I can't."

"You must. I insist. You can return after you have tended to your needs."

Magellan allowed herself to be escorted away by the young maid who'd been assigned to help her. The woman showed her to a guest room where a warm bath was being readied. A tray waited for her on the table with hot tea and finger sandwiches. Magellan all but inhaled the little rectangles filled with dilled cream cheese and smoked salmon. Then she ate two buttery shortbread cookies and chased it with a cup of tea laden with milk and sugar. Nothing had ever tasted so good.

Another cup of tea later, the hot bath was ready. The smell of fresh citrus soap made her want to weep. There was even a rinsing tub to start. With the maid's help she was able to get the worst of the dirt off before she submerged herself in the sunken tub. Then the woman helped shampoo her hair with a lavender-scented soap and left the room to give her time to soak.

Magellan closed her eyes with a blissful moan and lay in the water for a long time, letting her mind wander. Rhys had to recover. They were not through the labyrinth. They still needed one more part of the song. *He will recover*, she tried to convince herself, willing it to be true. Then she would figure out who she needed to meet in 1799.

She lay back in the water, too tired to think anymore. The maid came back with a fresh gown and undergarments she said belonged to the earl's mother, who was in London. The gown was a completely different style than what Magellan had worn in 1829. This one had a Grecian silhouette with an empire waist and was infinitely more comfortable. There was no corset either. The maid swept up Magellan's hair, even though it wasn't yet dry, and wove it into a crown on her head.

Magellan rose, anxious to return to Rhys. "Thank you for your help."

A footman came and instead of escorting her to the infirmary, he took her to the salon where the earl was waiting. Godwin stood and bowed. He had changed for dinner. His eyes gleamed with appreciation when he saw her. For a moment he looked terribly like Rhys.

She asked him, "Could you show me the way to the infirmary, please?"

"Later." He waved a regal hand. "He has nursemaids aplenty seeing to his needs. Right now he is sleeping soundly."

"I would still like to check on him."

"After dinner, I insist. We have much to talk about."

Magellan smiled faintly, desperately wishing Rhys were here with her. She did not want to be the one to explain this all to his father. What if he took it badly? Should she tell him who Rhys really was?

They arrived at the dining room, where a footman held out a chair for her while Godwin waited for her to sit first. He took a seat beside her at the head of the table. It was just the two of them and an army of footmen.

He said, "I admit I do not recognize the fairy nymph I met this afternoon. I would have to say now it must be Aphrodite who has come to visit Hereford Manor."

Magellan gave a startled laugh, meeting his dancing eyes. Was Rhys's father flirting with her? And where was the countess? Rhys's mother was noticeably missing.

"Thank you, and thank you for the borrowed clothes."

Godwin brushed aside her thanks with another wave and dismissed the servants, telling them, "Please leave us, and close the doors."

Magellan swallowed, trying not to panic. It felt a bit like waiting for the Inquisition, because the interrogation was about to begin. She stared at the table instead of Rhys's father. An assortment of dishes had been set out so they could serve themselves. Godwin prepared her plate while he said, "I thought it might be more practical to serve ourselves so that we may talk freely without other ears listening."

He placed a full plate before her and surprised her by getting straight to the heart of the matter. "You are correct. The stone circle was supposedly built by Merlin. There is a family legend that the center of Hereford's labyrinth protects a doorway to other times. My grandfather told me once he met a *traveler* who walked out of the labyrinth claiming he was from another century. I always thought it a fanciful story." He fingered his wineglass. "Why don't you tell me your version and then I'll decide."

His eyes were keen, his words an open invitation, and her angst suddenly melted away—and she knew, just as she had been fated to meet Rhys, she'd been fated to meet Godwin too.

Perhaps it was the candlelight or the excellent 1790 vintage wine, but over the course of dinner Magellan told him everything. The words poured from her easily. Instead of starting the story with the day the aurora borealis arrived in New York, she started with her childhood, with her being adopted by two elderly historians, her years being taught by Garesh, her discovery she could play any instrument without faltering, and Garesh gifting her the ring before he left.

She recounted the day the aurora borealis arrived, how the Earth's poles were attempting to flip, and how she'd played the pipe organ and ended up in the past. She explained waking up in the labyrinth and meeting Rhys. She did not say exactly when, because Rhys was wearing the family signet ring and was the Earl of Liron in 1829.

"Rhys is my son," Godwin said quietly.

Magellan hesitated and nodded.

"How many children do I have?"

"Do you really want to know?" she asked softly.

Godwin slowly shook his head with a poignant smile. "No, forgive me. Do go on."

Magellan left out any mention of the countess, Cecil, or Vivianne, and when she mentioned Gwynedd's diary being the key to it all, Godwin started to laugh. He tipped his head back and laughed out loud. He couldn't seem to stop, which in turned caused her to stop talking. Was he drunk? They had gone through quite a bit of wine. Perhaps she should resume the rest of the story tomorrow. She hadn't even mentioned the song and why they'd been propelled through time.

"So my son is translating this diary? Which I take it means he knows Old English?" Godwin was asking her.

"Yes. He's very good with languages."

"I should hope so if he's the heir to Hereford Library." Godwin smiled to himself as if enjoying a private joke. "What happened to this diary?"

"It was stolen from us in Frankfurt. That's how Rhys got wounded."

"*Ah.* And the Ley Lines, you say, brought you here."

"Yes, after 1570 where a doctor tended to him." She had yet to get into the specifics.

"How much do you believe in destiny, Magellan? A little or a lot?" Godwin had a mischievous glint in his eye. He and Rhys might look similar, but Godwin's personality was nothing like Rhys's. He was much more playful.

Magellan hesitated. Such a simple question, and she'd drunk her fair share of wine too tonight. "A lot."

"Excellent. Then follow me." Godwin nodded and stood up, offering her his arm. "I have something I need to show you."

He led her from the dining room down the hall to the east wing. She knew the way. They were going to the library.

He told her, "I take great pride in Hereford's library. We have one of the finest collections of ancient texts in all of Europe, which is why I am always acquiring more." He hesitated, and suddenly Magellan felt full of anticipation when he said, "I recently acquired a book."

He led her to the table by the alcove. The same desk Rhys would use in thirty years.

And there lying on top was Gwynedd's diary surrounded by fresh notebooks and a stack of dictionaries.

Magellan couldn't speak, too choked by emotion.

The triskelion carved into the leather gleamed in candlelight.

"You have it," she whispered.

Godwin's sharp eyes gauged her reaction, missing nothing. "You're saying this book was stolen from you in 1165?"

She nodded, afraid to touch it.

"It recently came up for sale from a collector. Given Hereford is the guardian of Merlin's stone circle, I am quite taken with any stories revolving around him and the Druids. But I have never read a personal account about his sister."

Magellan reached out and traced the triskelion with her fingertip.

"The diary just arrived today. Right before you, in fact." He raised his quizzing glass to his eye and stared at her to make his point. "I believe that is what would be called divine timing."

Magellan nodded, tears welling in her eyes. The diary had come back to her. Godwin had unknowingly retrieved it for them with what felt like destiny's hand. She had long since begun to believe Gwynedd was a part of her. And it seemed Gwynedd's triskelion was too.

Gwynedd, Merlin, and Taliesin had been a triskelion over a thousand years ago. *Two comets and a North Star.* Now Magellan felt as if she had found the missing piece of their journey. And it wasn't the diary. It was Godwin.

# Chapter 41

𝄢

## Rhys

The first thing Rhys saw when he opened his eyes was a bouquet of red roses. A vase sat on the table beside him. For a moment he had no idea where he was. He was lying on a bed. His whole body hurt. A thick padded bandage wrapped around his entire chest—then it all came back to him, chasing the boy, the knife.

*Magellan!*

In a panic, he tried to sit up, but the pain stopped him.

Were they still in 1165? Where was she?

His eyes darted frantically around the room. It took him a moment to realize he recognized this place. He was in the infirmary at Hereford Manor. He was back home. But how?

Alarmed, he sat up, not caring about the pain, and tried to get out of bed. The room spun, and he fell back, unable to control the dizziness as black spots intruded on his vision. His whole body was shaking with weakness.

Where was everyone? Where was she?

As if he'd called her to him, Magellan walked into the room. At first he thought he was dreaming, because she didn't look like herself. She was wearing a dress decades out of fashion. Her hair was styled differently too and swept up into intricate curls.

"Rhys!" She ran to his bedside and put her arms around him, tears in her eyes. "Rhys."

"How . . ." He couldn't get the words out, his throat too dry. He tried again to speak. "How did we get back home?"

She pulled away from him with an odd look. "We're not exactly home." She gave him a glass of water to drink and helped him sit up. He winced at the movement but was too thirsty and guzzled it down.

"How long have I been asleep?"

"A week." She bit her lip, as if hesitating to say more.

He couldn't fathom the lost time. "What happened in Frankfurt? We were at the church." He'd begged her to leave him, and she had refused. Where you go, I go, she had said.

"We ended up in Florence in 1570."

If he wasn't lying down his legs would have given way. "*Florence?* In 1570?" How could that be? He had no memory of it. He felt untethered, as if his thoughts were floating about him and he couldn't grab hold of them.

He tried to focus as Magellan told him how they'd ended up in another church. A kind priest had taken them in. He'd brought a doctor to heal him, but the man had only made it worse. While Rhys lay fighting for his life, she had found the Florentine woman who had the song, Maddalena Something—he didn't recognize the name—and then the Ley Lines had brought them here.

He could see in her eyes she wasn't telling him the full story. What she must have gone through alone or how she had gotten them here. He had so many questions, he didn't know where to start.

"What do you mean we aren't exactly home?" His eyes went to the window. He could see the gardens from here. Throughout his childhood he'd paid countless visits to the infirmary. Usually, his father would bandage his cuts and scrapes. Godwin had enjoyed playing nursemaid. He had a fascination for human anatomy to add to all his other fascinations and had always said he would have been a village doctor if not for his title. The bed in this room was used only for the worst of injuries or most serious illnesses. Rhys must have been in bad shape if he didn't remember being brought here. He frowned. Why had they returned home when Magellan only had four parts of the song and needed the fifth?

"We're not in 1829."

He almost missed her words, so deep in thought. His eyes flew back to hers and he saw her hesitate again.

"Rhys . . . your father is alive. We're in 1799."

He felt his breath rush away from him, as if all the air had been sucked out of the room. 1799? He hadn't been born yet. His father hadn't even met his mother.

*His father* was here.

"We arrived in the labyrinth?" Rhys asked her, though he already knew the answer. Of course they had. It wasn't as if they could have knocked on the front door. "You met him?"

She nodded, a soft smile forming. "He's the one who's been tending you. He fancies himself a doctor."

Rhys lay back on his pillow overwhelmed. He'd been unconscious for days, missed the Renaissance entirely, and his dead father who he had mourned was playing nursemaid to his knife wound. It was all too much.

"That's not all." Magellan leaned forward and took his hand. The light in her eyes took his breath away. "He has the diary."

"What?" That announcement cut through every other thought whirling in his head.

"He bought it from a collector. It arrived the same day we did. He's been in the library translating it. We'll be able to read the final pages."

Her shocking news caused a strange sludge of emotions to churn within him. The first one being *shame* he was the one to have lost the diary. *Embarrassment* his father was cleaning up his mess. And *jealousy*

Godwin was translating the last of it and not him. Rhys was the diary's translator and faithful scribe, and he had failed. He had failed in his one duty for Magellan. He closed his eyes, suddenly tired, even though he'd been asleep for days.

Magellan was oblivious to the self-pity and criticism currently consuming him. She offered him some broth, which he sipped gratefully. He felt as weak as a newborn lamb.

"I should go tell him you're awake." She made a move to rise, and he grabbed her hand.

"Not yet. Please. I'm not ready."

She sat down again and squeezed his hand in understanding. "Of course."

"Tell me, what happened in Florence?" He tried to change the subject. Anything to keep him from thinking about the meeting he would soon be having with his father.

While Magellan told him about Father Giuseppe and her time with Maddalena, Rhys tried to listen, but his thoughts kept wandering. What would he say to him? Magellan was still holding his hand, and he wasn't sure he could ever let it go.

"Thank you, for saving me." He kissed her hand. "I'm sorry for Frankfurt. I should have taken your concerns more seriously about . . . the darkness that would come after."

Gwynedd had warned them about the lower dimensions. What had happened was something he still couldn't fathom. All he knew was after Magellan had played the song, a dark force had entered the labyrinth, hunting for the light.

"No, I'm sorry. I should have insisted we buy a horse first so we could leave right away or none of this would have happened."

"It's not your fault," he said firmly. "I was the idiot."

"We were both not thinking clearly," she amended. "But that is all in the past now. Literally seven hundred years ago."

He gave her a weak smile, exhausted. "Does he know who I am?"

"Yes."

What a quagmire. He took in her outfit again. "Is that my grandmother's dress?" She cut a dashing figure in a 1799 dress.

She grinned at her attire. "I believe it is. Godwin lent it to me. He said she's in London."

*Godwin.* She was on first-name basis with him. "How long have we been here?"

"Four days."

Four days. What had she and his father talked about for four days?

"Godwin is almost finished with the translation." She had a smile on her face again when she said his father's name. As if they shared some private amusement.

She had met Godwin without him. Talked with him. Probably taken meals with him. Had sat in the library with him and watched him translate the diary—the diary he had lost! All while he was unconscious in the infirmary.

His eyes strayed to the roses. They were wilted. *Four days.* Magellan saw where he was looking and went to the vase.

"I should go pick some more. They're from the labyrinth. Godwin said he didn't mind." She gathered the rose bouquet in her hand and turned away.

The image of her holding the flowers struck him like a lightning bolt. It was the painting. His father's painting.

Of course. He painted her in 1799.

The Lady of the Labyrinth had always been Magellan. That smile, her hands. No one had hands like hers. The painting had been of her. Rhys could just never justify how until now.

A feeling of panic rose up inside of him, this time powerful and unstoppable. Were she and Godwin in love with each other? Had his father tried to kiss her?

"Has he painted you yet?" he asked, his voice barely a whisper.

"Painted me? Your father paints?" She looked impressed. "He truly is like Leonardo da Vinci, a real Renaissance man."

Rhys couldn't stop the fierce scowl on his face. "I'm sure he's enjoyed spending time with you." His father had always been a flirt with the ladies, and his mother wasn't here yet. A young Godwin must be an even bigger flirt. Botheration!

"You're not jealous, are you?" Magellan stared at him in wonder. "He's your father!"

"So? He's young and dapper and a real Renaissance man."

"Rhys," she admonished him gently. "You're being ridiculous."

He fell back on the pillow with a sigh, admitting to her, "He's going to paint you."

"Me? Are you sure?"

His gaze trailed over her face. "I found the painting after he died, and I always wondered who you were. You're standing in the labyrinth holding roses. When I first met you, I thought you resembled her, but there was no way you could have been from 1799. But you are."

Astonishment filled her face. "Which means this has already happened. Your father met you."

"What do you mean?"

"When you were growing up, he knew his whole life he would meet you in 1799 before you were born. What's unfolding now has already unfolded in your time."

The thought gave him a headache. He hadn't considered that aspect yet, but Magellan was right. His father had lived for years having already met him. Even before meeting his wife, Godwin had met his son and known Rhys would travel in time in the labyrinth. And here Godwin was reading the diary. Soon he would know everything. He would in fact know Gwynedd's whole story before they did because he was the one translating it.

Why had Godwin never shown him the painting of Magellan before he died? Why had he kept her arrival such a secret? Even as he asked the question, Rhys already knew the answer. Godwin had said nothing and let life unfold as it should. He'd prepared Rhys for the future only by encouraging his love of languages and history. He'd encouraged him to be a seeker, and he'd always told Rhys that one day he would travel far and help change the world, perhaps even save it.

Rhys had believed him for years, until he had consigned those ideas to the realm of fantasy. Yet here he was.

"What do I tell him?" he whispered.

Suddenly he felt a presence at the door and turned to see his father standing there.

It was time to meet a ghost.

# Chapter 42

## Rhys

"You're awake."

Rhys was speechless as he stared at his father in the doorway. So young. He was so young. Rhys had never seen his father this full of vitality. He must be somewhere near his own age. A man in his prime, hearty and hale.

Godwin came forward, his gaze trained on Rhys in fascination. "I've never met you, but you've surely met me I would hope." He had a twist of a grin on his face.

Rhys still could not answer. All the agony and sadness from his loss was returning full force and stubbornly wedging in his throat. Here was his best friend back from the dead in a younger incarnation of himself. His heart hurt to look at him. He finally forced out the word "Yes." Then he motioned to his wrapped chest. "Thank you for saving me."

"Never trust a Renaissance doctor." His father tried to make light of it. He had always loved humor.

Rhys was afraid he was going to cry, so instead he laughed. Soon they were all laughing. Magellan was the one who quickly brushed away a falling tear.

Rhys cleared his throat. "I hear you have the diary and are translating it."

His father nodded, ringing for tea, and he took a seat beside Magellan. They were both staring at him, looking fresh and clean—and beautiful together side by side. When does he paint her? And why?

Rhys tried to focus on the matter at hand. "How much has she told you? About our . . . purpose."

"She said I was to read the diary first. Then she would explain everything."

A familiar promise. Rhys cocked an eyebrow at Magellan, and she had the good grace to blush. It was the same carrot she had dangled in front of him. It seemed like a lifetime ago when he had thought she was stark raving mad and living in a fantasy world. They locked eyes.

"Well." Godwin interrupted their silent exchange and stood up. "I'll excuse myself to the library. I'll have someone come to help you get clean and changed into fresh clothes. We'll talk more later. Do rest."

Magellan stood up too. "I think I might go to the parlor and play the piano."

Godwin grinned at her and then at him. "Have you heard her play? She is exceptional."

Rhys couldn't decide whether to choke on laughter, sputter in anger, or die of jealousy all over again. Had he heard her play? Magellan gave Rhys a rueful look.

"Yes, I have," he simply said.

His father nodded and left. Rhys felt Magellan's gentle fingers brush the hair away from his brow, and immediately his ire lessoned.

"Don't be cross," she said softly. "He doesn't know what we've been through."

"Has he tried to sit on a piano bench with you?" The moment he said the words he wanted to take them back. Oh, that was a horrid, horrid question brought on by another wild swing of jealousy.

"Rhys Sherwood!" She put her hands on her hips, looking adorable in his grandmother's dress.

"Forgive me." He took her hand and kissed it. "Truly." Deciding it was best to change the subject, he asked her. "Are we here for someone, do you think? The fourth woman."

She nodded, now looking pensive. "I think so. But I have no idea who it could be. No one here in 1799 comes to mind. I need to finish reading the diary first."

"I'm sorry I lost it." He looked away from her. Frankfurt still seemed like yesterday. What she must have gone through. He knew she had left out the grisly details in her account. While he had been unconscious and of no help, somehow she had found the song in the Renaissance and delivered them both here—where the diary had returned to her again. Unknowingly retrieved by his father who'd had no notion of its power. That fact alone was incredible. Rhys could no longer deny the book's magical effects. Gwynedd's diary was tied to Magellan like a cord.

What did the last pages say? What were Gwynedd's final words to Magellan? For it had become apparent Gwynedd had written the diary for her. Rhys didn't begin to understand the mechanics behind it. Or know if Magellan was truly Gwynedd. He wasn't sure he believed in reincarnation or had given the idea much thought before now. Until he'd met Magellan, he had lived every day within the boundaries of his own life. Yet always yearning for something more, though never quite knowing what more was. Had he always been a part of this story? Had he known on some level he would meet Magellan and go on this journey with her? Now he was almost afraid to know what else Gwynedd had to say.

Magellan had only one more piece of the song to find. When she did, he didn't know what would happen. A feeling of trepidation gripped him. *Torschlusspanik* was the German word for the fear of running out of time to do something important before "the gates close." And he couldn't help but feel with a certainty in his bones, their journey in the labyrinth was about to end.

# Chapter 43

## Gwynedd

When I returned from my pilgrimage to Stonehenge, I was stunned to discover my father had arranged to have me wed King Tutugal's son Rhydderich in a political alliance. Even though it was well known Rhydderich's affections ran to men, not women. I was the daughter of a great chieftain, and it was my duty to accept.

I considered running away until I met Rhydderich. He was a towering, magnificent warrior, striking with dark hair and a powerful countenance. Immense intelligence shone in his eyes. Rhydderich had heard tales of my time with the Druids along with rumors that, like my brother, I had been born with magic. My love for Taliesin was already well known and Rhydderich did not take offense, for he had his own lover. Yet both our fathers were still determined our lives be bound together.

In life there are *waymakers*, those souls who enable you to accomplish your life's work. Rhydderich and I quickly found we were each other's. Instead of husband and wife in the truest sense, we became best friends and confidants. I carried his secrets, he carried mine, and we forged a partnership together.

I could not have accomplished my life's work without Rhydderich, nor his without me. When his father died and Rhydderich became king, he crowned me queen with the name *Languoreth*. The Golden One. For he knew I possessed a ring from the Golden Age and a connection to the world's glorious past. As Rhydderich's queen, I was afforded incredible freedom and protection to travel the land and visit the stone circles. For Merlin and I had much to prepare for in the future.

Merlin was the one who bestowed my husband his name, "Rhydderich the Generous," for there was no better king with a more valiant heart. Years later when Rhydderich died in battle as a wizened old soldier like my father, I retired my duties as queen. I left Partick and built a house in the forest to become a sanctuary for myself and my brother.

In our lifetime we saw the Druids' island destroyed in battle. I watched Cathan's beloved observatory and all its wonders go up in flames. After Cathan's death, Merlin became the last High Druid, the equivalent of a living library. During the course of his life, my brother's gift of seeing the future slowly drove him mad. As his twin, only I understood the depth of his pain. He lived his final years at our hidden sanctuary in the woods, where Taliesin finally joined us when he retired his duties as Bard.

Now in the twilight of our lives, we three have been united once more. Two comets and a North Star. Together we have begun to sift memories and record our knowledge to help ensure the future has a chance against the incredible odds we all face.

The ability to remember our previous lives was lost long ago after the Golden Age ended. My brother Merlin, who foresaw the future, told me when the time came to enter the labyrinth and retrieve the song, I would not have these memories to guide me. My life and the time I live in will seem as far away as a distant star.

I have broken every Druid law to leave behind an account for my future self. Taliesin was the one who suggested it, for words are forever tied to their writer. He and Merlin have promised to help safeguard the diary until the time comes to find the song. I have left as much instruction within these pages as I can, although I do not know how the future will unfold. Just as I cannot fathom why Garesh, the immortal sentry at Stonehenge, needed a lock of my hair. What I do know is we are part of a greater plan, spanning millennium all the way back to the last Golden Age before the galactic war, to keep the Earth whole and alive.

To give you some sense of the scope, I will share with you the first history lesson I was taught during my time with Cathan, and that is of the Great Year and the Map of Time.

Merlin and I sat with Cathan at his enormous table, where he spread out ancient maps of the galaxy. We listened, spellbound, as he explained, "Our planet's history spans a farther distance than we can imagine. The Great Year is twenty-four thousand years, the time it takes for Earth and the sun to spin around the galaxy once, like an ever-turning wheel." He showed us the cycle an astronomer had meticulously charted. "Half the time the Earth is descending in a twelve-thousand-year night and the other half ascending in a twelve-thousand-year day. Within this cosmic night and day, our hearts and minds are greatly affected."

My finger traced the path of the world. "How so, Cathan?"

"Where we are in the cosmos will determine what age we are in. The Golden Age is the pinnacle of human enlightenment. Every ancient culture remembers this time, when men and women were perfectly empowered, before our slow descent to the Silver and Bronze Ages and on to the Iron Age. Then the ages rise again, and round and round it goes, the rise and fall of civilizations—the rise and fall of history—and the rise and fall of magic."

Merlin and I were born in the Iron Age, the darkest age when the world's light is most dimmed. But even in our barbarous time, as my brother and I are testament to, magic still exists like the seedling that refuses to die.

Cathan went on to teach us how thousands of years ago at the end of the last Golden Age, survivors of the Great War came to our island for sanctuary. They were the ancient magicians who first came and laid down the megalithic stone circles that stretch across the land in an array of geometric wizardry. They intimately understood the language of the Earth, the power of the Ley Lines, and those pathways of energy connecting time and space.

Millennia later when wandering Celtic tribes began to arrive at our shores, they encountered these keepers of the stone circles. Cathan explained, "They called us the Wise Ones—they called us wizards—and over time we earned a new name: the Druids, which simply meant *those who know the trees*, for our power had dwindled. We had become only the keepers of memories."

Stories were told of the Druids, mystics in white robes who could talk with the trees. Travelers came as far as Alexandria, Egypt, to see for themselves the megalithic stone circles the Druids protected, which were as mysterious as the Great Pyramid in Egypt.

When word of the Druids reached Rome, the empire lusted for our lands, which sat at the edge of the known world. The Romans came to conquer and rounded up every Druid and Druidess—Healer, Teacher, and Bard—they could find and executed them in mass slayings. They chopped down the ancient groves and forests. They burned the schools and massacred every person on the isle of Ynys Mon, the Druids' heartland. After the massacre, the new Roman governor made it against the law to draw near a stone circle. It did not matter what the stones were for. Rome wanted to erase the Druids so not even our memory remained.

The Romans occupied our southern lands for four hundred years. When their empire fell, they left just as quickly. The Druids, few as they were, came out of hiding, though only a small group remained.

I often think of Cathan as I write these words. His beloved island, the last Druid sanctuary, is gone, and the ancient world he taught us so much about is almost forgotten. The great stone circles remain only as ghostly relics of a lost age.

To history's probing eyes, I am the sister of a wizard and the wife of a king who lived in the Dark Ages. From history's narrow vantage point—written by men—I am a woman, defined only by the men around me. But in the turning of the Great Year, this too is fleeting. For as the wheel turns and the ages rise, women will embrace their power once more and transform the world.

If we can keep the Earth spinning.

One guardian gave us the power to save this planet. She gave us her song and the labyrinth to find it.

The song has not been played in over ten thousand years. Assembling its parts will not be easy. For with each part you find, the labyrinth will splinter and ultimately break.

You must find the parts by Winter Solstice. Once you return to your own time, you will need to gather instruments from around the world. Musicians will come forward to play, answering the call in their hearts. In the final moment, the guardian's son, Horus, will bring the song's last part to make it whole.

The task ahead may seem daunting, but we are all waymakers to keep this world spinning.

When the song is played, every atom on this planet will sing.

*Every atom.*

The resonance will stabilize the poles and create a higher dimensional field for the entire world where nothing discordant can exist. As the Earth shifts to a higher vibrational frequency, lower vibrational frequencies will fall away. Hatred, anger, shame, despair, and fear will dissipate. The forces seeking to destroy this planet will no longer be able to reach us. Our resonance will be too powerful.

This is what we have been working toward for millennia over lifetimes, and the hour is near.

---

As I write these final words, the lifetime I claim as my own is fading. I am an old woman now looking ahead to the horizon, and my heart is as heavy as the stones of Merlin's beloved circle he has built for us.

For today, Taliesin and I laid my brother to rest.

Merlin said this would not be the first nor the last time he would die before us. Though we are always connected through time, I miss him already.

I laid a yew branch on his grave. The yew tree signifies death and rebirth. The end and the beginning. The oldest of the trees, only the yew can stand alone in the darkest grove without any light.

We are all in the dark now. Stay strong, stay the course, and remember, like music, the soul is all-powerful and never ending. One lifetime is but a star in the sky of the soul, and the soul is as vast as an endless sea.

# Chapter 44

## Magellan

Gwynedd's final message echoed in the chambers of Magellan's heart. She could feel the love behind the words. Magellan handed the page to Rhys. They were reading the last of the pages together.

Two days had passed since Rhys had woken. Only today had Godwin finished translating and called them to the library. Fortunately, Rhys felt well enough to leave the infirmary and move into a bedroom. He wasn't anywhere near fully recovered, and to his ire he was being pushed around in a wheelchair belonging to Godwin's late grandfather, but he was improving.

Now they had read the diary in its entirety.

Rhys put down the last page. Godwin was sitting behind his desk at the alcove. He looked crumpled, tired, but pleased with himself. He'd been sequestered in the library for days feverishly working on the translation.

Magellan recognized his handwriting. This was the translation the Liron Institute had delivered to the Morgan Museum—or would deliver. She fingered the pages. "I've seen your translation, in the future."

"You have?" His face lit up. "However did that occur?"

"The Liron Institute delivered it and the diary to the Morgan Museum on my birthday."

Godwin peered at Rhys over the brim of his little glasses. "Do you hear that, dear boy? We have an institute in the future. How marvelous. So!" Godwin took off his glasses with a dramatic pause. "If I'm to understand this correctly"—he made a circular motion to the pages—"the Earth is in the throes of being destroyed, and here we are, reunited inside an ancient labyrinth to find a song that was hidden millennia ago by a planetary goddess—who happens to be secretly buried at Stonehenge, mind you—who went against 'cosmic forces' to save the Earth. And she has entrusted women, with Gwynedd, i.e., Magellan, as her fearless captain, to reassemble the song when the time comes, and tasked a Sumerian immortal to help because extraordinary circumstances call for extraordinary measures. Does that about sum it all up?"

No one said a word. Godwin wasn't asking for an answer. Instead, he laughed and laughed and laughed.

Magellan and Rhys glanced at each other.

Then Godwin said, *"Liron."*

Magellan waited for him to explain.

"The Earls of Liron. Guardians of Hereford Labyrinth and a stone circle created by Merlin himself." Godwin then said to Rhys, "A title usually denotes a place on a map, but our title does not. Have you never wondered why? It was bestowed upon our family by the first king of England. Do you know what our namesake means, dear boy?" Godwin had taken to calling Rhys "dear boy" in jest, though Rhys was presently five years older.

Rhys shook his head. "No, dear Father, would you care to enlighten me?"

"Liron means *sing to me.*"

Magellan could feel the prick of tears sting her eyes and couldn't stop them.

*Sing to me.*

Godwin leveled his gaze to her. "Now. Magellan. Have I earned the right to hear the rest of your story? Tell me of the song you and my son have been seeking. I take it that is why you are here in 1799."

Magellan nodded, her anxiety about their quest returning. They had come so far. Centuries in fact, being propelled by a force beyond their understanding, and they were almost out of time. She stared at the ring on her finger and held it up for him to see. "This is Gwynedd's ring, and the symbols match the labyrinth's standing stone. Garesh gave it to me."

Astounded, Godwin took her hand to study it. *"Know the way."* He looked up at them both.

Magellan felt Rhys's fingers lace in hers. She stared at their joined hands, feeling the strength flow between them. Together they had made the journey. She truly couldn't have done it without him, and now they needed Godwin's help to finish it.

She told Godwin everything. About Fanny Mendelssohn, Hildegard of Bingen, and Maddalena Casulana. She tried to explain how the song was a symphony, and she was gathering the bones of it but would need countless musicians to bring it to life.

Godwin fingered the pages of the translation. "And the final part of the song was left to her beloved son, *Horus*." He stared at the library's walls, lost in thought. "Incredible."

"What is it?" Rhys asked.

"Horus." Godwin jumped up, galvanized, and headed to the bookshelves. The library was filled with thousands of books on towering shelves, and yet Godwin strode up one of the staircases to a top shelf with purpose. He soon came back down, carrying a thick tome, and set it on the table next to them.

Magellan read the gold lettering on the binding, *Myths of Ancient Egypt and Sumer*.

Godwin began explaining in a great rush. "Like Sir Isaac Newton, I believe the ancient world possessed technology and wisdom long since lost. Newton's unorthodox beliefs on the matter only came to light after his death." Magellan was nodding along, although she had no idea where this was going. He said, "I even have one of his notebooks in my alchemy collection, as well as some of the burnt pages recovered from the fire in his laboratory—"

"Father."

"You're right. I digress. Napoleon's unfortunate pillaging and exploits in Egypt aside, his surveyors there discovered that like the stone circles, the Great Pyramid holds mathematical codes. I believe there is a direct connection between the ancient Egyptians and Sumerians to the Druids and their megaliths. Gwynedd all but confirms it in her diary."

Rhys was frowning. "How?"

Godwin tapped on the large book he'd just laid on the table and began to carefully turn its pages. "First, the music and math she details in her diary is very similar to what Pythagoras wrote on what he learned from mystics in Egypt. Second, all mythologies around the world are in fact quite consistent with each other. Isis, the Goddess of Love and Queen of the Heavens, goes by many names: Ishtar, Inanna, Astarte, Esther. She is the most powerful of the world's pantheon and the last superbeing to live in this world before the end of the Golden Age."

Magellan wasn't looking at the book. She was looking at Godwin, his intensity giving her goose bumps. He slid the book toward them to show the image he'd found. On the page was a painting of a goddess riding a lion with sunbeams bursting around her head.

"*Horus* was her son. Part man, part superbeing, the last ruler on Earth connected to the heavens. Connected to the galaxy and the cosmic worlds we were once a part of before whatever galactic battle transpired. And according to Gwynedd, Horus has the final piece of the song."

They all stared at the book.

"So!" He clapped his hands, like a professor concluding his lecture. "It seems we are on an ancient quest for the goddess Isis. A quest that began lifetimes ago."

The whole idea seemed impossible. As impossible as Magellan sitting in an earl's library in 1799.

If, somehow, she did assemble the song in its entirety, she had to find Horus and the last part when she got back home. Then she had to get the world to come together to play it. She had no idea how she was supposed to do that. She was just one woman. Yes, her capacity for music was beyond the normal spectrum. But now Godwin was talking about goddesses and superbeings from other planets and ancient myths being real.

She stared at the painting of Isis. The goddess who supposedly loved humanity so much, she refused to give us up.

"Who are you here for?" Godwin broke the silence, asking the question that had been circling her thoughts for days. "Do you know?"

"No, not yet," she admitted. Her mind was drawing a blank on women composers in 1799 England.

"Well, you must find out quickly. December is upon us," Godwin pointed out, and Magellan felt her stress level rise.

"She will." Rhys reached over and took her hand. He gave it a reassuring squeeze. "You will."

She wanted to tell him she was not only worried about not knowing, she was worried about when she did know and the Ley Lines took her back. Would Rhys come with her?

Godwin gave their joined hands a perplexed look. She and Rhys were acting way too familiar with each other for his 1799 sensibilities.

Godwin stood up, announcing it was time for dinner, and rang a bell for one of the footmen to come and wheel Rhys. He gallantly offered Magellan his arm, and they all made their way to the dining room.

Dinner had already been set on the table, and Godwin dismissed the servants again so they could talk freely. Days ago, he had explained to the household staff that Rhys was a distant cousin and Magellan was Rhys's wife. The couple had journeyed to Hereford Manor but had met with great misfortune on the way. Their carriage had been robbed by highwaymen, with everything stolen, even their trunks.

Godwin had spun the tale with relish. The unfortunate couple had made it to Hereford Manor, hobbling pitifully on foot, with Mr. Sherwood mortally wounded. Certain he was dying, Rhys's last wish was to visit the center of the labyrinth where he had played as a child with his beloved distant cousin. The staff had listened solemnly and accepted Godwin's outlandish story that sounded straight from the pages of a gothic novel. His dearest cousin from childhood and lovely wife had been given separate bedrooms near each other while Mr. Sherwood recovered. And if anyone noticed the remarkable resemblance between the Earl of Liron and his distant relation, no one mentioned it.

They ate in silence until Godwin finally said, "Well, there's no denying the fact I am Merlin," he announced as if commenting on the pea soup.

Rhys choked on his wine.

Godwin winked at Magellan and said to her, "And I do look on you like a sister." He slapped Rhys heartily on the back to help him stop coughing. "That makes you Taliesin. Noble Bard. Gwynedd's devoted lover. Master poet. Writer of romantic myths. And a Druid shaman who, like Merlin, could prophesize the future if you read the histories."

Magellan met Rhys's eyes across the table. For all of Godwin's outrageous statements, the three of them had been brought together by some kind of divine providence. The Ley Lines had reunited them within the pathways of the labyrinth. They were each from different times, yet tied together by the quest and an ancient diary that alluded to previous lives they could not remember.

"It is an enticing thought." Godwin swirled his wine. "What if we *could* remember? Not just one lifetime but all our previous lives? Every soul memory. What if there was a medicine . . . a drug . . . that could enable all our memories to return?" Godwin sat back, contemplating the idea. "Like lost dreams. How I would love to know."

It was a tantalizing thought. Magellan had never considered having lived a life before this one—or living one after this life ended. The whole idea of reincarnation challenged her sense of self. If every life was a new identity, with each one came a new nationality, a new race, religion, culture, and set of beliefs. To have a myriad of lifetimes allowed no single life to define oneself. No single set of beliefs out of countless others were better or right. Suddenly the ego wasn't so important.

Magellan had been too busy living her own life to contemplate another one. She had met people she felt an affinity for, as if she already knew them on some level, but was it because of a past life? Did forgotten memories from previous lives leave their echoes behind?

Gwynedd had written how meeting Taliesin had filled her with the sense of *hiraeth*, a homesickness for a place one can never return to. Perhaps the feeling was homesickness for a lifetime one could never remember.

Gwynedd believed she and Taliesin had loved each other before. Just as Magellan knew she and Rhys shared soul memories on some deeper level, and she didn't need a drug or a pill to feel it. She could not explain the love she felt for Rhys, or the affinity she had for Godwin. They all three had come together to fulfill this mission, and there was still one more woman to find.

---

Magellan spent days in the library reading about the history of England, trying to figure out who the composer could be. When she became too overwhelmed, she would play the piano in the salon. There was no grand conservatory yet, no Streicher piano, no harp, or collection of instruments. Rhys told her in private how all those things came later after Godwin married Birgit. The two newlyweds had brought a trove of instruments back with them from Vienna.

When he said that, Magellan gasped. Suddenly the last piece fell into place.

*The countess was from Austria.*

Of course! At that realization, goose bumps rained down her body like a waterfall. The last piece of the song was waiting for her in Austria. And she knew who had it. Another woman with immense musical talent who had been eclipsed by a famous brother. Like Fanny with Felix Mendelssohn. Like Gwynedd with Merlin.

Magellan's hands grew still on the piano. It was well past midnight. She had been playing for Rhys and Godwin after a particularly long dinner. She'd known their time at Hereford Manor was ticking down. The clock had finally stopped.

Rhys was staring at her in concern. "What is it?"

"When does Godwin meet the countess?"

Godwin shot up out of his chair as if he'd sat on a sharp object and interjected dramatically, "Not a word! I don't want to know anything about my life."

"But—"

"It's not negotiable. I know my son. His name. His face. I've seen the man he will become. It is enough!" He went over to the mantel and turned his back on them to stare into the fire in the hearth. "It is enough," he repeated quietly.

Magellan stared at Rhys, wanting to say more. She would have to wait for Godwin to leave the room.

Rhys's mother was from Austria. Godwin must meet Birgit there.

She saw the moment Rhys realized it too. The light in his eyes.

"We have to go to Vienna," Rhys announced with urgency, sounding breathless with understanding. "Right away, the three of us."

Godwin was livid. "I told you I cannot know—"

"And you don't need to know anything besides that," Rhys shot back. "But you do have to go to Austria before the end of the year. I'll say no more on that front, except it's imperative you go, and we need to go too."

Godwin choked on a disbelieving laugh. "You're bamming me! I take it I did not pay enough for your schooling when you were younger. You do know Austria is at war with France? It was just declared this spring, and Napoleon has returned from Egypt."

"Trust me. I do know my history. It's going to get much worse after Napoleon declares himself emperor in 1804."

"What?" Godwin looked horrified.

"The war will be long and bloody. But we still must go," Rhys said stubbornly. He turned to Magellan. "Who is it we're meant to see?"

"Mozart's sister," she told them, her cheeks flushed with excitement.

"Mozart's sister?" Godwin sputtered with surprise. "Mozart has a sister? Can she play music?"

Magellan made a grimacing face, as if she'd bitten into a sour pickle. She then went on to explain not only did Mozart have a sister who could play music, she was a prodigy too like her brother. However, unlike her brother, she had been forbidden to perform as she grew older because she was on her way to becoming a woman.

Maria Anna Mozart, better known as Nannerl, had been born five years ahead of Wolfgang. She played the harpsichord like a master, the violin in secret, and her voice was called "the golden voice." She composed her own music, though no compositions survived her death. Growing up, she toured with her brother until she was eighteen and was then forced to "retire." When she was thirty-three, she bowed to her father's wishes and married an older man who had been widowed twice before. She was to care for his five children. The man was a magistrate, and they lived in the tiny town of Saint Gilgen in Austria. This woman, who had toured and played concerts in Munich, Vienna, Paris, London, Switzerland, The Hague, and Germany, had been consigned to a quiet life of obscurity. She gave piano lessons while her brother dazzled Europe and later the world, securing his place in the bowels of history. Wolfgang died young in 1791, but his music and name would live on, while Nannerl's would become a side note: *Mozart's sister*. Never a person unto herself.

Only later did the twenty-first century begin a search and rescue through the past, resurrecting women forgotten in history books like digging for gold. In Magellan's lifetime there'd been a whole discovery and celebration of women composers and musicians, and Nannerl rightfully had taken her place with the rest. These women carried inside of them music so powerful it could change the world.

Godwin was pacing. "You want to just go traipsing through the fighting? There is a battle in Zurich going on right now!" He looked to Rhys as if he could talk him out of it.

"I do not want to do anything of the sort. But we're meant to go." Rhys put his hand in hers in a show of solidarity. "We have to brazen it out."

"Brazen it out? Brazen it out?" Godwin passed a hand over his face and let out a pained sigh. "Lud."

"Godwin," Magellan pressed the point home, "this is not up to us. There is a greater plan at work. The woman we need is there." *As well as your future wife,* though she didn't say it.

"Well, the *greater plan* has chosen a bang-up inconvenient time. The War Office has warned against travel. It will take careful planning to organize the journey for us. We can't just go waltzing across the Continent on a whim!"

"This is not a whim, and it can be done," Rhys said. "It will be done, for I know you already did it."

"Not another word," Godwin warned him and then let out a long-suffering breath. "Fine!" He threw up his hands in surrender and began pacing again as he formed a plan. "I know alchemists in Europe. I will have to write to them to give us shelter, escort, and protection. It will take time."

"We don't have time," she reminded him.

"Then I'll write quickly," Godwin retorted.

"Excellent, for we *are* going," Rhys stated.

"I will write my letters." Godwin gave them a stern scowl. "I will have to introduce you as husband and wife."

Rhys's cheeks turned pink as he said, "Then perhaps there is time for you to visit the Archbishop of Canterbury? I believe you liked to boast how you were friends."

Godwin looked from Rhys to her and laughed out loud. "Truly?"

Rhys nodded. "I would hate to make a liar out of you, Father."

Confused, Magellan glanced from Rhys to Godwin. "Why does he need to visit the Archbishop of Canterbury?"

"I'll let you explain it to her." Godwin winked and went to leave. "I have a trip to Austria to plan and an archbishop to woo." He shut the door on his way out, giving them privacy.

"Why does he need to see the Archbishop of Canterbury?" she asked again.

Rhys suddenly looked bashful as he came and sat beside her on the piano bench. It was the first time in days they'd been alone.

He took her hand and kissed it. "Only the archbishop can grant a special wedding license so couples may marry immediately without having to wait for banns to be read."

She stared at him. A silent "Oh" forming on her lips. The shy, tender look on his face made her want to laugh and cry at the same time. "Are you asking me to marry you?"

He took both of her hands in his. "I believe I am."

Magellan stared at him, speechless, breathless. She had too many conflicting emotions coursing through her to focus on one. She had been hurtled across centuries chasing a song but never considered she would get married along the way.

She met his eyes, seeing the beautiful light within them.

Married in 1799. It was mad. It was crazy. But then, she had surrendered her sanity a long time ago, perhaps that day at the church in Manhattan when she opened a time portal with Bach. Considering all that had happened since then, marrying Rhys in 1799 before heading to Austria to find Mozart's sister made absolute perfect sense. She fleetingly thought, she only wished Crystal could be here to witness a wedding across centuries.

With a "Yes," she launched into his arms.

In music there is no greater power than a love song, and the Earl of Liron—guardian of the labyrinth, protector of the diary, and the beautiful soul she had traversed time with, a man whose name meant *sing to me*—was hers.

# Chapter 45

## Rhys

Rhys knew his father met his mother at a New Year's Eve ball in Vienna—or would meet. Godwin and Birgit fell in love during the remaining minutes of 1799 over the course of a waltz. As a child, Rhys had heard the tale countless times. He'd never in his wildest dreams imagined he would be the one to propel the story.

Godwin never would have gone to Austria without him. Rhys never would have been born. It was a circular time event, perhaps even a paradox if he thought hard enough about it, though he tried not to. Just like the painting of Magellan.

Until Rhys saw the exact moment Godwin would capture on canvas. He was standing beside his father in the center of the labyrinth. Magellan was wearing the same pale-pink dress as in the painting, another borrowed gown from his grandmother's closets. Her hair was down. She was holding red roses in her hand and waiting at the standing stones for their wedding to begin.

She and Rhys had decided to be married in the center of the labyrinth. There seemed to be no better place. Godwin had gone to

London and returned with the special license and the nearest town vicar, a spritely elderly fellow who was clearly in awe of Godwin, the infamous Earl of Liron. The man was honored to be performing the private ceremony for the earl's relation.

Magellan had just finished picking flowers for her bouquet when she turned to Rhys and smiled at him. It was *the smile*. The image captured on the canvas that was burned into his mind forever.

Godwin was standing beside him and said he would paint her portrait to capture the day. Then all at once Rhys understood. The painting had been a gift from his father. A wedding gift. Rhys didn't tell him he'd already seen it and found the painting after he died.

Rhys swallowed the lump in his throat. "Thank you. I'm sure it will be beautiful."

The ceremony was brief. The town vicar conducted the wedding with gravitas, as if he had a huge audience and not three people. He most likely could not wait to get back to the village and share his adventure.

"Dearly beloved," the vicar began.

Rhys and Magellan repeated their vows to each other, their hands joined. The sun was shining down on the labyrinth that day, the stones their cathedral. Rhys stared into the green of Magellan's eyes and knew in his heart he had loved her before and would love her again.

In a blink, the ceremony was over.

"My countess," Rhys whispered into her ear and kissed her fully on the lips, causing the vicar to gasp. Magellan threw back her head and laughed. Then she wrapped her arms around him and kissed him again. Godwin wiped a suspect tear from his eye and hurried the shocked vicar back to the house. Rhys and Magellan left the labyrinth last, strolling hand in hand.

The household staff was waiting at the manor to congratulate them. They had prepared a lovely wedding breakfast, not daring to ask why the eccentric young couple were getting married a second time.

After many toasts in the dining room with the vicar, they sent the man home in a carriage half foxed. Then it was just the three of them. They were all on the way to being drunk themselves more from the day and not the champagne.

"You told me, Father, I could not get married until I read the diary in its entirety. You made me promise. Now I understand why." Rhys could feel himself getting emotional. Godwin had lived through this time with them and then he had raised him as a young boy, knowing they would sit at the table together and celebrate his wedding day.

"To 1799, a most advantageous year!" Godwin proclaimed, and they all clinked glasses.

"To 1800," Rhys teased, knowing his parents' meeting was not far off. "You have no idea how your life will change."

"Not a word." Godwin pointed a finger threateningly at him. "Not a word." He was adamant that Rhys and Magellan could not share anything about his future and risk unraveling the past altogether, and they had sworn they wouldn't.

Magellan raised her glass. "To a safe journey to Austria."

They would leave in the morning, strange honeymoon that it would be. It had taken Godwin almost two weeks to arrange the passage for their trip to Vienna, with their staying at alchemists' estates along the way. Rhys tried not to worry about the date, but the days of December were ticking by. Tomorrow, finally, tomorrow they would be on their way.

On that note, Godwin bid them good night. The newlyweds were led to an apartment of rooms in the east wing, prepared just for them. When Rhys shut the door to their suite, he wrapped Magellan in his arms. They took turns placing tender kisses upon each other's faces like a love song just beginning to play. Then they gave themselves to each other in the most exquisite melody only lovers can make.

As Rhys drifted off into a languid sleep, the boundaries of their bodies still blurred, he had never felt so complete. A blanket of peace descended over him, and he dreamed of *the song*. He heard its grand symphony. He saw an audience of thousands, hundreds of thousands, all singing. The people were an open sea of faces surrounding an enormous stage in the shape of a circle as big as his labyrinth, perhaps bigger. Starlight beams were everywhere, harnessing light. Magellan was onstage, leading the musicians. Then she turned to him, her eyes shining. He felt like he was soaring within the music, yet he could feel his feet rooted to the stage.

Because he was there.

*He was there.*

And in that moment, standing in the center of the stage under the lights, playing the song they had journeyed to the heart of a labyrinth to find, he found the perfect word for her from all the words that defied translation.

*Kara sevda*, blinding love.

# Chapter 46

## Magellan

For the first time, Magellan dreamed of the song being played in its entirety. When she woke up, she could still hear the notes echoing inside her. Rhys had been with her in the dream. He had been onstage beside her as she led countless musicians. He'd been there. The dream had been so powerful, like a clear vision of the future, and it filled her with hope. Was it a sign he would return with her? That they would make it out of the labyrinth together? She had to believe it, or she would lose all courage. She clung to the fact she could feel the song inside her, propelling her to go on.

The whole symphony was a planetary puzzle. The melody was purely Western classical in its mathematical harmonics and symmetry, but she could hear the formidable African drumbeats that would carry the notes and make them soar. She could hear the spaces within the song being filled by an Eastern pentatonic scale. Chinese used five notes instead of seven, and Indian music's foundation was a seven note *saptak* scale put into ragas. Gwynedd had been right when she said the whole world would play it. Magellan still had no idea how she could make that happen, or how she could give birth to the symphony growing in her like an unborn child.

Now they were on their way to Austria with Godwin. The resounding echoes of the carriage's wheels and clattering of horses' hooves on the cobblestones were deafening. At times the carriage shook like tiny little earthquakes. They were traveling in Godwin's state-of-the-art travel carriage, pulled by six horses, with a smaller carriage following behind them. They had quite the entourage. They had a coachman, two groomsmen for the horses, Godwin's personal valet, and a maid, a sweet woman named Clara who was married to the coachman, to help Magellan. Then there were all the trunks. The carriages were unmarked for safety, without the Liron crest, and they stopped only when necessary to rest and water the horses. Still, the twelve-hour journey down to the coast felt endless.

During their time couped up together, Godwin asked so many questions about the future and what life was like. Questions only a scientist would think to ask. Questions about the evolution of industry and medicine, traveling to the stars, and mastering the chemistry of matter. He was vindicated and delighted to know there was a periodic table of elements where the elements fit together like puzzle pieces. Magellan didn't know much about the periodic table except the basics she'd learned in high school chemistry, but she did her best to explain.

For Godwin the year 1800 was weeks away. The grand turning to a new century, and with it would come changes and inventions beyond the imagination: electricity, the battery, steam engines, photography, movies, anesthesia, vaccines, trains, and automobiles. A hundred years later at the beginnings of the 1900s, the Wright Brothers would learn to harness the air. Then came the moon and space. And here she was stuck in a carriage after traveling dimensionally by sound, by a means that had once been used thousands of years ago—and her ticket expired on Winter Solstice along with the rest the world's. She tried hard not to think about it.

Finally, they reached the port town of Dover, on the southern edge of England. They stayed at an inn for the night and then got up early to take a ferry. Godwin had secured a private yacht to make the twelve-hour boat ride across the channel to Calais. He explained they needed a boat big enough to take his carriages and horses. He refused to use any other carriage, believing it would not be reliable. His was custom made and one he had designed himself.

Magellan had no idea the trip would be this involved, and the enormity of what she was attempting hit her. She was journeying across Europe in a whole other century, and it was taking precious time. What she wouldn't give for a car or a plane. In the carriage, they couldn't be traveling more than fifteen miles an hour. Sometimes it felt like she could jog to Austria faster.

With all the trip preparations and travel time, Winter Solstice was only a little over a week away. They were cutting it close, but they couldn't get to Austria any quicker. Godwin had planned the trip down to the last minute.

Rhys and Godwin explained to her how now was not the time to be an Englishman traveling on the road. France was currently at war with England, Austria, and Russia. For safety, Godwin reserved their own private dining room whenever they stopped at inns to have a meal. And when they arrived on the Continent, they only stayed at private estates. He had called upon a whole network of alchemists to help them get from one city to the next. When she asked Godwin how he knew them, he simply said, "We're all Freemasons."

She didn't know what that meant. She also didn't know what to make of Godwin's explanation to their hosts along the way as to why he was traveling to Vienna. Whenever he was asked, Godwin would grin and announce he was "on a mission for the goddess Isis." His alchemist friends would laugh, and the conversation would move on.

Ironically, at every estate they stopped there was always talk of Egypt at the dinner table. All of Europe was currently enraptured. Magellan learned the details from Rhys. Last year in a grand imperialistic move,

Napoleon had embarked to Egypt with 400 ships and 30,000 men. He brought with him 150 engineers, scholars, historians, and surveyors to study the land and bring back marvels from the ancient world. Much of the looting was being consigned as "cultural exchange."

Napoleon was determined to leave his stamp there as well. He established the Institute of Egypt in Cairo with divisions in physics, math, political economy, literature, and the arts. He commissioned artists to capture Egypt's ancient temples and ruins on paper. And one discovery made in July in the town of Rosetta was a granite stone inscribed with three languages, which would enable scholars to understand ancient Egyptian hieroglyphs.

"They are calling it the Rosetta Stone," a man who they were dining with explained. "I hope it proves useful."

Magellan caught Rhys's rueful smile. Even thirty years later, Rhys knew the Rosetta Stone's importance. How she loved their shared looks and secret communications across the dinner tables. They were both interlopers in a time where they did not belong. She rarely spoke at any of their stops. In 1799 she was simply the adornment, the wife. She really had no idea who they stayed with or if anyone was famous in history. They were all scientists of some sort . . . chemists, astronomers, or physicists. Although the term *scientist* wasn't used yet, and science had yet to become an official profession. Scientists were called philosophers, and the conversations between them always turned to invention and the latest discoveries being made. She wondered what all these philosophers would think if they knew she was on a mission to save the world with a small group of female musicians.

1799, much like 1829, could not have been more confining. The lack of opportunity and freedom for women was stifling. Fortunately, every house had a piano to help her escape, since music was the amusement of the day, and Magellan was always able to play. Only Rhys knew she would go stir-crazy if she didn't. He often mentioned to their hosts that his wife "played a little" and asked if they would mind her entertaining them. Sometimes she couldn't help but slip in something more modern, like a little Frank Sinatra, Louis Armstrong, or Billie Holiday. Rhys and Godwin always seemed to know when she did and would fight to hide their laughter.

When it was just the three of them traveling in the carriage, Godwin was full of questions about the song. How did she see all the parts coming together? What kind of instruments would she need?

How could she explain she would need every instrument? She would need all the strings and wind instruments ever made. She would need an army of drums, the heartbeat within the song. She would need human voices with incredible power like Wren's. *She would need whales.*

Magellan gasped at her own revelation.

She would need whales!

She didn't know how she knew, but she did. The world was 70 percent water. Of course whales were part of the song. On impulse she took Rhys's hand and squeezed it. For the first time, the song's full dimensions were crystallizing in her mind. She had three movements of the symphony. Now she needed the fourth. The grand finale and rousing conclusion. She didn't know how much of the fourth movement Nannerl had, because Gwynedd had written that the final part would be delivered by Horus. How that would happen or when Magellan didn't know. She would have to return to her own time to find out.

Would Garesh be there? Would he return to help her? He had been the one to prepare her for this journey from childhood and given her the ring on their last day together. Now she was on her way to get the last piece of the song, which felt like arriving at the labyrinth's center.

Magellan looked out the window at the sun, feeling like they were chasing the light. They needed to make it to Nannerl before the Earth's longest night or there would never be another day again.

# Chapter 47

𝄢

## Rhys

Rhys held Magellan's hand. The gravity of what they were doing felt like a burden they had been carrying with them in the carriage for days. Today was December 19, and they had only two days until Winter Solstice. Every second was precious. Rhys did not know what other worlds were out there in the universe or how the Earth factored into such a vast cosmos. All he knew was this world was on the brink of being annihilated, with the past, present, and future gone forever.

Now in hindsight, Rhys understood every life lesson Godwin had tried to impart to him before he died. How knowledge was true power and love was the answer to life's greatest question. Rhys had never been more full of love and conviction to save the world. If Magellan was the captain of the ancient ship, he would stand beside her on the bow.

Godwin broke their silence to go over the plan once more. "We will find an inn at Salzburg to stay for the night and then make the journey in the morning to Saint Gilgen to find Nannerl. After Magellan retrieves the song, we will travel northeast to Yspertal, the ancient Druid stone circle in Austria, which lies halfway between Salzburg and

Vienna." They needed a powerful place where Ley Lines were sure to cross to ensure she got back home, and they needed to avoid people given the danger. Godwin thought an ancient Druid stone circle in the middle of nowhere seemed the best bet. He went on. "Magellan will play her music on the journey to fend off whatever malevolent sounds she hears."

In Frankfurt, Rhys had not heard the hellish noise Magellan had. His hearing had vanished, eclipsed by the shadows. When he had asked her to describe it, she had shaken her head and told him she did not want to think on it. He could only imagine and stressed to his father, "Once we have Nannerl's part of the song we cannot waste a single moment." He had already imparted to Godwin the dangers to come after the song was played. "We will get in the carriage and ride without stopping while Magellan plays." He squeezed her hand in reassurance.

Right now, he was trying hard not to think about what would happen when the time came to leave 1799. He hoped with all his heart he would be going with Magellan to her own time. He was relying on the blind faith of a dream.

Still, in quiet moments when his thoughts drifted, his heart would clench. *Viraag* was the Sanskrit word for the crushing anguish from being separated from the one you love. He couldn't help but feel life was about to take her away, and he would lose his father again as well.

After Magellan retrieved the song from Mozart's sister and they made it to the stone circle, Godwin planned to make his way to Vienna for New Year's Eve. Even more stressful, Godwin was still resisting the trip to Vienna due to the war, preferring to return home to Hereford Manor.

Rhys would not allow it.

"But why must I go?" his father asked, sounding like a petulant child.

Rhys let out an impatient sigh. "Well, if you must know . . ."

"Not a word!" His father pointed at him.

Rhys was at the end of his patience. "You once told me before you"—he stopped himself from saying *you died* and swallowed the lump in his throat. He began again. "You once told me that it was my duty to live my life and love with an open heart. To not die regretting that I didn't. To be everything I was born to be. Well, you are no different. Trust me when I say the best years of your life begin in Vienna at the stroke of 1800."

Godwin stared at him a long moment. "You're telling me I will find love in Vienna?" He barked out a laugh and his eyes slid to Magellan, who was trying hard to keep a blank expression. Then Godwin glanced back at Rhys. "And not with just any woman I take it, from the grave look on your face like you've swallowed a goose. Is that where I meet your mother?" He threw back his head and laughed with glee. "Of course, now it makes perfect sense. It would be most inconvenient for you if I decided to return to Hereford Manor. I certainly can't miss that New Year's ball, now can I?"

Rhys simply gave him a nod. Magellan was looking from him to Godwin, her mouth pursed in amusement.

"What is she like?" Godwin smiled, his bad mood forgotten.

"I thought you didn't want to know," Rhys reminded him.

"What if I pick the wrong lady? You'll never be born. Or you'll be born a Siegfried or Albert and we'll never be here in this carriage." The threat, although made jokingly, lingered between them with an unsettling silence.

Rhys still held his tongue. Should he meddle with the past? Or technically the future of the past?

"A hint," Godwin prodded. Now that he knew he was soon to meet his future wife, he wanted to know. "Only a letter. The first letter of her name is all I need."

Rhys deliberated. There couldn't be any harm in that.

"B."

"B?" Godwin looked enchanted by the possibilities. "Barbara. Beatrice. Battina. Briaca . . . So! I will have to go hunting through a ballroom in Vienna for the lovely and mysterious B." Godwin stared at him with a devilish smile. "Then I will ask the beautiful B to waltz. Does that sound about right?"

Rhys stared into his father's eyes, a heavy poignancy sweeping over him. Suddenly his father's lifelong endearments for his wife took on a whole new light. When Rhys was growing up, he often heard all the little nicknames Godwin had for Birgit.

*My Beautiful B, My Beloved B, My only B.*

It had been for *the letter*. His father's sole clue Rhys had given him.

Rhys could feel tears prickling behind his eyes. "Indeed."

"Excellent. Say no more. We will not tempt the Fates with any further discussion on the future with my beautiful bride to B," Godwin said, giving a last and final play on the letter.

Rhys met Magellan's eyes. Hers were soft in understanding, and she took his hand in hers again. He saw his father studying their joined hands, his eyes on the Liron signet ring marking him as the earl in his own time. His father held his gaze, the light of laughter in his eyes dimming, and then he turned to look out the window.

Rhys desperately wanted to tell him about the accident, to plead with him to be careful in his laboratory, that his quest to discover elements was pure madness. But his father had already made him swear not to meddle in his future or try to change what had been done, for they were meddling with time enough.

Sunlight glinted off the carriage's glass window, and Rhys looked out at the lush countryside. 1799 marked the eve of the Napoleonic Wars, which would soon rage across Europe until the Battle of Waterloo in 1815. Even as they made their way to Salzburg, Rhys knew the Coup of 18–19 Brumaire, which had happened in November, had placed Napoleon firmly in power. The fighting would begin in earnest in April when France went on the offensive. By then his father would be back in England with his mother at Hereford Manor, and he would be born in 1803.

Rhys had studied the war during his time at Eton, and Magellan had told them of future wars, even bigger than Napoleon's, which was hard to fathom. A war given the title "World War," not once but twice. Wars fought with advanced weaponry, all made possible, his father had pointed out, by the discovery of elements. Magellan's periodic table of elements she had described was indeed a puzzle humanity would use in the future for good and evil. Which is why Rhys always thought it apropos *live* spelled backward was *evil.* The shadows, the force from the lower dimensions that had found them when the labyrinth splintered, felt devoid of life and love, which is why it was so terrifying, because Rhys never wanted to be without either.

He thought back to Gwynedd's diary about the Great Year and the Map of Time, how the world had a long day and a long night and right now the world was in darkness. What would happen when those hungering for war and destruction were faced with the power a goddess's song could harness? Gwynedd had said every atom would sing and be lifted to a higher vibration where darkness could not exist. The song would not only save the planet but humanity. Which must be why the guardian at Stonehenge had hidden the song in time with women.

Now they were on their way to find Mozart's sister, a woman forgotten by the world while her brother rose to fame. Rhys had been stunned to hear the tale. If not for Magellan, he never would have known about the sister's life. He could not look on music the same way again because of Magellan, just as he could not look at women the same. Half of the world were women, and they had been forced into obscuring their light, which only helped keep the world in darkness.

*Toska* was the Russian word for great spiritual anguish, a sense of longing without knowing the cause. Was the world in anguish because life was out of balance?

When Magellan returned to the future with the song, she would have in her possession the incredible power to bring the world back into balance. To keep the poles from breaking. To keep an entire planet spinning.

Rhys took her hand and kissed it. She looked over at him with a soft smile. Godwin had his eyes closed and was dozing.

"We'll need to find you an instrument to bring with us to Nannerl's," he said quietly. "Perhaps there will be a shop in Salzburg."

She nodded and looked out the window, her eyes distant. "Yes, we should find something," she murmured.

The views of the Eastern Alps were dazzling as they came into Salzburg, but Rhys's eyes could not stray from her. Every minute together was becoming more and more precious. No single word in any language he could think of could describe the yearning in his heart to hold on to this moment forever.

# Chapter 48

## Magellan

The moment was pure magic. A breathtaking view of the Eastern Alps surrounded them with medieval and baroque buildings nestled along the Salzach river. Magellan felt like she had stepped right into *The Sound of Music*. She could almost imagine Julie Andrews somewhere off in the distance spinning with her arms wide, singing "the hills are alive."

On a whim she launched into *The Sound of Music*'s "Do-Re-Mi" with a giggle.

Godwin opened his eyes in surprise. "What on earth are you singing?"

Magellan didn't want to stop to explain. She was high on time travel, or maybe it was the stress. They were less than forty-eight hours away from Winter Solstice and the end of the world. Or maybe Salzburg's pure 1799 air was making her batty. She didn't know and raised her voice louder, proclaiming *me* was a name she called herself and *far* was a long way to run.

Rhys broke out laughing, and Godwin told him, "I believe your wife has lost her senses."

"Yes, it's adorable." Rhys was leaning away from her to get a better view of the performance, his hand over his mouth in astonishment.

She crooned how it would bring it back to *"doe,"* ready to Do-Re-Mi again. There was something therapeutic about it. Maybe she'd been cooped up in this carriage with two earls for too long. Maybe she'd finally lost it. She sang louder, encouraging them to give it a try. "It goes in a loop. See?"

Soon she had them both singing. After a few rounds, they knew the lyrics and began to have fun. By the end Godwin was belting it out the loudest. He seemed to have missed his calling for the stage.

"What are we singing, by the way?" Rhys asked between laughs.

"It's from a musical that was made here. Or will be made." Magellan never thought she'd be in Salzburg. She'd traveled more on this trip than she had her whole life. Perhaps whoever named her Magellan knew she would too. It was a provocative thought she tucked away.

---

They Do-Re-Mi'd all the way to Salzburg. When they reached the town, they found a charming inn on a long, narrow cobblestone street filled with confectioners and vendors in the shopping district. Salzburg's city hall and many of the surrounding buildings had been built in the fourteenth century, and every stone felt as if it had earned the right to stay there forever.

While Godwin went to take care of the carriage and secure their rooms for the night, Rhys and Magellan set off to find a music shop. They didn't have to look long. It was just down the street, the store a small space crammed full of instruments. Magellan ignored the racks of violins and other string instruments to approach the woodwind section.

"I need an oboe," she told Rhys with certainty.

The oboe was similar to a flute in sound and made of wood with a double chamber to move the air. Unlike other wind instruments, the sound didn't need to stop when the player paused to inhale. An oboist could play, while inhaling and exhaling, thereby never breaking the momentum of the sound. Although the modern oboe made its debut in France in 1657, the instrument actually dated back thousands of years. A symphony tuned its orchestra to the oboe, and the instrument was relied upon by a composer to pierce through any song with its clarity. Magellan felt she would need an oboe if she was going to battle the vortex waiting for her on the other side.

Rhys turned to the shop clerk and asked for his help in German.

This would be the last instrument she would play to go home. She forced herself not to panic at the thought of what the future might bring. Anxiety came from either fearing the future or regretting the past, and she wanted to stay fully in the present, in her heart, and experience every moment she could with Rhys.

The shopkeeper helped her choose an oboe and fit the mouthpiece specifically for her, and she gave it a try. Her fingers flew across the metal keys. She focused hard on the breathing dynamics, trusting her instincts to coax the sound. She played part of *Swan Lake*, even though Tchaikovsky wasn't alive yet.

Everyone in the shop stopped what they were doing as she played the iconic melody. When she finished, they all erupted into applause.

With a sad smile, Rhys told the clerk they would take it. He knew what this instrument was for and what it could do when she really played it.

---

They walked back to the inn holding hands, with Magellan clutching the oboe to her chest. Godwin was waiting for them when they arrived. He had been able to secure a private dining room for them and had ordered a feast. *Like a last supper*, though Magellan tried not to see it in that light or she would lose her appetite.

Tonight, she, Rhys, and Godwin wanted to celebrate reaching Nannerl. They had champagne and wine. Many toasts were made to much laughter. Rhys teased Godwin, saying his Beloved B was really a "P" and Godwin should question his hearing. Rhys almost had Godwin believing it and then confessed he was kidding. A short food fight ensued.

The meal was incredible. They gorged on mushroom dumplings, Wiener schnitzel, savory crepes with ham and spinach, and a ragout made of pork and sauerkraut. They sang "Do-Re-Mi." A lot.

Magellan had never laughed so much or so hard in her life, until she remembered tomorrow they would set out together for Saint Gilgen at first light on Winter Solstice eve. Everyone seemed to be thinking the same thing, and the mood turned somber as they stared at each other over the flickering candlelight.

Godwin raised his glass for one final toast. "To Gwynedd, Taliesin, and Merlin, two comets and a North Star. May their journey continue."

They clinked glasses in solidarity and drank the last from their cups.

Later when Magellan and Rhys reached their room, in many ways it felt like stepping into their first room that night in 1165.

Rhys shut and locked the door and then they were in each other's arms, falling back on the bed. They were chest to chest, their hearts beating in time as they tried to memorize each other's bodies.

Tomorrow was the great unknown, but no matter what happened, Magellan had to believe their love was a Ley Line that would lead them to each other again regardless what time the world existed in. Because love, like music, was timeless.

# Chapter 49

## Magellan

The next morning Magellan played the oboe the entire way to Saint Gilgen. She needed to play; her whole body was knotted with nerves. She felt like a pied piper leading Rhys and Godwin to the center of the labyrinth and its end. The two men had become everything to her. Now she might possibly lose them both.

Stubbornly, she played only love songs: "I Will Always Love You," "Unchained Melody," "Endless Love," "Can't Help Falling in Love," "Nothing Compares 2 U," "Buy Dirt" . . . It was her best of concert, with music chock-full of sentimentality and every tender emotion that made life worth living—because love made life worth living. Everything else was just the chorus.

Godwin and Rhys were both quiet, letting her have her way, seeming to understand she needed to vent. When they stopped to picnic somewhere, Magellan barely ate, unable to taste a thing. She was trying desperately not to cry.

Godwin broke the silence. "When did you leave in your time?"

Magellan thought back. The Halloween wedding seemed so long ago, and yet the day was branded in her memory. When she told him, she added, "It was the week after my birthday."

Rhys startled in surprise. "When is your birthday?" he asked softly.

"October 24th. The aurora borealis showed up that morning." She saw him swallow and nod, his eyes going to Godwin. She explained, "It's when I heard the song's opening. The diary arrived at the museum that morning too from the Liron Institute."

Godwin had parchment out and was scribbling notes of what she was saying.

"They even had my phone number," she remarked.

"What is a phone number?" Godwin asked, and Rhys was the one to explain it to him, which Magellan found touching.

Godwin frowned at her. "So with these numbers we can hear your voice anywhere in the world?"

She almost added "and see me," but Godwin already seemed confused.

He asked what her number was and wrote it down. He had the diary tucked away in his jacket for safekeeping. They had decided he should be the one to keep it, since he was the one to show it to Rhys in the future.

Godwin told her, "October 31st is the ancient day of Samhain and, legend has it, the one day of the year when the veil of the world is at its thinnest."

"In my time," she said, "we call it Halloween. Everyone dresses up in costume and eats candy." She attempted to grin at Rhys and bring lightness back into the day. "I thought you were in costume when we first met. Everyone at the wedding was."

"And I thought you were straight out of a fairy tale." Rhys kissed her hand. His fingers gently stroked the edge of the scar on her arm that peeked out from the sleeve of her gown. "I'm sorry I didn't believe you."

She stared into his eyes, feeling a sense of déjà vu, and the words bubbled up within her. "Please believe me next time."

He frowned at that, not understanding. She didn't understand either or know where the thought had come from.

"All right, lovebirds," Godwin declared, packing up his papers and supplies, "that's quite enough."

"Ten days to go, Father." Rhys stood up, helping Magellan to rise.

"But how will I know it's her? How will I know?" Suddenly Godwin seemed unsure.

*"Kilig."* Rhys said the word like a professor schooling a student. Then he went on to explain. "A word from the Philippine Islands to express the sensation when you stare into her eyes."

"Kilig." Godwin tested the word as he boarded the carriage.

"Kilig." Rhys nodded to him and winked at Magellan, making her smile. How she loved watching the two of them together.

Rhys spent the rest of the carriage ride regaling them with all his favorite words that defied translation: *firgun*, the Hebrew word to express the feeling of joy when something good happens to someone else; *merak*, a Serbian word to describe the feeling of bliss from life's simple pleasures; and *jijivisha*, the Hindi word to describe the deep love of life.

Magellan held his hand, listening to him share words from around the world, words that filled her with hope and the yearning to keep living. She wanted Earth to never stop spinning. She wanted babies to be born and for the sun to rise again and again. The determination inside her hardened as they neared their final destination. Life and its infinite expressions had to go on. If every atom could sing, the song should never end. She squeezed Rhys's hand and wondered if a word existed in any language to describe such a wish.

---

When they made it to Saint Gilgen, the town looked straight out of a storybook, with gingerbread houses nestled on the waters of a glacial lake surrounded by an alpine forest. They found Nannerl's house in the center of town near the main square. Magellan could only think the large two-story rectangular sterile white building looked like a hospital.

As they walked up the drive, she clutched her oboe and couldn't help but hum a soft tune to calm her nerves. She was walking between Godwin and Rhys. Neither said a word as the moment drew near.

When they reached the door, Magellan let the hum go with a deep, calming breath.

"Ready?" Godwin asked softly. She gave a nod, and he knocked, taking the lead. They'd already decided on the plan. The Earl of Liron, his cousin, and wife were wayward travelers and paying a courtly call to the town magistrate. The men would distract Nannerl's husband to give Magellan time alone with her.

A housemaid dressed in a cap and apron answered the door. Magellan didn't understand German, but Godwin was being his charming self and before long they were shown into the salon, where the woman asked them to wait with a shy blush. The room was a modest living room and had a harpsichord in the corner.

Magellan took a step toward it, but Rhys tucked her arm in his. "You can't play it yet, my love," he reminded her, and they all took a seat to wait. Magellan tried not to fidget, but her body felt coiled with anticipation.

Minutes later the salon door opened again and there she was.

Nannerl.

Magellan could feel tears springing to her eyes and furiously blinked them back. Rhys gave her hand a gentle squeeze. Magellan felt like she would recognize this woman anywhere. Nannerl carried herself with quiet grace and looked to be about fifty years old.

Following behind her was a much older man, stooped with age. Only the men spoke, with German flying back and forth between them. Tea and coffee were brought in. They sat facing off across from each other on two sofas, Godwin, Rhys, and Magellan on one and Nannerl and her husband on the other.

As the men continued their conversation, Nannerl met her eyes several times. Her gaze kept drifting to the oboe case in Magellan's lap. Godwin finally said something that made Nannerl's eyes light up, then she spoke for the first time.

Godwin looked over to Magellan. "I mentioned how much you were admiring the harpsichord and told her you played a little." He winked. "She's invited you to play it."

Magellan wanted to laugh. How alike he and Rhys were. The men stood, and Rhys reluctantly let go of her hand. "Her husband is going to show us the square."

She gave him a nod and swallowed. The time had come.

After the men left, the women stared at each other. Magellan made a motion, asking if she could play, and Nannerl nodded.

Feeling like a sleepwalker, Magellan set down her oboe on the sofa and crossed the room. She tried not to think about what would come after she played the parts of the song she knew and instead focused on the here and now, standing in front of Nannerl's beautiful harpsichord alongside her.

Was this Nannerl and her brother's? The one they'd learned on when they were children? Nannerl and Wolfgang had loved each other dearly, made up secret languages only they knew, and traveled across Europe together. They had been kindred spirits, two prodigies from the same coin. But only one side of the coin had been allowed to shine.

In two years' time, in 1801, Nannerl's husband would die and she would move back to her hometown of Salzburg. She would become a music teacher and pass away in 1829, months apart from Magellan's first arrival in the labyrinth. And although Nannerl's brother's music would be immortalized around the world, none of Nannerl's compositions would survive her death.

One of the greatest pianists and musicians ever to live would take all her music with her to the grave—except for this song.

Magellan laid her hands on the harpsichord and began to play. She didn't just play the song's beginning; she played Fanny's part and

Hildegard's part and Maddalena's. All the women were with her now. With their parts of the song, they had also given Magellan a piece of themselves. They had given her their courage. Their resilience. Their unshakable faith that they could do anything in this world. Nothing could stop them, not even themselves.

Nannerl listened in wonder and sat beside her. Then she laid her hands on the keys and began to play with her. Suddenly they were in the midst of a duet, their hands in perfect harmony as Nannerl gave Magellan her part of the fourth movement, like handing over a flame. The movement's authority was visceral, a vast, sprawling piece of self-reckoning that could keep the tableau of humanity intact. The harmonies ringing in Magellan's mind were an epiphany, a pure distillation of power. Magellan only prayed she was strong enough to hold it.

The symphony contained the harmonics of the Earth. Just as one note could be divided into an infinite number of notes, this song was for all life and every heartbeat. Magellan almost faltered under its vastness, but Nannerl held her gaze as they played, her eyes bright with understanding. Every song has a moment of forgiveness, like a doorway to allow anyone entry, and this song had infinite doorways. Magellan and Nannerl walked through one door together, forgiving the world and themselves for their faults. Then they were soaring together in the music, touching life directly at its source, and for a moment they were transported to the place where prayers live and all answers exist. They played on until Magellan had the song resonating inside her, like a star ready to be born.

When Nannerl struck the last note, the echo stayed in the room. And stayed.

The sound persisted, becoming an ancient gong heralding the end of a long journey. Magellan held her breath, waiting for the echo to fade, only it didn't. The vibration built and built until the floor began to shake and tremor.

Magellan and Nannerl looked to each other with wide eyes as every piece of porcelain and candlestick in the room rattled and fell over. The shaking continued, gaining momentum. Nannerl jumped up with a cry and ran upstairs, calling for someone.

The tremors became violent. The labyrinth was breaking.

Magellan heard unearthly screams in the distance. The vortex had found its way in.

She had to get to Rhys and Godwin. She grabbed her oboe from the couch and dashed from the house.

Outside the sky was a dark, ominous canopy, with storm clouds rolling in like an army. The ground wouldn't stop shaking. Magellan stumbled several times as the wind whipped at her clothes. Thunder cracked, and within its reverberation she could hear horrific cries from human voices, a chorus of wails and words spoken in every language with echoing despair that went on forever. The air itself was becoming charged by its sound, growing louder and more powerful.

She ran down the path and saw Rhys sprinting toward her, with Godwin not far behind.

She launched herself into Rhys's arms. They quickly ran their hands up and down each other's bodies, reassuring each other they were still there.

"Thank God." His voice was shaking.

"We did it. I have it. We have to leave right now." Their plan to ride to the ancient stone circle didn't seem feasible anymore. She was already thinking of nearby places where she could open a Ley Line. "We can't make it to the circle. It's too powerful this time."

Rhys was nodding and looking frantically around. "There's a small church. Perhaps—" Before he could finish, a bolt of lightning struck the tree right beside her and she screamed. Her dress was on fire.

Godwin yelled, "Drop to the ground!" Rhys pinned her down, trying to put the fire out with his own body. Godwin yanked off his jacket, screaming at him, "Move! Move!" and he used it to smother the flames while Rhys held on to her.

Magellan writhed in pain. Her feet and calves were burned. The sounds were now circling her like a predator, the screeching assaulting her ears. She tried to cover them and chant, but she was in too much agony.

"Get her to the lake!" Godwin yelled. "Quickly!"

Rhys swooped her up and took off running. Godwin was right behind them, holding the oboe. The ground continued to shake as the labyrinth broke further, allowing the shadows to pour inside the world with their screams.

Everything was a blur. Rhys ran the length of the pier to the water's edge and plunged her legs in. The water was ice cold. She cried out but immediately felt numbing relief.

Rhys was beside himself. "Is it helping?"

She nodded, unable to stop shaking. Not from the pain but from the shock. Her teeth began to chatter as the sky opened up like a widening crack in a wall and rain fell on them in a stinging curtain.

Behind Rhys, through the rain she could see humanlike figures coming toward them, pouring in from more cracks in the labyrinth. Ear-ringing thunder clashed in the sky, sounding like cannons of war. With each crashing boom, the screams grew louder. An army of beings were arriving out of thin air, slipping into this time, along with more shadows than Magellan had ever seen in a wave of darkness. The sound turned deafening, a torrential onslaught seeking to destroy atoms at their core. She began her deep hum to ward it off, but it was too powerful.

The song had opened countless doorways to lower dimensions. Shadows and misshapen figures entered along with gales of sound. Thunder boomed and lightning raced across the sky. The labyrinth was being destroyed by this force, and it would be the end of the world if she did not leave it.

In the distance, murky figures marched toward them like a moving "valley of the shadow of death." Were they human? From the past or the future or from another world? Magellan had no idea what she was witnessing.

Rhys breathed in. "My God." There was no way to get to the carriage or the church. They were pinned at the shoreline.

Desperate, Magellan picked up her oboe and launched into playing *Flight of the Bumblebee* by Rimsky-Korsakov, the fastest-moving medley of notes she could think of for the instrument. She played in a flurry to block the violent discord bombarding her. The piece's original tempo was two hundred beats per minute. She was playing it even faster to create a whirlwind of sound, but it wouldn't hold as a defense forever.

Rhys turned to Godwin. "What do we do? We're trapped."

Godwin stared at the water, his face riveted. Then he said, "That is why miracles were made." Magellan didn't dare stop playing as she watched Godwin spring into action with urgency as he worked to untie one of the small boats from the pier.

"What are you doing?" Even as he asked, Rhys hurried to help him.

Godwin quickly untied the rope as he explained in a rush, "This is Lake Wolfgang, named for the man who came here a thousand years ago. A man who supposedly could perform miracles." Godwin turned to them with a brilliant light in his eyes. "And I would bet our whole library collection this water is on a Ley Line." Godwin fought to steady the boat. "Quickly now."

"Don't stop playing," Rhys told her as he carefully helped her into the boat and climbed in after. "I'm going to row us out."

Magellan was too terrified to stop. She knew if she did, the vortex would destroy her. There was no question. Its sound was towering above her and pushing down on the resonance of her oboe like a g-force, trying to break through. Her fingers played faster, and she fought to steady her breath to keep going. She focused on the continuous string of sixteenth notes with steely determination. The power in the notes' harmony was unbreakable. She just had to be unbreakable too.

The boat made a dangerous wobble but didn't tip. Godwin gave the bow a strong push. "Row, Rhys! Don't stop!"

The swarm of shadows and figures were descending like locusts. It was not the goodbye any of them had envisioned.

"I will see you in the next life!" Godwin promised her as he began to jump from moored boat to moored boat to get away from the pier and the coming horde. But the path was taking him farther and farther away from them.

Magellan's eyes were blinded with tears. She was unable to say goodbye to him, to say any words. She had to keep playing even though the pain was becoming too great. In this moment they were a triskelion, three interlocking spirals about to break apart.

Godwin called out to Rhys, "And I will see you when you are born!"

"Get to Vienna!" Rhys's voice choked on the words as he fought to row away from shore.

"Get as far out as you can to the center!" Godwin yelled from the shoreline. The wind was fighting them, the boat rocking dangerously as Rhys struggled to paddle. The storm was trying to push them back to the pier, where a swarm of bodies now gathered.

Hell's orchestra surrounded her, battling her oboe and its purity. The horde began jumping into the water one by one like a herd, all with the same mind to stop her.

Rhys yelled over the gusts of wind, "You must play the song!"

The song was the key to going home, and she was terrified to play it. Right now she was the bumblebee in flight. If she played the song, would Rhys fly with her? Would he be left here? Or would he go back to 1829 without her, forever apart? Or would he be there with her when she woke up on the other side?

The fear of the future was about to take her breath away.

There was so much she needed to tell him. It was all happening too fast. She needed to hold him again. To tell him she loved him. It wasn't supposed to have ended like this. She couldn't hold back the grief rising from the deepest chamber of her heart. She wasn't ready.

He seemed to know what she was thinking. She didn't need to say the words.

"You will never lose me," Rhys promised as he pushed on with the oars. They were about to go into an abyss. The water around them was becoming like tar as the cesspool of shadowed forms rose up in a hellish tidal wave on all four sides. "Where you go, I go, Magellan. Do you hear me?" he yelled. "Where you go, I go."

She nodded. Her tears would not stop falling, and her breath was about to falter. The fear of the future was too great. The pain in the world was too great. She didn't know if she could survive it.

He yelled, though his voice was dimmed and sounded far away from her over the battle of sound raging in her ears. But she heard him. "I had a dream of the future. I was with you onstage when you played the song. I was right beside you."

Hope flared in her heart. She'd had the same dream. To hear Rhys did too filled her with faith—a faith she grabbed hold of like a lifeline if she was going to get home.

A shared dream could be a life lived together.

Tears filled his eyes too and ran unchecked down his face. "Play the song, Magellan. Play, my love."

She nodded and surrendered. She surrendered her thoughts, her fear, and climbed back into the seat of her heart. Never taking her eyes from him, she seamlessly shifted, no longer the bee flying away. She was a force, full of love.

*Trust the compass of your soul,* Gwynedd had written. One life was not the whole story, and a soul's journey did not have an ending.

Magellan played all the song's parts she had inside her, buoyed by the women who had gifted their strength to her. She blew all her breath into the oboe, sending the notes valiantly into the dark.

By the end of the first movement, the tower of water bearing down on them froze as the ring on her finger lit like a lantern. And the mountains—a part of a much more ancient stone circle—bore witness to the miracle at hand.

The song made the water shimmer as its sound pushed outward like a supernova, reordering time and space to eclipse the darkness with the light. Magellan played on and Rhys released the oars, no longer needing to row as their boat headed toward the horizon like an ancient burial at sea.

They were leaving the labyrinth on the oars of sound. In this moment she was the captain of an ancient ship and as powerful as the magicians of old. Her voyage into the labyrinth had ended.

Magellan held Rhys's eyes as she played. They did not dare look away from each other as they sat in shimmering brilliance, existing in a moment both finite and infinite while the labyrinth folded peacefully around them.

Her body fading, she could no longer feel Rhys beside her. She could only see his eyes and his light shining. She could see the love, and she had to believe the Ley Lines connecting their souls would lead them to each other again.

She gave her breath for the final note, and the remnants of her fear fell away as she tuned her heart to the world. She was not alone. She was never alone, but a part of an enduring symphony. She felt Earth's power rush through her and the labyrinth release them, propelling her back to her own time, where humanity was waiting on the eve of the darkest night for a song to sing—a song holding the power to illuminate every atom with the force that spun atoms to *Life*: *Love* and *Music*.

The most ancient triskelion of all.

# Acknowledgments

Thank you for reading *The Last Labyrinth*! I am full of joy to be sharing this story with you. This book has been years in the making and feels like a dream to have it finished. The story kernel began from my dad encouraging me many times over the years to consider writing a book about Merlin. Finally, when I was ready to explore the possibility, I discovered Gwynedd in my research and the journey began. Thank you, Dad. This book could only be dedicated to you.

Next, a huge thanks to my agent, Alec Shane, and the team at Writers House. Alec, thank you for your fantastic story insights, high energy, and for finding *The Last Labyrinth* its home. To my editor at 47North, Elizabeth Agyemang, I knew from our first Zoom you were the partner for this story. Your passion and care for Magellan and Rhys were what I had hoped for. Then Clarence Haynes came aboard as editor, and we were a trio. And to add to the book love, Clarence's debut solo novel, *The Ghosts of Gwendolyn Montgomery*, came out during the editing of mine. Congratulations, Clarence! I can't thank you enough for all your help in bringing this story to life. Between that first call and the end of the editing process, it has been wonderful working with you both.

I'm grateful to the entire 47North team who had a hand in the book's creation. A huge thank-you to my exceptional copyeditor, Jon Ford, for his perfect eye on every detail along with Ashley Little, Rachel Norfleet, Tara Whitaker, and Jessica Poore with final edits and proofing. Thank you so much to David Drummond for designing such a stunning cover! Special thanks as well to the production team led by Andrea Nauta, marketing manager Chrissy Penido, and PR manager Allyson Cullinan.

A big thank-you to my film rights agents, Debbie Deuble Hill at IAG and Tom Ishizuka at Writers House. And Will Plyer for helping to keep my website running. Also special thanks to author Stacy Wise for giving the manuscript an early beta read, Emily Mallin for her help, and Julia Burke for her amazing eagle eyes on the last read!

While writing this book, many people helped with my research and were a fantastic support on so many fronts: Thank you to Monika Telszewska, Maciek Telszewski, Diana DiMartino, and George Holly; Sergei Galperin, a first violinist with the Houston Symphony, for being a great musical resource; Asitha Ameresekere, Luke Burke, Sean Cooper, and Geraldine O'Shea for my Great Britain research; and Brooke Summers-Perry, the president of Houston's Women in the Visual and Literary Arts, for my character research for Magellan's anxiety. Thank you, WiVLA.org too. It has been wonderful to be a member of such a supportive group of women. The themes for WiVLA's showcases this year were *Resilience* (shout-out to Denise Bossarte!) and *Rise*, which were perfect reflections to the running themes in the story.

While busy with edits, I taught a creative writing summer camp for Writers in the Schools called Magical Worlds, where I was surrounded by exuberant young writers brimming with stories and a deep love of books. They were so inspiring. Cheers to all twenty-three *Fantabriaectolovians*! Please keep writing and sharing your stories.

As a lifelong writer, I am so grateful I get to work with so many fantastic people in the book world who are as passionate about storytelling as I am. From the publishing side to the bookselling side to book clubs, bloggers, and book lovers who help spread the word. It is an honor to be a part of this circle.

Loving thanks and big hugs to all my family and friends, and to my son, Kenzo, the crystal flower you gave me was my good luck charm while writing this book.

The discovery process for this story was very much like a labyrinth. I loved every turn and pathway. I'm going to circle back to what I said at the beginning, because I do love circles (and kaleidoscopes ☺). I'm so full of joy to hand the book over to you now. Thank you to all my readers for taking the journey with me. Until next time ❤. Let's make some music!

# About the Author

*Photo credit © 2025 Glen Carpenter*

Gwendolyn Womack is the *USA Today* bestselling author of *The Fortune Teller,* the award-winning reincarnation thriller *The Memory Painter, The Time Collector,* and her YA debut thriller *The Premonitions Club.* Gwendolyn lives in Houston, Texas, with her family and is an adjunct faculty member at Houston City College. When she's not writing, she can usually be found immersed in a good book or photographing kaleidoscopes. For more information, visit www.gwendolynwomack.com.